The Bliss

Jacqueline Navin

JOVE BOOKS, NEW YORK

This is a work of fiction. Names, characters, places, and incidents either are the product of the author's imagination or are used fictitiously, and any resemblance to actual persons, living or dead, business establishments, events, or locales is entirely coincidental.

THE BLISS

A Jove Book / published by arrangement with
the author

PRINTING HISTORY
Jove edition / January 2003

Copyright © 2003 by Jacqueline Navin

Visit our website at
www.penguinputnam.com

ISBN: 0-515-13466-X

A JOVE BOOK®
Jove Books are published by The Berkley Publishing Group,
a division of Penguin Putnam Inc.,
375 Hudson Street, New York, New York 10014.
JOVE and the "J" design
are trademarks belonging to Penguin Putnam Inc.

PRINTED IN THE UNITED STATES OF AMERICA

10 9 8 7 6 5 4 3 2 1

Titles by Jacqueline Navin

THE BLISS
MEET ME AT MIDNIGHT
THE FLOWER AND THE SWORD

Prologue

London, England
March 1816

Leah Brodie sensed something amiss at the ball. Even before she saw the Wicked Earl, before her observant eyes registered the way the crush around her bristled at this uninvited guest, before she heard the first whisperings of shocked indignation, she felt the vaguest sensation of alarm—or delight—come over her in a lazy, prickling wave.

She searched for the source of the feeling but found nothing to cause the indistinct whisper riding lightly along the back of her neck. She would later wonder if it weren't some fanciful imagining to which she was prone. Perhaps she hadn't felt anything at all.

True, the night was a cool one, as it often was early in the London season, but it was no breeze that raised a shiver. The warm press of bodies at the marquess of Steele's ball made that blessing impossible. Guests were crowded shoulder to shoulder around the parquet floor of the ballroom, watching the dancers and talking.

Some wore bored expressions, watching the activities

around them with little interest. Others flashed smiles while their eyes darted rabidly about, anxious to take in each and every detail, which would be pored over, analyzed, and picked apart upon the morrow's morning social calls.

Edmund Harwith had Leah cornered by the potted palms. Handsome, possessed of a title and a substantial fortune, Harwith had seemed engaging at first. As Leah was supposed to be looking for a husband, after all, she had met his request to be presented to her with a beguiling smile and a flutter of eyelashes, just as she'd been taught. However, her pleasure faded the moment Harwith had begun to address his conversation to her breasts.

It happened often. She had the sort of figure that turned men stupid. Early in this, her debut season, she had decided that any man whose eyes drifted downward as if her chest possessed the ability to converse, was immediately discarded and in the future avoided at all costs.

This she had been preparing to do when she felt the first ripple of tension. It drew her shoulders upward. Her hands curled tight in her kid gloves, enough to strain the meticulous stitching. Harwith faded into unimportance.

She noticed the people around her were slowly falling silent. Their bodies grew stiff. Heads came together, then up, alert and craning. The air grew crisp with the snap of opening fans behind which comments, curt and rough with urgency, were fired.

Something was wrong. Something was happening. People seemed frozen, fixed, as in a painting. And then a movement caught her eye.

She saw a man, a very tall man, with dark hair worn rather too long than what was strictly fashionable. It gleamed with rich luster by the light of the hundreds of flickering candles that were reflected into millions by the crystals and mirrors and gilt in the room. He was half turned away, so that all she could see of his face was the jutting angle of a sharp cheekbone.

Behind her, a woman gasped. A man's voice growled, "Good God. I don't believe it. It's . . . Waring."

Waring? She knew that name. She'd heard it mentioned many times, always with disdain. The earl of Waring—known best as the *wicked* earl of Waring—was a notorious murderer!

Most young ladies would suffer an attack of the vapors at the mere suggestion of such an infamous character. Yet Leah—to her mother's great despair and her own frustration most times—was not like other young ladies. Never more apparent was that fact than now, as she threw aside any semblance of decorum and stood on the tips of her toes, arching to get a better look.

A murderer . . . imagine! It was simply the most exciting thing!

Waring never glanced her way, thwarting her. Once, just before he exited the room, he flashed a look over his shoulder, and she could have seen his face plainly if a woman with an immense coif had not stepped into her line of vision right at that very moment. Leah caught only a glimpse of narrowed eyes moving fiercely among the crowd, as if searching each and every face. Above was a high, noble brow, unlined. His complexion was dark.

He turned away again and strode into the other room. Harwith called after her as she began to move away, following without a thought. She wanted to see his face.

Wondering at the perversity that drove her to shamelessly stalk a man who, it was said, had murdered his own father, she threaded through the crowd of guests. She had no means to explain why she did these sort of things. Impulses had a way of springing up inside her. Knowing one's faults, however, gave no mastery over them. Sometimes she wished it did, times when trouble found her as a result of brash action.

Other times, she rather liked being the way she was. It was a bother getting scolded so much, but she often considered that she'd shrivel from boredom if she listened to all the lectures, pleas, scoldings, and exasperated pronouncements of doom her mother had doled out over the nineteen years of Leah's life. Of the two evils—trouble or boredom—she considered the latter the worst, so she shrugged fatalistically and kept pace with the Wicked Earl.

She circled a group of men gathered in a tight knot, absently apologizing to one of them when she trod on his foot.

"No, no, you have the wrong of it!" one of them was saying. "My grandson knew the boy at Oxford and says he is solid. There are many who know him to be innocent."

Another voice, angry and impatient, snapped, "Now how can you say that, when he was in the house, *alone*, when the body was found? And why did he run off, I ask you, unless he was guilty? He has been out of England for nearly a year."

"Would that he stayed away," a disgruntled voice sneered. "We don't need his sort among us."

"I heard it was a burglar that did it," a fourth man chimed in. "The window was broken, was it not? The inquest said it was the burglar who murdered the father."

"Oh, bosh, Clarence. Honestly, your naivete is astounding. The Wicked Earl was imprisoned for the murder of his own father, and that is incontrovertible fact. They wouldn't have locked up a peer unless they had damned good evidence for it, eh!"

Leah left the heated voices behind, continuing her pursuit. Waring did not look at all villainous, she thought. At least the back of him did not, which was unfortunately all she had been able to get a clear view of. His smartly tailored coat was quite the fashion. It stretched wide across his broad shoulders and hugged his narrow waist. His height was in his legs, lanky and long as he moved with sure, purposeful strides. Pantherish, she thought, a word she knew from her favorite cousin, Daphne, for she often used it to describe the heroes in her titillating stories. Leah loved Daphne's frank and thrilling tales. If her mother knew half of the things she knew from these, she would be livid.

And this man seemed like something straight out of one of them. A genuine man of mystery. She sighed and pressed on.

He stood for a moment in the doorway to the card room. He seemed to be looking for someone. Leah stopped as well, as her mind raced with questions, possibilities. Was he engaged in some secret assignation—another murder perhaps, or perhaps a *lover*. A woman who had abandoned him when he'd been jailed, perhaps. Did he seek the unfaithful woman to reunite their unrequited longing or punish her for her betrayal?

Really, this was *too* much like Daphne's adventure tales. She shivered in delight and crept closer, passing close to a pair engaged in an argument.

"There was a cut on his hand, proving he'd broken the glass to make it look like theft was the thing. My brother's estates are very close to Waring's, and he had it straight from the constable, I tell you. A cut right across the back of his hand, Castleton. What do you make of that?"

"As if that proves anything," came an answering sniff. "It is rather more significant that he was cleared of charges by men who knew more about the particulars than you *or* your brother."

"Well, at least he is taking his leave. The nerve of the man to come in here like this, as if he had a perfect right to be among God-fearing folk."

Indeed he was leaving, Leah noted in alarm. Having inspected the card room, he was now headed straight for the door. Leah took up her chase once again.

By the time she worked her way around the gossipers, the earl had already passed through the door and descended the marble steps into the street. His carriage waited, the door held open by a smartly liveried groom. He stepped inside without a backward glance and disappeared into shadow. The door closed and the carriage pulled away.

Leah sighed, flouncing slightly. Now she would never get to see him!

The man without a face stayed with her for a long time. He passed through her dreams, occupied her fantasies, always thrillingly elusive. For a while. Then she met Carl Enders and Mother decided she should choose a husband.

As for Waring, he did not appear again at any balls or society events. Soon, the ton forgot him and the stir he had roused the night he had stalked through Steele's ball died down, replaced by other topics of interest, fashions, and news items, and most of all scandals. Society loved scandals. It seemed almost everyone had a turn at being gossiped about.

Leah's turn came just as the season closed.

Chapter 1

THE SLEEK ARABIAN mare felt like a dream. She moved like quicksilver under Leah as they climbed the verdant dell toward the moor. Her body matched the rhythm of the beautiful beast as the mists parted before her. Like a veil giving way in welcome, it embraced her.

At the lip of the slope, she paused. The Yorkshire Moorland was a landscape of harsh colors and bleak shapes. It was nothing more than a wide expanse of large, flat hills hovering over the lands below, like a shelf upon which God might rest to survey the gentler regions of his creation.

Covered in heather and ugly scrub, pocked with jagged gray granite tors that rose up like giants from the flatland, it seemed an alien vision, as if from another world. She liked that, Leah did. In another world, she could be another person.

She whipped the Arabian into a gallop and set off for Madigan's Tor.

This was not home, at least in the sense that she had been born here or belonged to any residence hereabouts, but she wished it was. She *felt* it was. She loved this land, especially now when spring was new and wet and tenderly green and the sense of renewal was all around her and all through her.

After the vigors of the polite world, she had craved this respite. Now, alone on these wild lands, she drank it in deep, cleansing breaths as if she could dispel the last vestiges of the choking smog of London, and with it, all the restrictions and nasty reproofs of the bon ton.

How she *needed* this land. Especially after . . . she groaned, wishing she'd stop thinking about it. Her first season had ended in disaster. It was fortunate Cousin Daphne had offered for her to come for a prolonged visit in Yorkshire. Leah was glad, knowing she'd be in her favorite place with her favorite person on earth when she needed it the most.

The combination had worked to ease her already in the few days since she'd arrived. She rarely brooded over the whole mess with Carl anymore. Sometimes, though, despite her best efforts to put the episode behind her, she couldn't help but think about it, and always with a sick feeling in the pit of her stomach.

It wasn't Carl that upset her. She didn't miss him. She didn't really regret anything she'd done, either, which she'd never confide to another soul. She should be remorseful, and she'd tell Mother she was when she returned to her family, but secretly she knew she would do the very same thing again, consequences be damned.

Wait. No, there was one regret. If only she'd had a chance to kick him again after she'd poured the cheese soufflé over his head. She would have really liked that.

Realizing she was grinding her teeth, she kicked the horse faster and let the wind whip her hair loose as she raced across the heath, feeling suddenly as if she could outrun her memories. The bite of the morning chill caressing her scalp felt good, cleansing, and her hair fell loose. It caught the light, glossy curls tumbling. Swirls of gold and chestnut and deep sable streamed behind her.

Then she realized she shouldn't be riding so recklessly and reigned in her mount. Slowing to a more decorous trot, she pinned the smart little riding hat with the plume back into place.

See, this was the sort of thing that was always snagging her into unfortunate situations. She was thoughtless, impetuous, giving into impulses no well-brought-up lady should have.

Making an effort to behave herself properly, she proceeded at a more sedate pace. Belatedly recalling Daphne's frequent warnings of bogs, death traps that could sit undetected, looking no more dangerous than the next of patch of earth, but could swallow a horse and rider whole within minutes, she scanned the ground. Bosh. She didn't see anything.

This strange, ugly land, even with its marshes, soothed her. Stroking the horse's neck, she let her gaze wander to the sky. It seemed to hunker over these highlands in bilious piles of gray clouds, like ethereal mountains. Or as if heaven were right there and all she had to do was reach up her hands and she'd be able to touch it.

She stroked the horse's mane and murmured, "How I do love it here."

The horse nickered, as if in response. Leah laughed and took up the game. "Not that I didn't have a perfectly delightful time in London, mind you," she said with prim confidence. "I was quite a success. I assure you, that last little problem"—she grimaced as her mind slid quickly over the subject—"will pass and next year I will be welcomed back. Mother assures me it will all come to nothing, and besides, Carl deserved it. He did. Even the duchess said so, and she always says only good things about people."

Her shoulders drooped, suddenly tiring of the show of bravado. She admitted, "But it is good to be done with all of that. I so love not having to be so bloody, blasted correct all the time."

She clapped a hand over her mouth, then laughed at herself. "Oh, my. See, I am with Cousin Daphne only three days and already she has me swearing."

Laughing carelessly, she tossed her head. It was a gesture so reflexive she did it even here, when there was no one to appreciate it. "Well, the devil take it—I like swearing! That's odd, don't you think, to like a thing like that? Does it make me bad, do you think?" The horse was mute, as if too polite to comment.

Leah shrugged. "Odder still is talking to a horse. I don't normally speak conversationally with horses as a rule, but today . . . ah, my mind is restless and whenever that is so, it usually means my mouth is similarly occupied."

The wind had picked up. She glanced at the gathering clouds. Could a storm take form so quickly? She should head back, perhaps. Daphne had mentioned the weather could be unpredictable on the moors.

She turned the horse with a reluctant sigh, dallying a bit as she allowed the horse its head to pick her way among the gorse. "I only have a few weeks here. Then I have to go . . . I think to Cumbria. At least it is family we are to visit first, and I adore my niece. From there on, however, we are to live like veritable gypsies, traveling from one house party to another. It is the way of the bon ton. I prefer home. Yet, I don't really have a home, not anymore. I cannot even remember the last time we were actually in residence at our own house."

The moor had grown quite charmless under a sky that was becoming much too dense for her liking. She felt a sudden shiver of unease, as if there were darker things on these flatlands than mere ugliness or the threat of a drenching. And they were watching her.

She kicked the mare into a trot, suddenly anxious to be back at Barstow Cottage. Awaiting her would be a nice fire, a hot cup of tea, and a cozy chat with Daphne. Perhaps even another story. She hoped Daphne would oblige. It was a day for adventure, she thought.

THE DANGER SHE sensed came from a cluster of gnarled dwarf trees that had twisted out a miserable existence near the base of a mammoth tor. A dark man waited there. He stood tall, with long legs braced apart, as still as the unquarried stone around him. His hair was whipped wild by the wind and an ankle-length mantle spread out and around him like the wings of a bat.

At his eye he held a spyglass and watched the woman cross the untamed moorland. The toothless man to his right hissed, "There she is, my lord."

"Yes." Morgan Gage's voice was soft, edged with the tiniest degree of tension. It was the only indication that his emotional state might differ from the calm exterior.

"She's alone today," Morgan said, stroking his chin with long fingers as he lowered the glass and shifted his gaze upward, taking in the overhung sky. "Hardly the kind of day one felt was too glorious to miss by staying indoors." He paused, deep in thought, before looking down at his companions, suffering each one to bear the scrutiny of his firebrand stare.

The three men he had hired were pinched-face with tension, the promise of impending violence glazing their eyes. Like a trio of wild horses gnawing impatiently at the constraints of their bits, they stood poised, ready to be unleashed on the unsuspecting female.

Morgan savored the brigands' heightened state, pausing just long enough to bring them close to agitation.

Then he said, "Go get her," and turned away. "And woe to you if you harm one hair on her head."

He would meet up with them later when they brought her to the house. His stomach tightened and he felt his body shiver powerfully in anticipation.

⁓

LEAH SPOTTED THE men as soon as they emerged from their rugged shelter, coming fast and hard across the scrub. Their lack of stealth was intensely terrifying, as if they had all the confidence on earth and it mattered little if she knew she was their prey. It took only an instant for her earlier sense of unease to blaze fully into a searing blast of ice-cold panic. She turned the mare and kicked her into a run.

Remembering the bogs, she disregarded that remote danger in light of the men pursuing her—and, yes, they *were* pursuing her, as she ascertained by a quick glance over her shoulder. This certainty edged out all other fear. She dug in her heels and went for as much speed as could be attained on an English ladies' sidesaddle.

The wind ripped at the pert little bonnet on her head and pricked tears into her eyes as she leaned into the horse, willing her to take flight. The Arabian indeed flew, but she was young and small and not able to outrun those who pursued. The sound of them, very close now, filled Leah's head with thunder.

A large, rough hand closed over her shoulder, ripping a shriek loud and shrill enough to call down the slumbering angels charged with her care. Then suddenly, she was yanked backward and off the racing horse.

Everything became confused. She hit the ground hard. Before she could recover her breath, they were beside her. She struggled but she could not prevent her ankles from being bound together. With amazing swiftness, a rag was stuffed in her mouth and a neckerchief tied over it to stifle her cries. Her wrists were tied behind her, and then she was hauled up by rude hands and thrown over a horse.

Pain jolted through her in the awkward position. It sliced fresh and raw once they were under way at each movement of the muscular beast across which she was thrown like a sack of barley on the way to market. Or a young lamb to the slaughter.

She had difficulty breathing, both from the tightness of her stays and the gulping sobs choking in her throat. Fighting to remain conscious, remain aware, she felt rain and turned her bruised face upward, wanting the cold drops to revive her, save her from the depths of darkness that tried to suck her under.

She managed to endure the short ride without succumbing and when they stopped, she was yanked down and dragged inside some kind of dwelling. Once inside, she noticed little before she was brought into a room. The door slammed, leaving her quite alone.

Leah rolled onto her back and wriggled until she was sitting up. Her chest burned with the effort; she needed air desperately. Her stays were pinching into her sides as she lay in this awkward position, making breathing difficult. The sound of rain was fat and heavy against the closed shutters.

It took a moment for her to calm herself. When she did, she saw she had been provided a thin straw pallet upon which to lie, an unconventional courtesy from men who had given no thought to comfort thus far. She dashed a glance about the room.

Upon a slender table a greasy candle flickered madly, sending the stench of animal fat into the air to mingle with the subtle sour odor that she realized, to her disgust, was coming from the bed. Thoughts of vermin raised the fine hairs on the back of her neck. Over in the corner was a chipped earthenware basin to serve as a chamber pot, she supposed.

Wet from the rain, she felt the chill of her dampened clothing beginning to seep into her bones. There was no fire here, not even a place for one. It wasn't from the cold, however, that she took to violent shivering. She knew what these men wanted from her.

It was like something lifted straight from one of Daphne's stories—full of vivid details no gently bred miss should ever hear—about abduction and ravishment and rescue. She wasn't supposed to know what ravished meant, but she did. She knew exactly what that meant, although some of the words Daphne used referred to procedures and parts that were still rather vague. In any event, she knew enough to feel the black tide of fear rising swiftly within her breast.

She heard voices. Men's voices, some sharp and high in agitation, another calmer, deeper, speaking in cultured accents. She tried to listen, but no words were audible. Presently, she heard a door open and close, heard footsteps outside and the sound of horses riding away.

Had she been left alone?

The answer came when the door swung open. She made a piteous peep, the only sound possible gagged so tightly as she was, and popped her eyes wide to stare at the intruder. The rectangle of gray from the lesser gloom outside filled with a gigantic form. It paused, and then advanced.

The stingy light caught the form, bringing into view a face. A dark, angry face. Great hulking shoulders eclipsed the candle in the space of one step. The glimpse of him was too brief, but it left an impression of dark hair softly curled and worn long. She thought she had noted a white lawn shirt and dark breeches. From his silhouette created by the backlighting, she could see they were closely fitting and that he wore Hessians polished enough to gleam even in the dimness.

This was not just a man. This was a *gentleman*. His clothes spoke for his social position and—dear Lord, please let it be so—his character. She was saved! Her heart swelled with the violent blossom of hope. This man must have seen her abduction, followed her captors, and was now here to rescue her.

His next words, and the tone with which they were spoken, doused that hope as effectively as water drenching a feeble flame.

"Are you surprised to see me?" His voice was made of gravel, harsh and soft at the same time and it multiplied the tremors going through her. She shrank against the wall, wishing the shadows that crowded around her would swallow her whole.

She watched him, as still as she could make herself. "I've been waiting to talk to you . . . *privately* for a long, long time, Glorianna. I apologize for all of this fuss and bother, but it was the only way. I only hope you aren't too put out with me, but as I will explain, there was no other way."

He stopped in front of her, so close that she had to tilt her head back to see him. The light hit him from the side, so that his face was only an impression, vague and distorted by shadow. She could see a large blade of a nose, high-cut cheekbones with long hollows underneath. A wide, mocking mouth twisted over a square jaw. It was such a hard, uncompromising face, all planes and angles and power. Heavy brows obscured the color of his eyes, but the shadow of their lashes stretched in spikes across a clean-shaven cheek. The light touched a line along the left temple that was red and puckered, running from the outside of the eye down back to the ear. The angry scar added a more sinister flare to a face that needed no such enhancement.

He ran his thumb along it as he stood over her, but otherwise he was motionless. It was a gesture she guessed he did not do on purpose. She had the impression all of his awareness was directed exclusively on her. "I imagine you are uncomfortable, and that is not my wish. I will unbind you, starting with that gag. We need to talk. That's all this is about, really. A healthy airing of misconceptions and lies. It's time for truth." He paused for effect. "Tilt your head forward so I can undo the knot. And please don't scream. There is no one to hear you, and I warn you my nerves are already quite on edge as it is."

She did as he directed, bowing her head. The feel of his fingers prying at the tight knot felt like the brush of velvet along the back of her neck. A wave of tremors danced ruthlessly down her spine.

When his task was finished, his hands took the neckerchief away and pulled out the rag stuffed in her mouth. She took a few gulps of nourishing air and worked her jaw with relief.

With each breath, she felt herself swelling with rage and indignation.

"Now, Glorianna," she heard from above her still lowered head. "I want to know why you have been avoiding me."

Throwing her head back, she closed her eyes and shouted, "I'm not Glorianna, you damnable bastard!"

Chest heaving, she lifted her eyelids. The man was perfectly still and looked quite shocked. She could see his eyes now. They were pale brown shot with shards of glittering gold. Then the brows shot down once again and the startling orbs were cast back into shadow. He ducked his head toward her, leaning in close, muttering something she couldn't hear but knew was an epithet by the tone he used. Turning to the table, he snatched the candle and held it near her face.

In the presence of his intense inspection, she prepared to spout further invectives. "You've obviously abducted the wrong woman, you damned addle-pate," she began. "Of all the audacity, the bloody incompetence! I demand you release me at once. The devil take you, I—"

He cut her off, exploding with a vehement, "Bloody Christ!" and stuffed the smelly neckerchief back into her mouth.

The man turned. Paused. Turned back. Wiping his hand over the sweat collecting on his upper lip, he swore again. He spun on his heel and left.

Leah spit out the filthy cloth and drew in a breath to scream. He had told her not to, she suddenly remembered, and this recollection made her pause.

Strangely, her fear had gone. The appearance of the man with the hard face had dispelled the intense terror that gripped her out on the moor. It defied reason, and she knew it, but somehow the cut of his clothes, the clipped syllables with which he'd spoken had brought a touch of the familiar into this bizarre circumstance. He was a gentleman. This was, inexplicably, a measure of comfort.

Immediately on the heels of this came the frigid wash of indignation. He was a *gentleman*. He should have been the hero. Gentlemen were always the heroes in Daphne's stories. They saved the females from *the clutches* of the villain, who was always some uncouth person, usually with a physical deformity and a foul mouth. Leah had a fair idea what "clutches" meant, as these rescues always occurred just before the poor woman was about to be given the bliss.

Well, she knew one thing. The bloody blackguard would not get *her* virtue—that valued prize that society cloaked in nearly sacramental significance. Anyone knew that blackguards and other nefarious people were always plotting to give innocents the bliss, thus leaving the helpless girl bereft of any value, worthless, cast off, shamed. . . .

She stopped the direction of her thoughts, feeling a fresh flood of fear. She liked the indignation better and she willed it to come back. It made her feel stronger, less vulnerable, but how could she ignore the fact that she was . . . Oh, God.

Aloud, in a threadbare whisper, she uttered, *"In his clutches!"*

On that alarming note, the man entered once again.

His hair stood on end, as if he'd been running his hands through it. His face was still shadowed, but she could tell he was in a very different frame of mind than when he'd come in a moment ago. Gone was the smug triumph, the sublime superiority, but he was still as tall, still as broad, still as menacing as before.

Her whole body reacted to his presence, from the quickening of her heartbeat to the incremental rise in her temperature.

She had a quick mind, but she was not known for it. At least, she tried not to be. To demonstrate intelligence would have been detrimental to her carefully constructed reputation. Rather, her devotion to melodrama—which she had found men thought adorable—and flair for gaining attention even if she had to use a heavy hand were skills much more effective in attracting admiration.

In short, she was a woman who was ruled by emotions. Therefore, she wasn't inclined to exercise a great deal of caution at this moment.

"I demand you untie me at once," she snapped.

He held up a single finger. It meant for her to be quiet. She took no heed. In fact, it only incensed her. "You blasted devil of an idiot!" she blurted. "I absolutely refuse to be tied up like this a moment longer."

He shook his head, huffing out a mirthless sound, a rough sort of chuckle. "Where did you learn to talk like that?"

"I'll tell you nothing, not one little thing, you evil cur. Not even the most insignificant of details. I despise you for being the disgusting brigand you are, you must know that, and I refuse to cooperate with you in the smallest manner, rotten son of a whore that you are—"

"You know, we will get through this much quicker if you dispense with the swearing. Your facility with gutter language would be stunning on a fishmonger's wife, let alone a debutante, and I am duly impressed. But I'm anxious to resolve this fiasco. Now let us converse sensibly before I lose my temper."

He was immutable. But Leah saw this as a challenge more than a deterrent. She looked at him sullenly and said, "You will get nothing but grief from me, sir, as you are beneath contempt and deserve nothing of my respect. Sensible, you say? What is sensible is to cut you, as I shall indeed apply myself to doing." She turned her head away from him, demonstrating her snub, with a jerk of her head.

When he didn't respond, she slid her eyes back to him without moving another muscle. He was regarding her with one thick brow raised. It made his saturnine face seem almost human. "You must be either very, very stupid or quite mad."

She whipped her head back around to face him. "Mad, am I? Mad! Oh, that is rich, you filthy bugger. Am I the one lurking about the moor like some evil predator, abducting innocent women?" Seeing his narrowed eyes, she thought better of this tact. She brought her chin up, hoping it would shore up her flagging courage to at least look defiant.

Her voice was noticeably less strident, however, when she spoke again. "You haven't even . . . I'm still tied. Damn it all, will you at least free my *legs*? My . . . my . . . *feet* are pricking terribly." It was humiliating to speak the words *feet* and *legs*. A proper lady never referred to her lower extremities in the presence of a man.

He burst out with a harsh bark of laughter. "You swear like a cockney dock worker, and then blush when saying 'legs.' My God, you debs are simpletons." He raked his hand through his hair. "All right. I'll untie your legs. But I'll give you the devil if you cross me."

"I believe you should also be warned," she muttered as he bent over her bindings. She was trying to keep up the front all heroines when abducted were known for, but, dear Lord, the man was laying hands on her! She gulped. His fingers were actually touching her ankles, and without a single apology.

Why did it bother her so much more than when those three cretins had wrested her into these ropes? They had touched her much more boldly and yet this incidental brushing of his ungloved hands resounded through her entire body.

He angled a look up to her while his fingers pried open the knots. His eyes caught the light, startling her. The bits of gold embedded in those glittering brown pools looked the color of liquid honey poured fresh from the hive. "Really. And just what am I to be warned of?"

Her voice came out rusty. "You best not try to take the bliss."

He frowned, confused. "The bliss?" He seemed to be trying to puzzle this out when she realized her feet were free. Without stopping to weigh the wisdom of her actions, she kicked up and out with all the power she had and caught him in the jaw.

He let out a sound that was sort of a husky "Ooomph!" Covering his face with his hands, he ducked to protect himself from another blow.

She wasn't interested in punishing him, however. On her feet in a flash, she jumped up to the bed. He lunged for her as she back-wheeled on the flat mattress until her hands, still bound behind her, touched the wall.

"Goddamn bloody lunatic!" He slapped one hand back over his face, the side that wasn't cut with the puckered scar, the one she'd kicked. "Get down from there before I wrap my hands around your pretty little neck and snap it like a twig."

"I'll cut off your balls before I let you give me the bliss!" she shouted on a burst of inspiration. It was taken straight out of Daphne's stories. The people in them were always spouting things like that.

His hand dropped away. "What did you say?"

Did she say it wrong? She was suddenly disconcerted. It was ridiculous that she would be concerned about embarrassing herself given there were far more relevant worries to think about, but she was never really clear on some of the finer points of the things Daphne told her. She had, for example, no idea what exactly "balls" were. She knew men didn't want them cut off from wherever they grew, and to say one would do so was guaranteed to intimidate the most villainous of men. "Y-your b-balls. I'll cut them off. I will. You better not touch me."

"Where on God's earth do you get these things?"

"That's none of your business, you blackguard." That was good. When uncertain, retreat behind indignation. Mother had taught her that.

"You are the most deranged creature I have ever met." He shook his head, still amazed.

"You have insulted me five times now, not counting the assault on my person your men perpetrated upon me out on the moor. You are a . . . a . . ."

He cocked a brow. "Used up all your expletives?"

"Beast!"

Clapping a hand over his chest, it made a solid thumping sound just above his heart. One corner of his mouth hitched up, making him look like the devil himself. "You've wounded me deeply."

She swallowed, distracted by the way his body was so large across the shoulders. She hadn't ever met a man with quite as much breadth to him. A memory stirred. She tried to chase it, but recognition eluded her.

He stepped up onto the bed, his look pure aggression. She squeaked and tried to slide up the wall.

"I am beginning to find your antics, though initially amusing, increasingly annoying," he said. His voice, low and rich, vibrated in the air like a growl. "I want to know who you are and what you were doing riding this morning." He cocked his head, as if an idea had just struck him and a new rage crackled in the air around him. "Did Glorianna send you?"

"I-I don't know any Glorianna. I'm telling you nothing more. So, can you just let me go free, isn't that right?"

"Not yet."

"Why? What do you want from me?"

"A little quiet if you can manage it," he snapped harshly. "By Christ, do you always talk this much?"

She felt chastised. It was a sore spot and it drained her dry. She averted her eyes. "I have a tendency to chatter when I'm nervous. Mother tries to signal me if it gets to be too much."

He gave her a meaningful look. "I wish she were here. Has it occurred to you that things will go better if you cooperate with me?"

Ire thwarted reason once again. "Oh, you'd like that, wouldn't you? Well, I happen to be utterly uninterested in making your life more simple."

"Even if it complicates your own?" he shot. His gaze flickered over her before he turned away, as though suddenly disgusted with the entire matter. She had seen that arrogant gesture before, she'd swear it. The light didn't reveal much, but as it spilled over his hair, catching the gleaming darkness alight, she was struck with sudden recollection.

The gleam of light on dark hair, the sharp angle of his cheekbone, the tall, lithe body with that singularly fluid way of moving . . . "Oh, God!" she screeched.

He turned back.

"I know you! You're him!"

A murderer.

His brows forked down. His eyes darted over her, squinting to get a closer look. "Have we met?"

"No, but I know you. Everyone does. The earl of Waring."

Her thoughts ran wild. If he killed his own father, how easy would it be for him to dispose of an impudent little debutante who had somehow gotten tangled up in his evil plans. She pressed harder up against the wall.

Jabbing his fingers into his hair again, he raked hard, muttering, "Christ!"

In Daphne's stories, the women were always defiant and brave. But, oh, she didn't feel defiant and brave, not anymore. All her resolve to stand firm against him was crumbling. She could feel heat coming off his body. It was heady with faint traces of soap and horse sweat and it swept into her head and swirled around her brain.

She tried her best, though, not to show anything of the emotion coursing through her. This man was like a wolf. If he smelled fear, she'd be devoured. To give in to him would be to betray herself and feed his power.

So she said, in the most dangerous voice she could muster, "Let me go now, you vile cur. If you don't, I shall run you through, gut you and roast you, then feast on your entrails."

He looked at her, no longer amazed, it seemed, at her unconventional outbursts. Somewhat lazily, he asked, "Is this before or after you remove my testicles?"

"What?" She frowned, confused.

"Balls," he clarified.

She blinked, not wanting him to realize her ignorance. So she replied, "After."

"Ah. I was hoping before, as I'd surely expire from the roasting process, thus making the removal of my private parts significantly less painful."

She gasped, jerking back as if he'd struck her with those hands that were clenching and unclenching into fists at his side. "*Private parts!* You, sir, are insufferably disgusting. This is really going too far. You will not speak to me with such disrespect, referring to your . . . your . . ."

"Balls."

"Balls? You mean, balls are . . . private . . . um . . . Oh, God. Oh, my God!" Her knees buckled and she crumpled against him.

Chapter 2

THE LAST THING Morgan expected from this absurd girl was that she would collapse into tears. One moment she was hissing and spitting like a cornered she-cat and the next she had flopped forward onto his chest and begun making wretched gulping noises that made him wince to imagine the state of his cravat.

He was rather particular about his appearance as a rule. His three-month incarceration and the abysmal conditions he'd been forced to endure had left a lasting impression on the merits of cleanliness and well-laundered clothing.

His shirt was of fine lawn, starched slightly, pressed to perfection. As she sobbed against it, he rolled his eyes heavenward. It was merely a gesture. He had long since stopped looking for answers from that quarter.

For the sake of his wardrobe, he placed an arm loosely about the girl's shoulders and tried to pry her off. When she didn't budge, he sighed in disgust. "What are you blubbering about?"

She raised her head just enough to be heard. "I can't believe you let me say that awful word."

"Let you?"

"You should have told me what it meant." This renewed her tears. He bore her hysterics in stoic silence, resisting the urge to set her on her heels. She finally subsided, snuffling as she drew back from him.

"I need a handkerchief." She said it like a child, with a delicate sniff that was so piteous he nearly growled.

"I have none," he said curtly.

She looked down, angling her face into her shoulder to rub her nose against her dress. Her hands were still bound behind her. God, she looked completely pathetic.

"Oh, bloody hell. It's ruined anyway." Unwrapping his cravat, he held it up to her nose. "Blow," he instructed. She did so delicately into the fine cloth. "Now turn around," he muttered, "and I'll untie your hands."

As soon as she was free, she wiped her face and wadded up the ill-used cravat, then wrapped her arms about herself, like a waif gripped by a chill. But the look she gave him was all woman—enraged woman who might melt a polar cap with one blast of those mercurial eyes. They were large, almond shaped, and soulful enough to put an ache in the heart of a man less cynical than himself.

She said, "I know what you want. I'm not your ordinary miss who has been sheltered all her life."

No ordinary miss? "I'd noticed."

He'd noticed a great deal. Her hair, for example, was all different shades of dark blond and chestnut blended together. She was surprisingly tall. And athletic. Lord, she'd leaped up onto that bed like a sprite. She'd kicked hard, too. Hurt him but good, the little termagant. Lithe, long-limbed. Not exactly the look that was currently in fashion, but he'd not favored the soft, pampered missishness that was the rage of the bon ton. There was something alluring about this woman that defied detection to one feature. Rather, it was the inconsistent sum of her parts, the contrast and contradictions. Her strength and vulnerability, her wisdom and hopeless naivete.

Indeed, she was no ordinary miss at all.

How he'd mistaken her for Glorianna was inexplicable. But she'd been on a horse riding the moor as Glorianna always did—the only time she was allowed out of Blackheath Hall without Sanderson dogging her heels.

There was little resemblance, but he supposed the mistake was understandable given the distance from which he spied her. It was true that this girl was much taller than Glorianna, but she'd been seated upon a horse when he'd spotted her. Her hair was not the same color, but she'd been wearing it tucked up under a hat, as any lady might. With his blood boiling for the long-awaited chance, his anxiousness had led him into error.

"I know what you want." She said it quietly, with a hint of mystery.

He raised his brows. What was this?

"I know about the bliss," she told him.

Folding his arms over his chest, he queried. "What, perchance, would that be?"

"Oh, please. It is what all you villains do to your captives. You . . . force yourself on them. You give them the bliss. I *know*."

Warring reactions gripped him. He recoiled at the accusation of rape. He'd *never* forced a woman and didn't like the implication he ever would. But his body's response to her had been immediate and powerful.

What had she called it? The bliss?

The term was both melodramatic and so blatantly sexual it landed like a punch to his sternum when he thought of it. The *bliss*, for God's sake.

It would be nothing less than that, he thought suddenly.

All right. He wanted her. Depraved though it was, he wanted to kiss her until she was no longer unwilling. She would cry out for him, begging him to take her and when he did . . .

It would be bliss, he was most certain.

"I think I've had enough of this ridiculous conversation. Come," he said, spinning swiftly away from her and heading toward the door.

He opened it for her. Not turning around, he said. "I'll

take you back up to the moor. You can find your way home from there."

"But you . . . I thought . . ." She stopped in her tracks and stared at him. He lifted his finger and silently ordered her out of the cottage.

She must have sensed the leashed emotions in him—lust, and fury at himself for that lust—for she ducked her head and dutifully hurried in the direction he indicated. He let her pass, and her hair brushed his cheek, filling his head with the scent of woman. For a fleeting moment he thought his knees were going to give out.

He summoned his senses back to function with an act of will. He would be worse than the most useless of fools to let his body's reflexive reactions rule him. He took her outside.

"Hurry up," he muttered as he stalked toward the tethered horses. With the storm clearing, the air had a sharp, crisp tang. He filled himself with it, hoping to chase the cobwebs in his brain. They were muddling his thoughts.

But the master web spinner was right behind him. He felt her presence acutely despite his outward appearance of ignoring her. He didn't glance back, he didn't say a word. He figured the less he spoke, the better.

He waited beside her horse, knowing he would have to help her mount. She looked wretched, her fashionable riding habit crumpled and torn, smudges of dirt marring the fine peacock-blue material and discoloring the smooth creaminess of her skin. She still wore that absurd hat with the feather sticking out of it, although it hung at a rather despondent angle on a tangled mass of hair half out of its pins.

Her state of dishabille was incredibly sexy. He was guilty and angry all at once, overcome with a desire to rip out that damned hat with the feather and crush it under his heel.

She paused in front of him. "Why are you letting me go?"

"Don't you wish to go?"

"Of course I do. But, you said you wouldn't."

"What I said was not yet. I had to think about the whole mess. But there's no reason to keep you. You are of no use to me. And I don't think you will tell this to anyone. After all, you yourself spoke of wanting to keep this out of the gossip mills. I promise I shall not speak a word about this entire incident, if you don't. So we shall have a little alliance, you and I."

She made a sound like an indignant hiccup. "An unholy one, you cloven-hooved cur!" she said and grabbed the reins of her horse. They tangled on the branch. She yanked, but they only snagged tighter.

Wordlessly, he leaned forward and with a flick of his wrist, set them free.

She tossed her head and sent her curls tumbling as she led her horse away from him, clearly wanting no assistance. Her pride was served well by the use of a fallen log as a mounting block. Her athleticism was remarkable. She swung easily up into the saddle.

He had to admire her, fool though she was. Raging fire, subtle beauty. A face dominated by Madonna eyes and framed by hair burnished with gold where the sunlight hit. A body that made his mouth dry, with high, firm breasts, a slender waist, and a delicious curve filling the sidesaddle.

Tightly, she said, "I suppose I am expected to be grateful to you."

With deliberate insolence, he tore his eyes from their admiring wandering and drawled, "You might be. It could have gone worse for you today."

She flushed, then tried to scoff. "You wouldn't dare! You forget, I know who you are."

"True. Which reminds me you never did tell me your name."

"As if I would. Besides, what does it matter? As you say, we are soon to be rid of one other."

"I'd like to have something to call you when I think of you."

She reacted to that. Taken aback, her tone changed, softened. "You shall think of me?"

"From time to time I might. It will serve to act as a bitter remedy for rash action and remind me of the follies of pride.

I was far too sure of myself this morning, a mistake I'll take care not to repeat."

He watched her spine go rigid. It was movement both fluid and regal and he couldn't help admire the gesture for all it irritated him.

Her eyes sparkled as she shot, "And what of you? How shall I think of you when I recollect this dreadful encounter?"

Her tension caused the mare to skitter sideways. He grabbed the pommel of her horse and held it steady. "But you know my name."

"I know your *title*. I suppose I can refer to you simply as 'my lord' when I think back on this fiasco, but something in me rebels at such a courtesy, as your behavior had demonstrated you to be unworthy of it. I think I shall stick with 'bloody bastard,' which has a much more satisfactory ring to it, to my mind."

He chuckled. "My name is Morgan. That is no secret. Perhaps when you recall the more kindly aspects of our meeting, you will think of me by my given name. Now. You see how easy it is? We can be civil to one another. Why don't you try it, and tell me what name I might pin to my memories?"

Peering down at him, her lips curled. "As it would happen, my name is Morgan, too."

He was surprised at his explosion of sharp frustration.

He wanted to know her name.

He shook his head. "You are a prime piece."

"And you are a—"

"My God, you are the most stubborn thing I've ever . . . Just give me a name, goddamn it!"

"Blackguard!"

He stopped, looked at her. Grinned. Letting go of the pommel, he moved over to his mount and swung up into the saddle. Bringing the massive gelding alongside her pretty horse, he shot, "Mind if I call you Blackie for short?"

M ORGAN TOOK LEAH up to the moor in silence. Along the way, she wondered whether Daphne had missed her, and if she was worried. It had been nearly four hours since she'd ridden out.

What would she think when Leah told her she had been abducted by the mysterious earl of Waring? Would she think it a wonderful adventure, or would she be scandalized? She couldn't imagine Daphne being scandalized, but from experience Leah knew she had a curious ability to push her loved ones to their limits.

She wouldn't tell her about this. Daphne, for all of her liberated views, might feel obligated in view of Leah having been left in her care, to inform Mother, and Mother *must not know.*

There was no point, in any event. It hadn't been so terrible, after all. In fact, the earl of Waring had proved *rude,* yes, but quite reasonable in returning her promptly. And, as he had noted, it was not to her credit to have the meeting known.

So she would keep it as her secret. And his.

The thought of sharing a secret with this man was strangely exciting. She glanced nervously at his stoic profile and wondered if he were truly a murderer. Surely, such a nefarious creature would not have dealt so fairly with a helpless victim such as herself.

She had a feeling he would laugh at her thinking of herself in those terms.

"Are we close to Madigan's Tor?" she asked. She didn't mean it to sound challenging, but somehow it did. She tried to soften it. "I mean, that is close to where your men grabbed me. I can find my way home from there. It's just that I'd like to know how far away we are, how much longer we'll be riding."

He was curt. "Why don't you just relax?"

"Relax? I have just been terrorized!"

He snorted, clearly disbelieving she was so affected.

"But of course, I wouldn't want to cause *you* any inconvenience over the small matter of my inconsequential feelings. So, I'll just *relax,* that's what I'll do. Why, I'll just pretend that this is my normal jaunt through wild moorlands with a notorious earl who has abducted me and tied me up and struck a devil's bargain to ensure he doesn't rot in prison for the crime. What a jolly idea, then, I'll just relax and enjoy."

"Have it your way, Blackie."

"Don't call me that."

His head turned toward her and his glare nearly knocked her off her horse. "Then give me something else to call you."

The very fact that he wanted it was reason enough to defy him. "You know I will not."

His smile was like a wolf's. "So be it. Blackie."

Gnashing her teeth, she choked back complaints and rebuffs as they continued on their way. It occurred to her he hadn't answered her questions about how much farther they had to go and if he were taking her to Madigan's Tor. She wouldn't humiliate herself by asking for details he was obviously not going to give, but it infuriated her that he had dismissed her so easily.

Morgan halted at last, leaning forward on his pommel and looking down over the dells. He had taken them to the edge of the moor, and she recognized the meadows and the walled pastures of farmland. She was close to Barstow Cottage, Daphne's home. It was nested in the woods to the north. Behind her was the tor, she could see now, although she hadn't noticed it before since they had come across the heath from the other direction. He had taken her even farther than she had asked.

"Pretty land, Yorkshire," he commented, swinging his leg over his horse and landing neatly on the ground. Coming to her side, he took the reins from her and offered her his hand to help her dismount.

She drew back. There was an intensity in his dark gold eyes as he reached up for her that gave her pause. She didn't think he meant her harm. It was just . . . she couldn't have said what made her reluctant to place herself in his hands. He settled the matter by pulling her down as easily as if she were a kitten being rescued from a tree.

For her dignity's sake, she didn't give in to the urge to struggle. This left her a bit breathless once she was on her feet. She continued to stare at him, studying the harsh planes of his face, the grim lines, that angry, frightening scar until she realized that he'd released her.

Taking a step back, she had to find something to do. She slapped at the wrinkles in her riding habit and began to fuss. "Just look at this. I am an absolute mess! This was my favorite riding costume, torn to shreds. Bloody hell!" When she looked up, Morgan had one brow cocked. "What?" she accused with sullen defensiveness. "I had it specially made, for goodness sake. It cost a fortune."

"That is distressing. However, as I see it, Blackie, we can stand here and fluff your skirts some more, or end our association and get you returned home. It's completely up to you."

She looked doubtfully down at the cozy farms that led to Daphne and her pleasant cottage. Why was she suddenly reluctant to leave him?

His voice brought her head back. "Come here. I have some last instructions for you."

Her body reacted as his hands settled on her shoulders.

"Remember our bargain," he said. "I will keep this entire episode to myself, and you . . ." He paused, and his gaze fastened on her lips. As if it were disconnected with his present thoughts, he muttered absently, "Will keep your mouth . . . shut."

He didn't say anything further. He kept staring at her, though, and she was thinking how much she wanted to say something smart and crushing and stomp off but she couldn't move somehow and he kept staring and staring.

And then he bent his head and he kissed her.

He kissed her directly on the lips, with her body pressed full against his and his arms locking her in place so that she couldn't struggle. His mouth sealed over hers, demanding submission. She went limp, with shock, with reaction, with the hot, liquid feeling that curled inside her and held her fast.

It was Leah Brodie's first taste of desire.

A ND FOR MORGAN, it was an instant fever. He hadn't anticipated that.

How could he have guessed she'd lean into him like this, as if eager for him to prolong the contact, increase it even? It made him gather her tighter into his arms. He hadn't intended this. It was supposed to be a quick kiss. But a slow spiral of pleasure snared him the moment his lips descended upon hers.

Her mouth was soft. Silk against his own. She mewled and he felt his stomach clench as passion tightened its grip. She was pliant in his arms. God, he could feel the crush of her breasts firm and full against his chest. He moved his mouth, savoring the contact of his lips on hers. The taste of her was pure sweetness and heat mingled together.

The perception of that sweetness reminded him of who she was—what she was—and that gave him the ability to pull back.

Her eyes remained closed, her lips pursed and rouged from their contact. He felt the protest of his inflamed lust as he put space between them. She may not be an ordinary miss, but she *was* a virgin, he was certain of it. And although he might not be a gentleman any longer, goddamn it all, he had some honor left to him. He knitted the remnants of it together and stood firm against that irresistible invitation.

"Blackie?"

Her eyelids swept up and he was staring into those haunting eyes. They were direct, soft, and deep, and had him completely taken in so that when the blow came, it actually surprised him.

"Christ!" He jerked back, astounded with the force with which she struck. He'd expected she might be angry, pre-

pared himself for perhaps a slap, but she'd got him good enough to bring stars dancing in his peripheral vision.

Damn her. That was twice now she'd hit him!

"How . . . how . . ." Her lips trembled and she stalled, apparently speechless.

"How dare I?" he prompted in a low voice.

When she swung again, he caught her hand and spun her around so that her back was pressed up along his side. Her derriere nestled rather nicely against the side of his hip, brushing tantalizing touches along his manhood and doing nothing to lessen the pressure there. That was not to be endured, so he shifted her and steeled his mind against the distraction of her ample breasts curving against the inside of his arm.

His groin throbbed painfully. He released her and she whirled, looking wild and feral—a spitting cat cornered and ready to fight. For a moment, he just stared at her, caught in an unreasonable admiration for the reckless pride of hers. And then, inevitably, it began to annoy him.

"K-kee . . . keep you . . . your hands off me!"

He pulled himself together, speaking low and gruff. "Go home, Blackie. Console yourself with the likely fact that we shall never see each other again."

"If I am lucky enough for that to be true, it will still be too soon!"

"I am quite certain. Run along."

"Run along? Run along! See here. I am not a child, to be dismissed."

Leah watched his gaze rake down her body with merciless deliberateness, flaring a renewed heat inside her. Sharp, tingling darts of pleasure for which she absolutely despised him stirred within. She choked on the bitter blend of fury and humiliation.

She had let him kiss her.

She had kissed him back.

She wanted to strike him again. But the memory of his nimble move last time, how she ended up wrapped in his steely arms, frustrated her. She glared at him. "You are too vile to be endured," she said, "and I shall be relieved to be quit of you, but before I go I have one last thing to say to you."

Her body felt beaten from the inside, as if the sensations he had evoked had been a physical assault. He seemed to be staring at her mouth and her heart tumbled at the thought of him kissing her again.

He said, "Well? What do you have to tell me, and heaven be praised if it truly will be the last thing."

She had forgotten what she meant to say, which really disappointed her since she had been thoroughly looking forward to giving him the dressing-down he deserved. She cast about for something else instead.

"That . . . well, simply that you are vile. And I am relieved to . . . er, be quit of you. Which I already said, I know. But I repeat it now—for emphasis!"

"Do you care to add that if you never see me again it will be too soon? For emphasis."

"You feel quite superior, don't you?" she challenged. "It's all well and good for you to best me under these circumstances. I'll allow I am not adept at this coarse battle of wits. Unlike yourself, I have been gently reared. Your parents have obviously neglected to teach you how to comport yourself in polite society. Therefore, your mockery of me and complete disregard for my welfare is testimony to your lack of proper rearing—"

"Have a care, Blackie," he interrupted darkly. "I'll not tolerate slander against either of my parents. My choices are my own, as are my faults."

"And they are legion. You took shameless advantage of me, my lord, in that . . . that . . . dreadful kiss as well as the other liberties you and your repellant cohorts perpetrated upon my person during this odious episode. And I submit to you that you should be ashamed of yourself."

There was a dull silence, during which she watched him. He seemed carved of stone. Nothing gave him away, but a sense beyond the evidence of her eyes told her he was struggling with something very deep and disturbing.

He spoke at last. "I have no doubt that I shall indeed do that. In truth, that emotion is the bane of my life. It should give you no small comfort, I imagine, to know it. Now go home."

She swallowed, not knowing what to make of this. He remained unmoving, unblinking.

Having no alternative but retreat, she grabbed the pommel and turned toward the mare. She felt his hands lift her foot to help her mount. She ignored the heat his touch produced, flipping her hair back out of the way of the reins once she was seated.

He gripped her saddle for a moment, holding her in place. "Good-bye, Blackie."

She didn't answer him. She refused to even look at him.

Pulling the horse around, she raced down to Daphne's cottage, away from the Wicked Earl of Waring.

Morgan.

Chapter 3

LEAH'S CARRIAGE DREW to a halt in the circular carriage-way at Glenwood Park, the splendid country estate of the viscount and viscountess de Fontvilliers. They were, of course, simply Julia and Raphael to her mind, her sister and brother-in-law. As she was welcomed in the center hallway, she found her other family members had already arrived the previous day.

Her mother embraced her, then held her at arm's length and inspected her, smoothing back an escaped tendril of her hair before smiling. "Feeling better?"

She meant the business with Carl. But Leah was thinking of the earl of Waring.

Desdemona was both a harsh taskmaster and warm giver of approval when her daughters met her lofty standards. Leah had lived for those accolades but now, standing in the circle of her mother's arms, she risked the ultimate censure as inexplicable tears pricked at her eyes.

Swallowing hard, she willed them away. "Much better, thank you."

Her mother was doubtful, her shrewd eyes holding Leah's for a heartbeat too long until her husband, Francis Brodie, intervened. "She's just been a bit homesick for her family, Mona," he said, coming up to embrace her. "Just as we have been for her." His hug was crushing.

"Just so," Leah managed.

Her auburn-haired eldest sister came forward. Julia Brodie Giscard, the viscountess de Fontvilliers, was slender and tall, like Leah, with the same willowy, long-limbed frame inherited from their father. "I'm so glad you are finally here. We've missed you."

"Hello, Julia." They embraced. Turning to the tall figure hovering at her sister's elbow, Leah greeted her brother-in-law. "Good day, Raphael."

Raphael executed a respectful bow while offering a rather remote smile. Leah was in awe of the viscount, for he was an imposing man, both physically and in his demeanor. Handsome and taller than even her father, he had an air about him that she had never warmed to.

She didn't really understand everything that had happened three years ago when he and Julia were married so suddenly. She only knew there was some kind of urgency about their wedding and her sister had been desperately unhappy for a while. Since she and Julia had never been close, Leah had never learned the particulars. Whenever she asked, her mother's mouth grew tight and she shushed her with one of her most imperious looks.

She didn't see why it was all still a secret. It had turned out splendidly. These days her sister was the object of everyone's envy. She had a handsome, desirable husband who was titled, as rich as Croesus, and doted on her to a degree that was downright embarrassing at times. They had a beautiful baby daughter, Cosette, who was six months of age and the most adorable creature any of them had ever seen. Their fabulous home in the beautiful Cumbrian Lake District was always bustling with their whirlwind schedule of friends and pet charities. If there were a blemish in Julia's perfection, it was that she was too perfect.

"Does anyone have any word from Laura?"

The sister between Julia and herself, Laura, had married

an affluent man whose business interests took him abroad. They currently lived Ceylon so that Nicholas Rawlings could oversee his father's coffee plantations.

Julia said, "I had a letter from her just last week. It is in the parlor. You can read it for yourself."

She felt a twinge of neglect that Laura had never written to her. The close relationship between her two older sisters had always been a source of resentment. Then again, Leah considered that she had never taken the time to compose a missive to Laura, either. She just now realized that her sister might be lonely and perhaps chatty letters from home did much to cheer her. No doubt Julia wrote them in droves. Perhaps she had been a bit selfish to think of her own wounded feelings and not what it must be like for Laura so far from family.

They retired into the drawing room and Leah inquired after her two younger sisters, Hope and Marie. She was told they had gone to the nursery for a quiet rest after an outing earlier this morning.

She read Laura's letter to Julia and dashed off a reply while tea was served. Her father dozed. Raphael sat next to Julia and touched her every chance he got. Desdemona pretended not to notice, but Leah couldn't tear her eyes away from the naked affection being demonstrated before her.

They shared the bliss, didn't they? Strange, she'd never thought of it, but of course they did. And she thought of Morgan Gage and what it would be like to be sitting here with him, her family around her, and him touching her like that. She didn't know how Julia could bear her husband's touch so stoically; Leah was certain she herself would melt into the chair cushions if it were Waring touching her.

Taking two pastries, she hid them in the folds of her dress and excused herself. On light feet, she crept up to the nursery. Marie and Hope were awake, Hope reading aloud to her sister from a storybook.

"Hello, ladies," Leah said as she breezed in with the sweets she had pilfered.

"Hello, Leah," Hope said brightly.

Marie, the youngest, sprang to her feet. "Yummie! I love tarts." She grabbed hers and took a big bite. Through her mouthful, she said, "All we get for tea is bread and jam."

"Which is only fitting, as you would gorge yourself on pastries if given the chance. You must eat your good food first, and then the sweets."

"I don't see why," she mused, taking another bite.

"Life has so many rules," Hope observed, nibbling at her tart.

"How true." Leah sighed, sitting beside the pretty blond.

"How is Cousin Daphne?" the little beauty asked Leah in between bites.

"She's very well," Leah replied. "She sent you presents. When my bags are unpacked, I'll fetch them for you."

"I want to go to visit her," Marie said. The only one of the five with dark hair, she was a stark contrast to Hope in every way. Dark versus fair, challenging versus complacent, mischievous versus serene. And yet the two were best friends and constant companions.

Julia and Laura, Hope and Marie. Leah, in the middle, the only one without a best friend. She used to feel sorry for herself. It was the excuse she made to tattle on her older sisters and boss the younger ones around. As she'd grown, she'd grown less combative. It was then she realized that what she had wanted was a connection like each one of her sisters had, with someone at least.

She had Cousin Daphne, she supposed. It wasn't the same, though.

"You have crumbs on your chin," she told Marie. "You are too young for Cousin Daphne. You will go when you are older."

"I want to go now."

"Well, you cannot."

"You sound like Mother," Marie complained, licking the last of the tart off of her fingers. "Hope, can I have some of your tart?"

Leah intervened. "Marie, it's not fair of you to always

gulp down your food and then ask Hope to share simply because it takes her longer to eat it."

"I don't mind," said Hope, breaking off a generous portion and handing it to Marie. Looking smug, the little girl downed it in three bites. Hope still nibbled and Marie, eyeing the small piece left to her sister, caught Leah's reproving look and scowled.

"Tell us one of Cousin Daphne's stories," Marie demanded as she settled back.

"Are you sure you don't want me to finish reading the book? No? Very well. I'll tell you a story."

Both girls settled eagerly into comfortable positions snuggled up against their sister. Leah smoothed her skirts, thinking. Then she began.

"Once there was a lonely girl who took a ride on the moors one day. Little did she know that a man waited there for her—waited to take her away for he thought she was another woman, a woman whom he hated. He wanted to punish this other woman, for she was his wife and she had betrayed him bitterly and he wanted to make her sorry she had done so. So he grabbed the innocent girl thinking she was his evil wife and took her to his lair where he had laid a fresh bed of straw, for even though he was angry and bound on vengeance, there was a kindness in him that he never allowed anyone to see."

Marie's mouth rounded. "Oh, my, Leah. This is a very exciting story. Tell us more."

THE BRODIE YEARLY visit to Glenwood Park lasted three weeks. Leah's days were filled with playing with Cosette, relaxing with her family in which she revelled in not having anything special to do, and occasional picnics to the nearby scenic lakes, or tarns, for which the region was known.

Desdemona took the girls shopping in the village once or twice. The younger children had a wonderful time exploring the surrounding woods and taking tea with the grown-ups, which was a treat. Their governess was not in attendance, so they were free from lessons for a while. It was a time to be looked forward to all the year, culminating in the tradition of a large country ball attended by Julia and Raphael's neighbors and local friends.

Leah found the comforts of her family eased her preoccupation with the notorious earl of Waring. But she dreamt of him at night, and sometimes, when caught in a quiet moment, she'd wonder if he'd found the woman he was looking for— this Glorianna—or if he were still searching for her on the moors. Did he think of her as she did him, if only, as he had heartlessly quipped, to remind himself of the folly of pride?

She was in the parlor answering correspondence from some of her London friends one day when Julia came in. She made small talk, then ventured, "Is something the matter, Leah? You've been so quiet. I get the distinct impression something is on your mind."

Had she been that obvious? Leah replied briskly, "I suppose if there is any difference in me, it is the maturity of having gone through a season. I am of marriageable age, you know. I am a woman now. Should I not act differently?"

"It appears more," Julia said with a small smile, "as if something is upsetting you. I hope that unfortunate episode with Carl Enders is not still bothering you. Leah, I know we've never been very close. I suppose I have some blame in that, but frankly, you didn't make it very easy to like you sometimes. You were always trying to get me in trouble."

"Well, it never worked. Mother always doted on you. And you and Laura were thick as thieves."

Julia's eyebrows lifted. "Were you jealous?"

"Of course not—"

"I'm sorry if we left you out. I never realized it until now. Frankly, I thought you didn't like us very much."

Leah shrugged. Tattling was her way of evening the odds, pointing out her sisters flaws so that hers were not so glaringly obvious. It was true, she hadn't been very pleasant to her sisters, but not because she didn't like them. She had been in awe of them and afraid to show it.

Leah said, "How could I not like you? You were perfect and Mother adored everything you said and did. And Laura never failed to make her laugh. She is always sparkling and witty."

"And you were the worst spy!" Julia declared, and laughed.

"I know." Despite her remorse, she chuckled, recalling some of her more outrageous antics. "It was awful of me. I am sorry now, Julia, truly I am. I suppose it is true that I was rather a brat to you and Laura."

Julia was surprised at Leah's honesty. "Well, now that we are grown, I'd like us to be friends."

"I'd like that, too, Julia. But I'm not upset about Carl, really I'm not."

"All right. Are you nervous about the ball, then? It will be your first time out in society since that night, I know, but people are so much different here in the country. More forgiving. I suppose it is because they are all so eccentric themselves, or maybe because they have more with which to occupy their minds than gossip. In any event, I think it is the perfect start to ease back into the public world."

"I am sure you are right," Leah said, letting Julia think this was the reason she'd been pensive.

But her sister was far too perceptive. "You know, as I've been watching you these past days, I had cause to remember a time when I myself was rather quieter than was my normal habit. I had a great deal of secrets then. It was when I had first met Raphael. I was so confused . . . and I thought it possible that you might have found someone. . . . Of course, I could be wrong. I wish you would tell me, Leah, because you show all the signs of a woman pining for a man. Will you trust me with your secrets?"

Leah was silent for a long while. She decided it was hopeless and sighed. "I met the earl of Waring when I was at Cousin Daphne's house. It was an accidental meeting, but . . . quite memorable. He was kind to me . . . sort of. But he was very rude, too, and I was—I am!—furious with him and wish I could stop thinking about him because he said he would never think of me, except to ponder his regrets and that was a very hurtful thing to say, don't you agree?"

"You can't stop thinking about him?"

"Well, seeing as he was insufferable, I should say not."

Julia's expression was inscrutable. "He has a shadowy reputation. Mysterious. It might make a woman feel . . . romantic?"

"He is very much the opposite. He was a swaggering, arrogant lout, completely annoying. When he kissed me, I hit him. The nerve of that man, as if I would like it!"

"He kissed you?" Julia cried.

Leah stopped, shocked at her own stupidity in blurting that out. "Yes," she admitted.

Julia stared at her for a moment. "He didn't do anything further, I hope. What I mean is, he was not rude or untoward? Oh, bother, I will simply ask outright—did he take liberties?"

"Oh, no. He behaved very honorably, Julia. Other than the kiss, I mean. Which was . . . Well, it wasn't awful. But, anyway, don't worry. He didn't harm me."

Julia relaxed visibly. She gave Leah a long look. "And did you like it?"

Leah's jaw went slack at the question. Julia prodded, "You said it wasn't awful."

"No. I suppose a man like him would know how to kiss a woman senseless. How to hold her just right so that the clouds seemed to spin."

"Is that what happened when he kissed you?"

"Yes," Leah admitted. "Why are you asking so many questions about this? It is humiliating."

"I am trying to determine, Leah, whether you are infatuated with him."

"Absolutely not!"

Julia gave her a disbelieving look. "I know the signs. You call him a bother, yet you defend him. You cannot stop thinking of him. And his kiss made you weak and light-headed. They are the signs, you know."

"But surely . . ." She stopped. "You don't really think it could be so?"

"It seems distinctly possible."

"It's true, then. Oh, Julia!" Leah closed her hands over her eyes and exclaimed, "This is by far the worst thing I've ever done!"

O N THE NIGHT of the ball, Leah was nervous after all. She hadn't thought she would be, but facing everyone again, even all new faces, sent a cloud of butterflies into wild flight inside her stomach.

Without making a fuss, Julia stayed close at hand, smoothing out the first hour with effortless conversation and light-as-air gaiety that belied any concern. Introductions were made with no sign of anyone having heard anything about Leah's London debacle and her dance card filled up quickly. After a while, Leah began to enjoy herself.

She had taken special care with her appearance tonight, thinking it would shore up her confidence to know she looked her best. Her satin gown was her favorite, elegant and subtle in shades of cream and taupe. Matching rosettes rested in her chestnut hair, arranged artfully into a crown of soft curls.

Her brother-in-law came up to her and struck a bow. "I see you aren't dancing this dance. Care to give me the honor?"

"Julia told you to make certain I would not be a wallflower, did she not? You can tell her nearly all my dances are promised. I am merely having a rest."

"Nonsense," he replied smoothly, taking her hand in his and leading her out to join in the waltz. "It is my pleasure."

Fontvilliers was always arrogant. It usually annoyed her, but she didn't resist as he swept her in a semicircle and rested his hand on her waist.

He danced wonderfully and she let herself be led by his expert direction.

"Julia has been concerned about you," he said.

She avoided his eyes. "We have spoken. I believe she is reassured."

"Ah. Well, that is good. What concerns my wife concerns me."

"Don't you think that a tad presumptuous?" she quipped.

"Not at all." He absolutely refused to be insulted. "When someone owns your heart, you will see how it is. A man and a woman become connected in an integral way, and what affects one's happiness is twofold the worry for the other."

"It sounds dreadfully intrusive," she deadpanned.

He grinned. She had to admit, Raphael was a devastatingly handsome man, and even she wasn't immune to that grin. "You will see," he repeated. "Isn't there anyone who interests you this evening?"

She made a moue of distaste and refused to comment. Raphael's good-natured chuckle loosened her mood and she smiled. He was rather charming, even halfway likeable if one could get past his snarling exterior.

Suddenly, she went stiff in his arms.

Not noticing right away, Raphael said, "Thank you for the lovely dance. Your reluctance was unfounded, was it not, for I didn't tread on your toes once. Leah?"

She couldn't answer. She could only stare. Raphael gazed down at her, but she kept her eyes fixed over his shoulder, to the tall man who had just entered the ballroom.

Waring was here.

In her sister's house, just like he'd come to the Steele's ball, unapologetic and brazen as you please, standing on the edge of the floor and sweeping the crowd with his daggerlike gaze.

Had he been a figment of her imagination, she would have conjured him thusly, bold and stark and full of contrasts. He was dressed to perfection. A crisply starched shirt and cravat showed like snow against the pitch of his tailcoat and the dark richness of his hair. Unlike his nearly mystical appearance in London, however, she could see him head-on, watch his hazel eyes flit from face to face, find her and trap her with a stare that caught her breath in her throat.

Raphael's grip on her tightened. "Are you well?"

Before she could recover, he followed her gaze. "Who is he?" Raphael asked. He had picked up her tension. It showed in his voice.

"No one." What a stupid answer! "A friend," she amended.

He returned his attention to her. "Did you invite him? You seem surprised. More like shocked."

"No. Yes. I mean . . ." She was never a good liar, so she chose a neutral version of the truth. "I didn't know he planned to attend."

Raphael released her. "Who is he?"

"The earl of Waring," she said quickly and began to move away before he could respond. "I'd best see to him." She struck out blindly, intent only on removing herself from Raphael's all-too-knowing eyes.

When she looked up, Waring was gone. She looked swiftly around her. Raphael was still frowning, following her with that inscrutable gaze of his, so she exited the ballroom and passed through the hall and went into the dining room. It contained long tables laden with filled champagne flutes and canapés. A well-dressed crowd milled among the delicacies. Waring was not in here.

A figure moved beyond the French doors and she followed. The moment she stepped into the darkened terrace off the dining room, she realized she was flushed with excitement and chagrin. Here she was chasing him again, feeling the same fluster she had felt that first night, the same excitement and urgency.

A whiskey voice muttered low into her ear, "Good evening, Blackie."

She whirled, coming almost nose to nose with Morgan. His angular features were devoid of any expression, save a wry twist to his sensual mouth, as if he knew the effect of his sudden appearance and relished it.

The stone baluster was behind her, and she reached back to wrap her fingers around the cool marble in order to steady herself. The feel of it in her palm penetrated her dazed state, and she clung to the sensation like a touchstone. Her heart fluttered against the wall of her chest like a trapped starling.

He said, "Your servant," and held his white-gloved hand out for her. Years of training prodded her to move. She placed her own ivory-clad hand in his. It looked very small. She had never felt small before. She was tall, her hands long-boned and graceful, but in his larger palm, her hand looked elegant and feminine.

He bent into a smooth bow. "Thank you for not denouncing me," he said, straightening. "I was not sure if you would or not."

"Why are you here?" she blurted.

His smile was slow, insolent, melting her bones. "Why, I came for you."

She blinked.

"May I have this dance?"

"Dance? Oh. Um. I thought you wouldn't . . . you came out here."

"I thought it best our reunion take place in private. Now that we've said our hellos and you haven't fallen into a fit of vapors—or temper, which is what I thought more likely—I'd like to dance with you. Will you?"

It was one of those moments when her mouth disobeyed her better sense. Besides all of the reasons she shouldn't dance with him, there was first and foremost the problem with her body. It didn't seem to be able to move. And yet, without consulting the dance card dangling by its string from her wrist, she answered, "Yes."

She shook off her shock with an effort, scolding herself silently for acting like such a ninny over the man. She concentrated on doing simple things, like moving her feet one in front of the other and calming her rattling teeth.

They attracted notice immediately. Heads swiveled, eyes tracked their progress through the house to the ballroom. Darting a glance to Morgan, she saw he appeared unconcerned at this.

"People are staring at you," she said.

"Yes. That tends to happen when I enter a room. Does it disturb you?"

"No. No, not at all." She cast a look around her and wondered what on earth she was doing. She was mad to be seen openly with the notorious earl. But how could anyone expect her to resist him?

The new dance started up and he escorted her onto the floor. With a deft snap of his wrist, he whirled her about to face him. He bowed. She curtsied. He crooked an elbow and she placed her hand over his. They lined up with the other dancers.

She spoke for his ears alone. "How did you learn who I was?"

"It was relatively simple," he answered. "I just had to make a few well-placed inquiries on who might be visiting relatives in the neighborhood. Despite the dire state the gossips would make my situation, I do have a few remaining friends who would help me gather such information." He broke off when the dance took them in a circle with another couple.

When they came together alone again, she said, "So what do you want with me?"

"Ah, Blackie, you are so impatient."

"I don't like you to call me that."

He inclined his head with satirical patience. "Very well, then. Miss Brodie."

It was time to promenade, and as she moved away from Morgan, her eye caught the notice of a young marquess scowling at her from the edge of the dance floor. She had promised this dance to him, she just now recalled. Quickly she turned her face away to avoid him seeing her. Morgan must have noticed, for he immediately looked over.

"It seems," he told her quietly, "that despite your having savaged a defenseless man in public merely a few months ago, you still have your male admirers. Did I steal his dance? Poor fellow. Ah, I cannot blame his being irritated. You are enchanting."

Holding his hand, she circled around him, damning him

for the flush his praise produced. "Just what do you mean by saying you came here for me?" she fired.

"Merely to join the legions of men who clamor for your favors."

Her heart stopped cold in her chest. Could it be he felt as she did? Had he not been able to forget her, just as she'd been unable to put that kiss out of her mind? Did he lie awake as she did, recollecting every word they spoke to each other?

"Excuse me," a voice said, intruding on her reverie. "I believe Miss Brodie has forgotten that this is my dance."

The man who had issued the softly spoken challenge was the marquess who had been glowering at them from the edge of the dance floor. He addressed himself not to Leah, but directly to Morgan, and there was more than a touch of challenge in his tone.

Leah made a move toward him, hoping to diffuse the situation. Morgan closed steely fingers over her wrist. "Miss Brodie was feeling ill in any event. She is in no condition to dance. You may tell the rest of the bucks who signed her card that she will not be available anymore tonight."

With a gentle yank, he pulled her away from the marquess, who was so taken aback he didn't think to make a scene.

"What are you doing? Where are we going?" she hissed. People were watching them.

"To take in the air. It is excellent for clearing the head when one is ill."

She didn't bother to argue with him that she wasn't ill. Or perhaps she was after all. Her stomach was queasy and she kept having to blink a light-headed feeling away. But he didn't know that, of course. The ruse was meant to get her in private.

The thought nearly buckled her knees.

Once they reached the garden, she pulled her hand out of his grasp and presented him with her back, arms folded, head cocked with indignant cool. She didn't care for his doubletalk and his high-handed mauling, and she'd let him know it, too.

He was silent for a long time.

The night was overcast. The waning moon set frothy clouds aglow, lending an eerie, supernatural effect to the sky. Around her, the sounds of evening were a gentle chorus and despite her irritation with Morgan, she listened in appreciation to the mellow sound. She filled her lungs with the scent of jasmine and roses, closing her eyes for a moment to steady herself before saying, "You seem to have a penchant for party crashing. I saw you that night at Steele's ball. That was how I knew you on the moor."

"I see." She heard him take in a long breath, let it out. "That sort of rudeness is not my usual habit, but there is much in my actions these days that is out of the ordinary. I had had a rather bad day and I was feeling rather urgent."

"You were looking for someone. Dare I guess . . . was it Glorianna?"

"Yes, it was Glorianna. In any event, I am once again present at a ball uninvited. This time, however, I am looking for you."

"I should tell Raphael to remove you. I don't know why I didn't."

"Maybe you didn't want to. I was hoping you'd at least be intrigued, that it would stay your calling the footmen to drag me off until I could speak with you."

"What is so important that you would ruin my evening?" What a lie that was. His appearance was the most fabulously exciting thing that could have possibly happened that night.

"I understand you had a bit of difficulty this season. Some problem with a fellow . . . Carl Enders, I believe it was."

She whirled, her outrage throwing off the haughty airs she'd affected. "Do you need so desperately to hear about it? What a gossip you are!"

"I heard you kicked the poor devil. And that you poured soup on him."

"It was soufflé."

"No doubt he deserved it."

"He was kissing Lady Leonora Danvers under the rose arbor, mere hours after calling upon our home and requesting my father's permission to ask for my hand. I was expecting to become engaged that night."

"And be the one kissing him under the rose arbor. Did you love him?"

"That is none of your business."

Studying her for a moment he pronounced, "You don't appear heartsick. And I think you wouldn't stop at soufflé if it were your heart and not just your pride that was injured."

"You think you know me, do you?" The strange thing was, he was exactly right, but she was not about to admit that.

"Do you think of him?"

"Yes, and often, but only in slightly better terms than I think of you."

"Ah. So you think of me, do you?"

"You are conceited!"

He shrugged. "When you think of that day on the moor—"

"What day on the moor?"

His smile was sudden and startling. "I would imagine you could conjure the memory if you gave it a fair amount of effort."

"Indeed, I never do, not even to 'contemplate the folly of my pride,' as you might have done from time to time."

He chuckled. It was a warm, rich sound, and it hit her like heat. "I think I must have hurt you when I said that."

"You could never hurt me. I would have to care what you thought of me for anything you had to say to hurt me."

"You know, you are not as adorable as you think with that show of arrogance."

"And you are not so charmingly mysterious as you would hope to be."

His patience left him. "By God, you are a bloody trial. You'll never give the tiniest measure, will you?"

"Will you?"

"I shall tell you what I'll give you. A proposition."

She tossed her head, savoring having gotten under his skin. "How bold you are to assume I'd be interested in any sort of proposition from you."

His voice was hard. "You are here with me, are you not?"

That left her sputtering.

He stepped into the silence smoothly, crossing his arms over his chest and peering down at her from along that sharp, fine nose of his. "My proposition is this: You have suffered a rather substantial amount of damage with that entire Enders affair. Not only did you exhibit a scathing temperament and lack of restraint, you allowed everyone to learn he spurned you. That can blacken the most pristine debutante's reputation *permanently*. If you had played it differently, you could have quietly disassociated him and come out much better for it."

"I have no regrets about what I did." Her tone was sullen and defensive and even she knew it sounded false. "Anyone would have done the same."

"No, my dear Miss Brodie, they would not have, not if they had any sense, which I am sorry to say you do not. Courage, yes, and intelligence, indeed yes. Reckless pride and defiance . . . oh, in spades, my dear. But sense, well, that is something you cannot lay claim to. And so it has cost you dearly. In fact you are on the racks with the wags."

"I don't give a fig about what anyone—"

"You lie horribly. Your chin comes up and you look like a child with chocolate smeared all over her face insisting she had nothing to do with the missing bonbons." His tone and his face were soft with gentle amusement. "Now, don't be offended, and don't snap at me, for God's sake. For once, listen."

She crossed her arms over her chest but kept silent.

"Consider that your reputation will be much enhanced if you debut on the summer parties with a new beau. Someone possessed of a title and a fortune and all the things the marriage market values. He must be someone for whom others will envy you, and you, my dear Miss Brodie, will be gloriously vindicated."

"And that man would be . . . ?"

"Myself, of course. A business proposition, Miss Brodie,

is what I offer. It would benefit us both mightily, I think, if we should pose as a couple."

She made a strangled sound as her eyes rounded with shock.

"Speechless?" he purred. "How delightful. The last time I found you that way, I had just finished kissing you. The effect didn't last too long, I am sorry to say."

When she managed to find her voice, it rode a note of stifled rage. "Pray tell me why you propose this ridiculous idea?"

"By posing as a suitor, I can give you back your social desirability. It shouldn't take too long, I don't think. After all, my reputation may be tarnished, but I am a peer, and my attentiveness will erase the stain of Enders's rejection. In turn, my association with you shall mean I will not have to resort to the tedious task of party crashing any longer. Your family is considered good ton and can provide the sort of help I need to give me entrée into the type of parties I desire to be invited to."

She took a moment to digest what he was saying, and then she struck upon something. "This has something to do with Glorianna, doesn't it? You wish to see her at these parties—that is why you wish to reconcile with the polite world."

"Ah," he said with a nod, "that nimble mind of yours."

She sneered. "Not quite so senseless as you supposed, am I? Why do you seek her so desperately?" She paused, braced herself, and asked, "Is she your lover?"

"Good God. She is my stepmother, in fact. My father's wife." His jaw set, turning his lips white with tension, and he jerked his gaze to the side, out over the lawns terracing down to the ponds. "The only family left to me."

The mood had changed in an instant. His body was no longer draped in insouciance, but rigid. His face was tight and the scar glowed in the patch of moonlight that drenched the garden.

"What do you want with her?" When her only reply was a dark stare, she said, "You had best tell me. I won't help you to harm anyone or be party to anything untoward. I mean, it is all very suspicious. Why do you simply not call on her if you wish so badly to see her? Why resort to such measures as kidnapping ladies off the moors and all of this subtlety?"

"Because she will not see me. Her husband interferes to keep us apart."

Her new husband probably didn't want her to see anyone connected with the old tragedy. Or it had probably occurred to him, just as it had to Leah, that they might have been lovers. "Why is it so damned important?" There was more than a twinge of jealousy in her tone.

"Because I want my life back," he snapped. She closed her mouth, astonished by this. "And she is the only one I have left."

He seemed to struggle for a barely perceptible moment before bringing himself under control. "My father," he began in a calmer voice, "was killed last year, murdered in his own house. The official verdict was that he'd been stabbed to death when he caught a thief in his library, presumably in the act of burgling the place."

"You," she began, then paused. Screwing her courage to the sticking place, she continued, "were arrested for the crime."

"Yes. I spent over three months in prison. You have heard as much, no doubt. You also know I was cleared of all suspicion. But the killer was never caught. That fact combined with the incriminating nature of some of the circumstances that transpired the night of my father's death have left the stain of doubt in many a person's mind, however. It has made me something of a pariah, I am afraid."

"Well, you left England. That made you seem guilty to some." She blushed at his look, then shrugged. "I may have heard a few things about it."

"I am certain you made it your business to know everything you could find out about me. I know I would have in your place. Yes, I went to the continent after the inquest was concluded, but this was not any attempt to elude justice. It is not unusual for me to travel. Anyone will tell you I do so a great deal overseeing properties left to me by my mother in

France and Italy. I returned only last month after arranging for their sale. I don't have the desire to spend long weeks away from England any longer. I am needed here, at home. Perhaps had I realized that sooner . . ."

"What do you mean?" she inquired when it didn't seem he was going to finish.

He took a long breath, as if bracing himself. "If my father's murderer was not a random thief, if it was someone he knew and knew well . . . I might have forestalled this tragedy by realizing the danger. I might have warned him." His face appeared drawn, as if the weight of this guilt he spoke of bled the life's blood from his veins.

"You stayed on the continent for a very long time after the inquest verdict," Leah observed. "Nearly a year."

"To my great regret now that I see what damage my absence has done. After fighting to escape the gallows, it was a welcome diversion. The amusements of Paris and Rome can provide a necessary antidote to thinking too much."

She swallowed. She would *not* feel sorry for him. "I still don't know what you want with this Glorianna."

"In my truancy as her friend, she has been left vulnerable to an unscrupulous man. She recently married. The man is Randall Sanderson. He is my cousin, someone I know well, to my regret. We despise each other. He lived with my father and myself when he was younger. There is a long history there, one I am not going to explain at this moment, but suffice to say that when I heard they had married I returned home immediately out of concern for her well-being. We were close once, she and I. In my absence, we drifted apart, but I shall not allow any harm to come to her."

"Why should harm come to her?" Leah's eyes widened. "My God, you don't think your father's murderer would do anything to her?"

"There is no reason to think she is in danger, but I wish to assure myself of that personally."

"Well, if your cousin won't let you see her, then can you not simply follow her, speak to her when she goes on morning visits or shopping or some such thing? Or . . . or contact a friend of hers and slip a message in secretly."

"Randall always accompanies her, even when she visits friends or shops. He closely supervises every aspect of her life. This is Glorianna's way. She is a woman who depends heavily on a man. It was so with my father. The only time she seeks any time to herself is her morning rides upon the moors when she is in Yorkshire, and that is only because she loves it so and neither my father nor Randall can keep up with her."

"Oh. That's why you thought I was she . . . yes, well, now that the kidnapping tact has failed, you propose to travel a more conventional route."

"That is my plan." He was thoughtful as he spoke, as if they were conferring over the matter. "I am easy to control when branded an outsider, as I was in London. Randall is present for any activities that take Glorianna out of the house and into the public eye, but he cannot possibly oversee each and every private moment. The summer parties, with houses filled to the brim with guests, milling about, groups going off every which way according to their interests, will no doubt give me the opening I need."

"Then what will you do?"

He paused. "I am not sure. That must seem amusing to you, but I truly don't know. She might not trust me. I suppose the first order of business is to see what can be done."

Leah studied him, mulling over whether or not to believe what he was telling her. She felt he was being truthful, but also knew there was more than this to the tale. "If I understand correctly, you suppose that if we are known to be romantically linked, you will receive all the invitations I do. And that will get you in to these parties, the parties where Glorianna will be attending and roaming freely, at least some of the time."

"Exactly so. Very simple, I think, and hardly a huge undertaking. It should not put you out much to accommodate me."

"But this charade may gain you nothing. I don't recall ever meeting a Glorianna. We may not share the same group of friends. We could spend all summer going every single place my family is invited and still not come across her."

"She's been in mourning, remember. She's only just now begun to step out in society again. That could be why you have not yet made her acquaintance. However, I do know her family is acquainted with the duke and duchess of Cravensmore. I remember her speaking of them. They are special friends of yours, are they not? That is why I have reason to believe that you might have one or two engagements in common in the coming months."

Leah blinked in surprise. "In fact, the Cravensmores sponsored both my sisters' seasons and this year for me. How do you know all this?"

He smiled. "I make it my business to know all about any partners I take on, and that is what I am proposing here with you, a mutually beneficial partnership. Oh, don't get spiny on me again. You cannot fault me for acquainting myself with the facts."

"What facts?" she asked, suspicious. What had he heard about her?

"Your father is a banker. He's well-known for his acuity with trade and investment. His consortium has made him a wealthy man, and his investors have profited as well. He revived the duke of Cravensmore's weakened fortune and a deep friendship that formed between the two men led to the Cravensmores all but adopting your family."

It annoyed her that he knew so much about her. It flattered her, too. She shrugged. "Anyone knows that."

Morgan continued, "And your mother is hell-bent on good marriages for you and your sisters. So far, she's been successful. Your two older sisters have made spectacular matches. I should think she'll be delighted with a wealthy earl as a suitor for the impetuous, wayward Leah, who just might have ruined her chances of following in her sister's footsteps with an inconvenient show of temper?"

"How cruel you are!" she exclaimed. He *had* been listening to gossip.

He was unapologetic. "I was merely pointing out the

facts. Here is another one you should consider, Miss Brodie: A liaison with me would be advantageous for you. You should at least consider my offer. It costs you nothing and offers much gain."

"You flatter yourself." Her voice was scathing as she stepped away from him. "You are quite the controversial figure."

"So is Byron, and he is all the rage. In this matter, we will be exactly what the other needs. Why do you hesitate? I have been very clear with you, laid everything out as simply as I can. My motives are stated. I would think they recommend me to a favorable response."

"Well, they do not. I find them offensive. You seek to use me most blatantly."

"Why do you pretend to protest? You will accept my offer in the end."

Her chin came up and she challenged, "You cannot possibly know what I shall do."

"Very simply put, my dear Miss Brodie," he said, leaning into her so that their noses were nearly touching, "you cannot resist."

She thought briefly of striking him. The smirk on his face was too much to endure and she wanted desperately to wipe it from his arresting features. She wouldn't, however. She had dared it on the moor, when the cause of right had been so staunchly on her side, but she wouldn't ever dare it again.

Through gritted teeth, she asked, "And why, my lord earl, shall I not be able to resist you? Do you imagine yourself to be so *irresistible*?"

"Not at all, Miss Brodie. It is not the potency of my charm that has me convinced you will not refuse me. Rather, I refer to the irrepressibility of your nature."

"How dare you presume to speak about my nature. You have no knowledge of me—a few hours' acquaintance under extraordinary circumstances is hardly sufficient to make an accurate judgment of a person. And, as it happens, you are quite wrong if you think I will follow your lead."

"Am I? Then you are delighted with the vapid amuse-

ments of the ton, I presume. It wasn't boredom I saw on your
face when I watched you dancing as I came in. It wasn't a
flush of excitement that colored your cheeks when you
danced again with me." His grin was maddening. "Come,
Blackie. You cannot deny the prospect of an adventure interests you."

He was absolutely right, he knew he was absolutely right,
and it embarrassed her to the tips of her toes. "You could not
be more wrong about me," she shot back, shamelessly lying.
"I will not be your accomplice in this heinous scheme. For all
I know, you wish to finish what you started when you killed
your father and take away the last witness, who is this Glorianna. Perhaps she has good reason not to speak with you.
Perhaps she is afraid of you. And perhaps she has cause to
be."

She immediately regretted her outburst. A change came
over him, swiftly and without warning. Tension crackled in
the air as his expression darkened. "Listen to me, and listen
well, you little fool. I did not kill my father. Consider that if
you had been in the company of a *murderer,* my dear, your
family would be weeping tonight, not dancing. I didn't harm
you. And damn you for it, but you weren't afraid of me for
one moment, were you? It might be more convenient if you
were."

"It seems to me yours is a ridiculous ambition, this plan of
yours. I cannot see how it will work."

"You are quite correct. It is very likely a hopeless quest."
His hands fisted, then relaxed, twitching as he stared at her.
She was caught in the power of his face for a moment. It was
all there, naked for one brief moment—his uncertainty, his
desperation, his grief, and his determination. She felt overcome all of a sudden.

He said, "But perhaps I have nothing else."

And then the illusion—had it been an illusion?—was
gone. He was thrown into shadow as a cloud passed over the
silver moon and the glimpse of boiling emotion disappeared.

Part of her wanted to run, to take flight now. She could
flee into the ballroom and lose herself in the crowd. She

could put the tormented earl of Waring out of her mind and forget everything she had just heard.

But his voice came softly from the darkness that had descended. "I need you, Leah. I need you to help me. And you need me."

I need you.

Her heart hammered. She wet her dry lips with her tongue as those words echoed in her head, in her heart. What a silly twit she was, she thought and tried to master the swell of feeling that left her trembling. He didn't mean it the way she wanted him to.

She could barely speak, forcing the words out in a rusty voice. "The thought of you pretending to be in love with me. It is humiliating."

"No one would know."

"*I* would know. And . . . and *you* would know."

His eyelids lowered to half-mast, giving her a quelling look. She braced herself for some whipping comment, but all he said was, "There are more important things to consider than the irrelevance of bruised feelings."

"Then what is relevant, my lord? You seem so bloody clear about all of this, would you kindly enlighten me?"

"The only point that we need address ourselves to, my dear Miss Brodie"—he narrowed his eyes and leaned forward—"is simply this: Will you do it?"

Chapter 4

Morgan held his breath as he waited for Leah's answer.

The moon emerged again, pouring silver light over her as she visibly wrestled with indecision. That luxurious mane of chestnut hair, duly tamed for the beau monde, made his hands itch, wanting to touch it, rip it loose, see it fall wild as it had been when he'd first laid eyes on her.

His chest tightened. She was having that effect on him again, the one that made him altogether too aware of her in ways he was absolutely not going to acknowledge.

He understood his reaction well enough. From the first ignominious meeting, he'd been aware that he desired her. However, that moment of weakness when he had given in to that same urge that gripped him now and he had kissed her would not be repeated. He hadn't conjured this plan as an elaborate ruse toward seduction. Not to say the idea may not have tempted. . . .

But, damn it all, he was a moral man. *Still* a moral man, despite it all. He'd not use an innocent badly. Their bargain would be struck and fairly adhered to. A business arrangement, a mutual exchange of favor—and that was the end of it! This feeling of wanting . . . well, that just would make all of this that much more complicated. His life was already complicated. This he would keep simple.

He felt a wave of distaste at his own actions. He was all but exploiting her unfortunate circumstances, forcing his false attentions on her. He crushed the feeling, hardening himself against it. Sometimes innocent people got hurt in this world. Good God, he of all people knew that. As long as he didn't touch her, it would mean nothing. He hadn't lied when he'd said she'd benefit from their arrangement. And if he was using her in the bargain, so what of it? He had nothing to feel badly about.

She hadn't answered, apparently considering his offer. He could almost hear the battling voices of reason and zeal inside her head.

Come on, Blackie.

"Yes," she said at last. "I will do it. Not because I need any aid from you . . . but it might prove diverting. These summer months are so boring." She tossed her head like a snooty filly. "House party after house party. It should be interesting, at least, to have a bit of an intrigue to occupy my mind."

Sharp, hot relief shot through him. "Very well," he said, matching her cool tone. "We will start as soon as possible. I will call on you tomorrow."

He was about to offer a bow and take his leave, when she said, "There are a few provisos, my lord, I wish to have as part of our understanding." She angled a coquette's glance up at him.

A fist closed tight, low and deep in his gut. She didn't know what that look did, he'd wager, but she was incredibly good at it. "And what would they be?"

She snapped her fan against the palm of her hand. "Firstly, I insist that this charade be the most sacred of secrets. No one, absolutely no one besides the two of us must know of it."

"Absolutely."

"You will conduct yourself in a manner than will convince all and sundry that you are extremely enamored of me. *Extremely,* my lord, do I make myself understood? You see, I am used to excellent solicitude from my suitors and expect nothing less. And you will behave as a gentleman at all times. You will treat me with the utmost respect, even in private. Especially in private."

"I most heartily agree."

"I may be your accomplice, but should any of our little arrangement be revealed, you shall make certain that I am regarded completely as an innocent."

He fought with the corners of his mouth. How could such a face harbor such a canny mind? "Done and done. Is there anything else?"

He'd meant it as a taunt, but she tilted her head and gave the matter some thought. "One more thing. I will not be involved in your scheme any further than that. I will do nothing to get you together with this Glorianna person. I will not be enjoined to accept certain invitations or make any choices in my companions to favor your cause. If luck puts us in the same places, then so be it. I will allow you to attend me, but *that is all.*"

"Which is very gracious of you, I am sure," he growled. She batted her lashes at him, innocent as a lamb. It seemed sincere, but with this one, you never knew.

"Then our deal is done?" she asked loftily.

"I am in the unenviable position of having very little say in your requirements. In any event, they give me no pause. Our deal is struck, Blackie."

She preened a bit, pleased. "Very well. You may call on me tomorrow if you are eager to start. Arrive after luncheon and I will receive you. That is, if Mother allows it."

She placed her finger against the pillow of her bottom lip and began to gnaw delicately on the nail. "It might take some convincing. Your reputation is a bit muddled, and she won't like that. You are an earl, it is true. Oh! You said you were rich? Because if you are, it will recommend you favorably, very much so. Still . . . I must decide on just the right tact. . . ."

"I have trust in your persuasive abilities to do your best with such a liability as I present," he responded drolly. He tried not to look at the glimpse of her strong white teeth nibbling like that, or the moist pliancy of her mouth. "From what I've observed, you could whittle away the confidence of a zealot."

"You do not know Mother," she countered with a bracing look. "Well. Perhaps Julia could be of help. I must think on it."

"I shall rest these machinations in your capable hands and take my leave now," he said. "Unless you notify me otherwise, I will pay a call on you tomorrow."

"Oh. All right, then. Good evening. My lord. Shall I call you my lord?"

"In polite society, I think it will serve better than your usual manner of addressing me as 'bloody bastard.'"

She laughed, then caught herself and sobered. He bowed and walked into the house.

He was strangely agitated as he headed back through the ballroom. Eyes followed him, prickling his skin like tiny bee stings. He had lied to Leah when he told her that their stares didn't bother him. He hated them.

Polite society—what a jest. Rude, cruel, they were like maggots, the worst of them were, swarming over scandal and devouring it with lavish delight, not caring whom they destroyed in their paths.

He expected some would close ranks and freeze him out, but others would back him. He still had some in the world who believed him. He prayed it was so.

His carriage arrived in the semicircular driveway and he got in. His haunted thoughts followed him into the darkened interior. Pressing against the luxury of the squabs, his thoughts returned to Leah.

He hadn't told her the truth. Not all of it, anyway. He was still enough of his father's son to feel a pang of guilt about that. Sanderson had not taken away all his honor.

He was after justice, he reminded himself. He need think only of justice. Nothing else mattered. Not even Leah

Brodie. Yes, he enjoyed her spirit and lunatic courage. But not too much. He mustn't like her too much. She was merely a means to an end. He refused to allow her to become a distraction.

Once under way, the well-sprung conveyance proceeding along the country lane toward the village at a fair clip, the pressure lifted off his chest in slow degrees. Just stay focused, he told himself as the weight eased. He would find Glorianna and speak with her, heal the wound that had ripped that last connection to family away. But there was more, much more to be done. Sanderson's lies had to be exposed. Morgan would not rest until he'd see his father's killer exposed and punished. He had to. He had to make it right, and lift the burden of his own damning guilt.

No matter what the cost.

L EAH SAT WITH her mother and her sister Julia, watching her tea grow cold and gnawing on her thumbnail.

"Stop that," Desdemona commanded, not looking at her. She was conferring with her eldest daughter, with whom she was discussing whether or not to allow the earl of Waring to call upon Leah.

Julia was saying, "I have heard both good and bad of him, Mother, and both sides hold strong opinions."

"That makes him a walking, breathing scandal just waiting to explode upon us all." Desdemona collapsed back into the chair.

Leah cringed. Although it might be true this could lead to disaster, she had no liking for hearing the man who stalked her dreams referred to in that tone of disgust.

Trying to think of something she could say to defend him, she offered, "He has been nothing but honorable." Which was true, sort of, if one didn't count the kidnapping incident. And the way he'd kissed her. She didn't dare look at Julia, who knew this, adding with a bright note of hopefulness, "And you know, he is awfully rich."

Her mother sighed. "While it is true that he is quite the dashing figure and perhaps has a romantic quality that wins defenders, he also has many detractors, so many in fact that I simply cannot imagine any good coming of an association."

Julia handled this objection easily. "I find it unbelievable that any man could be all the wicked things that are whispered about the earl. My goodness, to listen to the incredible claims made against him, it makes Raphael's old reputation seem saintly."

"And the earl *is* very rich," Leah chimed.

Julia bit her lips to stifle an inopportune smile. Sobering quickly, she said to her mother, "Yes, very rich, and a peer. His family lines are quite distinguished."

Desdemona mulled this over. "But what if the rumors persist? And what if, God forbid, there is truth in them? The fact remains that he quarreled with his father, and so it is very likely that when he was threatened with being cut out of the will, he—"

Without realizing it, Leah stood up. "He is not a murderer!"

In the silence that ensued, she stared back at their shocked faces. Julia's expression was particularly pained.

Blast and bloody hell, I've gone and ruined everything, Leah thought and sat down again, struggling to compose herself. Taking up her sewing, she smiled apologetically and spoke, this time more sedately. "It seems to me ill-advised to make important decisions solely to appease the nastiest tongues wagging in the ton."

"Well put, Leah," Julia said, bestowing an approving smile. "Raphael is impressed with the admiration Waring inspires among men Raphael holds in esteem."

Desdemona looked from one daughter to the other and sighed. "I wish your father were here. I am simply too confused to decide."

Francis Brodie had left that morning for London for business. However, Leah thought it strange that her mother would feel it necessary to discuss this with him. She ruled the family quite effectively on her own, as her husband's work took him away from his family more often than he was present. As far as Leah could tell, her father was never consulted about anything regarding decisions, large or small. It was odd her mother would pine for him.

"Madam?" a maid said from the doorway. In her hand was a salver. Upon it lay a calling card with the corner bent.

Leah could see the name printed in bold script as the tray was laid before her mother. It was Waring.

"I want to receive him, Mother," she said urgently.

Desdemona looked at her, then at Julia, who prodded, "I shall ask Raphael to have him come to the library after we've taken tea. He can speak with him directly."

After a moment, Desdemona said, "All right. Show him into the crystal parlor, Molly. Leah, go and change your dress."

MORGAN TURNED FROM the window when Leah entered the room a while later. He was dressed in riding breeches of buckskin tucked into knee-length boots. A loose-fitting shirt billowed from his shoulders. His cravat was arranged in the fountain style, appearing soft, yet held its shape perfectly.

He had looked devastating in his formal wear last night, and yet this more rugged style held an appeal that was earthier and somehow more . . . dangerous.

Mother entered behind Leah and greeted the earl, asking him to be seated as she called for tea. Leah sank into a chair, disappointed seeing she was not going to get much opportunity to speak with Morgan.

Desdemona, an adroit conversationalist, began the usual polite inquiries into Morgan's state of health, whether he was enjoying the current run of splendid weather they were having, and had he had a pleasant ride out from the village.

Morgan replied in brief but pleasant phrases. He was clever enough to pose a few questions that resulted in Desdemona doing most of the talking. He listened patiently. Not once did he look at Leah.

In a very short while, a maid entered the parlor and told Desdemona that the viscountess wished to see her mother in the nursery on a matter concerning Cosette. It was a fairly surefire ploy Leah and Julia had concocted in order to give Leah some time alone with Morgan. The only thing to distract Desdemona from her duties by her daughter was the prospect of being needed on behalf of her granddaughter. She was up out of the room with a quick apology and a swish of her skirts.

"I suppose you took care of that. Very clever." Morgan pushed himself to his feet. "We must work quickly as I imagine she will return as quickly as she is able. There is a certain amount of information I need from you, and I thought it best we get started immediately so that when opportunities present themselves, we can move posthaste."

He moved to a escritoire set up against the wall, pulling a sheaf of papers from a pocket of a greatcoat, which he had flung on the back of a chair. "Here is a list of the major parties coming up in the next two months. The starred items are the events Glorianna is likely to attend. The ones with two stars are those that I suspect she would have in common with your family."

He pushed the papers toward her. She glared at him, but he didn't notice. He seemed to be avoiding eye contact.

He went on. "I wish you to go over these lists so that I can see if my assumptions are correct. If there is anything you have doubts about, I suggest you question your mother. I want to know as soon as possible what your itinerary is. We should conclude this initial piece of business quickly so that I can anticipate the likely scenarios."

Oh, yes. How silly of her to have forgotten. Theirs was a *business* arrangement.

She snapped up the papers and looked them over. Flipping through them, she shot off comments and shoved them back at him, one by one. "We wouldn't be caught dead at the Henshaw house party. My mother considers her demimonde. You haven't marked us down for the duke of Sanderburg's event. You should. We don't like the Kinstons. There is a bit of a rivalry among their daughters and we Brodic girls. Hmm. Let's see. No, we do not favor the Bellingham regatta, too raucous, Mother claims. Oh, dear. You do not have us down for the Cravensmore ball. Obviously we would not miss their celebration." Shoving the last paper back at him, she kept the tartness in her tone. "Is there anything else you require? I wouldn't want to take up too much of your time."

"What a splendid show of spleen." He finally looked at her.

"Not at all. This is how I am when doing *business,* that is all."

"You *are* put out!" Damn, he appeared to be about to laugh at her.

"Why would I be? You came in here and charmed my mother, who is bloody hell hard to charm—believe me, I know. You do not offer so much as a hello, or a go-to-hell, or jump-in-a-lake to me, and then began whipping out papers and shouting orders. Dear me, how unreasonable of me to have gone into a tiff. Most women would simply adore such treatment from their *beaus.*"

He was insufferably calm. "I do not recall shouting."

"Oh . . . *spout,* then, if I've gotten the word wrong. Spouting off instructions as if I am no more than your servant."

"I regret if I neglected the usual pleasantries, but . . ." He frowned. "This isn't a real courtship, Leah. To me, it is a sort of business deal. I suggest you regard it in the same light."

She went rigid. "I am well aware of that, my lord. However, I fail to see the necessity of forgoing even the semblance of courtesy. It is, after all, part and parcel of most *business* dealings."

"Please accept my apology." He did not, however, sound contrite. What he was, she was quick to note, was scathingly mocking, with eyelids at half-mast and the corner of his mouth curled up slightly, just enough to give him a heart-stoppingly rakish air.

He sat down in a chair and leaned back, bringing one

ankle to rest on the other knee, looking exceedingly comfortable. "Are you not going to ask if I wish to take another cup of tea?"

"I assumed you would order me to do so if you wished it."

He flashed a quick smile, a real one this time. He should smile more often, she thought. It erased the chiseled lines that made his face look so stern all the time. But he probably liked the intimidating mien better. A man who smiled so little obviously valued his remarkable ability to overawe, she thought waspishly.

Well, he wasn't intimidating *her*, she decided, and squared her shoulders against the creep of disquiet at his changed mood. He was sitting there, smug and content, merely staring at her. "What are you doing now?" she blurted.

"I'm prepared to *visit*."

Rolling her eyes, she exclaimed, "Oh, please!"

"I've admitted my error; I've apologized." He was calm, reasonable, which was just so very infuriating. "May I put myself at the mercy of your hospitality?"

Wordlessly, she grabbed his cup and sloshed cool tea into it. Handing it to him, she shook off the droplets of moisture, sending them onto the rug and onto his person. She asked, "Do you want a biscuit?"

"No. Thank you."

She took her seat and stared at him directly. "Did you have a pleasant ride up from the village?"

"Very."

"And the inn, do you find it acceptable? What is the name of it?"

"The Yellow Swan. And it is quite comfortable, thank you for inquiring."

"I don't believe there are yellow swans. Where does that come from?"

"I believe it is symbolic, although I don't know the meaning."

"It should serve to be of some interest. Perhaps you should ask the innkeeper."

"Perhaps I will."

"So. How do you like my hospitality so far?"

"I haven't sampled the tea as of yet, but your conversation is scintillating."

"Can you do better?"

"I should think so." He placed his cup on the table by his arm. "Why don't you tell me about yourself, Leah."

"Please do not patronize me. You are not interested so why pretend?"

"Because we have to pass the time some way, and I might as well get to know you. It would be expected, after all. Imagine the raised eyebrows if we were to be conversing with another couple and it was revealed that I didn't even know the most rudimentary facts about you. Where you grew up, for example—I should know that."

She clenched her jaw, annoyed. "I was born in Hampshire, but moved to Surrey when a small girl. I am nineteen years of age. I've just had my first season. It is rather old for a first season, but Mother and Father wanted me to wait, although I never understood why."

"Perhaps they didn't wish to lose you to the world just yet."

"I am quite certain that isn't it. Mother is not like that. She loves us, of course, but is not overly affectionate. I think it was because . . . well, sometimes I get the feeling that Mother does not quite trust me to control my temper. I don't always find it easy to know the right thing to say and exactly how to say it. And I have a tendency to . . ."

Stopping herself short, she flushed hotly. What was she doing?

Pulling back from the confidences she had been about to spout, she glared at him. His eyes danced. "Please go on, Miss Brodie."

"I doubt I need list my faults for you."

"But they are such charming ones that one can hardly make complaint of them. In fact, one might consider the same piquancy that you say your mother sees as a fault as merely strength of character. Which, I have always thought rather challenging. I enjoy a challenge. Women who simper try my patience, but a quick mind, even when it comes with a tendency to snap, can enliven a man's enjoyment of the fairer sex."

She glowered. "My, my, my lord earl, you see what effect your flattering attentions has on making me positively giddy. I fear I am all tongue-tied as a result. I know!" She clapped her hands together and widened her eyes with innocent surprise. "Let us talk of *you* instead."

"I do not like to talk about myself." The lines of his face deepened. His tone had changed.

It was her turn, however, and she was not giving it up. "Nonsense. All men love to talk about themselves. I, too, must have knowledge of you, as would be natural in any courtship. You yourself said so."

"Very well. What do you wish to know?"

"I want to know about your scar," she stated boldly before she could stop herself. "I was noticing that it didn't look very old, like it was from childhood or something like that. Rather, it has a more recent appearance. Naturally, my curiosity is aroused."

"My scar." The words were flat, angry. His hand moved involuntarily to the weal, thumbing it absently as if he were suddenly self-conscious. "You like to play foul, don't you, Blackie?"

"If you are sensitive about it, all you need tell me is that you would rather not speak of it, and we won't. I just wanted to participate in this marvelous spirit of getting to know one another better, that is all."

"I am not sensitive about it. And I'm afraid the tale of how I got it is not all that exciting. I tripped into a stone wall. The sharp edge of a stone caught me at the temple."

She didn't believe him. "You were lucky," she replied. "You could have damaged your eye."

"Oh, yes," he drawled in a dark, low voice, "I was very lucky."

It was driving her insane not to press him on the details, for therein, she was certain, lay the story she wanted to know.

She wouldn't get anywhere with him, she knew, so she took a different tact. "Do you live in Yorkshire?"

"I have a hunting lodge in the woods near Leyburn. I live there now. I grew up in the midlands, at Hatham House. It's rather neglected now. I don't keep up with it."

"And do you often abduct women on the moors thereabouts, or were you just beginning your life of crime when I met you?"

He worked his jaw, a sign of his annoyance. "Do you want to know something, you little minx? You've quite a wicked tongue on you. You had a right to be angry with me, I admit I was rather curt today. But now you are just being obnoxious."

She stood. "Well, it has not been the most auspicious beginning, but at least I now know my instructions, and limitations. I am not to ask anything of you. No questions, no information, not even the most idle of inquiries will be tolerated. I, however, am to speak freely about myself and tell you everything you wish to know. I think I understand you quite rightly, my lord. Ah. Now that we've that settled, I believe I shall insist we end our visit. I believe I've had about as much of your delightful company as I can stand for one day."

She was halfway to the door when he called, "Leah."

Pausing, she waited without turning. He said, "Look over the invitations listed on those papers. When we speak again, I will expect you to be able to give me facts. Take care and I will call on you again within the week."

Her traitorous body reacted to the promise of seeing him again, and soon, with a shimmer of anticipation thrilling her even now, in the throes of anger. "With new lists and strategies to be discussed, no doubt. I shall look forward to it with great intellectual curiosity. Good day!"

———

MORGAN NEVER SLEPT well anymore.

Turning onto his side, he punched his pillow. He considered rising. If he thought it would help, he would dress and go downstairs to the inn's common room, but he'd only end up prowling.

The pile of letters he'd written out earlier tonight were sealed and printed with the proper direction, awaiting tomorrow's post. He was tempted to go over them one more time, but knew he would only be worrying at a bone. He had done all he could for now. It was up to each person to decide if and how they were willing to help him.

As he twisted restlessly in the sheets, he thought perhaps he should use this time to lay down the finer points of his upcoming plan of action. He still wasn't certain yet what he intended to do. There were too many contingencies. Much depended on the responses he received from his letters. And, of course, Glorianna.

Would she be angry at him? he wondered. Did she hate him for abandoning her? There was a slim chance she was the one who had returned his letters and refused to see him time after time, perhaps furious with him for his long absence. He decided it was more likely her husband was diverting Morgan's attempts to reach her without her knowing.

Morgan was positive, however, that she had no knowledge of her new husband's hand in making her a widow. Neither she nor indeed anyone suspected Randall Sanderson could be capable of killing. Even Morgan's own father had refused to believe in the evil that Morgan saw in Randall.

Evan had resisted Morgan's complaints about Randall through the years, and it had lead to frequent arguments. More recently, when Morgan had returned home from a trip abroad to find Randall once again staying at Blackheath, dancing in attendance to his father's beautiful young wife, he'd immediately seen the dangers but his father staunchly disagreed. Evan ignored Morgan's warnings and would not ban Sanderson from the house. He had resented Morgan's observation that Randall's devotion to Glorianna was not as it seemed.

Bitterness twisted a tight knot in his gut as Morgan remembered the hot, angry words he and his father had shouted to one another. The last words they spoke.

He should have tried harder. He should have *made* his father see what Sanderson was.

But Randall was skilled. He posed convincingly as an affable, even somewhat foppish fellow with an entertaining quality that had won him many friends. Even the prince regent found him diverting, it was said.

Morgan wondered how Glorianna would react when he told her what Randall had done. Should he even try? Would she believe him?

Restless, he twisted in the sheets, not wanting to think on this bitterness anymore. A face came into his mind's eye just then, a woman's face comprised of facile features that could change swiftly under the fascinating influence of emotion. Certainly a more pleasant diversion, but he didn't want to indulge in thoughts of Leah, either. Therein lay the path to disaster, he thought. But his mind was active tonight.

The idea occurred to him of going down to the taps and getting some ale but he rejected that, too. He wasn't tempted by the lure of alcoholic amnesia. He'd spent his recent travels trying that tact. No bottle held enough solace, nor any woman for that matter. He'd exhausted himself trying.

The far-off chime of the mantel clock downstairs tolled the quarter of the hour past three. Outside, an owl hooted. He closed his eyes.

He felt himself dozing at last. Memories crowded in the moment he let his guard down, rising like smoke in his head, and images followed.

Ten years of age. His father as he'd been then, tall and robust. Standing in the hall of Hatham House, he looked sternly at his son. Morgan had just received a new pony, and had left it for the groomsman to return to the stables after riding. His father didn't like that. Morgan always hated to disappoint his father, even then.

Evan Gage sent him to the stables to brush the horse and return the saddle and bridle to the tack room with the admonishment, "You take care of your own, Morgan. A Gage knows the value of hard work."

He fought with grief, half awake, half asleep, feeling the chill of wetness in his lashes, on his cheeks.

I am, Father. I shall take care of my own.

Random flashes, of his mother and his sister, of their funeral and his father's white face full of grief. There was such pain blazing in his eyes as he'd uttered the fervent promise that they would always have one another. Always.

Then, happier times playing with friends, and snippets of village fairs and the years spent at Harrow—all of these came and went. He smiled against the ache that always came with remembering the happiness of his past.

He remembered when he had been twelve years old, and had taken his little boat out on the river by himself.

Yes, that was a particularly vivid memory. He was not supposed to go fishing alone, but the adventuresome spirit of youth chafed under the restriction. Being a fairly typical boy, rules seemed not to be as much limitation as enticement into the forbidden.

It had been a fine day, a clear day. The placid blueness of the water lanced across green meadows and wound through forests as high as cathedrals. He'd left shore and set out, dreaming of Coronado and Vespucci, both of whom he happened to be studying with his tutor at the time.

Fat clouds had come in quickly from the North Sea. The brilliant water dulled with the fading light, a film sealing away its previous sparkle. He began to grow uneasy as the wind kicked up. Morgan had turned toward shore, already nervous at the speed in which the weather had changed.

But the river was fitful, so choppy he couldn't row against the flow. He tied off the boat on a root erupting from one of the banks. The trees waved madly as he began to walk homeward. A stick struck his cheek and drew blood. In the irony of hindsight, he recalled now how he had fretted that the cut would leave a scar. It hadn't. The wound that marred his face had come years later.

A gust of wind sent him staggering backward. He had begun to grow afraid. Softly, he'd begun the Lord's Prayer, ran through it quickly and then began it again, this time slowly, trying to focus on the words to give him courage. The third time his voice sobbed it out and halfway through the fourth repetition, he made up his mind he was going to have to find shelter.

It had been a miserable night spent wet and shivering by the river under a leaking bower of shrubs. He woke alone and shivering the following morning. As he emerged from his shelter, he saw the encroachment of the tide at his feet. He had slept unaware of the possibility of his hideaway being flooded, trapping him inside.

Starving, freezing, he had wanted to flee inland, away from the dangerous swirling water. But they would be looking for him along the river, he had had sense enough to realize. He waded along the flooded shore, fighting demons that would visit him again as an adult, during long months spent in a prison cell. Demons of despair, rage, and terrible, terrible fear.

When he spotted his rescuers, he waved his arms and fell to his knees, drained instantly from the effort of shouting. The most piercing part of the memory was the lovely warmth of his father folding him into his arms. He'd never seen his father weep, had never imagined a time when the great man would succumb to such a show of emotion, but he had felt the wetness of his tears and heard the hitch in his father's voice. "Goddamn you, boy. You are in for a most wicked thrashing when I get you home."

He hadn't gotten a thrashing, though. Once home, his father administered three lifeless blows before his hand went limp and he told his son to go inside and see his mother. To this very moment, Morgan could recall the sour taste in his mouth as he walked into the house. The strange tone in his father's voice had been much worse than the well-deserved beating would have been.

Morgan blinked, waking all at once.

The familiar ache of loss dug its fingers into his heart. *Father.* The pain of it felt good. Clean, true, vitalizing.

I will take care of my own now. I will take care of every-thing. I will make right what I did.

Even though it was too late. And revenge did not eradicate guilt.

Chapter 5

RAPHAEL LOUNGED ON his bed in the grand master suite of Glenwood Park, his hooded eyes watching his wife. "I don't understand why you are getting involved in this."

Julia, who was seated at her dressing table taking down her hair, glanced over her shoulder at him. "I told you, Raphael, I cannot explain it. It is simply something I feel. She's quite overset about him. I've never seen Leah this way."

She had dismissed her maid earlier, knowing he enjoyed watching her dress—or rather undress—for bed. His belly tightened as she shook out her auburn hair and it caught the light like dark copper satin. He wanted to touch already, and this was just the start of the show.

He said, "His reputation is abominable."

"You are one to talk. In his case, there is far less fact to support the accusations than there was for you."

"That doesn't mean he is innocent. This is no small infraction he's being accused of committing. By God, he might be a murderer."

"I don't believe that. Neither do you, or you would be objecting more strongly. I mean, really, does it make any sense at all for a guilty person to be seeking vengeance? A true murderer would want to let still waters lie, correct?"

"If he is so blameless, why did he run out of here today before I could speak with him? Leah cannot be too careful. Her reputation is already questionable and her judgment is hardly sound. For God's sake, she drenched that fellow in pudding."

"It was soufflé." Julia sniffed. "And you must try to understand that she is a tad impulsive, true, but that doesn't make her wicked."

"Well, I still say she . . ." He forgot to finish his sentence, for Julia stood, the clinging silk of her dressing gown making his mouth go dry. He knew she was naked under her wrapper.

After the birth of his treasured daughter, his wife's body had only grown more voluptuous. Her breasts had retained some of their increased size once the baby was weaned. They were firm and round and a constant temptation for his lust. Her stomach had returned to its former flatness, but her hips curved in a new lushness he couldn't seem to get enough of. He certainly didn't have any complaint about her body before, but making love to her now was like discovering her all over again.

She looked at him, eyebrows arched with mild annoyance. "Why are you objecting to helping Leah?"

He cleared his throat with a bit of effort. "I do not object so much as I am puzzled by this sudden friendship you've struck up. You've never been particularly close."

"That is true, and I regret it," she said. "I suppose Laura and I were always such good friends to one another, we shut Leah out. It must have hurt her terribly."

"But that's not the reason why you want to do this. You are caught up in the romance of it all. Admit it. Come and tell me what is going on in your devious little head." He patted the mattress beside him hopefully.

She gave him a mischievous look and stepped behind a dressing screen to doff her wrapper and put on a negligee. The candle she brought with her threw her shadow on the framed decorated paper painted in the Oriental style. In silhouette, her naked form was revealed to him as she slipped off the silk robe. He smiled silently, knowing *she* knew damned well he could see her.

That was all right. He'd make her pay for his torment.

She called, "I suppose I want to help her because I believe I know something of what she feels. Was it so long ago that you've forgotten?"

"I've forgotten nothing," he said throatily.

"Leah has always seemed . . . well, rather unsettled. Maybe he will help her to be happy, Raphael. Can I fault her for trying to find what we have, what Laura has found with her Nicholas?"

Her long elegant arms reached over her head as the gown fluttered down around her. The outline of her body was still depicted clearly in the shadows, the paler shadow of her nightgown only a suggestion of a garment. His breathing quickened.

She seemed to be tying some ribbons. Why was she fussing with damned ribbons he would have no patience to untie?

He had no more interest in their discussion. "Your logic is flawless," he said by way of accession.

Julia blew out the light and came out from behind the screen. He sucked in a short breath at the lavender negligee. It concealed very little. Strategic placement of embroidered appliques clustered to preserve the most basic of modesty. The skirt was full and swirled when she walked, revealing high cuts that showed off her long legs.

She struck a pose for him. "Do you like it, Raphael?"

"Very nice," he purred.

As she moved toward the bed, her golden eyes dipped to where the sheet rode low on his naked hips. His aroused state was plain to see.

Resting her knee on the bed, she reached out to take his extended hand. "Won't you please help?"

"Very well. Invite him to dinner," Raphael said. "Then I can speak to him alone over port and cigars and all that manly nonsense and judge for myself."

Leaning over him, she hesitated just before her lips met his. "Thank you, Raphael."

"And now, viscountess, about that tantalizing show just now . . . I believe I have a point to make about the hazards of tempting a lusty husband."

Her free hand slipped down his front, dipping under the sheet. The smile that curved on her lips was pure sex. "Oh. I do see your point, Raphael."

L EAH HAD SOLVED the problem of Morgan Gage.

She had thought she would scream when he had come the last time, armed with lists and issuing orders. She had been furious—she still was. More important, she was a bit worried. Why was it he appeared to be immune to her? Not that she had any great conceit about herself, but she happened to have garnered a great deal of male admiration during the season. No less than five proposals of marriage were proffered, none accepted, of course. Whether too old, not wealthy enough, or smitten lads who made her nervous with their worshipful stares, they were all politely, but firmly refused. Even Carl Enders didn't inspire her affections. So, why then, did the fates have to curse her with the one man she wanted to notice her was immune to whatever charm she could lay claim to?

He didn't even see her as a woman at all, but as a conspirator, a *business* associate! Such thoughts kept her in an agitated state for a full two days after Morgan's visit until the answer came to her.

She was in the nursery with her sisters when Marie announced that when she grew old enough to go to balls, she wanted to have as many suitors as Leah. "Tell me how to get beaus. It is so easy for you to make a gentleman like you," she pleaded sweetly.

Leah's made-up elaborate instructions were meant to amuse her sister. She stressed that one must always "cross one's eyes when being presented to a gentleman as they find that intriguing." Demonstrating how to walk when entering a ball—knob-kneed and pigeon-toed with arms dangling—she had them rolling on their backs and clutching their sides. Soon she was in the same condition as they attempted to imitate her tutoring.

But the entire little episode had gotten her thinking. That was when she realized she'd been going about this all wrong!

She'd been so stupid. She had to face facts. The kiss on the moor had not affected him the way she had been affected. The feelings that had overpowered her and reduced her insides to ash were obviously not reciprocated. As a result of this, and the hurt she felt, she'd been piquant, snide, sarcastic, and altogether her least pleasant self when dealing with him.

That, she knew, was no way to catch a beau. Even the most inept at the art of flirtation knew *that*.

She was resolved to do much better this time. And she knew she could.

Today, as she readied herself for an outing with Morgan— an innocent little drive into the village—she chose a lovely muslin gown of seafoam green and creamy yellow, cut in the empire style. The soft drape of the expensive fabric needed no embellishment. The bodice was lower than what should be worn for day, but she wasn't going to bother with that minor concern.

She had good breasts, that she knew. In Daphne's stories, the men always enjoyed ogling the woman's breasts. Therefore, if she were pledged to do her best to attract his interest, she would put them on prominent display.

As she sat to get her hair dressed, she began to wonder precisely what ogling meant.

Her hair was done up in a cap of curls, and she'd begged Debra, her maid, to leave some long tendrils to trail enticingly down her back. She thought they looked just slightly wicked. That delighted her. She wanted to be daring today.

With her sooty lashes and dark brow, a bit of powder was all that was needed to lighten her complexion fashionably. Mother abhorred the use of cosmetics, so she had no rouge for her lips. She bit them mercilessly, then surveyed the effect.

She was quite pleased. Then she frowned, thinking perhaps her bosom could be more prominent. She called for Debra.

"I want the tapes tied more tightly," Leah instructed, taking off the dress so that the corset could be retied.

"But, miss, you can't show that much of your bosom until after—"

"I'm wearing a shawl with the dress," she said impatiently. "I want to have some shape."

"Miss Leah, you have ample shape."

"More tightly, please, Debra."

She endured the procedure and examined the results.

Behind her, Debra said, "They look like they are ready to spill out if you take a deep breath."

"Don't worry, Debra," Leah answered in a thin voice. "I can't take a deep breath. Oh, all right, loosen them a bit. I do want to be able to talk. But not too much!"

They quibbled about the tightness of the corset, but Leah prevailed. Putting on the dress, she was satisfied with the effect. She draped the shawl over her shoulders, wanting to wait for just the right moment to unveil herself and astound him with her feminine assets.

Debra looked at the décolletage warily. "You . . . look lovely, miss."

She plucked at her gown, arranging it just right. Smiling at her reflection, she said, "Thank you, Debra. You've been a great help."

A knock sounded at her bedroom door and another maid stepped in. "The earl's downstairs, miss. He's got the phaeton ready, and it's a beauty."

Leah's stomach flipped. He was here.

She almost lost her courage at the last moment. Then she squared her shoulders and said, "I will be down momentarily. Have him await me in the hall."

Then she sat upon her bed. She intended his wait to be a long one.

MORGAN WAS VISIBLE irritated when she descended the staircase into the center hall. She could tell by the way he worked his jaw. His silent, intense stare almost made her trip over her own feet as she headed toward him.

Thankfully, her recovery was smooth and she completed the rest of her journey without spilling onto the floor.

He'd been sitting on one of the chairs lined against the wall. When he saw her, he came to his feet, his movements smooth and insolent. She supposed he wasn't pleased to have been kept waiting for three-quarters of an hour.

"I believe, Miss Brodie, that I distinctly told you one o'clock," he said tightly.

"Good day, my lord," she murmured, sinking into a curtsy. She placed a hand over her decorously draped shawl so that it didn't gap. That little surprise was for later.

"Forgive my tardiness." She angled a look up at him, a gesture she knew made her large eyes appear even larger. "I suppose I dallied over my toilette. I wanted to make a good impression after our last meeting, which I fear did not go very well. I hope you consider it worth the wait."

He regarded her suspiciously, no doubt puzzled at this blatant turnabout in her attitude. She felt a swell of delight at the fact that she'd been able to surprise him. That was a good sign.

She was bitterly disappointed when all he did in response to her flirting was cast her a strange look as he headed for the door. "I've a phaeton waiting in the forecourt. We should go."

Her confidence wavered for a moment. She hugged the shawl about her.

Courage! she told herself. This was no time to falter. Safety was staying at home and clinging to Mother's skirts and letting Morgan dictate what he required of her as if she were merely some lackey. If she ever wanted to get the upper hand and deflate his blasted and infuriating arrogance, she was going to have to take a risk or two.

He helped her into the small conveyance and climbed in beside her. Taking up the ribbons, he started them out, setting the pace at a breezy clip. The team was beautiful. She noticed he was particular about his clothing, his horses, his equipage. They always looked to be of quality and meticulously maintained.

They drove in silence. The road was a scenic feast and Leah, who loved the outdoors, let herself relax a bit and enjoy it. This area of England was known for its beauty, and it was in full glory now, with the season of spring bursting upon trees and driving gaily colored flowers out of the ground to bask in pale lemony sunshine.

Leah was surprised how effectively the silence in the carriage and the gentle swaying motion lulled her. She would not have thought this sense of contentment was possible in Morgan Gage's presence, but as they drove in silence, she began to feel at ease.

She wanted to fill her lungs with the tangy, fresh air, but when she attempted to do so, she felt the pinch of her stays and had to stop before the dancing lights on the edge of her vision blocked out consciousness. This damned corset, she groused silently. The blasted thing was too tight! She shifted uncomfortably, pulling on the undergarment as much as she could without drawing attention.

She longed for comfort. As much as she enjoyed fashion, it didn't suit her to be tied up like a Christmas goose. What she really enjoyed, she reflected as she tipped her head back and took in the clear, startling azure of the sky, was the wild and free feeling she felt sometimes when she could throw it all aside. During her rides on the moor, for example, when it seemed as if she could touch heaven and the entire world lay far away.

A hare darted across the road in front of them, followed by perhaps half a dozen miniature tufts of fur. A mother and her babies. Leah sat bolt upright and exclaimed, "Oh, Morgan, look! Aren't they darling?"

He hadn't as yet spoken to her. He must still be angry

about being kept waiting so long. "Not to mention delicious. With carrots and turnips, a parsnip or two."

She was preparing an acid reply when she remembered she was supposed to be enchanting. She swatted at his arm playfully and cried, "Oh, you are just too naughty to tease me! But I don't think I want to contemplate harming bunnies today, you silly man."

He didn't seem enchanted. He seemed to think her daft, by the sideways look he sent her.

He said, "I think we should head directly into Hawkshead. We could take tea there, stroll about a bit. Be seen. The sooner we are established to be keeping company together, the sooner the tongues will start wagging. This will get the word out about our association."

The disappointing reminder about their "business" doused her enthusiasm momentarily. Usually, men loosened up considerably when she touched them incidentally like that and referenced them as "naughty." They seemed to go limpid at that word.

"What a fine, ingenious idea," she replied, determined not to be daunted. She added her sweetest smile. "Although a picnic would have been glorious. I do love picnics." Reaching for her hat, she adjusted the angle to keep the sun off her face. "I remember this time when I was a child, before Father worked so much, my two older sisters, Mother and Father, and I went to Dartmoor to visit Father's aunt. We went on a picnic and had the most splendid time. Laura fell into a marsh. Oh, we fished her out quickly, but she was sopping wet and began to cry. I cried, too, because I thought that it was unfair she had gotten a swim!"

She saw he wore a slight smile, grudging though it was. "So you were always incorrigible," he said flatly.

"That word! That was the very thing they always called me."

"It's a frequent one given to persons who have a certain zest for life."

She was surprised out of her false flirtation. "Do you think I have zest?"

He almost chuckled. "I think you have it in abundance, Miss Brodie. I would imagine that for you, the worst thing imaginable is to live an ordinary life."

"I don't know. I don't think I'm all that different from most girls."

He spiked his brows, sounding droll. "Take my word on it. You are."

Suspicious, she queried him. "That can be taken two ways."

"I find your distinctive nature engaging," he assured her.

It was the first nice thing he had said. She went warm inside and let her head fall back, tilted upward so that her hat did no good at all in warding off the sun.

She sighed. "I wish everyone saw it so. I am afraid there are those who view it as more of a problem than anything delightful."

"I suppose your family has had a time of it with you, especially a mother who has the ambitions yours has for you."

This was true. Leah was surprised at his acuity. "Mother only wants the best for us," she replied. "I know she does. We have to be very careful, you know, we Brodie girls. We aren't really ton, as you know. Not by birth. We are merely guests of the duke and duchess of Cravensmore."

"Yet I believe you've had more success than the most richly endowed heiress dragging a plethora of titled ancestors in her wake."

She preened under the compliment. "Well, be that as it may, Mother stresses that we must always be above reproach. No hint of scandal of any sort must touch us."

"But wasn't there something a few years ago with your eldest sister and her husband? Something about a wager . . . ?"

Leah chewed her nail. "Yes. I wish someone would tell me what that was all about. Anyway, Mother says the most important thing is that we remember that we are guests among the upper echelons of polite society and never take the honor for granted."

"And how did she take the Carl Enders episode?"

"Oh. That was dreadful. She . . . didn't understand. She was distressed, as you may imagine."

"Poor girl. I suppose she was hard on you."

"Quite the contrary. She didn't say much. That is worse than any of her dressing-downs, those ponderous silences of hers. I felt wretched, of course. Of all of us, I have been schooled very carefully in the essential rule that one's behavior be controlled."

"Is that because you have the most difficulty following the rule? I imagine it is anathema to a spirit like yours. It is inevitable you would rebel from time to time."

"My goodness, I didn't know that you went through so much thought. About me. It . . . well, it quite surprises me."

His mouth twisted in a wry smile and said, "I can't take much credit for being too brilliant. You see, I may have heard the term *incorrigible* a few times myself as a boy."

She giggled, overcome with happiness. It was working. He was *very* different than the last time. Her charm was *working*!

"Somehow, that does not surprise me one whit," she said and was pleased when he broke into another of his genuine smiles.

She liked it when he smiled like that. He looked like a different man. A man untroubled. "Well, who would have guessed," she observed. "We finally have struck upon something in common."

"You make it sound like a true wonder."

"What is a wonder is that we are not arguing. Therefore, I hardly dare tempt my good fortune and continue the conversation."

"Oh, come now. Surely we can do better than ten minute's worth of civil talk. It may take a bit of effort, but I think we are up to it."

"Are you pledged to behave yourself? No taunts, no dissembling? Can you make me the promise to refrain from insult?"

The look he slid her was slow and pensive. "I will if you will. *And* no swearing."

She jerked her head as if offended. "Honestly. Well, I suppose if you are such a prude, then very well, I shall watch my language."

How handsome he was. She hadn't thought so at first. He had a hard face, true, but the harshness was eased somewhat right now and she'd had hints of what it might look like unlined with care.

Turning her face up to the sunlight, she ignored the risk to her complexion to enjoy the warmth. She was feeling so comfortable that she was practically reclined, her long legs out in front of her, crossed at the ankles. She pulled herself upright with a frown, tucking her feet out of sight. She had quite forgotten herself.

She pulled her thoughts upright, as well. It would do no good to indulge in romantic fantasies. This was a man who challenged her at every turn. He had to be managed, she reminded herself, lest he gain the upper hand again.

Hawkshead was a very large village. It was still quaint, with mellow stone paving in the street and pretty multipaned bowed windows in all of the shop fronts. Signs hung over each door, announcing the wares or services offered within.

A cobbler stood in his doorway, nodding to them when they drove by as he cut into an apple and popped a slice into his mouth. A few ladies Leah knew from past visits to her sister's home waved to her and she waved back.

Morgan drove them to the carriage house behind the inn. Once they debarked, Morgan pulled her arm through his and set out for a very public promenade along the cobblestone streets.

Leah felt a vague disquiet at this show of solicitude. It was all pretense, all show, cleverly calculated to gets tongues wagging with the news that Leah Brodie had a new beau—no other than the earl of Waring. And yet she had agreed to do this.

Still, a tingle of shame burned below her skin. It eroded the sweet euphoria she had enjoyed on their ride.

Morgan, too, had lost the good mood. Ramrod straight, he walked with studied casualness beside her, his eyes moving from side to side, watchful and gauging everything. He held tension in every inch of his body.

Sometimes it frightened her, all of that bound energy in him. What burdens weighed on him? she wondered, reverting him all too quickly to the hard, intense-looking person striding beside her now.

She was distracted by the greeting of two women, a mother and a daughter. She knew them as Julia's friends, but couldn't place the name right away.

It would come to her. She was very good at people. Something tugged at her memory—the woman had a son in military service. Tom? No . . . Aha! "And how is Francis?" Leah inquired politely.

The woman—her name was . . . Delia Parham, that was it—exclaimed, "How kind of you to ask. Why, he is fine, my dear, just fine. He's with his regiment in Belgium."

"A beautiful country, Belgium," Leah said and turned politely to Morgan. "My lord, have you ever been there?"

Stiffly, Morgan answered, "I have."

He was not going to make this easy. He looked morose and downright unfriendly. "Have you met Mrs. Parham? No? Oh, dear, how rude of me. Allow me to present her. Mrs. Parham, the earl of Waring."

A single heartbeat of uncertainty pulsed in the air as Morgan went absolutely rigid. Then the woman smiled and dipped into a curtsy and eagerly introduced her daughter, Mabel. Leah made a mental note of the name as she watched Morgan closely. He was too stiff, she despaired silently. Willing him to lose his chilling reserve and at least make an effort, she tried to catch his eye and signal him. She knew from experience he could be charming if he wished to be. He had to dredge up some semblance of that charisma quickly.

Although she never succeeded in catching his eye, he seemed to read her thoughts. A smile snapped into place, and he took Mrs. Parham's hand and bowed over it. "Your servant, madam," he murmured.

When he'd straightened, Leah sent him a look of approval. He raised his brows back at her as if to question her ever having doubted him. The four chatted a bit before Leah and Morgan excused themselves and moved on.

"I thought you were going to freeze them out," Leah admonished once they were out of earshot.

He seemed somewhat contrite. "I expect the worst when meeting people for the first time. I am not normally so sensitive, but I have been subject to some astonishing rudeness recently from people who have heard . . . certain rumors."

"Ah. So you admit you are prickly."

"I do not recall saying the least thing about being prickly."

"Yes, you did."

"I said I was cautious. Guarded."

She sighed and toyed with the fringe of her shawl. "Semantics, my lord. Merely a quibble over the precise word, but the meaning is still the same. You push people away, and not only on first meeting."

"Words are powerful, and one must take care at all times lest their meaning be mistaken. Misunderstanding is—" His head snapped around. "And . . . what do you mean, 'not only on first meeting'? Are you making complaint of my companionship, Miss Brodie?"

"Only when you stalk along the street glowering as if ready to fend off attacks from wild creatures."

He scowled. "I was hardly glowering."

She couldn't suppress a smile. "My lord, you are standing here glowering while you insist you do not glower. In any event, you cannot argue that you have to appear more . . . normal. Smile, relax. Appear the congenial fellow."

"Now I am told I appear abnormal," he muttered to the sky.

"Well, not freakish. It is just . . . You look like a military man on a march to battle. Oh, here comes some friends of Julia's. Now remember—less fierce and smile. Remember to soften your—hello, Dame Harriet!"

They chatted, Morgan being much more amicable than she'd hoped. As they left her, she commented, "See. That went very well."

He sighed, mumbling something under his breath. The air

of exasperation he wore was too liberally laced with amusement to take offense. His look was not as dark by half than it had been before, so she let it go without comment.

"I loathe to swell your head," he said cautiously after they walked for a while, "but I must admit you are adept at the social graces. You make people feel at ease and comfortable. It is quite amazing to watch. You have a gift, but do not expect the same of me."

"You do very well when you put your mind to it. If you were only less prickly, you'd see that."

"I am *not prickly.*"

"You are, Morgan. As prickly as a porcupine."

He looked balefully at her. "Do you realize that I am not considered good society, Leah? This is precisely the reason we are doing this charade in the first place. The fact that some provincial ladies have been civil to me does not change that. It will be much different when we are submerged among the bon ton."

She thought about that. Glancing up at him, she said, "It must be terrible. I hadn't really thought about it before. . . . To be an outcast, to feel unwelcome everywhere you go. I always have my family. They would always close ranks around me and shield me from the very things you have to face every day."

"It is not . . . a pleasant thing, no." The arid quality of his voice made any more words unnecessary.

Seeking to change the mood, she asked if they could step into the draper's shop. While she browsed, Morgan waited with his arms folded by the front door, like an impatient sentry.

She was grateful for the break from having to converse with him as she picked up items and examined them. The goods were of excellent quality, she was surprised to see. There were some exceptionally pretty ribbons and a collection of small rosettes in a shade of champagne exactly suited to one of her favorite dresses. She admired them and moved on, not having any money with her today.

Leah, intent on admiring a blue swatch of silk, did not notice Morgan pointing out these items to the shopkeeper. When a young shop assistant took the material from her with a smile and said she'd add it to her purchases, Leah objected.

The shop assistant said, "But my lord said that anything you admired should be packaged for you and sent to the Park."

Leah turned sharply to Morgan, who was looking bored as he flipped through a stack of sketches for frock coats. When he caught her eye on him, he looked hopeful. "Are you ready to go?"

She felt so strange. It wasn't that she didn't appreciate his being so generous. She was. But, damn the man, it was so achingly like something a real suitor would do, and how pleasant it was to imagine him her indulgent lover. . . .

"Yes," she said, walking swiftly to the door.

What had she expected? She railed at him when he was cool, and now that he played the attentive beau, she felt worse.

She was just going to have to get over this silly nonsense. A business deal was just that—business. Curse her for her impetuous, romantic nature, she'd agreed to this and there was no sense mooning over everything that just wasn't enough and it was no good, simply *no good* imagining how different it would be if this were not merely pretense, but real.

Ah. But she had her plan, didn't she? Perhaps . . . Well, perhaps he'd look at her differently. That's right, she had ways to charm him.

Outside, she turned to him and touched his shoulder, giving him the benefit of her widest, most beguiling look. "Thank you for your thoughtful generosity."

He narrowed his eyes, immediately suspicious. But as they resumed their stroll, he seemed less stern, not quite as haunted as he'd been before.

They paused outside the milliner's shop. The window was a wild melange of elaborate and tasteless headwear, flush with plumes and ribbons and tufts of yards of tulle spilling every which way.

Morgan said, "Do you wish to go inside?" It was apparent he dreaded the answer.

"Heavens, no. This stuff is dreadful. Is that an orange bird sitting on that green hat? Oh, on second thought let's do go in. It will be fun."

She pulled him inside, although in fact he didn't resist so very much. He even smiled tolerantly—perhaps even the tiniest bit amused—when she plopped an audacious confection on her head, made a moue and asked him how he liked it.

He appeared unmoved, drawling, "You look like you have an ostrich sitting upon your head."

She frowned. "Yes, of course, but the question is—does it look good up there?"

That was when she heard his rich laughter for the first time. When they spied the shopkeeper stalking their way with a murderous expression on his face, Leah hastily replaced the offensive headdress and they beat a hasty exit out onto the street. Behind them, the square-bodied matron fluffed the hat and muttered soothingly to it.

"Good God," Morgan growled with a backward glance through the shop window, "I think she concocted the thing out of a departed pet."

The humor was so unexpected that Leah laughed outright. It wasn't the practiced twitter she usually affected, but the way that came naturally to her—loud and a bit raucous. Of course, she almost fainted because her damned corset was so tight, it was difficult to take deep breaths.

As for her vulgar show of hilarity, Morgan appeared not to mind the way she laughed. His eyes sparkled, and it seemed he might actually like it, but it was difficult to tell because he looked away so quickly.

He said that they should go to the tea garden for some refreshment so they headed back in the direction of the inn where Mrs. Hanover's Tea Emporium nested just one door down.

They entered and greeted their hostess, who rushed out from behind a counter piled with an assortment of cakes and biscuits to greet them with a wide smile. Leah looked around, rather breathless at the startling room in which they found themselves. The place was a riot of neoclassical décor, pillars and busts of cheap plaster, and an abundance of potted plants that was rather exotic, almost hedonistic.

"No wonder Mother never brought us here," she murmured as they were shown to a table set with fine linens and delicate china. It was in the corner, almost cut off from the rest of the place by a dense grouping of palms. Leah looked about at the other patrons, none of whom were paying them any mind.

"Your order?" the proprietess inquired, indicating a printed menu lying on the table.

"High tea," Morgan said, not even consulting his.

"Yes," Leah agreed, smiling as the woman hurried away.

They were left in marvelous privacy. Seated on the cozy cushioned chairs, Morgan settled back and offhandedly observed that the place reminded him of the forum. She laughed, replied with some comment or other, and they relaxed together amidst an easy atmosphere.

Leah decided that despite their inauspicious beginnings today, overall things were proceeding quite well now. Splendidly well, in fact.

It was time.

She removed her shawl.

"The day has grown quite warm," she said, sighing as she folded her hands in front of her and gazed nonchalantly about the place. "This is an adorable shop. I like it very much. Oh, I am just now reminded to ask you to stay to supper. The viscount de Fontvilliers himself insisted. He wanted to see you before, but I forgot to tell you. I promised this time that I would tell you how dearly he would like to speak with you. I do hope you can make it on such short notice. I am afraid Raphael can be a bit overbearing, and will not be put off any longer."

She turned to find him staring at her and her breath ran

out. His hazel eyes were dark, nearly brown, hot and intense as they bored into her. His gaze kept dipping to the prominent display of her bosom and she had the most profound certainty that he was rather impressed with what he saw.

Strange that it should thrill her like this, making the very marrow of her bones vibrate with excitement. Male attention to her décolletage had annoyed her before. Now, the touch of his gaze on the gentle swell of bosom that pushed over the top of her dress tingled. She was overcome with a sudden awareness of her femininity, feeling somehow very small and delicate and vulnerable to the masculine interest pulsing off him.

He said, "Put your shawl back on."

She blinked, the pleasure draining out of her in a sudden wash. "What?"

"You look indecent."

She laughed dryly, trying to dismiss his crushing command. "Why, you sound like a prude. Honestly, Morgan, I hardly think it is your place to tell me what to wear. I like this dress, and I am quite comfortable."

It wasn't true. With the corset constricting her like this, she could barely touch her back to the seat cushion. And she creaked with every movement.

"You know fashion far too well for me to lecture you on that being the wrong sort of dress for day. I wonder why you would commit such an obvious faux pas?" He sat forward suddenly, so suddenly she squeaked, drawing back sharply. She remembered how he had come after her in the hut on the moor, his eyes holding the same blaze of fury they did now.

Through a stiff jaw, he said, "Are you trying to seduce me, Blackie?"

Chapter 6

THE QUESTION HIT her like a blow. She stammered, staring helplessly as it dawned on her that he wasn't stupefied with desire at all. He was incensed. Her glorious display of feminine assets had not moved him. Her flesh crawled with humiliation. Without a word, she leapt to her feet and hurried through the front door.

He was right on her heels, catching her on the cobbled walkway that ran along the main street. She whirled on him, eyes brimming with tears. "How could you?" she flung in a hurt voice.

He held a warning hand out in front of him. "Don't you dare start. I cannot countenance weeping!"

"Do you take pleasure in treating me in this outrageously humiliating manner?" she cried, dashing away the tears that had splashed onto her cheeks. Fresh ones replaced them instantly. "Is it that you find my very presence loathsome—is that why you are ashamed to be seen with me? Oh, what sacrifice you make! What a martyr you must think yourself to have to pose the suitor to such a repulsive hag as myself."

"What the devil—" He cut himself off, looking about sharply and modulating his tone. In a voice meant for her ears alone, he said, "Come back inside this instant. People are beginning to stare, goddamn it, and it would hardly do either one of our causes any good if you were overheard bleating about our little arrangement."

"I want to go home," she demanded, ignoring him. "Take me home at once!"

"Oh, bloody hell. All right. Calm down, will you, your color is high. People will think you are about to take a fit."

He pulled her by her arm as he turned to stalk toward the carriage house in back of the inn. Leah trotted beside him, clutching her shawl and snuffling. "I can hardly breathe," she complained, "and you've overset me terribly."

"Perhaps if you were laced more loosely you wouldn't be fearing an attack of the vapors."

"How dare you speak of undergarments to me, you uncouth brute!"

He rolled his eyes and muttered something. "Just wait here and try not to faint. I'll fetch—"

"I'll not stand out here and provide a spectacle for passersby."

"You should have thought of that before you ran out weeping. Very well, come along then. I don't know why you have to be so ridiculously emotional all the time."

"Emotional?" she gasped. She caught the gaze of a woman shocked at the outburst and lowered her voice. "A woman dresses for a man and he tells her she looks vulgar."

The words came low through his clenched jaw. "I didn't say that. You look anything but vulgar. You look elegant and appealing as hell, and you damned well know it. My God, you are displaying everything you have—and I'll give you credit for it being quite a bit—for everyone to see."

"I just wanted you to like me!"

He stopped, his gaze shrewd as he turned to her. "You wanted me to want you."

She jerked upright. "I *certainly* did not. I just want you to treat me with respect."

"That is balderdash, Miss Brodie. You want me panting at

your heels like all your other conquests of the season. Here's the phaeton. Get inside."

She threw off his helping hand and climbed in on her own, not caring if she looked ungainly. It was better than having to bear his touch. He rounded to the other side and leaped easily into his seat. Taking up the ribbons, he set them in motion with an angry jerk.

"Stop that infernal crying, damn you," he snapped after a moment. "And don't think I am giving you another cravat to snivel all over!"

"You are the most beastly man I've ever had the misfortune of knowing. I wonder if you care about anyone."

"What you wonder is what you have to do to ensnare me like you've ensnared your legion of enamorata."

"Enamel-what? I don't know what you are saying half the time, and I seriously doubt you do, either."

"You know what I'm saying well enough. Your little ploy was not successful. The magnificent vision of your bosom has failed to reduce me to slavering idiot. And now you are put out because of it."

"It might shock you, sir, but you are not the center of my universe. I chose my dress today to please myself."

It didn't trouble Leah to lie, although she didn't do so as a rule and when she did, she hardly ever did it well enough to convince. But she was desperate, and humiliated, and she'd be damned if she were going to let him go on thinking . . . well, the truth. With a toss of her curls, she finished, "Your delusions of your importance are pathetically false."

He pulled the phaeton to a stop now that the road had turned and they were out of sight of the village and alone on the stretch that led to Glenwood Park.

Leah fished in her reticule for a handkerchief. "I can't believe you've made me cry. Again! No man has *ever* made me cry. You are positively barbaric, and I . . ." She looked up, her voice trailing off.

He was staring at her again, hot and intense. But there was something in him besides anger.

A curl of apprehension tightened in her stomach. She felt

exposed, and her eyes rolled downward to find her shawl had slipped to her shoulders. She didn't move it back into place. She didn't move at all. She didn't dare look up at him because the very real certainty came over her that she had tempted a tiger and had gone too far.

"Goddamn it all, you little idiot," he said, and she felt him move. His leather-clad hand slipped under her chin, pulling it up as his mouth came down roughly over hers.

The kiss was hard, shocking her with fire for an instant before the first wave of pleasure leaked into her veins. The feel of his lips was like velvet, just as she'd remembered it. She'd thought perhaps she'd embellished that first kiss in her memory, making it impossibly glorious. But she hadn't. She'd not exaggerated one thing, not one little thing about the feel of his mouth on hers.

Desire rose swiftly inside her, white-hot, sparking an ache somewhere she couldn't define. He moved his mouth over hers, the friction sending her into a tumult of tremors. His hand touched her hair, his fingers digging into the carefully arranged curls.

She wanted to rip out the pins and feel her hair falling around her, around them. Everything felt suddenly sensual; she felt sensual, incredibly aware of her body.

Slipping her hands over his shoulders, her fingers curled into hard muscle. When he shifted position, leaning further over her and pressing her back into the cushioned seat, she felt the muscles of his back flex under her palms. The power of him sent a thrill down to her toes. His masculine body was so different from the slender softness of her own.

Her breasts tingled as they were crushed against the hard wall of his chest. Even through the layers of material, the hotness of his flesh burned like a fever.

He released her and they gazed at each other, panting breathlessly, still holding one another. She was terrified he would speak, that he would tell her they should stop.

She didn't want to stop.

"Morgan," she said, reaching for him. His hands closed over her wrists and held them away.

Dark-lashed lids, pretty enough to belong to a woman, swept down as his gaze lowered to her heaving chest. She mewled, a sharp sensation of pleasure knifing through her at the bold look. The ragged sound of his breathing filled her head and she closed her eyes, surrendering, wanting him to touch her. *There.*

His voice was hoarse. "We're alone in the middle of the country and I'm kissing you. You need to think about what we are doing."

"I'm . . . not terribly good at that."

"Why did you entice me?" His grip tightened, becoming almost painful. "Why did you display yourself for me?"

She opened her eyes to find him peering intently into her face. "It wasn't like that. I just wanted . . ." What had she wanted? This? Somewhere, some part of her *had* wanted this very thing. Oh, God, it was true. And he knew it.

She had longed for him. She had wanted him to want her, just as he had accused her of doing.

As much as she wanted him.

"What did you want? Me to make love to you?" His perception was so shocking, so chillingly accurate that it sobered her instantly with a cold flood of humiliation.

"You conceited oaf!" She pushed at him. Her fury chased the last of her ardor. "I don't want you. I was just curious. What's the crime in that? Isn't a girl allowed to be curious? Honestly!"

"What was it you were curious about?" he challenged, and there was a new hardness in him. He leaned in closer, not giving her the space she craved. "About the bliss or whatever the hell you call it?"

"I, sir, am a lady of gentle breeding and I'm most certainly *not* curious about the bliss!"

"You are a liar. Listen to me, Blackie, I've long since discarded society's rules. So if you think I'll play by those rules, you are wrong. Don't make me your protector. I'll fail you, and then we will both be done for."

"I don't need you to protect me. I can take care of myself."

"Can you? Then let us put you to the test."

That smoky voice held her paralyzed as he kissed her again. Her heart jerked in her chest and she tilted her chin up, forgetting all her brave words of independence, meeting his mouth and kissing him back with all the passion he had stirred to life.

He ran his tongue along her lips, shocking her, then ducked his head to brush a tantalizing kiss along her jaw, tasting her there, too. Oh, God, it was decadent, it was delicious! With a soft moan, she let her head fall back to allow him more access.

Aware that his hands had slipped under her shawl, her breath hitched and she froze. She did nothing to stop him. He closed long, strong fingers around her breast. It felt incredible. She hadn't known, hadn't suspected, that a man could touch a woman and make her feel like this.

She sighed, settling into the caress. Then his fingers touched her aroused nipple through her bodice and she gasped. Tight, hard pleasure stretched like a cord from her breast to the juncture of her legs, exploding into a pool of heat, and a new ache asserted itself, shocking her out of her lassitude with a surge of alarm. All at once aware of the foolish risks she was taking, she sat up abruptly, nearly knocking the two of them off the bench seat of the phaeton.

She had lost her head, lost every bit of sense she ever had. What had come over her? She twisted free, pressing her hand to her forehead as if the pressure could chase away the disconcerting pleasure he had conjured.

Her head began to clear as she struggled to fill her lungs with much needed air. He let her go, turning away, and she felt a ripple of loss shake her even as she clung gratefully to the side of the phaeton, her back to him.

"Th . . . that was despicable," she managed to say after a moment.

"You asked for it." His voice was a tight growl.

"I-I didn't. I merely asked for—"

"It was killing you that I wasn't tripping over myself trying to please you, was it not? God, you debs are drunk with your own power. I am more than a few years beyond the callow youths who've danced attendance to you all season long, but I am just as susceptible to a beautiful woman. Yes, I want you. I just don't want the games. Now that you have proof of your rather potent charms, does it change anything?"

She wrapped herself in her arms, suddenly cold despite the mildness of the day. "It makes me afraid of you."

His glare pinned her to the seat. "That's good. I think you should do well to be very afraid of me. It will teach you not to dabble in flirtations you cannot control." He ran his hand over his chin. "God, what a mistake this is."

They were silent for a moment. Then he said, "But we are already well under way with our grand deception. We have much to gain, both of us, but perhaps even more to lose should we continue. What do you say, then, shall we turn back now or make a concerted effort to control ourselves?"

"And have everyone believe I have been scorned yet again!" She was infused with a renewed energy born from a flood of indignation. "When we break off this ruse, it shall be I who decide when and how, Morgan, and only after we have done what we set out to do to repair our reputations. I, sir, am no coward. I will not retreat. I am certain I can manage to control myself. See that you do the same."

As for the bravado of those words, he allowed them to slide on by without so much as a raised brow. "Good," he replied. "Then we shall just have to endeavor to forget this ever happened. And"—his voice deepened—"understand that it will not happen again."

They drove home without another word spoken between them. In the tension, Leah's thoughts sped over jumbled, troublesome thoughts. She had gotten snagged in her own net. She had tried to entice him, and it was she who wound up losing her head.

But he had, too. He'd even admitted it.

The thought should make her happy, but she didn't feel happy. By the time the Park was in view, she was as confused and miserable as she had ever been in her life.

As to the supper invitation offered by the viscount, Morgan told her curtly that he regretted he had to decline. She was relieved despite the complaint she knew she would get from her family. She didn't know how she could have borne his company one second longer if he had accepted.

They didn't so much as look at one another as he handed her impersonally down from the carriage and took her to the front door. The farewell he offered was studiously impersonal.

She paused at the open door and watched him take the phaeton back down the lane. She wondered what the devil she had done today.

And what had made her do it.

———

I FEAR I am playing with fire."

Leah looked at the baby seated in front of her. Cosette's eyes were huge and startling green, like her father's. On the whole, the child favored Raphael, startlingly so. Her doting sire even boasted his hair had been just that shade of pale blond until age had darkened it.

Placing the third block on the tower she was building for her niece, she clapped when Cosette swiped at them, knocking them down. The baby's soggy grin blossomed and she slapped her chubby hands together.

"Hurray!" Leah exclaimed, then built the tower again.

Cosette bounced with excitement as she saw the blocks piled together. Pointing, she cried, "Gah!"

Leah laughed, and leaned forward to snatch a quick kiss. "You are so adorable." Feeling the softness of the child, the fresh smell of her, she felt a rush of love for her sister's daughter. She had always liked children, always had a way to amuse them without much effort. But this baby affected her differently than any other child had before.

From the moment of Cosette's birth, Leah had wanted to hold her, cuddle her, play with her, and care for her. She'd wanted her in a possessive way that awakened maternal instincts inside her she never suspected she had. She'd even been a bit jealous of her sister for having such a perfect child. Maybe, she thought as she applauded Cosette's brilliance in knocking down the tower again, she would have a baby of her own some day as beautiful and charming as this.

And then, of course, she thought of Morgan. How she would adore holding Morgan's child to her breast, loving, nurturing him. Or her.

"Oh, God, what is happening to me?" she said aloud, and Cosette looked at her curiously, as if she didn't know the answer but was giving the matter serious thought.

Leah laughed, tickling Cosette until she giggled. Sweeping her up into her arms, Leah carried her to the window seat. Another of Cosette's favorite games was gazing out of the window that overlooked the terraced lawns all the way down to the forest that ringed the house. It wasn't the view that enchanted her. She liked putting her mouth on the glass, slobbering a great deal, and then smearing her hands in it to make a grand mess.

Curling her body around Cosette to keep her from tumbling off the cushions, Leah let her play. She rested her head against the cool glass and sighed as her thoughts resumed their tumble.

What was she going to do about Morgan? He was a man; he had desires. She knew about these desires from Daphne's tales. They made men want to take the bliss. It made them want to *give* the bliss. Oh, *Lord.*

Her heart began to pound. He had admitted he wanted her. She had wanted desperately for him to notice her, long for her, but then it had frightened her.

A shiver rippled through her and she gave a slight moan. Cosette looked at her, smiled her drooly smile and pounded on the glass.

And she *wanted* him to give her the bliss! But she couldn't and not just because it was wrong, or because it would cause a scandal, but because . . . because she didn't want it to be just *that* when not a word of affection or feeling had passed between them.

The happy child, finished with defacing the clean panes,

climbed onto her lap. Leah stared into the solemn little face. "Don't fall in love, Cosette," she said, then stopped cold as the words registered.

Was she in love?

How could she love him? Wasn't love something sweet and exhilarating that came from a man's devotion to a woman and her admiration of him? This wasn't love, this infatuation. It . . .

It was what, then? What else?

"Oh, *Lord!* I am in love with the earl of Waring? This has to be the most foolish thing I've done yet."

Cosette smacked her hand smartly against Leah's cheek. "Gah!" she cried.

Leah's eyes stung from the surprisingly strong blow. She wasn't angry at the little girl, however. She supposed it was just Cosette's way of trying to knock some sense into her.

I N RAPHAEL'S STUDY, two men sat across from each other. To an observer they would have seemed congenial companions, but both men—one dark, the other fair—knew that this was not an amicable meeting.

"My sister-in-law is young," Raphael said.

Morgan watched the viscount through the lazy haze of cigar smoke before his eyes. In one hand he held a finely rolled specimen of American tobacco that emitted a sweetly pungent aroma. In the other rested a snifter filled with aged scotch that smoothly slid down his throat and puddled into a sense of false warmth in his gut.

There was no warmth in Raphael's stare. The effects of the liquor were countermanded by the tension from his host.

Smiling slightly, Morgan responded, "She is nineteen, soon to be twenty. I believe she has currently made herself available for marriage proposals."

"Ah. Then you are of a mind to make a marriage proposal."

"My intention of deepening my acquaintance with Miss

Brodie is for the purpose to find out the answer to that very question, monsieur le viscount, as are all courtships." Morgan sipped his scotch and leaned his head onto the back of the chair.

Two cats, each one refusing to play mouse to the other.

"Not all, but your answer satisfies. Still," Raphael persisted, "you are substantially older than she."

"I am a bit puzzled, monsieur le viscount, in your meaning. I do not know your age, of course, but I would put it near to my own thirty-one years. And your wife is surely no more than a few years Leah's senior. The discrepancy between myself and Miss Brodie seems no greater than that between yourself and your wife, and yet you appear the most sublime of married couples."

Raphael didn't hesitate. "There is a question of maturity that makes a distinction between the sisters. Leah is considerably different than my Julia was at her age. Less . . . constrained, shall we say?"

"Ah, but maturity does not render one immune from scandal," Morgan countered quickly and Raphael's mien slipped a tad, enough to register the direct hit.

Morgan had made it his business to find out what lay behind the hushed-up circumstances of the marriage of the viscount and Leah's eldest sister. Despite the high regard in which the couple was now held, a few die-hard gossips still spoke of an outrageous rumor of a wager among Raphael and his former associates, a group of profligates who'd since parted ways. It concerned, it was rumored, his ability to win Julia from her previous fiancé.

From the reaction he received from his host, the rumors might come somewhere close to the mark.

Morgan pressed the advantage he'd won. "I will allow Leah is sometimes a frivolous creature, but she has a certain unexpected frankness that I like."

He repressed a smile, remembering her saying, *I shall run you through, gut you and roast you, then feast on your entrails.* "I find it can be delightfully diverting," he added, then took a long draw on the cigar.

"We in the family know her well." Raphael's words were spoken dryly, ripe with all sorts of meaning. "And that is why we are concerned. Leah possesses a certain willfulness that is a concern to her family."

"A woman with spirit, as are all the Brodie daughters." Pursing his lips, Morgan said, "Including your wife. You would no doubt agree with a preference for a companion who is of strong character. Let me be frank. Simpering misses are not of interest to me."

"I particularly wish you to know I would . . . *take exception* to Leah being caught in an unhappy situation. You must understand, it is a duty I feel as a male member of the family."

The threat was clear, but it didn't rile Morgan. He found he had some measure of understanding for the viscount's concerns. It was hard not to want to protect Leah, to shelter that vivid light in her that a harsh world might tarnish and dull.

"I do not need to be convinced of the rewards of family." Morgan spoke slowly and with sincerity. "It is a joy I feel most keenly in my loss."

He didn't speak of his family, he simply didn't. Nor did he make public his grief, but he admitted it now, the words like sand in his throat.

Raphael's speculative stare lengthened, then broke off. He directed it at his cigar and said, "And yet, we must confront the inevitable specter of the unfortunate rumors that surround you. There may be damage you do not intend, but may occur in any event. More scotch?"

Morgan tossed back the little bit in his glass and held it out. "Thank you."

The viscount de Fontvilliers and Morgan had not met before Morgan arrived tonight for the supper invitation, which had been emphatically worded in a note sent to the inn. In reality, it was a summons, one Morgan had been expecting. It was time to pass muster, another ring through which he had to leap successfully to gain his boon. Thus, he'd come to

Glenwood Park to give the Brodie family their opportunity to look him over.

They took no pains to hide it, either. The evening was more of an interview than a social occasion. After dinner, the men retired privately for a bit of plain speaking considered too shocking for feminine ears. Almost immediately after having been settled into the luxurious confines of Raphael's library, the grilling had begun in earnest.

What did surprise Morgan was his reaction to the entire proceeding. He'd been set for war. Yet, far from being annoyed, he found himself fielding Raphael's questions with tolerance. Perhaps it was because he rather appreciated Leah having such a concerned and protective family. He understood that. He even envied her that.

Or perhaps it was the viscount himself. Morgan did not resent his taking a leading role in protecting his wife's sister, or his methods. Raphael was a man who would be a formidable enemy. Under different circumstances, he might have proven an unfailing friend.

Raphael rose and carelessly splashed a liberal amount in his glass.

Morgan decided to get the worst of it over with, and took a direct tact. "You were of course referring to the rumors about my being a murderer, I believe. A curious burden for a man to bear, proving one's innocence. I am by this time well acquainted with the fruitlessness of the task, for you see, monsieur le viscount, all I can do is profess my blamelessness and leave it up to each person to draw their own conclusion. I did not kill my father, and I am most interested to find out who did."

"That seems logical. Any ideas?"

"None I discuss."

"I wonder, Waring," Raphael said at last, "how one can attend to two things at once. Looking for a wife and uncovering a father's murderer seems like an ambitious schedule for a man."

Morgan replied, "One does not choose the occasion when it seems imperative to deepen one's association with a woman." With a touch of laughter riding on his voice, he added, "Nor does one choose the woman."

"Such charm as my wife's sister possesses can be persuasive," Raphael granted.

"Indeed," Morgan said, schooling his thoughts to behave. Charming? My God, the woman was devastating. Perhaps, under different circumstances, a different time, a different *him*, he *would* have pursued her for solely his own pleasure. Maybe he wouldn't have been able to resist.

Emptying his glass, he laid it on the table beside him and stood. "I find it reassuring that Leah has such a caring family. I thank you for your hospitality and shall take my leave."

Despite their congenial words, there was no conviviality between them as Morgan left. He went into the parlor to say good evening to the rest of the family and bowed low before a very pleased-looking Leah. She asked permission, and received it, to walk him to the door.

There, he refused to get caught in those dark, dark eyes, and made the mistake of directing his gaze to her mouth, which only caused him to remember how tender it had felt against his. He tried not to notice her disappointment when he took her hands in his and said a quick good night, then left her with that cupid mouth pouting.

How crushing she could look. He wondered if she practiced facial expressions before a mirror or if they came naturally, without artifice.

Once outside, he breathed in deeply, filling his lungs with the soft, spring air moistened with night. He was irritated to realize he was aroused—aroused, from only saying good night to the little fox.

He was going to have to do better than this if he were going to spend an entire summer in her company and not succumb to the forbidden.

Chapter 7

THEIR FIRST FORAY into society came weeks later at Lord and Lady Farthingham's country estates where a large number of the beau monde gathered for a week of feasting, riding, gambling, dancing, and fierce competition in billiards. Mingling with the other handpicked guests, Morgan and Leah looked over the new arrivals as they filed into the resplendent drawing room of the manor house.

They had been among the first to arrive. Morgan had insisted. Eager to confront what awaited, he had been tense and uncommunicative during the interval in the coach. He remained guarded until Leah pinched his arm and sent him a silent look.

Thereafter, he masked his feeling better. He had thus far comported himself with stellar self-possession, that is if one didn't notice the way his gaze strayed to the door so often or how his body went rigid when a carriage drew up to the front. It seemed obvious he was waiting for someone.

Ah, well, Leah thought fatalistically, if he remained a bit formal, at least his face didn't resemble a death's mask any longer. He was engaged in conversation at present with some young men whom he had recognized from university. He appeared to be having a good time, apart from that eerie vigilance, but Leah noticed no one else thought him strange.

Leah headed to a group of girls she knew from this past season, swallowing her disappointment that she was not going to get to show off her new beau. Although happy that Morgan was having an easy time of it, she nonetheless would have preferred him at her side.

She had anticipated this day with relish. The gown she had chosen for her first appearance back in genteel company was a stunning confection of peach eyelet lace of a shade particularly selected to compliment her creamy complexion. It was demure enough for daytime wear—she wasn't going to make that mistake again—with frothy layers that fell so that the pinky-peach underskirt showed through the lace overlay. A matching ribbon caught the dress high under her breasts and fell with lovely suppleness around the gentle swell of her hips.

The young ladies among whom she sat admired it right off, but their compliments failed to elicit the usual degree of pleasure. Leah was too intent on keeping an eye on Morgan. The group he was with were getting rather loud, laughing frequently and doing those annoying things like slapping each other and guffawing that men inevitably did when finding themselves in good company.

Leah rolled her eyes. Morgan's tension had unwound considerably. He leaned a shoulder against the fireplace marble, a ready grin for the jokes being bantered about, looking very urbane and natural.

She felt a pang of jealousy. Morgan had rarely laughed so easily with her. And she had never seen him look so much at ease. Just as she was battling the first wave of disgruntlement at seeing him doing so well without her, a second wave crashed with the thought that if he enjoyed overwhelming success in getting himself into the good graces of the beau monde, then maybe he wouldn't need her.

Lady Sophie, one of Leah's closest friends, slipped into the seat next to Leah with an impish grin and tapped her on the shoulder. Leah roused out of her unpleasant thoughts and uttered a small cry of delight. She clasped Lady Sophie to her in an exuberant embrace.

Sophie was a petite girl, pretty with a lively personality and the sweetest disposition Leah had ever known a person to possess. The two had become fast friends in London this year. After the Carl Enders debacle, Sophie had written encouraging words in her letters.

Over tea, Sophie asked, "Forgive my rudeness in asking you, but I simply must ask if it is true? When we arrived, my father recognized the earl of Waring here and someone told us he is with *your* family."

As badly as Leah wanted to spill out the news that the earl was indeed here in attendance to her, she demurred. "The earl and countess where good enough to include him in the invitation when Mother wrote to tell him that he was visiting us."

"Who is he, point him out to me," she said, squinting around her. Sophie was too vain to wear the spectacles she so obviously needed for her nearsightedness.

Leah pointed out Morgan, feeling a swelling of pride come over her. *Mine,* she thought, then corrected herself. Only for the duration of their farce.

Ah, but at least she could enjoy it that long.

"The one with the dark hair. Oh, my," Sophie trailed off with a sigh. "Imagine," she said suddenly, "the Wicked Earl, right here within our midst. My mother declared she plans to cut him, but my father swore at her. He knew the earl in London, thought him a fine fellow indeed, and he promised her he would not speak to her for a month if she did so. It was quite a row. Oh, do tell—what is he like? Is he the gentleman or boor?"

Before Leah could answer, Lady Dahlia, the duke of Sydney's daughter, slid into the seat next to them. Leah didn't much care for Dahlia. She and her kin were the worst snobs, disdaining all but the most elite nobility. Leah was shocked that she deigned to join them, but supposed the lure of gossip had overcome her aversion to a common-born person.

"My father didn't think he would dare show up," Dahlia hissed, jutting her chin in Morgan's direction. "He was shocked to learn the Farthinghams had invited him. Imagine, a man like that. Why, I would not give him so much as a drink of water if he were on fire."

Leah gave her a freezing look. "It didn't stop your family from attending, I see."

Sophie fairly bounced in her chair. "I think it's *exciting* that he's here. He's something of a curiosity, and we are the first to talk to him."

Dahlia looked over at Morgan. Her glance stuck. "Yes, indeed," she murmured. A sly look came over her pinched face. "The man himself is rather . . . commanding. I can see why he is so controversial. He makes no allowance for his strained position, but enters the room with an air of . . . what is it? Well, it is not so much that he enters than he *imposes* himself on it. One certainly cannot fail to notice a man like that, can one?"

Leah clenched her jaw in frustration. While Dahlia regarded Morgan with a new predatory gleam—the sort eligible women got when an intriguing man of good looks and wealth, not to mention that all-important title, entered their midst—she was forced to remain silent and not stake her claim.

Morgan was hers! Had he forgotten her? Had he decided he didn't need her after all?

She drummed her restless fingers on the arm of her chair to keep from doing something impulsive. Like standing up and shouting, "Yoo-hoo!" to remind Morgan what he was about. Like pushing Dahlia into the sooty fireplace. Like bursting into frustrated tears.

Several other young ladies joined their group, all of them bubbling with curiosity about the elusive earl.

Leah sighed, narrowing her eyes, and willing Morgan to turn his head and witness her displeasure with him. Why was he over *there* when the proper place for a beau was at the side of the woman he adored? Even if he was only pretending to adore her!

Then the Baroness Klass—a notorious flirt if there ever was one—strolled with swinging hips and luxuriant smile right up to the knot of men. They nearly went into paroxysms at the arrival of the voluptuous female.

Morgan inclined his head as the introductions were made. She extended her hand with a look to melt an iceberg. Morgan took it in his and bowed low over it. Very low. Too low.

That did it.

Leah coughed loudly. Barked, actually, as if she'd swallowed the bone of a quail leg. Whole.

More than a few people turned her way, Morgan among them, and she cleared her throat. "Oh, my lord Waring!" she called sweetly, flashing a quick smile. "May I have your assistance?"

His eyes speared her as he hesitated. Not pleased was he, she noticed by his expression. He didn't want to come over, so she forced the issue by waving her hand at him.

For one tense moment, he did not move a muscle. Her mouth went dry and the first pass of hot panic flushed her from the neck up as she considered that he might not come. Finally, he excused himself from his friends. His walk was loose, lazy, full of insolent arrogance and Leah tensed, knowing she had baited his temper this time.

He executed an admirable bow before her, then nodded to the other young ladies. In his distinctive silky voice, he wished them good afternoon. Several of them twittered; those who didn't gawked.

"I'm sorry to disturb your *important conversation*," Leah said with a dose of tartness she was certain he would perceive, "but would you fetch me the cream? My tea, you see, it's not got enough cream in it and the tray is all the way over there."

He smiled, but his eyes remained dangerous. "How dreadful for you. I shall be back directly."

Lady Dahlia cast Leah a vicious look, ripe with jealousy and Leah sat up a bit straighter. Morgan returned promptly and handed her the creamer. "Thank you so much," she purred, angling a beguiling glance up at him.

His fingers brushed hers, lingered, moved slightly in

something suspiciously like a stroke. She felt the contact all through her. He did it on purpose. She was sure of it.

Her simpering smile faltered.

"Is there anything else you require?" he asked with convincing solicitousness. One might even think he meant it. She knew better.

He wouldn't care for her showing off like this. Perhaps she shouldn't have taunted him.

"Thank you so much, my lord, but no. I believe I shall be quite content now." She settled back with her tea, as if dismissing him. Several thundering heartbeats echoed in her ears before he murmured something meant to be a "your servant," bowed, and turned away.

Sophie, sensing that Leah was trying to send a message of proprietorship to the other woman, said, "My goodness, Leah, is he your beau?"

She shrugged. "We met at my sister's ball, and he called upon me several times. We had a lovely outing to Hawkshead a week or so ago, and I do admit I found his company very . . . ah, very stimulating." She snapped her mouth shut. Best not to speak too much about that outing, and the less said about how stimulating she found Morgan, the better.

"Your mother allowed it?" Sophie asked, astounded. "Without an escort or chaperone?"

"My sister and niece were set to go with us, but Cosette was out of sorts that day. My mother didn't wish to disappoint the earl, and Julia persuaded her to give special permission as it was merely a ride along public roads to a very charming village where Julia knows everyone. Country people are not like the ton in London, you know, and Julia has gotten quite used to their more carefree ways. Mother is quite taken with him. And my sister thinks him charming."

Lady Phyllida, the daughter of an earl who had recently announced her engagement to a doddering, arthritic duke, raised her brows. "Indeed, I can see why."

Dahlia's laughter was a delicate trickle of sound. "Oh, then he is merely a friend of the family."

Leah leveled a gaze at her. She loved having something to

hold over the snobbish Dahlia—was that very wrong, she wondered? Therefore, she embarked on the delightful challenge of turning her rival's complexion green. "It's true, we've all grown so fond of him. All of us. He so enjoys visiting us. He was at Glenwood Park nearly every day. What a charmer, he is. Oh, and a marvelous sense of humor, by my word!"

Here Leah paused and laughed softly while staring into the distance, as if remembering a particularly fond memory.

"He's amusing?" Dahlia clearly doubted her. "He seems rather dark."

"Well, of course. He's *dark,* yes. In an amusing way."

"He's not handsome, exactly," said Phyllida as she furrowed her brow. "But yet one can't seem to take their eyes from him, can they?"

Leah followed her gaze and they all fell silent, pondering the earl from across the room. "It's his self-assurance," she said softly, concentrating on the quiet confidence in every line of his body. "There's this air about him like he doesn't really need anybody. And yet sometimes, it seems like there is a depth behind his eyes that is very appealing and sad."

Sophie's shiver was delicate. "He is very alluring, yes. But I think he seems rather frightening, too."

"No. Not frightening, exactly." Leah tilted her head as she considered her "beau." Everyone waited, hushed and expectant. "Dangerous, somehow."

"Yes." Phyllida nodded when Leah didn't finish. "He's . . . so . . ."

"Mmm. Exactly," Leah said, knowing that despite the lack of a proper word for whatever Morgan was, Phyllida understood.

Leah caught Morgan's eye. He didn't look happy with her. No doubt she would get an earful later.

On impulse, she motioned him to her. He set his jaw, narrowed his eyes, and started toward her.

"Ooooh, my." Phyllida's moan was as sensual an utterance as a well-bred woman was allowed to make. "He is *definitely* so . . ."

Leah donned a look of stilted pleasantness as Morgan drew up to her. "My tea is cold, I'm afraid," she pouted. "My friends and I are having the most wonderful talk, and I don't want to interrupt, so would you be so good as to fetch me another cup? Thank you, you are a darling."

Morgan's face was still only for a moment before he cloaked it behind a smile as false as hers. He took her cup from her. "I'll get it for you right this minute. And I'll dash back immediately after it's poured so that you will not be afflicted again with the hideous burden of tepid tea."

Her spine went rigid. He was mocking her, and if he were any more obvious about it, she'd most definitely suffer a humiliating setback in front of everyone. "Please do not take it so seriously, my lord. If you hurry too much, you may scald yourself."

"I would consider it an honor." His tone was dry, and the women stared blankly, apparently thinking him absolutely besotted. He bowed and backed up a few steps before turning away, as if she were Queen Charlotte.

Leah forced a lilting laugh. "You see? I told you he can be so funny sometimes. He is always joking like that."

Doubtfully, Phyllida turned to watch the retreat of Morgan's broad back. She sighed. "He . . . is . . . just . . . so . . ."

Dahlia's eyes narrowed. "He's very wealthy, I had heard." She was deep in thought for a moment, and then said, "Mother has been wrong before."

Leah sighed and fought the urge to scream.

Morgan returned with the tea. Leah had heard the warning in his voice before, but she had a point to make to these women, so she took a sip from her cup and decided it could use a bit more sugar. He got it without a word. Then Leah asked him to fetch her shawl. When he returned, she basked in the admiration of the other women as he stood behind her and draped it around her.

His hands closed over her shoulders for a moment, and there was a hush and collective widening of the eyes as they all took in the gesture. Leah was taken aback by his willingness to play along.

Leaning over, he said, "Is there anything else you require, Miss Brodie? Some biscuits?" His breath was maddeningly warm on her neck. "A sandwich?" In a lower voice for her ears alone, he added, "Someone's head on a platter, perhaps?"

His touch was sapping her wit. "N-no," she answered. Everyone gaped as his mouth hovered a mere hair's breadth from her ear. She began to feel dizzy.

"Then leave off this damned show. I guarantee you won't like my performance if you keep at it."

Leah saw the other young women snap open their fans and begin to flutter them furiously. They hadn't heard him, but they'd seen him whisper something in her ear, and they would naturally assume it was some private endearment.

She donned a smile, resigning her game. She didn't dare tempt him further.

He stayed away from her until after the buffet luncheon was served. As she finished the last morsel of parfait, he appeared at her side. His fingers, immutable as warm steel on the flesh of her upper arm, pressed tightly as he inquired if she would like to accompany him on a stroll to view the famous gardens.

Leah's instinct was to pull away, knowing he only wanted to scold her. She told him no, thank you.

"Oh, Miss Brodie," he replied. "I absolutely guarantee you will regret it if you don't."

He didn't mean missing the flowers.

Leah swallowed hard and went with him. Outside, she walked briskly toward the colorful beds. "Yes, my lord, look at the daffodils. You were quite right—umph!"

With absolutely no ceremony he took hold of her and barreled them both behind a clutch of hedges. As she stumbled along, she exclaimed, "I know what you are going to say, and before you do, I want to just establish that all of this is absolutely not my fault!"

His top lip curled and he sent her a skeptical look. "God help me, I know I'm going to regret asking, but I can't seem to stop myself. How, pray tell, is this not your fault?"

"You were ignoring me!" she blurted. "And the other women were all giddy and staring, acting like a pack of bloody roundheels."

"Watch your choice of words, Blackie, we're not on the moor."

She cast an anxious look around her. She lowered her voice. "*Don't* try to tell me that you didn't notice what was happening. You are positively the rage, my lord earl, and loving it, I'll wager."

"Will you explain yourself?" he demanded.

"Please do not forget that if you become the new darling of the ton, *I am responsible*. And you were enjoying it, prancing around the parlor like a lion in heat—"

He looked at her in horror. "I do not *prance*."

"Phyllida was just *dying* over you, you had to have seen her. As for that Dahlia—I thought she was going to take a bite out of you."

He waited a heartbeat. "You are insane," he pronounced simply.

"I am most sane, sir, and well sighted to boot. And if you are going to be my suitor, then you best do it correctly and stop appealing to *other* women."

"I'm not interested in dallying with simpleminded debutantes."

The statement fell flatly in the air. In the deafening silence, Leah felt the steam drain from her as she realized how right he was. And how awful.

No, he wasn't here for simpleminded debutantes. He didn't care for any of them—Dahlia or Phyllida or that awful baroness, even. Or herself.

He was here for Glorianna. She wondered, and not for the first time, if he was in love with his dead father's wife. Was that what compelled him?

Suddenly she didn't want to talk to him anymore. She broke away, fleeing around a bend in the path that opened into a walled garden, where she saw there was a folly, a freestanding rotunda in the Greek style. She stepped inside, hugging a column, pressing her face against the marble to cool the lingering heat on her face.

Behind her, she heard his footsteps.

She didn't turn around. "Yes, Morgan, I know quite well that you have a very specific purpose for being here."

She heard the sadness in her own voice, as if she were forlorn and yearning. She didn't want him to think her forlorn and yearning. Even if she was. Pulling herself upright, she tried to shake off her mood. But she still couldn't look at him.

He said, "None of this is new to you. What has you overset?"

She turned. The scar that tore across his cheekbone was whitened again.

She thought of what it would be like to touch it, to try and soothe the bristling tension that caused it to stand out at times when he was upset. With her, inevitably. It seemed she brought out the worst in him—the worst in herself—whenever they were together.

Her lips trembled as she asked, "Is it so difficult to act the part of a man who finds me irresistible?"

"I'm not the sort of man who fawns," he stated, as if it were as immutable a trait as the color of his hair. "I wouldn't know the first thing to do."

She thought, *How I wish things were different,* and saw his reaction. She realized she had uttered it out loud.

"Leah . . ." He shook his head slowly, and his eyes lowered to her mouth. Her body responded instantaneously to the softness in his voice and the keen sharpening of his gaze. Prickly sensation quivered through her. Liquid weakness poured over her. Heady, lazy feeling weighed her down.

It wasn't fair that he could do this to her, and remain unfazed.

No. He wasn't unfazed. He wore the same expression she'd seen in his eyes when he'd kissed her on the way home from the village.

"Goddamn it," he muttered and backed away. "We are going back inside."

She'd humiliated herself again. Stepping off the folly, she

headed back to the house, taking long strides, wanting distance, wanting to run away from him and all the feelings he made her feel. They only twisted her reason and made her do awful, stupid things.

His hand closed around her upper arm. "Leah, wait."

The heat of his fingers bled into her, melting her and she wanted to turn to him right now and fling herself into the shelter of his arms, except it was him she needed to be sheltered from.

It took all she had to look at him.

He paused, searching for words. "I don't want to hurt you. I'm not . . . I've lived the past year . . . I spent months in prison, and I thought it was the last place I would see before I died. It changes a man. I am different from the men you've known, danced with, flirted with."

He expelled a long breath. "You and I are from different worlds, and I'm glad of that. I wouldn't want for you to know the things I've known. But, you must realize I am not the kind of man you need. You want someone who will give you the attention you deserve. A woman like you attracts admirers like a rose draws bees, for God's sake. You are absolutely right to think you should be doted upon, have someone who can sit with you and talk about things, who can take the time to explore that frighteningly agile mind of yours. Someone who can make you laugh. All I ever seem to be able to do is distress you."

She bit her lips, thinking, *Because I want you.*

"I am bound to disappoint you. I can't believe that is starting to actually bother me." His harsh laugh was full of scorn. "All of this nonsense we're mixed in, it isn't so important as you make it. Soon, this summer's adventure will pass, and you'll go on to dazzle the ton as you did before.

"Oh, you shall be restored to their bosom and spend long nights dancing reels and fending off proposals of marriage until you find yourself the perfect husband. Me . . . I will fade into memory, and this little game will be but a story you tell. I know you are fond of stories, aren't you? You will be the heroine, and you can tell them all of this odd little episode and how you were courageous and compassionate and amazing. . . ."

There was a vivid, horrible vision in front of her eyes all of a sudden. Of herself with a man. Another man who was not Morgan. Of sitting in front of children, not Morgan's children, telling them the story and holding her love still secret in her heart.

She bit her lips. Hard. And made the mistake of looking at Morgan. He looked stricken, she thought, but knew she was wrong.

"Bloody hell!" he muttered and jerked into motion, leading her back to the house.

M ORGAN AROSE THE following morning feeling extremely tense. Most of the guests had arrived, ready and eager for the week's entertainment, but Glorianna and Randall were not here yet. He had gotten word that they were among those invited and had responded that they planned to attend.

He wondered if the stragglers who would trickle in today and possibly into the evening would bring them at last. There was a sense of unease mixed in with his anticipation. He wasn't certain he wanted to confront them both this soon. Why did he hesitate? he wondered with scorn, and put the feeling out of his mind.

It proved stubborn. He felt rushed, all of a sudden, as if he, not Sanderson, were the one being caught unawares. Unprepared. Absurd, since he'd waited a year to find his way back home and to realize that he would never have peace until he knew the man who had murdered his father had seen justice.

The reason did not overtax his brain to deduce. Leah, of course, had occupied nearly all of his thoughts in the last weeks he'd spent with her.

As he rose to perform his morning ablutions, he reflected that he was not being entirely fair to blame Leah. She herself had made surprisingly little demands on him after that stupid trick she'd pulled in the village. Up until yesterday and that . . . well, her complaint was not without merit. His part of the bargain, after all, was to dazzle her friends with his devotion so as to effectively restore her reputation. It was just that it had been so long since he'd been welcomed in any home of good ton. Running into a group of his old school chums had been an unexpected pleasure, and it was good to feel his old self again.

Morgan's valet, Andrew, entered. He was a quiet fellow, precisely why Morgan liked him. No small talk or gossiping commenced when Andrew poured the heated water into the basin and began to lay out a freshly ironed shirt and trousers while Morgan washed.

After a few comments about his cravat, Morgan was left to his own thoughts once again as he sat back in a chair while his face was lathered with hot soap and the straight razor expertly wielded.

Randall Sanderson. He had to concentrate on Sanderson, not the delectable Miss Brodie. How many times had he schooled his thoughts thusly, always to fail? Andrew finished and Morgan wiped the excess soap off of his face and finished dressing.

He paused, looking at himself in the mirror as he donned his coat. His fingers touched the puckered line of skin on his cheek. His mood darkened. If he ever needed a reminder of all he had lost, it was this.

This was not a lark with a pretty maid. This was deadly business, and he had best get ahold of his errant brain and concentrate on exactly what he was supposed to do when he found himself face-to-face with his nemesis.

He didn't wish to arrive late to breakfast. It was going so well already, better than he'd dreamed. He'd not met any of the rancor and open hostility he'd encountered when he'd returned from the continent. Of course, London had been Sanderson's domain. He'd done an excellent job of spreading rumors and half-truths to make it appear that Morgan was the one guilty of his father's murder. Some still believed that.

But not everyone, it seemed. Randall's influence did not extend into the rural shires. What an excellent thing to note. His mind began working furiously over the possibilities this presented. His thumb ran up and down his scar.

"All done, sir," Andrew said, whisking invisible particles of dust from his shoulders with a little brush.

"I shall be down in a moment, Andrew. Thank you. That is all."

He adjusted his cuffs to show just the right amount below his coat sleeve, and wondered what it would feel like to take a man's life.

I T WAS LATE when Morgan arrived downstairs, but breakfast was still being served. Although country hours were much earlier than city hours, the night's revels had caused most of the guests to sleep in late and the day was rolling along lazily.

Morgan learned that the Farthinghams had a picnic planned for luncheon for this very afternoon. Although he considered it a ridiculous ado going on about packing some food in hampers and eating it uncomfortably on blankets spread on ant-infested meadows, he recalled something Leah had said, that she had enjoyed a picnic. She would. She seemed to thrive whenever she was outdoors.

He should take her. It would be the seemly thing for a beau to do. She entered the room just then, accompanied by a group of her friends who had probably been riding with her this morning.

Seeing her costume, he started. It was a smart peacock-blue riding habit with a hat that reminded him of the one she'd been wearing on the moor. The feather, however, was spry and graceful, not at all the ruined plume he'd mauled. The effect, now that he had it fresh and absolutely perfect, was very alluring.

He was struck by something different about her this morning. He realized almost at once that it was the first time he'd observed her without her defenses flared. Of course, she hadn't seen him yet. The moment she did, a shadow would come into her eyes and her smile would tighten.

He berated himself for his sentimentality. He had spent this morning getting focused on the true business at hand and steeling himself against this very sort of thing and yet. . . .

And yet he felt the contrast between his dark preoccupations of death and vengeance and murder and Leah's refreshing, effortless beauty. It made him feel . . . ugly. Inside. Not guilty, just filled with the ugly things that had happened in his life. The ugliness that lived inside him still.

When he looked at her now and all of that beauty shining out through her eyes, he was possessed of a longing he couldn't name.

Or, perhaps, dared not.

Leah caught his gaze on her and tensed, just as he'd anticipated. Her eyes dimmed; her posture grew rigid. She became uncertain.

He swallowed the bitter taste in his throat. Going to her, he inquired, "Did you enjoy your ride?"

"Indeed, my lord, it was very enjoyable."

"I . . . ah, there is a picnic planned for later on. I know you enjoy them. I thought you would like to attend."

She blinked, apparently stunned for a moment. Then she smiled. He felt his stomach plummet in a queerly pleasant manner at the unabashed pleasure on her face. "I would absolutely adore it!" she exclaimed. "I shall go change at once."

He couldn't suppress a soft laugh. "Leah, it isn't until luncheon. We're only half through breakfast."

But he was strangely comforted that he had managed to make her so happy. It didn't prove such a difficult thing, after all.

They set out in the early afternoon. There was a large group of men and women riding sleek mounts or nestled in open conveyances of all types. The procession crawled over jewel-green meadows under a sky of robin's-egg blue, the mood gay as the high-pitched voices of the ladies called to one another. The bass intonations of the gentleman rode under the sound, like a blending of choral harmony.

It was rather pleasant, Morgan observed grudgingly, though he didn't quite share the mood. Leah rode beside him and that, somehow, felt rather nice.

"Are you displeased?" Leah asked. "We do not have to participate if you are not of a mind."

Had he looked that dour? Probably. She kept scolding him for it, as well she should.

"No," he said, "I'm not cross. I just have a tendency to get lost in my thoughts sometimes."

"You look like you are in a funeral procession, not a recreational outing."

"How kind of you to point it out. As it is not my desire to remain the mysterious earl, or whatever the thing is they are calling me these days, I shall make more of an effort to comport my features into a more pleasing countenance."

"*Wicked* Earl of Waring," she corrected with mock innocence.

"Yes," he drawled. "How good of you to remind me."

"Oh, I'll be more than happy to tell you when you are doing anything wrong," she said with such an impish smile he had to reply in kind. They both turned away, but the smiles warmed, and lingered.

He found he suddenly felt much better. Trust Leah to not care a fig for the fierceness that seemed to drive everyone else away. Then again, she never did have any fear of him. And she never relented. Did that make her a fool or very brave? he wondered.

A group of her friends called to her and Morgan told her to go on ahead. He watched in admiration as she kicked the horse into a canter.

He fell in with a cluster of London swells, cursing his luck until their sophomoric humors proved surprisingly amusing. He relaxed and took their hilarity in the proper spirit, reflecting that the rowdy bunch was reminiscent of himself at an immature age when the world didn't weigh so heavily on his shoulders. He'd nearly forgotten.

Couples paired off quickly as they arrived at their destination, spreading their blankets and uncorking champagne. Leah selected a spot not too far from her mother's watchful eye and had the liveried under-footman set out the hamper.

"I brought all of my favorite foods," she said gaily as Morgan spread the coverlet, "and I would have brought yours except you refuse to tell me anything about yourself, and so I don't know what they are. I didn't want to intrude on your hallowed privacy, so I didn't ask."

Her sly little sideways look, the way she tilted her head just so, was calculated to disarm him. It didn't. Not much, anyway.

He told her, "For luncheon, I am partial to roast beef sandwiches on crusty bread and sliced cucumber salad made with dill."

She wrinkled her nose. "I brought chicken."

"Ah. My second favorite."

"My Lord, so much information at once," she declared, patting her hand over her chest and batting her eyelashes at him. "Dare I press my advantage and delve more deeply. Indeed—I shall do it. Please, sir, pray tell what is it you favor for dessert?"

"We don't wish to move too fast," he replied drolly, reclining on his side, propped on an elbow.

"Indeed, that is wise, for we do not wish to overwhelm my poor simple deb's sensibilities of which you say I have none—sensibilities, that is. Why, I fear I would be rendered quite incapable of speech."

Her eyes had turned iridescent in the sunlight, fracturing into various shades of fathomless brown. He liked the way they sparkled when she was being mischievous.

"We could only hope," he muttered.

She laughed freely, tilting her head back so that the creamy white column of her neck was exposed. Vulnerable.

Inviting.

It wasn't good to be noticing that. He dragged his gaze away.

Leah sighed and gestured in front of her. "Doesn't it seem like you can see forever from here? Look at that view."

He hadn't noticed before that the sloping dell offered a tremendous vista of the emerald vale. They were high on the hillside, with terraced fields below them and forests off in the distance. The horizon seemed leagues away and the scent of spring was heavy in the air as it wafted over them and down into the verdant valley.

She sighed and stretched out her legs. He could see her feet clear to her ankles. Her toes were pointed up, like a child sits. Grinning, he tilted his head back and felt the sun on his face.

He was beginning to feel fine.

"Look," Leah cried, springing to her feet. "They are setting up the targets for archery. Drat, I don't have my bow with me! Ah, I'll have to make do with one of theirs. You don't mind if I play, do you?" She was already striding toward the archery fields. She whirled, walking backward a few steps, and added, "Do find something amusing to do, Morgan. If you want to be less conspicuously wicked, you have to do less scowling and make more of an effort to *blend in*."

He wasn't alone for long. Other guests plied him with jokes and conversation and truffle tarts. He tried not to watch Leah, but it was impossible to keep his gaze from wandering to where she and the other archers were queued up before the targets.

Right now, she was leaning on her bow, talking animatedly to the another archer as she waited for her turn. Her hat had slipped back, exposing her face to the sun. She must like the feel of the sun on her skin, and a sudden image came to him of her relaxed, sultry, basking in its rays without a hat.

The voices of the people to whom he was talking faded away as his imagination took fire. He conjured a vision of Leah reclined, her hair loose and soft as silk and spread all around her. On her warm skin, a fine sheen of sweat glistened—

He forbade the thought, clamping down on it before it got any further.

It was much better when he was furious with her.

Leah shouldered up the longbow and threaded the arrow. He expected that she would be a skilled marksman. She had strength in her. He recalled how she'd leapt onto the bed in the hut on the moor when he'd kidnapped her. She'd kicked him but good—hard enough to make his head ache later that night.

Taking careful aim, she closed her eye and curled her tongue around her upper lip. His throat went dry as he fastened on the glistening pinkness as it swept over the plumpness of her mouth—

Jesus!

The arrow cutting through the air made a sharp *thwong* and embedded itself on the line between the bull's-eye and the first circle.

It was an excellent shot. He felt like sending up a cheer.

The shot, it seemed, didn't meet with her approval. She threaded the next arrow and took aim.

This one hit the red circle and her companions congratulated her. She let loose her last arrow, another bull's-eye and received renewed round of applause.

She looked at him, then, and saw him watching her. She sent him a bright, beaming smile and waved her arm while the sun drenched her in light. It was a decidedly exuberant, and *unladylike,* wave that made him chuckle warmly and shake his head. He waved back.

Imagine that unfettered exuberance in bed.

His stomach clenched tight and he cursed.

"Young Leah Brodie, eh?" one of the men said, noticing the interchange. "She's a beautiful girl. Many a man has had his eye on her this past year. She's a spry one, she is." He tapped his temple, showing he meant of the mind, not of the body, although Morgan mused that both were true. "Wouldn't mind spending a bit of time with her myself. I like a lively chit. Nothing like a bit of a challenge, I say, as long as it doesn't get too out of hand, and by George she's got a spark. . . ."

Morgan leveled a look at the man, stemming his gushing praise.

"Oh, not *now*, of course," the fellow rushed to reassure him. "Ha, ha. It is easy to see she is taken with you. I just meant that before you were calling on her, I'd thought of it. Didn't mean to tread on your toes, what."

Morgan eased the weight of his glare, satisfied. Wicked Earl myth be damned, he was going to send a clear signal to this man and everyone else that Leah Brodie was his.

"Yes," Morgan said softly. "She is *very* taken."

He supposed it should trouble his conscience that he was cheating Leah of an opportunity for real suitors, but it didn't. He hummed softly as he made his way back to their blanket when the archery challenge was over. Leah joined him and unpacked the hamper.

"Are you finding this amusing?"

"Tolerably," he said, taking the plate she offered and biting back the twitching of his lips.

"Did you ever go on picnics when you were younger?"

"We did. On the moors. My mother and I used to like to climb up on the tors and eat our sandwiches there. My father and sister would laugh at us, saying we looked like a pair of vultures, perched on the rock like that."

"I didn't know you had a sister."

"She and my mother died when I was nine. Fever."

"Oh, Morgan, I am so sorry, I didn't know—"

"It is all right. Really. It was a long time ago."

"I suppose that left you and your father very close. I know how fond you were of him. It must have been awful to lose him, too."

"Yes, we were close."

She reached out and took his hand. The gesture startled him. "I am so sorry for all of this, his death I mean, and everything that happened to you." She squeezed. "It's bloody awful, is what it is, and it shouldn't have happened."

He didn't respond right away. When he could, all he said was, "Thank you, Blackie."

She paused, chewing on her lip. "Morgan? I have been thinking about something."

"A sure sign of impending disaster."

The look she cast him was petulant. "I was wondering if it would be all right to ask you something."

"I am, as always, at your service."

"You said your cousin, Glorianna's husband, was a bad sort and you were afraid for her. I thought at the time you meant he was a coward and wouldn't protect her well if the killer came after her, but then it occurred to me that you might have meant *he* was the killer? You did, did you? You believe it was him."

Morgan turned away from her, studying the pastoral scenery around them. "And what if I did? Would you think me a lunatic?"

"No. Why would I?"

"Everyone else did. Of course, they'd been paid to say that. Nevertheless, I learned quickly to shut up about it. I'd survived the gaol once, I didn't think I'd have the same luck in an asylum."

"Paid . . . is that what happened? The officials were *paid* to arrest you?"

"There was some flimsy evidence to start. I was the one who discovered my father's body, or rather discovered *over* his body. His man came in and saw me trying to find a pulse. It was rather incriminating, alone with a dead man, blood on my hands. I had gone in to talk to him that evening and found him like that. I often think what might have happened had I come moments sooner."

"Oh, Morgan, you couldn't have foreseen what happened. Murderers rarely go about announcing what they are planning."

He gave a soft laugh, amused at the blend of tolerance and urgency in her voice. "I should have known, Leah. I lived with my cousin from the age of eleven. He came to us when his father died, thirteen himself at the time. His mother was my father's very beloved sister. She couldn't manage the boy after her husband died. She asked my father to take him, show him a firm hand. But it wasn't a firm hand Randall needed. There is something very wrong with Randall. It is as if a part of his soul doesn't exist. The problem was, he is so damned clever. He was always that way. He could gauge just what was needed, just what to say, and charm a snake.

"I alone saw the things he did, for he often didn't bother to hide them from me. After all, I could do nothing to stop him. Sometimes, he'd even crow about how clever he was. One time . . ." He flinched at the memory. He could still recall the acrid smell of smoke and the thick, stinging of white-hot air in his throat.

"One time he set a fire down in the row of crofter's cottages. I had seen him sneak into the house moments before the alarm was raised. I knew immediately he was responsible. The fire destroyed the home of one of the crofters who had caught Randall with his young daughter and told my father. Randall had his allowance cut off and his freedoms curtailed as punishment. The fire was his revenge."

He began to take deep breaths, as if his lungs labored under the emotions of that day. The panicked shouts of the men around him, the bleating of the livestock in the yards and how his chest had burned as he'd run to free the animals from the encroaching flames were blisteringly vivid. "Two lives were lost that day, a good deal of crops and valuable property."

"But didn't your father also realize he'd done it?"

"Leah, Randall Sanderson is more clever than you can ever imagine. There was no proof, no one saw anything. The incident with the crofter's daughter had occurred months before, but that bastard can hold a grudge, and wait to get his recompense, believe me. Oh, and on that day of the fire, he lined up with the water brigade hauling buckets until the sweat poured off him. He worked feverishly trying to save the remaining huts, the livestock, his face as black as a Moor's with soot and grime. He was hailed for his efforts. I got sick in the ashes. They thought it was lung poisoning from the smoke, but it was something much worse. It was the knowledge that I had seen evil. True evil."

Leah's face spoke of her horror at what she was hearing. "My God, I never imagined people like this existed. You hear about these things, but you just don't imagine it could ever be real."

"I didn't tell anyone. I didn't think they'd believe me. Hell, it was a damned hard thing to believe, I knew that. I made the mistake of confronting Randall myself."

"I suppose he denied everything."

"He did, but in a way so that I would know he was lying. It is all a game to him, a sick game, and he knew I was caught between knowing and no one to tell. My father never hesitated to discipline Randall or myself, but his one weakness was that determined to make good with his beloved sister's son. He could not accept the basic premise that the boy was just plain evil."

"It is still happening today—that terrible frustration you always felt. I mean, you know he did it, but no one will listen to you. And you can't provide absolute proof to have him arrested."

At Morgan's expression, Leah said hurriedly, "Oh, Morgan, I should not have asked about this. I am sorry to have gotten your mood so low. We were doing so well, too, having a wonderful day. I hope it hasn't upset you to talk about it."

"It hasn't," he said honestly. "I think it might actually have helped a little. I've never spoken to another person about it. Sometimes I wanted to, but there was never anyone I could trust."

"Really?" She smiled warmly, pleased. "Then I am honored that you confide in me. I shall keep every word to myself. You can trust me, too."

"Yes, I know I can. Blackie."

She was really very beautiful. Morgan couldn't keep himself from reaching out and touching a finger to the smooth curve of her cheek.

She darted a glance to where her mother sat watchfully.

Leah then lowered her eyes. He withdrew his hand with reluctance.

Sometimes he wanted very badly to touch her. Sometimes, he wanted a great many things.

"Morgan, can I just ask you one thing more? You are going to try to expose him, aren't you? I think you should. And . . . and I wanted you to know that if I can help I will. I know I said before I wouldn't but I will. You need only ask."

"I treasure that," Morgan replied solemnly, and with sincerity. Her wide eyes regarded him with unwavering faith and he wanted badly to be worthy of what he saw there.

But he was bound to a different course. She thought him an honorable man. He had been, once. But he'd done the same things in his defense that his enemies had done to him. He'd stolen and lied, and paid for men to look the other way. And now he was committed to a path of vengeance with as much disregard for the law as any felon.

He had no recourse in the courts. No one would open the case. Morgan's influence with peers was damaged. But he had one idea, one small chance to bring Sanderson down.

With stealth, with subtlety, he would build the case for suspicion against Sanderson. He would trickle the facts out deftly, seed them and watch them take root and flower, stripping his enemy of the strengths—his seeming innocuousness and high regard—that had held him above punishment. Then Morgan wouldn't need the law.

If there was a consensus of opinion that Sanderson might be guilty, then Morgan could call Sanderson out and no one would fault him. Cause for a legal duel would be firmly established.

And then he would kill him.

Chapter 8

L EAH DECIDED TO learn how to play whist, which wasn't to her liking but she stayed with it anyway. She favored outdoor activities, such as riding or lawn tennis, or bowling and pinions, but Morgan was involved in the billiards tournament going on at present and she wished to stay close to the house.

She was into the second rubber of the day when the viscount of Kingsley, who had come three days late with an heraldic arrival and profuse apologies, entered the card room and spied Leah. He threw his hands up and exclaimed, "Lud! 'Pon my word, hide the desserts for it is the inimitable Miss Leah Brodie!"

The room went instantly silent. Leah's head snapped up to gaze into the merry eyes of her tormentor, the thunder of her heartbeat deafening in her ears. She made a face of disgust when she saw who it was. Kingsley was an outrageous rapscallion who loved to shock. He also happened to be one of Leah's dearest friends.

Very often and quite dramatically in his trademark style of wit, he claimed to be a frustrated suitor of hers, but in truth their mutual affection was more of the nature of siblings than anything of a romantic nature. The look she gave him was one akin to a fed-up sister giving an annoying brother a silent warning. He burst into raucous laughter.

The gaping stares his outburst had caused transformed into fond smiles as others in the room recognized him as well. Despite his unconventional, and often outrageous, humor he was tolerated with fondness. Kingsley was always a much sought-after guest at all the ton's parties.

"I say," he went on, pointing his toe and folding himself into a flourishing bow before her, "as your most devoted servant, madam, I beg your leave to take up your cause. I declare myself your champion. Why, I have no doubt were I armed with a leg of mutton and turnip greens, I could do damage to the dastardly fellow in who played you false."

Leah had to laugh at this, especially when Kingsley brandished the imaginary leg of mutton in the fencing style and began a mock duel.

"And thenceforth, my fair, fair Miss Brodie, shall I be in your favor." Kingsley went down on one knee before her and folded his hands in entreaty. "Oh, I beg you, allow this honor to be mine."

She would have made a suitable reply, but a blur from the corner of her eye startled her, stealing the words. She looked up to see the towering visage of Morgan looming over the two of them. He looked thunderous as his eyes flitted first to Kingsley, then to her.

His scar was nearly white and his jaw was set in that straight, tight line that meant he was furious. Morgan grabbed her wrist and yanked her none-too-gently onto her feet. No sooner was she thus than he shoved her behind him and swung around to square off against Kingsley. His voice was low and threatening. "I have little care for your jokes, sir."

Leah tried to step out from behind Morgan, but she was shoved back into place by a strong hand on her waist.

"I say," Kingsley said with amused surprise, "you intend to devil me, do you?"

"Morgan." Leah tried to speak up, but he wouldn't even

glance at her. His hand held her in place. She pushed hard against it, but to no avail.

"Why, dear Leah," Kingsley drawled, a gleam of mischief in his eye, "why didn't you tell me you'd gotten yourself another chief admirer? Alas, my heart is broken into a thousand pieces, 'pon my word! Pray, present me to this brave challenger."

"I take exception to your mockery," Morgan growled.

"Morgan, it is all right!" Leah managed to extricate herself at last and stepped in between the two men. "Allow me to introduce my good friend, my lord," she said, trying like anything to catch Morgan's eye, keenly aware that he would think Kingsley's taunts cruel if he didn't know the fellow or the nature of their relationship. He must believe the worst, for he was as furious as she'd ever seen him.

Which was nice, in a way. She felt the warmth of his protectiveness.

She addressed herself to diffusing the tension. "This is the viscount of Kingsley. We are old acquaintances, my lord. He is a wicked tease, I am afraid, but there was *no harm* in him."

Kingsley inclined his head in acknowledgement of the introduction. "If you are jealous, you have cause to be so, for I am an ardent admirer of our young sprite and avow my everlasting faithfulness to being her friend. Have no care, my lord. I am merely clowning for the sake of diversion. I would not harm Miss Brodie, not for the world."

Morgan didn't move a muscle. "Miss Brodie hasn't mentioned you."

"Not mentioned me, what? Why, what's wrong with you, gel? I'd have thought I'd be the first thing out of your mouth, with being the object of your heart and all that. Come, let me take you on a stroll and I shall scold you."

He held out his hand for Leah. Morgan moved quickly, knocking it away before Kingsley saw it coming.

Leah bit her lips and ran her gaze about the room, taking in the faces watching the interchange with interest. Blast and curse it all, was Morgan insane making a scene like this? He was going too far with this. And damn Kingsley—he was enjoying every minute of it.

"Miss Brodie is unable to accompany you." Morgan took a small step so that his greater height towered over Kingsley. "She has a previous engagement. With me. So, if you will excuse us."

Kingsley rocked on his heels, pleased and not ashamed to show it. "Gads, I believe he'd fight a duel over the matter. As I'm a shameless coward, I must surrender. Do have a good time, Leah, darling, and try not to miss me too much."

With a waggle of his eyebrows and a deep bow he was gone.

Leah felt the tension tighten in the dull silence left after Kingsley's exit. Acting quickly she trilled a chirping laugh and pushed on Morgan's arm. "Oh, you actually had him thinking you were angry, my lord. What a jest."

Morgan blinked, as if coming to himself. She caught his eye and tried to look meaningfully at him without compromising her smile. His expression changed immediately as he understood they were being observed and overheard.

Leah went on, "Your pretense was monstrous good. Why, I believe you frightened him away. We shall tell him later it was just a bit of his own medicine back upon him."

"Indeed," he said, coming to the game better than she had hoped. "I admit the fellow is amusing. Still, I won't have him upsetting our plans."

"Our plans? Oh, of course, right, our plans. I . . . er . . . exactly what are our plans?"

He raised his brows. "It is a *surprise,* remember?"

"Indeed. Well, I would not miss it. I do so adore surprises."

His grin deepened to a degree that could not possibly be genuine. "And I adore surprising you."

"You do so often, my lord, and very thoroughly."

He bowed, as if accepting a compliment. "Your servant."

"Let us be off then. Oh. Where . . . that is, in what direction do we go?"

"This way, madam."

He grabbed her arm and led her outside, looking to all their observers as if he were being gallant. In actuality, his grip on her was just shy of being painful.

As soon as they were out of the house, he snapped, "Who the devil was that jackanapes? My God, did you not see he was mocking you?"

Leah didn't know whether to crow with happiness or slap him. She *was* angry and yet the glow from the knowledge that he was enraged on her behalf left her without any will to fight him.

"He was not mocking me," she explained with patience. "He is an impish fellow and no one takes him seriously. I know him well and for a long time; he is like a brother, nothing more. He did me a favor, drawing out the fact of the Enders disaster and making a joke of it. You know everyone was thinking of it and whispering behind my back. More, he allowed *me* to laugh at it. It was clever of him, really. Painful, but clever. Sort of like having a splinter taken out."

He dropped her arm and stopped in his tracks. "You are serious. Are you that desperate to be admired that even a bloody fool like that can charm you?"

"That is insulting. Now I am in an excellent mood so do not spoil it. I have been fortunate twice. Not only did Kingsley make his play, but my new suitor—that is you!—arrived on the scene and charged to my defense, all but beating his chest in a manly show of protection. Oh, Morgan, you achieved just the right degree of outrage and subtle threat. I am certain I shall be most envied among the wagging tongues tonight. This is marvelous. And, by the by, I was wonderful—calm and decorous. Wise, even, don't you think? It was a very admirable show altogether."

He blinked, bemused. "So . . . you think this was a good thing?"

"Indeed, I am not vexed. But I should thank you. It *was* good of you to leap so ardently to my defense when you thought I was being maligned. You were magnificent."

"Anyone would," he stated gruffly, still a tad confused. "It is not so great a thing."

"But you seemed angry," she said, laying a hand on his arm. "Not just pretense, either. I am sorry if he upset you."

His scowl deepened for a moment. "I thought he was hurting you." His eyes glittered. "No one will ever get away with that."

She tried to say, "Oh," but there was no breath in her. She wrapped her free arm tightly to her body to prevent herself from flinging it wide with joy. She trotted beside him in order to keep up with his long, loping strides as he set off again across the lawns. "Um. Morgan. Where are we going?"

"We can't right well show up back at the house. I said that we have plans. So, we'll have to make some plans."

"Shall we stroll? I like the woods," she suggested.

"Perhaps. Or . . ." He pointed to a small boat docked at a small pier. "We'll take it out on the lake for a while. That should do it."

What a marvelous idea. What a *romantic* idea. She feigned a casual air and replied, "Oh. All right."

The craft was small and light, most likely used for pleasure, not profit. It was devoid of the fishy smell a utilitarian vessel would have saturated into its boards. For that blessing, Leah offered a silent thanks. Morgan handed Leah in and climbed aboard, taking the oars in hand. With long, powerful strokes, he sent them gliding onto the lake and headed to the far shore, maneuvering easily on the glassy surface.

She enjoyed the sleek, slicing motion of the boat on the water. They didn't speak for a long while, didn't even look at one another. Morgan paused only to remove his frock coat and roll up his sleeves. He offered Leah an apology for the dishabille, but she waved him off. Taking off her hat, she tilted her head up to the bright orb of the sun and closed her eyes.

The joyful memory of Morgan coming so ardently to her defense shot tingles right through her and had her smiling without her even realizing it.

After a while, he said, "We should head back. It is probably close to tea."

"Or after," Leah mused. She felt contented, and not at all hungry. "I don't mind. It's nice out here."

"I don't want you to grow faint."

"I'm not the fainting type." Except when she tied her stays too tightly, but she wouldn't mention that.

"All right. Let's head up there. In the shelter of the pines on the shore, it's nicely shaded."

"Yes, let's do."

He worked, sending them skating into the secluded waters of the upper lake. Sweat glistened on his skin. Leah watched him covertly, her gaze lingering on the fascinating play of male musculature visible beneath the lawn shirt as he pulled the oars in each sure stroke. The boat surged, responding to his power, and she found she *did* feel a little faint.

When he was out of breath, he laid the oars across his knees. "Do you mind floating for a while?"

"Not at all. It is quite pleasant here."

They sat companionably until Leah asked him, "You seem accustomed to the water."

"I've had a boat since I was a child. I often go out onto the river when I am in Yorkshire. It relaxes me."

"I wish we could live in the country, but Father does too much business in London. I miss him when we're away from him. He is forever at work, however, and doesn't take even the briefest holiday. I suppose that is how we became monstrously rich—ooh! That was poor manners for me to say so, but it's true, nonetheless."

"I admire men like your father, especially ones who made something out of nothing. It's a trick to keep money, but more of one to get it in the first place. For myself, I am horrid at finances and such. I trust my father's man of affairs, as he happens to be excellent at these things. He sees to things quite adeptly, even brilliantly, despite his feelings toward me."

"Is he not faithful to you?"

"I'm afraid Mr. Humbolt is one of those persons for whom the subject of my guilt or innocence has not yet been resolved to his satisfaction. He serves the Waring estates for the sake of the love he bore to my father."

"I am sorry to hear that. I have often thought that it must be dreadful to have to contend with people thinking the worst of you."

"In case you haven't noticed, I am not a man of delicate feelings. But, I admit it has been excessively trying. It is like having one's whole identity taken. I am no longer seen as the man I was. When I walk into a room every face turns to me, and I would dare the meanest of souls not to be resentful of the conjecture in each and every eye as the crowd silently divides themselves into sides on the matter—guilty or innocent."

Morgan shrugged, trying to slough off the mood. "With Humbolt, however, it is more than inconvenient. The man worked closely with my father and I have long suspected he might have some information that could help me. However, I have been unsuccessful in winning his confidence."

She slapped her fists on her lap in frustration. "It is so very wrong that no one sees this Sanderson for what he is. It must drive you to madness."

He seemed to find something amusing, for he was looking at her with a soft fondness in his eye and a half smile. "If you have the misfortune of meeting the man, you will understand. Sanderson appears the last person one would suspect of anything ill conceived. Hell, I would like him myself if I didn't know what lies behind that hapless smile."

"If only Mr. Humbolt could be persuaded to listen to you!"

Again he smiled that strange smile and she felt herself flush under the warm regard. "You are taking this quite personally, but I appreciate your sympathy. However, I am not certain if anything will come of it in any event. The man might simply not have anything of value. I am not looking for anything specific. I was hoping for something in my father's business affairs that would seem unusual—transfers of money or something my father might have mentioned to Humbolt."

"Wait. I have an excellent suggestion! Why not lie in wait for him when he rides in the morning, and have men kidnap him and bring him to a shack—"

She broke off with a shriek because Morgan had taken the oar and used it to send up a splash at her.

"You beast!" she cried, shaking off her hands.

He looked smug and sublime. "You will dry. What, with you sunning yourself like a cat, I would think you'd like the cooling off. And your father can well afford a new dress, what with being rich and all that."

He was teasing. "I wasn't born to privilege, I'll have you know. When I was younger, we were in a different sort of circumstances. I was a country girl. I had chores. I milked *cows*."

He pretended to be aghast. "No."

"Oh, yes."

"And these chores. You performed them faithfully every day without ever being reminded."

"Oh, bosh, Morgan. I was incorrigible, remember?"

"Indeed, I am reminded of it often. So tell me some of the incorrigible things you did."

She didn't know what made her, but she complied, regaling him with stories from her "misspent youth," as he began to teasingly refer to it.

She told him of the day she got into her mother's rice powder and frightened her sisters into thinking she was a ghoul. He rolled his eyes when she confessed to charging a tuppence to her friends for a peek on the mating habits of her father's Manchester terriers. He howled until tears glistened on his luxuriant lashes while she related the catastrophe that occurred with the nursery paste and how her governess didn't speak to her for a week as a result.

He pronounced her a hoyden in such a way that it sounded like an endearment.

She sighed and shrugged. "I suppose that was exactly what I was."

"You still are." At her arch look, he sent one back her way and prompted, "The soufflé?"

"Oh. Yes. I should not have done that. I should have talked to him first. I wish I wasn't so impulsive. It is possible I misunderstood, but now . . ."

"Leah, Carl Enders is an abominable toad." Morgan's tone was sharp and final. "I made it my business to find out about him. You were lucky to have escaped marriage. I don't know what you were doing with him in the first place."

"You looked into him? When?"

"Never mind."

"Tell me what you learned."

"You mustn't spread gossip," he admonished, but she sensed she could persuade him.

"What, was he an ideal gentleman, wasn't he? He gave money to orphans and widows and I am an awful person for treating him so badly. No doubt the ton will never forgive me—"

"If you must know, when my man caught up with him, he was in an opium den with a pair of whores. Ugly ones at that."

Leah made a horrified face and covered her mouth.

Morgan regarded her with a more intense interest. "Why would you wish to marry someone like that, Leah? Enders is the worst sort."

She was still reeling from the revelation about Enders's disgusting activities. "I didn't know him very well. Mother knew his aunt. Mother . . ." She blinked and grimaced, touching on some tender memories. "Mother was getting very short with me when I received all those marriage proposals and I kept saying no. Father agreed with me and said I must wait until I met someone I believed would suit, but he wasn't there very often and there was no one who would suit. Mother grew more and more impatient and kept asking, 'What is wrong with this one' and 'What are you waiting for?' and then Carl arrived from America and he was very rich and an adventurer and Mother liked him and he was of a fine family even if he wasn't titled himself—"

"Take a breath."

She did, then let it out in degrees. She waited a moment,

then spoke more thoughtfully. "I just grew afraid, I suppose. I really didn't know what I wanted. I began to think that maybe I never would. I thought that since I usually make such a botch of things, perhaps I should listen to Mother. She wanted so desperately for me to marry, and Carl seemed perfect. She thought he was, in any event."

Morgan did something that shocked her. He leaned forward and took her face in his hands. "You must never do that again."

She had no idea what he was talking about, but it didn't matter because his eyes were reflecting the sparkling light off the water and they were soft gray-green. His mouth was soft, too. The hard lines of tension were gone, replaced by the ones of concern creasing his forehead.

"Do not ever doubt your own judgment," he said.

"But you said I don't have sense."

"But you have a good brain when you remember to use it. Most of all, though, you've got heart. Don't give it away so cheaply."

But her heart was already gone, and for the price of a single kiss. She closed her eyes, blocking out his face, afraid to look up at him because she had no skill at subterfuge. She was an open book and there was no way she could hide the emotion brimming in her breast.

"Thank you, Morgan," she murmured and sat back, slipping out of his grasp. Clearing her throat, she said, "And what of you, then? You admitted you were also incorrigible. I've told you all my confessions. What of yours?"

For the first time since she'd known him, he looked self-conscious.

"Well, I was more of an adventurer. Not any real imagination, at least nothing compared to you. Typical boy stuff, really. Camping in the woods, running off to the fair with friends, fishing and shooting, things like that."

"It sounds marvelous. I envy you your freedom."

He nodded, seeming a bit lost in thought. They were quiet for a space, companionably watching the shadows grow long. After a while, he said they should go. Leah sat quietly

as Morgan took up the oars again and sent the little boat gliding over the silent lake.

BACK IN HIS room, as Morgan awaited his valet, his mind
was occupied with the strange mood left from this afternoon in Leah's company.

They were much later in getting back than they should
have been. The ladies had retired upstairs for their rest and
the lengthy toilettes to prepare them for dinner. The house
was quiet other than the deep bass voices of the men milling
about between the billiards room and the library. The sound
drifted onto the lawns, through the French doors that were
opened to the breezeless dusk.

He'd sneaked her around the back and up the servants'
stairs. Creeping like footpads across the plush carpets, Leah
hadn't been able to suppress her giggles. As if it were some
delightful adventure. He'd wanted to scold her for her silli-
ness. But he'd wanted to laugh, too. He wished he could. He
wished he were able to lose himself in the fun of it all as she
had.

He'd taken her to her room, all the way to the door although it was very unwise to do so. They might easily be discovered. It had been quiet, however. No one had come along.

Why had he taken such a stupid chance, though? Was it so
difficult to leave her?

She'd paused with her hand on the knob and their gazes
had held. His awareness of her, always acute, had shot to a
frightening pitch. Every nerve screamed for him to reach out
and touch her, pull her close, take the invitation held in her
obsidian eyes.

To his credit, he'd resisted and left her quickly, coming up
to his chamber and ringing for Andrew. As he waited, he
played the afternoon over and over in his mind.

He should be thinking about Humbolt—finding a way to
approach the old fool and convince him to cooperate with
Morgan's investigation. His talking to Leah about the man of

affairs had gotten his mind working on how vital a source he could be if he could be brought round.

He was suddenly struck with the memory of Leah pounding her fist in frustration over the whole matter, and he smiled. Then another image followed, this one more vivid, of Leah sunning herself on the boat, loose-limbed, reclined, smiling into the sky.

Today she'd been happy. He might have made her that way. He thought so. And he'd felt happy, too, for a space. Even talking about everything, the past, his plans, all of it— it hadn't spoiled that soft, easy mood they had struck up between them.

Andrew came in, his face pale. Closing the door behind him with a soft click of the lock, he said, "Mr. and Mrs. Randall Sanderson are here, my lord. They arrived this afternoon."

LEAH WALKED AS quickly as she dared through the hallways of Farthingham Manor. She was very late. Mother had left the message with her maid, Debra, to meet her in the music room three-quarters of an hour ago.

She slipped into the music room—thank goodness the door was in the back—and sank into a chair. The other guests were smothering yawns as Lady Edna warbled an unrecognizable tune and sawed at her viola. Mother was seated up at the front, her back ramrod straight, her eyes glazed over so that if one didn't look too closely they would think her attentive. This was fortunate. Leah could say she'd slipped in right after the concert had begun and her mother wouldn't know differently.

The door behind her opened and a woman came in. She made no effort to be surreptitious as Leah had just done. Without arrogance, she looked about, smiling and nodding as she recognized certain people who half turned in their seats, probably grateful for the diversion. She held herself with an understated dignity, as dainty as a Dresden figure, as lovely as a Titian portrait.

Lady Edna stopped her song in mid-note and held out her arms. "My dear!" she exclaimed. She swung to her audience. "Please forgive me, but I have been beside myself with worry. I promise to return if I could take but a moment to—"

She didn't get to finish her sentence as the audience leaped to their feet with profuse assurances that it was indeed perfectly all right with them for her to take a bit of a break.

Lady Edna embraced the new arrival. "Glorianna, my dear, I have nearly despaired of your arriving at all."

Leah stopped breathing.

The woman answered in a voice as tempered as an angel's, "Our carriage threw a rod down in Garston Grange."

"How dreadful!" Edna cried.

Leah stood as her mind clicked into a furious whirl.

This was Morgan's precious Glorianna, whom he sought with unflinching determination. The woman with whom he was, one might say, obsessed. The woman for whom he had arranged all of this, this charade, this pretense of romance that she kept forgetting was farce.

And now she understood why Morgan felt so strongly about her. Glorianna Gage Sanderson, the former countess of Waring, was an incredibly beautiful woman.

She got to her feet and moved numbly through the room to the door. Her mother appeared by her side.

"We are all going into the salon," she said, taking her daughter's hand.

The exodus from the music room was nearly feverish. Everyone was desperate to make themselves scarce in case Lady Edna made good on her promise to return and complete her recital.

Somehow, Leah found herself in the gilt and mirror salon, surrounded by a garrulous crowd. The sound of laughter seemed tinny and far away. People spoke to her. She made responses vacantly.

Hadn't she feared all along that Morgan loved his dead father's wife? How could it be possible that a man would *not* love her? She was perfect. She was breathtaking. She was, after all, the admitted reason why Morgan was here.

A servant passed just then with a tray filled with champagne. She grabbed one and sipped it, her eyes peering over the rim to look for her mother. Otherwise occupied, Desdemona didn't notice.

Just to steady her frayed nerves, Leah told herself, and sipped again. It tasted good. Sweet and tangy, the fizz played delightedly on her tongue. She gave up sipping and drank fully.

It tasted good. She could already feel her limbs getting lighter. No, heavier. Something. Warm. That was it. Calmer.

She strolled to a corner of the room, positioning herself so she had a direct line of sight to Glorianna, and stared hard, memorizing the woman, feature by feature. She brought her glass to her lips as she did so, and discovered it empty.

How had that happened? Perhaps she'd spilled it. She'd get another.

"Miss Brodie?" a male voice said.

"Hmm?" She looked up to see a friend she knew from London, a handsome son of the earl of Guest-Havicum. He bowed low and she waved her new glass at him, splashing some champagne in his direction.

"May I present Mr. Sanderson. He spied you a moment ago and wished to make your acquaintance."

"Forgive me," another man spoke. Leah jerked her head in his direction, then had to pause to clear the strange blurring in her head. "I simply had to meet you, Miss Brodie. I have heard so many things about you."

She began to feel a tinge of alarm at her muddleheadedness. Vaguely aware that she should know the name, she held out her hand.

Mr. Sanderson took it in his and bowed low over it. For a moment she thought he might kiss the back of it, as in the French manner. The thought was instinctively repellant, although she didn't know why. Mr. Sanderson was a pleasant-looking fellow, with light hair and a slight build. Moderately handsome in that bland way some men had, men who held no interest for her; there was certainly nothing objectionable about him.

She tried to pull her hand away, but he didn't release it.

"You are lovely, Miss Brodie, if you will forgive my impertinence in saying so. Isn't she, Charles? Absolutely lovely."

"Miss Brodie is well-known for her sparkle," Charles replied with a smile at Leah.

This Sanderson fellow still hadn't released her hand.

Sanderson . . . Who the devil was he? Someone important, she thought.

He was speaking again, in that silky tone that made her want to put as much distance between them as possible. "You and I share a friend. A very special friend. Actually, he is really my cousin, but we've always been so close, I think of him as my friend as well. When I had heard of his spending so much time with you, I wanted to get to know you better as we have much in common."

Oh, my God! Randall Sanderson.

"I am afraid you have me at the disadvantage, sir." Her voice sounded smooth, thank goodness. No sign of her disconcert. "To whom do you refer?"

"Why, the estimable earl of Waring, of course. I do understand he's been very attentive to you of late, and I can see why. Honestly, Charles, I cannot remember when I've met a more engaging young lady."

And then he released her. Relief went though her and she wondered at her reaction. He hadn't hurt her but she still felt immensely grateful to be free of him. She snatched her hands close, rubbing her wrists where he'd held her as if his grip had chafed. Charles looked at her oddly.

She prayed that for once in her life, her emotions were not obvious.

"He mentioned you." She kept her voice even. "How pleased he will be to see you. Now if you will excuse me."

She made to leave, but Sanderson stepped neatly into her path. "If I might take just a moment further of your time. I simply must tell you how it gratifies me to see the good you've done. You see, my dear Miss Brodie, my wife and I are so very fond of the earl, even in light of . . . well, some problems in the past. She loved his father a great deal. It has distressed her that she and his son have not been able to share their grief."

He didn't appear to move in any noticeable way, and yet, Randall Sanderson seemed to be drawing closer with every word. Crowding her. It took every morsel of courage Leah possessed not to shrink away. Morgan wouldn't be very pleased with her if she acted the coward, she thought. It was an inane thought, for what did Morgan's pride in her matter, but it kept her back up and her eyes locked onto his direct stare.

"Morgan is a very complicated man, but a good one," Sanderson went on. "He's done so many strange, unexplainable things . . . but always with the best of motives. I am constantly assuring everyone of that fact. Ah, but I'm certain you know all about his finer qualities. Ah, my dear, you are a godsend for overlooking certain complications that remain unresolved."

He smiled and she felt a chill.

He wants me to feel frightened.

The thought was clear and sobering, putting steel instantly in her spine and clearing her head at last.

Leah silently blessed her mother for instilling the belief that every lady of quality should be adept in the art of obtuseness. It was a very effective tool in shutting the mouth of the most obnoxious person and diverting a tense situation.

She forced a smile, one of her most dazzling. "How kind of you! That is simply a lovely thing to say." Although she was instinctively loath to touch the man, she laid a hand upon his arm. "You are just so sweet, sir. I cannot wait to tell Morgan all about your good wishes for us. I know it will mean so much to him."

He looked at her uncertainly, not knowing if she were truly vapid to have misunderstood him, or playing him for a fool.

It didn't matter what he thought. All that mattered was that she extricate herself from him as soon as possible. She was still feeling raw, and she was afraid of this man. "It was wonderful to meet you, Mr. Sanderson. I look forward to seeing you again soon."

Sweeping past him, her heart pounded furiously as she wondered if he would attempt to detain her again. He didn't.

She began to breathe easier once away from him, wondering if the champagne going to her head had made the meeting more sinister than it was. After all, Charles had stood by the entire time and seemed not to notice anything wrong about the man.

Still, she felt a lingering unease as she threaded her way through the crowded room. A friend waved her over to join her, but Leah suddenly knew she wanted to be alone. She headed for the stairs. She was just starting up them when she realized she still held a nearly full glass of champagne.

She paused. She had only just overcome the effects from the first glass. Oh, bother—there could be no harm in one more. Besides, her heart still throbbed whenever she recalled the exquisite face of Morgan's Glorianna.

She swallowed it, savoring the warm, gliding comfort.

Deciding she couldn't face the confines of her bedroom, she looked about. The gardens were right through that door over there. She might make use of the night air to clear her head of the cloying thoughts and worries.

On the way out, a servant came out of the kitchen with a newly stocked tray of flutes asparkle with fresh champagne. Without a thought to his raised eyebrows, she took one in each hand and headed out of doors.

Chapter 9

MORGAN FIGURED THAT Sanderson was already aware of his presence. He would be waiting for Morgan to make the first move, braced for battle and probably calculating a counterattack.

Angry at himself for being caught unawares—spending the day in lazy idyll was the height of foolishness—he was concerned about Leah. Would she be afraid when she heard? How *would* she react if she were confronted with either Glorianna or Sanderson? If caught unawares she might be frightened. He could imagine anything from her squealing in horror to her brazening up to one of them and declaring some preposterous challenge on his behalf.

They were amusing, if slightly masochistic, imaginings, but he knew he wasn't being fair. Leah had a quick mind, not to mention a social adeptness that he envied. More than likely she could and would handle any confrontation like an old salt facing a squall.

Still, he decided to find her to give her warning.

As he moved through the house looking for her, he spied Sanderson immediately with some men out on the terrace. He felt nothing at seeing his nemesis. That struck him as odd.

Whenever he thought of the man, he always had felt a cold hardening in his chest. It was a clean, painful feeling he'd become accustomed to. Now, it was with a strange sense of calm detachment that he assessed the man's likeable veneer. It was his most dangerous quality. He had always been popular, but now he had parlayed his ability to please without seeming fatuous into a prominent spot among the beau monde.

He moved away, feeling suddenly better. Sanderson had reached mythical proportion of evil over the years when he and Morgan had been young and Morgan was unable to do anything about him. Now he saw he was just a man, a rather ordinary-looking one, whose exterior sheltered a corrupt soul. He wasn't untouchable. He was human and he was within reach.

Morgan could put a ball through his heart easily anytime he wished. But he would do it in his time, without censure and completely within permissible bounds. He moved on, continuing to search for Leah. He found Glorianna, instead.

Unlike his reaction to Randall, the feeling upon seeing her was swift and severe and took him completely by surprise.

Morgan froze in his place. She was sitting with a group of women, listening attentively with that serene expression on her face he recalled so well. Often in the past she had sat thusly in their drawing room at Blackheath while he and his father discussed some topic, a half smile on her mouth and her eyes shining. She had looked at Evan with such love, it had warmed the coldest January night.

She looked exactly the same, as if those years and a single, horrible tragedy had never occurred.

He backed out of the room, battling the confusion of his thoughts. He had missed her, and if he had been able to ignore the pain of the loss of her in his life before, it hit him all the harder now. He was reminded of his duty to her. He should have been here to protect her, not off courting forgetfulness in European drawing rooms. His father would have been gravely disappointed that he'd failed Glorianna. He had neglected his own.

He wanted Leah. He had to *see* her, needed to see her. Not wishing to examine the reason, he tamped down the roiling grief and prowled the rooms of the Farthingham mansion. She was not among the group playing whist. He poked his head into the parlor where her friends were gathered to find that she wasn't there, either.

He grabbed a passing footman. "Have you seen Miss Brodie?"

The servant shook his head. "No, my lord. Would you like me to send word to her room?"

"Yes, thank you."

He waited in the hall, feeling as jumpy as a cat. With Glorianna and Sanderson in the house, the place seemed charged, full of energy. He felt it in every nerve.

The servant returned. "I'm sorry, my lord. Miss Brodie was not in her room."

"Miss Brodie, you say?" another servant said as she passed, her arms full of stacked fresh linen napkins. "I saw her go into the gardens a while ago. She might still be there, my lord."

Morgan thanked her and headed outdoors.

He found her easily enough, sitting by herself on a bench near some hedges, out of sight of the house. Her wilted posture and somewhat rumpled appearance sparked a flare of alarm and Morgan quickened his step. His foot hit something and he looked down. An empty champagne flute rolled across the flagstone walk noisily.

"Leah?"

Her head snapped up. She gave a sort of "harumph" sound and tossed back the few drops left in a second glass, then squinted disapprovingly into it.

Morgan was incredulous. "What the bloody hell are you doing?"

She laughed, making it a rude sound. Flinging out her arms, she said, "I'm sitting in the garden. What the bloody hell are *you* doing?"

"My God. You're drunk!" he exclaimed.

"No, I am not. I'm merely glowing. Mother says that

women get a glow." With a flourish, she spread her arms again, almost throwing herself off balance to tumble into the bushes behind her. "I really like glowing. I think I'm a regular glowworm, you know, those things that turn into fireflies. Glowworms!" Then she dissolved in a fit of giggles. She lifted her skirts and pulled out an uncorked bottle of champagne from between her feet. Clanging it against the flute, she splashed a fair amount of the stuff into her glass.

"Give me that." He reached for the bottle.

She snatched it out of reach. "Get your own. There's plenty in the kitchen."

"What . . . what the *hell* are you doing?"

She unwrapped one finger from its grip on the bottle and pointed it at him. "I already answered that. You're trying to trick me, aren't you?"

"Leah, for God's sake, tell me what has happened. I know you well enough to realize you aren't out here throwing down Farthingham's finest French champagne on a whim. Talk to me."

"No!" she declared haughtily, then her mood changed abruptly. Her face crumpled and she chewed the inside of her cheek. "You were her lover, weren't you? I should have known. I am such a dolt, I—Morgan!" She cried out in protest when he darted in an unanticipated move and snatched the bottle from her.

It was only half empty, he was relieved to find out. He poured the rest out onto the ground.

She swiped at him. He evaded her easily. "What are you doing, you worthless . . . bloodsucking cur!"

"Too bad." He was smug as he dropped the emptied bottle onto the ground.

"How dare you, you . . . bounder!"

"I've already heard your amazing repertoire of epithets. They do not impress me, nor do I find them insulting. Amusing, yes."

"Amusing? You find me amusing! Oooh!" Throwing her head back, she announced, "I am not going to talk to you any longer. You are nothing but a . . . a worthless piece of sheep guts and I want nothing more to do with you. Not that you care, I realize. You don't need me now, anyway." She waved her hands in the air making dramatic motions. "And if you find you *do* need someone to help you, I'm sure Dahlia won't mind lending a hand. Or Sophie." Her shoulders sagged. She added miserably, "Or Phyllida."

He looked at her incredulously. "Did you just call me sheep guts?"

"Never mind." She waved him away. "I've just cast you off. Aren't you going to say something? Now let go of me."

"What the devil kind of thing is sheep guts to call someone? It doesn't even make any sense. I am not holding on to you, by the way."

"Well, good!" she shouted. "I wouldn't want you to get hurt because I mean to leave and you are not going to stop me."

He snatched her by her shoulders. "*Now* I am holding you. And I'm not letting go until I get an explanation for this foolishness."

She pouted for a moment, refusing to meet his eye. She was like a rag doll in his arms. At last she said, "She's very beautiful."

"Who?"

"Glorianna, you idiot! Your precious Glorianna. You're in love with her."

He gave her a shake. "Don't be ridiculous. She's my father's wife." He stopped. "I mean she was my father's wife." He jerked his head, indicating the empty bottle. "Is that why you got yourself potted? Are you jealous of Glorianna?"

"I can't believe what an idiot I am, that's what's the matter! I was so stupid!" He let her go and she went back to her bench and sat down with an inglorious plop.

He walked slowly, carefully, to sit beside her. "You are not an idiot. You may *act* in ways that are decidedly strange and incomprehensible to rational people but you are quite bright when you are not being foolish."

"You *abducted* me, for God's sake, and what do *I* do when you imperiously demand for me to invite you to be my suitor? Why, I invite you to be my suitor, that's what. Now tell me if I'm right in the head! And you say, 'Just pretend to be falling in love with me,' and what do I do? I agree! Without a care for anything but this bloody thrill that I feel whenever I'm with you. If I'm not an idiot, then what am I? Tell me!"

"Is that what has you so upset?"

"I don't understand myself anymore, Morgan."

He gentled his voice, intending to humor her. "You are as you have always been, Blackie. As courageous as a warrior, as generous and caring a person as I ever knew. You have a tender heart and so you were moved to help me. You didn't turn me away because you could no sooner do that than kick a wounded dog."

She looked at him, her eyes limpid for a moment. Then her brows furrowed and she let out a loud "Hah!" and stood. He jumped up. She jabbed her finger into his chest and announced simply, "I don't even like you half the time."

His brows jutted upward. "Really?"

"Yes. I think you are pompous. That's right. I also happen to think you have no sense of humor. Except sometimes you do and then you act like it's a high crime to let it show. I find that very unpleasant. *Very* unpleasant, Morgan. In fact, I find you unpleasant most of the time. Only . . ." She paused. She seemed suddenly sad, her shoulders wilting. "Oh, sometimes . . . sometimes you are most pleasant. When you are, I like it. You see? That is exactly the problem. Because *you* don't like it when you are nice to me, and then you are unpleasant again. I wish I could just let you see how . . . *unpleasant* I find you."

"You are doing a wonderful job right now."

She looked up at him hopefully. "Really?"

His voice was gentle. "Why, it's a veritable dressing-down. I am quite vexed."

"You don't mean that. You are only saying so to make me feel better."

"You've driven me to distraction. Frustrated me beyond words."

She seemed somewhat appeased. "I have?" Those soul-stealing eyes made him smile. She seemed so bloodthirstily hopeful.

"On more than one occasion," he vowed, his gaze lowering to her softly parted lips.

"That is very gratifying to hear. Morgan?"

"Yes?"

"Are you going to kiss me?"

He hesitated. "You've drunk too much. You wouldn't want me to take advantage of that, would you?"

"Oh, yes," she breathed, her eyelids drifting closed as the corners of her mouth turned up into a dreamy smile.

"Leah," he said, meaning it to sound like a warning. Instead, it came forth as a groan of longing. She answered with a soft sound of pleasure and wound her arms around his neck. Her teeth sank into her bottom lip, her eyes were closed and glistening as if tears were caught unshed in her thick lashes.

He wanted to kiss her so badly he was trembling. If he were a worm, he would. He would crush that mouth under his without mercy.

The prodding of desire warred with his self-control, feverishly urging him on. She was willing. She was everything he wanted.

He pushed her away. "Leah."

"I know. This is very wrong." She sounded groggy. He felt groggy, as well. Intoxicated as much as she was at the moment. "I think it is wrong for us to kiss, too. Morgan, is it wrong?"

"Yes."

"I know. Um. Morgan, why is it wrong?"

"We are in a garden. Anyone could come along. And second, you've been drinking too much. No gentleman, no matter how beautiful the lady, should take advantage of such an occurrence."

Her face lit up. "Do you think I am beautiful?"

He cupped her face in his hands and said, "Yes. I think you are very beautiful. I think you are the most beautiful creature I've ever seen." Then he stopped himself because it would be unwise to continue.

He dropped his hands and looked away. "I will take you to your room."

"Yes, of course." He helped her to her feet. "Good idea. But, Morgan?"

"Yes, you little fool, what is it?"

"I love you."

He couldn't answer her for a moment. He couldn't think of a thing to say.

There was the kind of silence that allowed for the faraway chirp of birdsong or the slap of the topmost leaves of the trees being blown together and remained huge and endless.

Finally, all he could manage was, "Oh, Christ."

"Do you hate me now? You do. You hate me!"

He steered her toward the back of the house. "No. I don't hate you. I could never hate you. Come on, now. I've got to get you inside."

"But I want—"

"Now." He was sharper than he intended. "We don't want you to be seen. If you were, this could turn into a disaster worse than the Enders thing."

"Do you want to know something? I like it when you call me Blackie." She erupted in a giggle that ended in a hiccup. "Do you want to know something else? When you kidnapped me, it was the most exciting thing that ever happened to me. I thought you were going to take the bliss. Do you want to know something else?"

"No."

"I wanted you to."

He gritted his teeth. "Don't say that."

"I know. That was bad." She worried her lip, an action he found exceedingly tantalizing. "I won't say it anymore, Morgan, I promise."

"In the kitchen door, there you go. Head on back to the servant's stairs, see, here they are. No, don't sit down." He called over his shoulder to the round-eyed cook standing behind the scrubbed oak table. "May I have a pot of coffee sent to Miss Brodie's room, please?"

"Yes, my lord."

Leah continued, "I often say things I shouldn't. I wish I didn't. It's terribly embarrassing. You won't remember what I said about the bliss, will you?"

"It's already forgotten. Watch your step. Here we are. I believe this is where your room is. Down this corridor, isn't it?"

"Morgan?"

"What?"

"I'm sorry I called you sheep's guts."

"It's already forgotten, Blackie."

"All right."

He didn't want her mother to find her in this condition, so she summoned her maid, whom Leah had told him she could trust. Her name was Debra, a solid, practical woman about his age with an attractive face and neat figure and a no-nonsense manner. He explained that her mistress had over-imbibed and he stressed the indiscretion be kept quiet, especially that Desdemona should not be told.

Debra said, "I think madam best not be troubled by such a trivial incident. She has far too much to worry over as it is," and they were both aware that she was agreeing to keep Leah's secret.

Morgan relaxed. "Then please take down a recipe for a tonic I will give you. It is an emetic, so although it will be unpleasant for her, it will cleanse her of the poisons she's already consumed."

"She'll not thank you for that, I'll wager," Debra said with a grin.

"No doubt, but it will get the alcohol out of her body more quickly." Morgan dictated the directions. "Plenty of water, then, after she's been purged."

"I grew up with five brothers, and all of them were fond of their gin," Debra assured him. "I know a few tricks of my own."

"I'll tell our hosts that she's suffering from the migrim. You should tell her mother the same thing if she comes to check on her. The symptoms will be similar. Just do *not* allow anyone to give her laudanum. They might try if they think it's the migrim."

"I understand."

"And get her to eat something once she's feeling better. She won't want to, but it will settle her stomach."

"My lord," she laughed, "I pray you not to worry. I will take excellent care of her. I promise." Her eyes were clever, and for some reason, the knowing look she gave him left him disturbed.

Morgan gazed down at the prone form on the bed. "She's going to feel wretched when she awakes."

"I'll see to her, my lord. I'll do everything just as you instructed. Now, you best leave me to it, so that I may get started. The sooner the better, I think."

Shaking his head, Morgan gave Leah one last glance. He sighed. "Silly twit," he muttered, and left.

THE TIME TO confront Randall came after dinner. When the men retired for their "smoke and politics," as his mother used to call it, Morgan entered the library, fetched a snifter of brandy, and accepted a cigar. Positioning himself by the window, a bit away from the others, he waited.

He had exchanged brief greetings with Randall earlier. After Morgan had gotten done with Leah, he had returned to the rest of the guests and approached him. He had made it a point to greet Randall with an air of the casual pleasantry expected from cousins who hadn't seen each other in a while.

Morgan had taken care, however, to not allow a single private word to pass, keeping the conversation light and dissipated among a few others who were gathered around them. He left after only a short interval, saying to Randall in parting, "We should make time to speak alone soon. We have some things to catch up on."

There was nothing sinister in those words, nothing anyone

standing close would perceive, but Morgan trusted Randall would hear perfectly well the understated challenge. It suited him to make Randall wait, knowing how poorly the man tolerated frustration. He had made himself scarce for the rest of the day.

He had no doubt, as he stood alone, peering out onto the torchlit gardens, sipping brandy, that Randall would seek him at the first opportunity.

A dark satisfaction curled the corners of his lip slightly as he heard the familiar voice declare, "There you are, Waring! I am deuced, I've been anxious to see you. I am absolutely dying to hear of your travels. We have missed you at Blackheath. Glorianna will be sorry she hasn't seen you today, I know she was looking forward to it more than a child looks forward to birthday presents."

Randall laughed, looking as innocuous as a pup. Morgan was well acquainted with how Randall operated. There was always a duality of meaning in every gesture. On the surface, for the benefit of those who watched all appeared pleasant. Yet a double entendre was couched in every phrase.

Their gazes locked. Morgan kept his features impassive, something he knew agitated his opponent. "Well," Morgan drawled lightly, "I am here."

Morgan took a step away from any prying ears and Randall followed. They kept their tones even, but each man's manner took a distinct turn.

Randall said, "The year since I saw you last hasn't been kind, Morgan. You have a hardness about you. I remember you so differently."

"I am different," Morgan replied. He fingered the cigar. "No one could go through what I did and remain unchanged. One might say quite accurately that I am a different man. And you, too, have experienced changes. Allow me to congratulate you on your marriage."

"I am glad you are pleased." Randall gloated unattractively. "Glorianna was worried it would upset you."

"I care only for her well-being," Morgan said meaningfully. "In fact, I am devoted to it."

"I try to do my best to please her. It has been difficult for her this past year, and I was there, by her side, day after day. I don't think she's completely recovered from the loss, you see. She needed someone to help her."

The tacit referral to Evan's death didn't have the effect Randall could have hoped for. Morgan shrugged and said, "I am sure you made yourself invaluable to her. You have the unerring instincts of a true parasite. Still, it must have been daunting, trying to live up to my father. I would have thought it was beyond you, but then, you always surprised me."

"My wife has made no complaint," Randall said tightly.

"Ah, but Glorianna never complains. That is one of her charms."

Morgan's gaze swept the room, ensuring they were not being observed. "Tell me, Randall, did you even tell her I'd written and called? It might come as a shock to her when I divulge that I've been trying to get in touch with her for months."

"She will understand my reasons. For her own sake, I kept you from her." He sneered. It was one of his least attractive gestures. "I will tell her I merely wished to protect her from your disturbed ranting. Everyone knows you were delusional after they let you out of that horrible prison. You were making wild, irrational accusations, and you know I cannot allow Glorianna to be subject to that."

The tone he used was soft and wheedling as if he were giving a sample of how he would persuade Glorianna that he only had her best interests at heart.

"Perhaps she will be touched. Or, she might begin to question your solicitude, especially when I can prove it is not ranting after all. Let us not forget the tidy packet of information entrusted to my solicitors. If not for that blessing, I might not be standing here today."

"What? That collection of lies?" There were tiny droplets of sweat forming high on Randall's forehead and across his upper lip. "No one would believe any of it."

"That pack of lies, as you say, kept me alive. Without it, I daresay I might have fallen into the path of a carriage on the streets of Paris, or perhaps met a bloodthirsty footpad in Rome. No doubt the documents I set aside as insurance against my life are the reason I am standing in front of you today. And you and I both know it doesn't hold so much as a half-truth."

"No court will hear your accusations," Randall sneered. "You have already tried that, and humiliated yourself in the process."

"Well, how could I have known how deep your pockets, or how widely you spread your bribes? You'd paid off every magistrate and constable in the shire by the time I put my case together. And let me not begrudge you your other plots. You have indeed been most clever in tainting my reputation. I am as good as convicted in most people's eyes, on 'evidence' that had to have taxed even your creative mind. And yet . . . and yet, Randall, I stand here today, in the bosom of the polite world. I am no longer scorned. You didn't do a very thorough job."

Sanderson seethed at the taunt. "Hiding behind the skirts of a debutante—I would have thought that was beneath you, Morgan. You used to have more pride than that."

"I used to have a lot of things. Pride is one of the few I have left. And I promise you, it will be a proud moment indeed when I stand over your corpse. Remember this and remember it well. *Nothing* is beneath me anymore. I will do whatever, use whomever, sink to untold depths to bring you to the justice you deserve."

He watched his nemesis, a man he'd squared off against countless times. The throbbing at his temple betrayed Randall's tension. "What the devil do you want?"

"I merely wish to see Glorianna. She is my family, like a sister, and I like a brother to her. I will see to my own. Not you or anyone else shall interfere with that which I cherish so well."

"That ridiculous saying of Uncle Evan's—*see to your own.* Well, she isn't yours anymore, Morgan. She is my wife now." Randall's face was almost purple. "You keep away from her. Or I will make you sorry. I am very good at making people sorry, Morgan. Surely you know that firsthand."

"What else can you take from me?" Morgan shot back. "You have done your worst."

"Have I? Did I mention that I had the pleasure of meeting Miss Brodie today? I must say she is incredibly lovely. In fact, I kept telling Guest-Havicum that very thing, and it occurred to me that such a lovely creature as that is so incredibly fragile. The world can be harsh and sometimes very unfair to the innocent. Don't you agree?"

Morgan felt his blood turn to ice, and yet his flesh seemed to blister with a terrible heat. The calmness in his voice was hard-won. "It would be a foolhardy mistake to involve Miss Brodie in what rightly lies between you and me. I can destroy you, Randall. If you know me at all, you know I would do it to protect anyone else from you, Miss Brodie *and* Glorianna most."

"You can't hurt me, Morgan. If you could, you would have done it already."

Moran gave him a brittle smile. "And you are not so certain of that fact as you pretend, or *you* would have destroyed *me*."

Lord Tedicum March, who was obnoxiously drunk, chose that moment to intrude on the pair.

"What's you two talkin' bout?" he roared, red-faced and sweating in the summer heat.

"Nothing. At least nothing of any great significance," Morgan said smoothly. "I shall let you have him, March. I trust you will find Mr. Sanderson as amusing as I have. Good night, gentlemen."

"My lord," Sanderson said, ever correct, ever composed when being observed.

"Well," Morgan heard March harumph behind him as he exited the room. "Doesn't like the drink, eh? Well, Sollopson, we'll take care of his share."

Morgan came out of the study like a man surfacing from under leagues of water, pausing under the great chandelier in the hallway to take in deep lungfuls of air. He felt sullied. He also felt shaken.

The bastard had met Leah, spoken to her. Somehow, that burned a fresh wound. He'd not wanted Leah touched by any of this filthy business. What had she thought—had she been frightened? Why hadn't she told him?

Promising himself that Randall would pay for threatening Leah, Morgan tried to stave off the desire to go upstairs to see her. He only wanted to reassure himself that she rested comfortably and was not troubled. In the state in which he'd found her earlier, she could have been terrified over Randall and been too incoherent to tell him.

His willpower held out until just around sunrise.

Chapter 10

LEAH'S ROOM WAS dark. Only the watery light filtering through the pale curtains from the waxing moon served as any sort of illumination, but it was enough to keep Morgan from banging his shin against the furniture as he stepped inside and shut the door.

The sound of her breathing was soft. He almost didn't hear it at first. Pausing, he strained his hearing. But a half heartbeat later, he was reassured. As soundlessly as he could manage he crept closer to her bedside.

He could make out her form and he smiled into the darkness. No serene repose for Leah, of course. She lay curled around the coverlet, her legs gleaming whitely in the moonlight coming in through the window and her arms thrown wide over her head. It was the most erotic pose he had ever seen.

The familiar wanting came over him. As usual, it was bittersweet. Something light and good came into his heart when he looked at her, and yet he could never have her.

Little fool, look at her, he told himself, wrapped in her dreams and knowing nothing of the world. Did she dream of him? Was that why her body lay like that, as if sultry restlessness had left her tangled and unsatisfied?

She thought she loved him. That made it harder. So damn much harder.

He sat gingerly on the edge of the bed. He wanted a moment to think, to figure out what the devil he was going to say to her, but she stirred. Blinking her eyes, she seemed to disbelieve them, then sat bolt upright. "Morgan?"

"Relax." He put his hand out to ease her back, then thought better of touching her. "I only wanted to make certain you were all right. How are you feeling?"

"Wretched." She clutched the coverlet to her, but not before he got an eyeful of her bountiful bosom outlined in silk-trimmed cotton. "I was dreadfully sick."

"And now?"

"Debra made me eat toast even though it was so hard to get it down. My throat was raw. But, I admit I feel somewhat better. My throat is still a little sore from . . . er, it just hurts a bit, but mostly I'm just tired. What time is it?"

"Nearly dawn."

"What are you doing here?"

He paused. "I needed to see you. Make sure you were all right."

"Of course I am all right. I didn't drink *that* much, Morgan."

He pressed his lips together to keep from smiling and said not a word in disagreement. "Leah, why didn't you tell me that Randall spoke to you?"

She scrubbed her eyes with the heels of her hands. "I forgot. Why?"

"It is very important. Please try to remember. I must know if he said anything to threaten you."

"I was a bit muzzy-headed at the time." She ran her hand through her hair. It was loose, gleaming as richly as a silk skein in the meager light. "I don't recall too much. I think he was pleasant, but . . . but in an unpleasant way. Does that make any sense?"

"I believe I know just what you mean. Exactly what did he say? Can you remember anything?"

"Well, he said I was lovely." She gave a rueful smile. "And he spoke of you. But . . . he didn't sound nice even though he was pretending to be concerned about how you were doing. I felt he was trying to intimidate me, but he didn't overtly do anything that would be seen as upsetting. It was more of a feeling I got from him, in the *way* he said what he said." She sat up straighter. "Why are you asking?"

"I spoke with him today. I am not ashamed to tell you that I am worried, Leah. I am very worried for you. He as good as threatened me with harming you if I tried to get close to Glorianna."

"Really? I'm actually flattered." He scowled at her, but she shrugged. She asked, "What are you going to do?"

His eyes slid sideways and his jaw tightened. "I'm not going to leave her alone. And . . . well, we will discuss that in a moment. Until I can think of what to do about you, I need you to take special care. I don't want you to be alone. Stay with your mother, or a group of your friends, at all times. And I don't want you riding anymore in the mornings."

"Morgan, really, I don't think—" Her spine stiffened and her eyes flew wide. "Oh, God!"

He was immediately alarmed. "What is it?"

"Now I remember, he spoke of you, about the rumors. Yes, it's coming back to me . . . I . . ." She stopped. Her hands flew to her cheeks and her eyes rounded in horror.

"Christ, I'll kill him. Tell me now—what did he do?"

"Nothing." Her thumbnail went between her teeth.

He grabbed her. "Tell me, damn it."

"No, it's nothing. It's not Sanderson, I . . ." She tried to turn away, but Morgan jerked her back. "I can't say it. It's too humiliating!"

What the devil? "Tell me, Leah, or I swear I'll shake it out of you."

Hanging her head, she muttered, "It's not Sanderson. It's you. What I said to you."

"To me?" He was confused for a moment, and then all at once, he knew.

She had remembered she'd told him that she loved him. He released her. "Oh. Yes. That."

She collapsed, curling back under the covers. "Bloody hell!"

"Leah, it is all right. I know you didn't mean it," he said gently. "You'd been drinking. People say things—"

"You arrogant bounder, it's true!"

He was stunned. She turned to face him. "It's true, and you know it. You've always known it, haven't you?"

He realized that he had. He'd simply made up his mind to ignore it, dismiss it just as he'd tried to pass off her blundered confession just now.

"Perhaps an infatuation," he tried hopefully.

"Oh. Does that make you feel better? All right then, we'll call it an infatuation. That changes everything."

"Then what do you suggest we do about it? You know how impossible the situation is."

"No. I really don't, Morgan. All I know is that I feel this way. And you . . . well, I don't know very much about you."

"I told you my favorite luncheon foods," he shot at an attempt at humor, but the look she gave him doused that idea.

She said, "All I know about you is that you wanted to get into society to bedevil Randall Sanderson and get close to . . . close to . . . *her*." Her face crumpled.

"I am not in love with Glorianna. The accusation that I am is singularly repellant. She is as a sister to me. I've told you this repeatedly. Blackie, I can only think of her happy with my father and it feels remotely incestuous to suggest I have any other feeling for her. But it is still a strong bond, and I will not forsake it."

"Well, all right. I was wrong. You cannot blame me, you know. I have had to reach my own conclusions. You never tell me anything and God forbid you explain yourself." She was sullen and defensive, not very attractive traits on anyone, yet with her luminous eyes widened for full effect, she looked so hurt and small and childlike that it pierced him. "I don't know why I have any sort of affection for you at all."

"Yes. You told me last night how you found me . . . what was the word? Oh, yes. Unpleasant." For no reason, he picked up her hand and kissed the back of it. "Poor Blackie. I haven't been very nice to you at all, have I?"

"You don't sound sorry." Now she had grown petulant. It was adorable on her.

"I'm not sorry," he snapped, but even he could hear that his voice held no bite. "It's how it has to be, that's all. Don't look like that, goddamn it, Leah, and don't you dare cry."

"I wouldn't cry over you," she declared in a wavering voice.

"Christ, Blackie . . . Don't you think I'd give anything to—" He cut himself off.

Her head came up. "What?"

"It doesn't matter."

She snatched her hand out of his and he immediately missed its warmth. "Leah," he said, "it doesn't matter because I am in no position to offer you anything. I have something I must do, am bound to do. There was never a future for us, you knew that. It's impossible . . . There's no room for anything else in my life, not now. Maybe not ever."

"Well, I'm not going to wait around for you."

"I wouldn't ask you to."

"Why not?" she flung.

"Because it wouldn't be right."

"Then it is of no consequence to you what I do? If I marry another man, lie in his bed, and let him touch me the way I know you want to?"

The pain slammed into him, knocking his breath from him. She saw the grief on his face before he could stop it. He couldn't meet her eye. And he couldn't speak.

"Because I will," she cried. "I won't die for pining for you or any such nonsense. I am no fool, and I am not your fool, Morgan. Yes, I will marry, and I shall have children. My life will go on. I will go on and I will try like the devil to forget you. Because I won't want to remember."

Emotion dug into him like claws. "Right. That's good." His voice sounded like his mouth was filled with sand.

"But before that . . . I want it to be you, Morgan. I want to know the bliss. I want to know the bliss with you. Then I'll forget. I'll forget you ever existed. Just this once, just once, to last us the rest of our lives. It's what we both want. Isn't it?"

Isn't it?

Hell, yes.

He said, "It's not what I want."

"No? Then you don't desire me. I thought . . . But then again, I was fainting in your arms and telling you I loved you and . . . oh, Lord, I can barely stand to remember all the things I said to you. And you *brought me to my maid.*"

"Damned right I did, even if it was the hardest thing I'd ever done in my life. There are rules about these things, you little fool. A man doesn't take a woman who is obviously not at her full capacity. You'd been *drinking,* and not just a little bit. Not to mention that you are a virgin. I have a personal rule about deflowering virgins."

"It sounds like too many rules to me."

That startled him, and he shut up. She was right. Too many damned rules.

And then she said, in a voice much softer, much more soothing, "And I think you have so many rules because you are afraid. Oh, I recognize the signs. I've spent my entire life being afraid," she said. Rising, she walked to the window. Her night rail floated behind her, soft and billowing as a cloud and in the moonlight, she looked like a wraith.

He rose and followed. "Not you. You have courage enough to send a band of Huns packing."

"No. I am afraid, Morgan."

"What are you afraid of, Blackie?"

"Hmmm." She ducked her head and a slice of silver light fell across her face. He wanted to rest his lips there and feel the smoothness of her skin against his mouth.

She lifted a shoulder. "Of never being . . . acceptable. Of never shining, or being special or anyone noticing me, other than to tell me my posture is poor or I'm daydreaming again. I suppose I just want someone to like me."

"What? That is absurd. Oh. I see. All those sisters. Have they been so hard on you?"

"Are you mocking me?"

"I'm asking."

She drew herself up and looked away. "It's nothing so terrible. I just . . . I'm the third daughter. Lost in the middle—a boring complaint."

He smoothed the hair from her face. He couldn't resist.

Her hair felt incredibly soft against the soft pads of his fingertips. He watched it sift through his hand, mesmerized by its sheen, its weight. "Not so boring. What happened, love?"

She hesitated for such a long time, he thought she wasn't going to respond. "Once I heard my mother talking to my aunt. She was talking about her sadness after I was born. She called it the 'black time.' My aunt had had to come and care for me. Mother couldn't rise from the bed for over a month, or do anything. She just cried. She . . . she didn't even want to see me. My aunt Margaret brought her to me, but she wouldn't even look at me.

"Aunt Margaret said it was the melancholia that sometimes comes after a birth. She said it must have been because I was the third daughter. She said Julia didn't matter because she was the first and my father and mother had known there would be other chances at a son. Then Laura was a disappointment and they began to grow anxious. Then me. It must have been a bitter blow. And then Hope and Marie, they were sort of anticlimactic. She had already accepted, you see, that there would be no heir. Mother said that perhaps Aunt Margaret was right, because she didn't lie in bed, listless, for endless days after their births. Just mine."

"God, Leah." He went to take her in his arms, but she stepped away. "When did you hear this?"

"I was eight years old. I was spying, of course. I always used to spy. Ever since then I thought I should try to make it up to her. Try to be good, make her happy she had had me and that I wasn't a boy."

"Christ."

"No, it's all right. I made up my mind to make her proud—the proudest of any of my sisters—by outshining them. I tried very hard. But, oh, Morgan, I'm not very good at being good."

"Don't say that, you foolish little . . ."

"I almost had it. This season, I did shine. I did. I became popular with the ton the way Julia had. But better. It was all going beautifully and then I dumped soufflé on Carl Enders's head."

"No, don't do this, damn it. Your mother loves you, you know she does. She'd lay down her life for you, fight a hoard of dragoons and a Bengal tiger to boot."

"Of course, my mother loves me. I'm just not very special, not in the way she values. I always fail when I . . ." Her face crumpled, and he knocked aside the hand she flayed toward him to keep him away and closed the distance between them. Taking her into his arms, he hugged her tightly to him, needing to take it all away.

"Oh, Leah. Listen to me. I want you. I want you very much—too much, damn it, I can't think half the time. And you are right, sweet Blackie. It scares the hell out of me."

She was sniffling softly. With a smile and a sigh, he untied his cravat and offered it to her in lieu of a handkerchief. This was getting to be a habit. Well, he would just have to spend a bit more on cravats.

"Th-thank you for saying that," she stammered.

He closed his eyes, struggling to cling to his sanity. Then he gave up, muttering, "Damn it, Leah," and tipped her head back and closed his mouth over hers.

Banking his hunger, he was determined to make the kiss tender, to express what blazed in his heart. How could he tell her that he wanted to protect her, heal her, save her? It made no sense, not even to him. So he kissed away her tears and softly, softly she melted against him.

He pulled away, tugging rebel strands of hair from her wet lashes. Her eyes were wide, filled with astonishment, and she was so incredibly beautiful his breath refused to come evenly. "You are the most bloody special woman I have ever met."

"I love you, Morgan. I know you don't want me to, but I do. I'm sorry."

He couldn't stop stroking her skin. It gleamed peach and cream and felt soft as silk. "No, Blackie, don't you dare apologize."

"But you don't like it that I love you."

"No. No, I don't. It makes things harder—er, that is to say more *difficult*."

She gazed at him and the devil himself would have found it impossible to resist the appeal in that face. "I'm nineteen, Morgan. I know what I want."

He smiled against his will. "All of nineteen."

"Old enough," she said and she was right.

"Show me the bliss, Morgan," she said. "Please."

He hesitated, still fighting with his conscience. And losing. Losing very fast.

"Your husband will kill me for this. But husbands rut tamely in darkened rooms. You are made for passion. You deserve passion, and if I've nothing else to give you, you stupid girl . . ."

"I don't want you to protect me and I don't want you to decide what is best for me. I just want you to do what you *want* to do."

He closed his eyes. "I couldn't begin to describe the things I want to do with you."

"You do?" Her smile was brilliant. "And what of that rule about deflowering virgins?"

He bent to kiss her again. "Well, I'm thinking of it more now of a guideline than an absolute rule."

She laughed, her lips curled against his. He grabbed a fistful of hair at the nape of her neck and bent her head back with a jerk. When he kissed her again, she was sweet and eager.

He backed toward the bed, pulling her with him.

"Wait. What of babies?"

He stopped cold. "What?" he said in a strangled voice.

"Daphne says there are ways to prevent getting a baby. In her stories—"

He shook his head in astonishment. "What sort of friend is this woman to tell such things to an impressionable young woman?"

Leah looked insulted. "A very practical one, I'd say. She argued that it was the not knowing these things that got girls in trouble."

He relented, laughing softly. "I cannot fault that logic. There are measures we can take. I will show you."

She relaxed. "Yes. Show me. Show me everything."

"God, Leah," he groaned, and pulled her tight up against him.

He saw her lashes sweep over her eyes, hiding their dark depths, saving him from drowning, but then her mouth touched his and he felt himself fall into her. He moved his hands down to her waist to pull her up against him. She felt so slender, so distinctly feminine. She filled his head with a rush and numbed his mind, suspending the nagging certainty that he was defiling something precious, something sacred.

But he couldn't stop himself. He needed her, needed this, so like a starving man he took from her, kissing her hard, pressing her back so that she was nestled among her pillows and he could feel her against his chest. His mouth worked hers, taking more, giving as well, tasting, biting gently until she moaned and still he had to *take more* because he'd waited so long.

His hand slid up her side, seeking her curves. He could feel her shudder as he skittered over her rib cage to her breast. Her small gasp came sweet and high and her mouth went slack under his. He touched his tongue to her lips, caressing them, stimulating the sensitive pad of her bottom lip. She answered him with a soft groan and the tentative touch of her tongue to his.

Her hands tightened in his hair, pulling at the roots. The pain stung, mingling with pleasure, becoming pleasure because it was all a part of the passion.

He broke off to look at her. She had gone limp in his arms,

her eyelids heavy, her gaze locked with his. Her mouth was swollen and glistening from his kisses. Her chest rose and fell in rapid movements, thrusting her chest into his hand. The pebbled peak grazed his palm.

"I'm not afraid. Morgan," she whispered.

"No. Don't be afraid."

His free hand cupped her face, keeping her his prisoner as his mouth played. He nibbled her lips, grating his teeth gently under her chin over the sensitive flesh of her neck. Down, tasting, gliding his mouth to feel her, biting her shoulder. She arched against him, moaning, her restless hands grasping and pushing him in turn.

His fingers worked furiously at the ribbons cinching her gown at the neck. When they were undone, he tugged viciously at the material, wanting her naked.

Splaying her hands on his chest, she tugged at his shirt. He helped her with the studs. He was thinking only about how her body would feel against his, flesh to flesh. He worked swiftly, kissing her, muttering things he didn't even know he was saying. The words came out of him, gentle words, loving words telling her how beautiful she was and how much he wanted her.

In the darkness, he shed his clothing, his body straining with the delay, making him impatient with wanting to *feel* her. He stretched out over her, bearing down to press her into the mattress. He felt every bit of her under him as he attacked the nuisance of her nightdress, getting the garment off as he traced the outline of her ear.

He moved to her breast. His mouth closed over a neatly tightened peak. She curled into him, her arms clasping him tightly. "Oh, God," she cried. "It feels wonderful."

She was so innocent, so honest. He'd never had a woman like this. Each and every sensation was a dazzling discovery to her.

He pulled back, wanting to see her body. She lay still for him, letting him look his fill. Her body was gorgeous, slender and long. Her legs went on forever. Her hips were delicately flared, her abdomen table flat. Between her legs, dark sable curls beckoned him.

His blood raged in his veins. The torment of every moment was exquisite. He ran his hands over her, touching her everywhere, then lowered his body carefully over her once again.

She stretched like a cat, reaching for him, sliding her hands lazily down his back and across his shoulders. He struggled to be gentle, for he felt no such languor in himself. He leaned on his elbow and followed the line of her hips to part the delicate folds. The moist heat of her inner flesh yielded against his fingertips.

"Open for me, Leah," he rasped.

She slid her thighs apart, slowly at first, but as he began to stroke, her body relaxed and he nudged her apart, giving him access to pleasure her.

"Oh . . . God . . . I . . . Morgan!"

He moved into her, invading her tight passage. Tilting her hips, she wordlessly invited him further, her hand locked on his forearm. He obliged, penetrating her until he felt the barrier of her virginity, then gradually withdrew.

Her eyes were glazed, staring up at him full of astonishment. Her lips were parted and glistening from his kisses. When he entered her again, she blanched with pleasure. He pressed upward while his thumb brushed her sensitive place nestled in the soft down, starting a rhythm meant to bring her to pleasure.

"This is the bliss," she gasped. He stroked her again. She lifted her mouth beseechingly and he took it again with his. Their tongues parried, and he commanded her with the kiss, timing each stroke in tandem to his pleasuring her until she cried out, jerking in delicious spasms as she lay in his arms. As her climax poured through her, Morgan thought he had never seen her look more beautiful. Then her tremors eased, and her body gradually fell back into the soft cushion of pillows.

He held her tightly, resting his cheek in the deep valley

between her breasts. Her fingers dug into his scalp, ruffling his hair.

She sighed.

Lifting his head, he traced the shape of her mouth with his lips. "Yes, that was the bliss, Blackie."

Chapter 11

LEAH STRETCHED DREAMILY. The famed bliss. It certainly had lived up to its name in every sense. She hadn't expected it to be like that—shattering, falling, being pulled apart in the most deliciously devastating way. And Morgan had felt so solid, so strong over her, holding her, saying those lovely things close to her ear, touching her and driving her wild and giving her such pleasure as she could never have imagined existed.

"Mmmm," she said. " I feel very wicked."

"I thought it was I who was the Wicked Earl."

"Then it must be contagious." She turned to him, smiling. "And we are not even finished yet, are we?"

"We can be. If you want it to be so."

Daphne had described the carnal act to her. At the time Leah had thought it repulsive and completely confusing, but Daphne had promised that when she felt the urge to lie with a man it would all make perfect sense and that she would crave the deeper pleasure that his penetration brought.

Leah wanted that deeper pleasure. She wanted to belong to him completely.

"I don't wish to stop. I don't want to be safe and good and

all the things everyone tells me to be. I want to do what I want. And I want you to kiss me, Morgan."

He obliged. She opened her mouth to him and floated away on the pleasure of his tongue sliding against hers.

She could hear her own heartbeat mingling with the rough sounds of their uneven breathing. Her hands roamed freely over his shoulders and back. She loved the way his body felt, the play of shifting muscle, the power in his every movement. This was Morgan, she kept thinking, and she wanted to cry.

But he hated it when she cried, so she kept kissing him instead.

He pulled back, staring down at her, taking in all of her, lingering, savoring. God, she must be the most wanton woman that ever lived, because she didn't feel self-conscious at all under the burning perusal. She shivered, reveling in the passion in his eyes.

"You are so damned . . . beautiful." His voice was hoarse. "Ah, God, Leah."

He pressed a series of quick kisses down her neck and parted from her, taking only a moment to rid himself of the rest of his clothing. Then he was back beside her, smoothing her hair out of her face with trembling fingers.

Leah let her eyes drift closed.

She felt him. He was rigid and hot at the apex of her legs. She spread her legs, shameless, wanting, and he leaned into her. Her flesh parted and he slid inside.

"You're hot," he gasped and eased in further. "Ready and wet and . . . ah, God!"

The feel of him filling her was astonishing. Her inner flesh stretched around him.

"You're tight."

Morgan was hers—she held him in her body. Woman and man, joined. She clutched at him, sliding her legs to wrap around his hips when his hands showed her how. He grasped her bottom and pushed harder. She moaned softly.

The sharp sting when he reached her barrier brought her out of her reverie.

She looked up at him. His face was grim. "Be sure," he said.

"I am," she answered. "Very sure, Morgan. Make me yours."

He held her face in his hands, kissed her hard, his mouth muffling her cry when he plunged himself fully into her, then lay very still.

She had braced herself, but it hurt in a way she didn't imagine. She didn't move, either, letting her body recover. Morgan said something she didn't quite hear. She thought it might have been, "I'm sorry."

That spurred her into action. She didn't want him to be sorry. Not for taking her virginity. It was his; she'd given it to him.

She moved, sliding her body out from his, then sheathing him again. She bit down against the sting, wanting only to make him not sorry. A guttural sound came from the back of his throat. The feel of his breath on her neck sent delicious ripples down her spine.

He moved with her, taking up a languid rhythm. She found that the pain eased, and she pushed against him.

"More," she urged. Her hands gripped the tight hardness of his buttocks, bringing him into her.

His body gleamed with sweat. She dug her hands into the thick muscle of his back.

He spoke her name, and she found she was no longer thinking of him, but of herself and the wild delirium taking over her body.

She felt him stiffen in her arms, then he jerked, driving himself in deeply, rapidly. She held on tight, delighting in his rapture as he climaxed violently. He said her name again, cried it aloud.

I love you, Morgan.

She didn't dare say it, but it filled her consciousness as he rode out the last spasms of pleasure. He at last lay still, his heart beating against hers.

LEAH DOZED LIGHTLY, waking when Morgan rose and began to dress.

"It's nearly morning," he said after he leaned over her to kiss her. "Sleep."

"I don't feel tired," she protested.

He laughed at her heavy lids, kissing each one in turn. Winding her arms about his neck, she kept him from rising. She reached up and kissed him with vigor.

"You are insatiable," he murmured.

"We can add that to incorrigible."

"And maddeningly desirable. Now let me go before Debra comes in here and wakes the whole house with her screaming at seeing me in your bed."

"Good night, Morgan." She sighed, letting her arms fall. Her look of contentment slackened and her eyes drifted closed as he crept from the room.

He paused at the door, staring at her one moment longer. "Good night, Blackie."

As soon as he entered his room, he rang for Andrew. The valet was prompt, even at this early hour.

"I want to speak to Spencer and Hallorhan as soon as they arise," he told Andrew.

The valet was startled at Morgan's wish to speak to his groomsmen. "Are we leaving, my lord? Should I pack your things?"

"No, Andrew. Just ask them to meet me in the forecourt before breakfast."

"Very well, my lord."

Andrew stopped, his gaze taking in the still-made bed. He turned back, raking a gaze from head to foot to take in his master's rumpled, half-dressed state. His voice held no inflection, however. "Is that all, my lord?"

"For now. Bring me up a tray as soon as the kitchen is awake. I am famished."

Andrew's eyebrows jutted skyward. "Indeed, I will do so posthaste."

Morgan frowned as the man left. Andrew was a Puritan at heart. During his service to Morgan, however, he had not been disapproving when it was apparent that Morgan had entertained a woman. Yet he never failed to appear shocked. That had always amused Morgan.

Today, however, he was not amused. He was not certain what he *was*. His body felt incredible, drained and tired and still full of restless energy. Making love to Leah had not eased his tension. He wanted to be back with her right now.

There was also the problem of his conscience. It didn't sit well with him that he had given himself over to his baser self. Leah was an innocent, but she had tempted him and he, as the more worldly person, should have . . .

What good was it to berate himself for giving in? He was only a man, for God's sake. What man would have denied a woman like Leah?

Still, he shouldn't have done it. If he were free to do so, he wouldn't mind in the least offering Leah exactly what she wanted from him. After all, she loved him. And she was incredibly beautiful and sensual. Making love to her would never grow dull. He would not find a better choice for a wife.

Plus, he genuinely cared for her. Apart from the desire, there was a deep affection he had not known before with any other lover. He admired her and felt a fierce pride at her quirky originality. No woman could match her.

Perhaps it was best, though, that marriage was impossible. What could he offer her—he was still not received by half the families of the ton and likely to cause a fresh scandal when he put a ball through Sanderson's black heart. His life was committed to a darker purpose.

He had work to see to, not this pie-faced mooning. He grew disgusted with himself. Spoiling wives and bouncing babies on his knees was not in his future.

But how strange the appeal of domestic life all of the sudden. He had never thought to *want* that sort of thing.

He vowed to put the matter out of his mind. That was not easy, however. His brain stubbornly clung to images and words and scents and feelings, leaving him with white-knuckled frustration until he had to admit the truth.

It seemed his night with Leah had only whet his appetite for more.

~~~~~~

Things were strange that morning.

Leah's family was completely out of sorts. Marie, Leah, and Hope were gathered for breakfast in their mother's bedroom, a request Desdemona made occasionally to keep some semblance of family amidst the social demands of their summer schedule. Leah was preoccupied—what with obsessing over each minute detail of last night and being subjected to subsequent shivers of delight as each bit of memory unfolded—and Hope was quieter than usual as well. Marie demanded more sugar in her porridge while their mother nibbled her toast and sipped her coffee, strangely distant and not putting a stop to the child's pestering.

Such tolerance was most unlike her mother. Leah felt a tremor of unease at this strange mood. Could she suspect what happened last night—was that why she was so preoccupied?

Of course not, she chided. If Mother knew, she would be storming like a hurricane, not wan and withdrawn like this.

She had to stop thinking like Daphne. According to her, women of lost virtue were always very noticeable. They were slatternly and wore filthy clothes. Their hair was greasy and their skin went bad with the pox. Leah had examined herself closely in the mirror, looking for any telltale signs this morning. She could see none. She wasn't really surprised, it was just that she thought it best to check just in case.

Because Leah *felt* very different, not at all as if she'd *lost* anything of value. Instead, she gained some wonderful secret knowledge. She was filled with a low-grade excitement that buzzed pleasantly in her limbs. Lord, she flushed crimson every time she thought of Morgan's hands on her, coaxing those incredible feelings.

"I do wish your father were here," Desdemona said in a weary voice.

Leah started. "What? Oh, yes." She cleared her throat. "I, too, miss him."

Marie stamped her foot and demanded, "And I! Why does Father have to work so much? I want Father."

Leah tried to give her a warning look, for her disrespect would surely earn her one of their mother's dressing-downs. She always hated when the little girls were scolded, even if they deserved it.

"Yes," Desdemona replied in a wistful voice, "he is always working, isn't he?"

Leah gaped at this response. The small lines around her mother's eyes and mouth seemed deeper, more pronounced today than she ever remembered. Again, Leah thought of last night and felt a flash of apprehension.

Not because she regretted it. She never would. She had given herself to the man she loved. If she never shared another moment with Morgan, she would hug the memory of last night to her heart for the end of her days and treasure it.

She regretted only that her mother would be devastated if she learned of it. Why did it seem to be that Leah's happiness had to be at the cost of risking making her mother miserable? Why did what she wanted have to be so different from what everyone else wanted from her?

"I don't like it," Marie said. "I want him here with us."

"Shh," Hope said, trying to divert her troublesome sister. "Don't be naughty."

Mother remained silent.

Leah was truly worried now. "Mother, are you feeling ill?"

"No. Only a bit tired," Desdemona answered.

Marie's bottom lip trembled. "I want Father. He always reads to me, and he is teaching me to play cards. Why can I never have Father? Where is he?"

"I shall tell you where our father is," Leah snapped, turning to Marie. The sternness in her voice caused the child's eyes to widen. "To earn the money that dresses you in that fine sprigged muslin you so love because it was specially made for you to look like mine. And those kid shoes that are the envy of all the other little girls every place you go. And all the other finery you enjoy and never make a note of, not even so much as to offer our father a thank-you. If you think it is a hardship on you with his not being here, imagine what it is like for him to be separated so much from his family. Now, I know you miss him. We all do. But no one more than Mother, so please think of her."

There was a short silence as three shocked faces stared back at her.

Hope tugged on Marie's arm. "Come, Marie. We shall play dolls and get your mind off Father."

Marie allowed herself to be pulled away. She was clearly awed at having her usually indulgent older sister speak to her so severely. It seemed to have worked, however. She complied with Hope and took up her doll.

Leah sighed, her impatience gone. Turning to her mother, she braced herself for a reprimand. "I'm sorry, but I thought she deserved it," she explained, "and . . . well, you didn't look as though you were up to it. Mother, what is wrong? I've never seen you like this."

"What a mood I am in of late." Desdemona smoothed her iron-gray hair. It was pulled up in a twist that flattered her long, plain face. Her features were strong rather than beautiful. Leah had some of that strength in her own face, softened by the symmetrical comeliness supplied by her father's family.

"I hate for you children to see it," she went on. "It is just that with all of these people about all the time, it's unnerving. Oh, I don't mind it most times, but it is tiresome having to be polite, make conversation, observe all the courtesies and intricate rules, all without a rest. I suppose I am just a simple country girl at heart and it's starting to show. But I tell myself this is everything and more that I always wanted for my daughter, so why am I complaining? This is foolishness, isn't it?"

"No." Leah was amazed. Desdemona had always seemed to Leah to be the penultimate ideal, a woman who had distinguished herself among her social superiors. She *was* a country girl, common born, who had risen to the ranks of the crème de la crème of the polite world. Now she was admitting that she felt *tired* of it all.

Leah said, "No, it isn't at all. I feel that way, too, Mother. Sometimes I hate all of these parties and social obligations and I want to just ride, like I do at Daphne's—on the moor with no one else around."

Desdemona patted her hand. "I know. You have such an independent spirit, but I have a great many fears for you, Leah. I don't wish you to be lonely, darling. It will be different when you have a husband. A good husband is a woman's partner. He can sense when she is overcome or overset or . . . well, if your father were here, he would say, 'Mona, we are taking the day to ourselves,' and make all the necessary apologies and arrangements before I knew I had reached my limit."

Leah smiled. "And we'd have a picnic."

Desdemona smiled, too, and her eyes crinkled in the corners. "I very much believe we would."

Leah's smile faded. "I always thought it was you who took care of everyone. Oh, I know Father takes care of the finances, but the family is your domain. You do it all."

"It may seem like that, but everyone needs someone to take care of them sometimes, don't they? It is true I take care of your father, seeing his favorite dishes are served for dinner and his newspaper is pressed every morning. Those small things to add comfort to his day. But he takes care of me in all the important ways."

"You've never spoken to me like this before. I like it, Mother. It makes you so much less fearsome."

"Fearsome? Am I so bad as that? Well, I had to be to keep you in line."

"Yes. I know. I am incorrigible."

"Were, perhaps, you were a bit. I suppose I can tell you now that there were times when it was difficult to keep a straight face when reprimanding you. Really, you were always an imp, but a lovely one. But now you are a woman. To be married soon." She made a wry face. "If you can ever settle on a husband."

Leah dropped her eyes, thinking of Morgan.

Thinking of last night.

It was inevitable that her mother would ask, "What of the earl? Does he seem of a marriageable mind?"

"We have not discussed it," she answered honestly.

To Leah's immense relief, Marie came up just then with a long face and creased brow. "I am sorry, Mother," she muttered. She glanced back at Hope who gave her a meaningful look and Marie turned back around with a grimace. "I was very wrong."

Desdemona remained serious. "I accept your apology, Marie. Finish your porridge and you and Hope may go up to the nursery to play."

"May we take a walk later?"

"Mother is tired today," Leah said, drawing the child over to her. Including Hope in her message, she said, "I would be happy to take you on an outing, *if* you finish your porridge and don't give Mother any more trouble."

The children agreed.

When she turned back to her mother, she found her studying her. "You are different today."

"Different?" Leah's voice showed her strain. She tempered it. "Oh, no, I am not different. I am just the same, Mother, really I am. I-I think today is just a strange day for all of us. None of us are quite ourselves."

"You admit you are not quite yourself, yet you insist you are no different than usual. Oh, never mind. My brain is tired today. Go on your outing and leave me to my rest."

Leah stayed busy with her sisters for the rest of that morning and into the afternoon, trying hard to resist the temptation to brood. Morgan was not the only thing on her mind. That damned Randall beast person had gotten under her composure. She hated to admit it, but she was more than a bit daunted by the fact that the man, whom Morgan believed to be incomparably evil, had cast his eye her way.

This morning, she had remembered his slick smile and gleaming eyes and a wave of deep apprehension had overwhelmed her. In Daphne's stories, the most intrepid heroines managed to secret a weapon on their person and produce it at the right moment to avoid getting ravished or throttled. She had no weapons, however. It would hardly be seemly if she asked her host or hostess to supply her with one.

Impulsively she picked up a letter opener that was lying on a small escritoire in one of the parlors and examined its edge. She had no idea if this would make a good weapon. Running the pad of her forefinger along the blade, she was surprised. It wasn't as sharp as even a dinner knife, but it might do some damage if she found herself in a pinch. She decided it would have to do and with a quick glance around, hiked up her skirts and slipped it into her garter.

It brought her no sense of security or safety. She hoped she wouldn't be attacked outright, in any event. It was difficult to believe even a nefarious character like Sanderson would dare such a thing. Besides, Morgan would protect her. How strange that she had such faith in him. She really hardly knew him. But she loved him. And she trusted him, with her heart and with her life.

So much to think about was making her head ache. She put aside her worry about being accosted because what she really had to figure out was how to keep her soul from shattering into a thousand pieces. She had traded her virginity for a single night of the bliss. It had seemed a fair bargain for an experience that was to last her the rest of her days.

Today she was very sure it was not going to be enough. Not nearly enough.

When Leah entered the rooms set up for a buffet dinner that evening, she joined a group of her friends. Dahlia was particularly biting, smiling coldly and raking her eyes down Leah's long form.

"My goodness, Leah," she sniffed, "how does your father

afford all that material? Each of your dresses must take a score yards of fabric. No wonder he never leaves the bank."

The reminder that her father, while not so crass as engaging in trade, was not a member of the idle rich was outdone by Dahlia's crassly pointing out how unfashionably tall Leah was. Of course, Dahlia and Phyllida, both petite and dainty, were the epitome of fashion. They smirked at one another as if in congratulations for the doubly condemning jibe.

"I think she looks elegant. Like a Greek goddess," Sophie said, giving Phyllida an arch look. "Moreover, I believe the earl of Waring likes her just the way she is."

Leah blushed, uncharacteristically speechless for the moment. The smug expressions of Dahlia and Phyllida faded and Sophie took Leah's hand and said, "Let's go sit over by the fire, Leah. I feel a chill in the air. It's making my skin crawl."

Turning with Sophie, Leah angled an arch look over her shoulder at the other two women. They appeared sufficiently vexed. When she turned back around, she found herself about to collide with a small, exquisite blond. She gasped, startled, then received a double shock when she recognized the woman. It was Glorianna Sanderson.

Flustered, Leah glanced about, desperately trying to find a decorous way not to have to speak to her. She didn't wish to face this woman. She was afraid of her, plain and simple. The woman had power over Morgan, and even if she did believe him when he claimed it was not romantic love, it was still the only hold anyone had over him. Which was more than she could claim.

However, there was nowhere to go short of fleeing. She grasped her hands together in front of her and tried to look pleasant as Glorianna came up to her.

"I know it is bad form to accost you like this," the woman said, "but if I had to take the time to find someone to introduce us, I might have missed my chance. You see, I am being rather naughty. I am not supposed to be talking to you." She wrinkled her nose and giggled, like a girl bent on mischief.

The gesture made a favorable impression on Leah. It

served to bring the woman down from the heights of a
paragon into the realm of someone Leah might like.

"I've been trying for two days to meet you," Glorianna
confided, glancing quickly around. She seemed a bit furtive.
"Will you speak to me? I'll wager introductions are unnecessary since we both know who the other is. Do you mind?"

"N-No," Leah stammered. "I just don't understand why
you wish to speak to me."

Glorianna's smile was beatific. "Splendid. I'll explain
everything. Come sit with me outside here. There is a small
terrace just outside these doors, and a garden beyond. It's
cool enough and we can be more private."

The two women passed into the terrace and down the flagstone steps. They headed for a gathering of stone benches
under a thickly leafed oak. Underneath was already filled
with shadows in the gathering dusk.

Leah sat, stretching her long legs out in front of her to
ease the pinch of her stays. When she noticed Glorianna's
decorous posture, her dainty feet curled under her bench so
that she looked not to have any, she felt embarrassed at her
own toes sticking out like some backstairs undermaid who
didn't know any better.

She straightened quickly.

Glorianna laughed. "Oh, please be comfortable. I am hoping we can be friends."

"It is very kind of you." Notwithstanding the invitation to
relax, Leah arranged herself more seemingly.

"Please call me Glorianna. I may have once been a countess by marriage, but my roots are far more humble than
yours."

"All right." Leah tried several different positions for her
hands, but they were too restless to sit calmly on her lap.

"Well, now that I have you here, I hardly know what to
say. I can hardly assail you with all the questions I have, so I
will begin with simply saying that I am overjoyed to hear the
news that you and Morgan are attached."

"Oh, we aren't attached. Not really, in the sense of any
permanence . . ." Leah trailed off. How was she to explain

her relationship with Morgan when she herself didn't understand it?

"Don't be modest. It is obvious his meeting you has been instrumental in his joining polite society again. Morgan has been through so much." Her eyes were sad. "I want him to be happy."

Leah began to relax, realizing that this woman truly just wanted to be friends. Besides, this was an excellent opportunity to gain some insight into the reticent Morgan Gage. "You were close, then?"

"Very. You see, when I married Morgan's father, Morgan and I were fond of each other. We share a bond because of our loss and I have missed that so much since he has been gone. I have missed him. We were all so very happy together for a time, he and his father and I. Then . . . since Evan's death . . ." She stopped, her features constricting in pain.

Leah was moved. "I am so sorry." Impulsively, she reached out for the other woman's hand, which Glorianna took gratefully.

"Does Morgan speak of me?" Her look was full of disarming appeal. "Does he speak of his loss?"

"I can tell you that he speaks of his father in reverential tones," Leah assured her. "And he feels keenly his loss, not just of his father, but of all of his old life. He does speak of you, too, and I know he longs to be reunited." She cleared her throat, forcing the words out. "He is most interested to talk with you, but has not been able to reach you."

Glorianna's eyes misted over. "Oh, I am not so sure he has even thought much of me. I suppose he has been busy paying court to you. I've heard everyone talking. They say he looks at you with devotion in his eyes."

Leah bristled with discomfort. "Oh, no, you mustn't think we are the *grande passion*. Morgan is devoted to enjoying your friendship again."

"I think you underestimate your appeal, Leah. Morgan is a very complex man, and he does not play the doting suitor, ever."

Unless it is a farce, Leah thought, but kept her lips pressed together.

"I will never know why he is so closed with his feelings," Glorianna mused. "Evan was a wonderful man, and he was never harsh with Morgan. But Morgan . . . he was always so intense, railing against the world, grabbing life and experiences with both hands, even as a child, to hear the way his father told it—and told it proudly. Yet . . . sometimes I wonder if prison did not break something in him. He was never the same after that."

"Why have you refused to receive him?" Leah blurted.

"I? Oh, I am dying to see him. It has been awful to not be allowed to do so, even to write. My husband has been reluctant to allow it, you see. He is very protective of me, especially since I took the death of my first husband so poorly. He fears Morgan's . . . er, problems would cause me distress."

"I can assure you his concern is misplaced. Morgan has no *problems.*"

Her eyes filled suddenly with tears. "Oh, my dear, Morgan was tormented by the way his father died. They had quarreled and he felt so much guilt. Randall explained it all to me. Morgan was out of his mind with grief, irrational, and for a while he sought to blame anyone. Everyone, even myself, was accused."

Leah's eyes narrowed. Oh, Mr. Sanderson was indeed very clever. No wonder Morgan had feared he'd be thought of as a lunatic. Randall had done a thorough job of besmirching Morgan with virtually every soul who mattered. And he had justified his isolation of his new wife by lying to her about Morgan's state of mind.

"I can assure you, Mrs. Sanderson, Morgan is not irrational. And he certainly does not harbor any ill-conceived ideas about anyone's guilt." Which, she thought smugly, was a very clever way of putting the truth.

"I am so happy. I have been so frustrated and so sad not to be able to speak with him, tell him all the things I've wanted to for so long. Imagine my joy when I learned he was here, in this very house, but Mr. Sanderson insisted on keeping me away from seeing him until he could determine whether Morgan had recovered from his terrible delusions."

"Morgan is as sound of mind as anyone I know. There is no reason for you to be kept apart any longer."

Take that, Mr. Sanderson.

"How relieved I am to hear it! I hope I can confide in you, Leah. I shouldn't complain when I know he is only concerned for my benefit, but such strict controls on my freedoms have chafed sorely. I just hope I can make him see reason. Randall is . . . well, he's sometimes overly jealous in seeing to what he feels is his protection of me."

I wager he is. She said, "Men sometimes are not very good at listening."

Laughing, Glorianna wiped her eyes. "Indeed, they tend to take over and dictate cures."

Thinking of Morgan, Leah said, "And they always think they know best."

"You know much for one so young. But some women have a gift of understanding men. Me, I have always been a fool in that area. I need a man in my life. I love the way they are strong and dependable. I admit I like a man to take care of matters for me. I am no good at it, it just is that simple. You . . . well, you are just so much more courageous."

"Oh, I don't think I am so wise. I feel like I do not understand the first thing about men. Or anything."

"But you hold a great attraction for them. Please do not think I was gossiping, but naturally I was curious about you when I heard Morgan was here as a guest with your family, and you are spoken of with much admiration, and amusement. It seems many are fond of you."

Leah shook her head, but still couldn't suppress a smile. "No doubt my friend Kingsley. He loves to play that tune. He thinks it plucks on women's sympathies to pretend he is my spurned admirer and makes him more appealing."

"Well, even if it is so, he is not the only one. That man right over there has been watching you the entire time we've been out here. I believe he might be smitten."

Leah looked over her shoulder with little interest. The

man was very tall, dressed in dark clothing and a plain cravat. He looked like a servant. Probably a footman belonging to their hosts. But there was something interesting about him.

Now she remembered. He had been in the garden this morning, when she had taken her sisters out for a stroll. Hope had pointed him out, mentioning something about his long face looking like their uncle Peter.

He *was* looking at her. No servant stared at a houseguest like that. She realized that he had been watching her when she had seen him in the garden, too. She hadn't thought much of it at the time. But now that he was here, standing by the wall and making no secret of his interest in her, she found it suddenly alarming.

And now she'd been caught in a clandestine meeting with Glorianna Sanderson. Her husband would be furious. Would he be murderous? Was this man his spy? His assassin?

She felt a sudden awareness of danger, of feeling uncomfortably conspicuous and very vulnerable. Standing abruptly, she said, "You must excuse me."

"My dear, is something wrong?"

"No. I . . . just remembered that I . . . I haven't seen Morgan all day and he had said he wished to speak to me, so I have to find him. He will wonder at my forgetfulness."

Glorianna was confused. "Oh. Very well. I fear I am to blame for keeping you."

"No, indeed, I enjoyed our conversation."

"I hope we shall be friends."

"I am sure of it." Leah looked behind her. The man was pretending to look about him in a show of innocence that was so blatantly false it sent a chill up her spine. "I must go."

She hurried into the house, her mind working fast. Morgan had told her last night that Sanderson had threatened her with harm. She had to find Morgan and tell him at once that she had spoken to Glorianna and that Randall's man was stalking her.

In the house, the guests were still gathering before dinner. Morgan was not anywhere to be found. When she asked after him, a young man told her he had seen Morgan heading out toward the stables a little while ago. Leah exited the house through the library door and took the path.

When she was half the distance from the house to the barn, she realized she had blundered. The path, usually filled with milling servants and guests, was isolated at this hour. She looked about, her heart beginning to thump heavily, a growing sense of dread settling in her chest.

She looked back toward the house. The man who had been watching her was coming down the path.

Whirling, she gauged the distance to the barn. She hesitated. There appeared to be no one about. She would prefer to run back to the safety of the house, but that way was blocked. Yet, if she continued down toward the barn, she could be trapped in the deserted structure.

She began to feel the sting of fresh panic. Her hand went involuntarily to her garter, feeling the solid comfort of the letter opener held tightly in her silk bindings. Should she make a stand for it now? The edge wasn't very sharp. Why hadn't she armed herself with a real weapon?

Making a quick decision, she stepped off the path and headed into the woods. She was fleet of foot. She would have a chance to outrun him, lose him in the thick foliage. She could even hide if she had to. It was her best chance.

Behind her, she heard the crisp sound of grass being crushed underfoot. He was right behind her. It sounded like he was running.

Fear exploded into blinding terror. She broke into a full tilt run, crashing into the copse and taking to the trees like a fawn.

Chapter 12

MORGAN RECEIVED A message to come downstairs right away. He was washing up and making a quick change of clothing after spending the afternoon in the barn. His horse, an ornery beast with a knack for aiming his kicks just right, had thrown a shoe earlier and Morgan had to be on hand to aid the farrier with the temperamental animal.

Throwing on his coat, he went out to the small garden where he met one of the pair of footmen he had assigned the task of guarding Leah.

Spencer explained quickly, gesturing to the now empty seating under the tree. Morgan listened grimly.

"Where is she now?" he snapped.

"Mrs. Sanderson has rejoined the rest of the guests, but Miss Leah has wandered off. Do not worry, my lord. Hallorhan is with her. Look—there he is. What the . . . what is he doing going toward the woods? Why would he do that? He couldn't be following her, could he?"

Morgan squinted into the distance with a sinking feeling of certainty that indeed he could. And probably was. Where Leah was concerned, there was no use in wondering the why of anything. If there was ever a chit who would be running into a wood formally dressed for a dinner at a peer's country house party just as the food was about to be served, it was Leah Brodie.

He muttered, "The little idiot . . . Go on inside, Spencer. I will handle this."

He set off after Leah and Hallorhan, plunging into the woods where he had watched the low-lying branches swallow the tall masculine figure. His shoulders relaxed as he caught his breath and scoured the surrounding greenery for a sign of them.

He caught a glimpse of Leah's pale blue dress. Grinding his teeth together, he set off after her. He didn't dare call out to her lest the sounds be audible from the house. He very much wanted to avoid alerting the others that he was chasing a wayward debutante around the deer park.

He peered intently through the thick clusters of bracken and shrubs, looking for a flash of blue. There she was—he saw her dress in swift snatches of bright color among the prolific green. She was running.

She must be terrified. It only now occurred to him what must have happened. He hadn't gotten an opportunity to tell her he'd set his footmen to watch over her. They must have done something to frighten her.

But why in God's name was she running away from the house, into the woods?

He sighed and swiped the stinging branches out of his way. One rarely saw sense in Leah's actions.

He passed Hallorhan on the path. The older man was huffing and puffing, his cravat loose and the dark coat he usually wore draped over his arm.

"Still got sight of her, my lord," the servant gasped.

"You're red in the face man, and ready to keel. Head on back. I've got her now."

The man didn't argue. He stopped, bent at the waist, hands on knees, and heaved in great gulps of air.

Morgan sped along the path. He could see her well now, racing away. He softly called to her.

She must have heard him, for she stopped, whirling about

with wide, desperate eyes. Her hair had worked itself out of its pins, and it floated as she whipped her head back and forth, searching for some way out. Her hands clutched in at her heaving chest and she was nearly doubled over. In her hand something glinted. Morgan stopped, seeing it was a small knife.

Her mouth was open and working, as if she were about to speak, but too terrified to make a sound. She was drawing in a deep breath. She was going to scream. Morgan raced forward, slashing his hands in abrupt cutting motions, trying to communicate the desperate need for her to be quiet.

Falling to her knees, she closed her eyes.

"M-Mor . . . Morgan . . . you . . . you . . . the ma . . . ma . . . man . . ."

"Quiet, Leah. Just catch your breath."

Then she held up the knife. That stopped him.

What the devil?

At first he thought she meant to threaten him, which was confusing enough, but when she turned it on herself, he went blind with fear. His only thought, the only reason he could comprehend for her actions, was that she was trying to harm herself.

Good God! She wanted to die because of last night. He had taken her innocence without a word of love or the future and now she was despondent. And she was going to do it before his very eyes to punish him.

He leaped at her, covering the distance in an amazing feat of panic-fed athleticism and knocked her back on her rear. In a flash, he had her pinned under him, her hands over her head. Grabbing her wrist, he banged it against the ground until she released the knife.

She continued to wriggle, making strangling sounds. Once she was disarmed, he freed her.

Leah grasped the lapels of the spencer that came just below her breast and fought herself free of it. Then she began to pull at the front of her dress.

Morgan's jaw dropped to his chest. He experienced an exquisite thrust of lust followed by an equally powerful certainty that he had descended to the depths of a worm to be looking at her with desire when she was obviously in acute distress. However, the unmistakable heat exploded in his loins, shooting down his legs, his arms, making his hands tremble.

She was stripping off her clothes.

Desire will atrophy a man's brain, his father had told him. It completely melted his as he watched her, astonished, fumbling for the laces of her corset.

"Hel . . . hel . . ." Then her lips pursed and opened, making a pathetic, airless "pah" sound.

And then the fugue popped like a bubble in his head, and he realized she was breathlessly trying to say "help."

Christ! She had been running through the woods like a fleet-footed deer, laced up tight in her tapes—she couldn't breathe!

Knocking her hands away, he sat her up and turned her around to access the buttons at the back of her dress. He didn't fool with the tiny seed pearls, although he was fairly adept at undressing women. He grabbed the little knife he had knocked away—Christ, it was only a letter opener!—and ran it neatly along the seam, opening the dress. He laid Leah back down.

Her head lolled as he set her upright again. "Don't faint," he ordered, working swiftly to pry open the cut tapes. Once he had done that, he gripped the sides of her corset and yanked.

Arching her head, she gulped in air as the corset gaped at last. She grasped his arms, her fingers digging into his muscles. "Th . . . ank yo . . ."

"Just relax," he told her, smoothing back her hair. Hunkering back on his heels, he cupped her head and brought her face up to meet him. She was still flushed, still out of breath. Her breasts heaved, threatening to spill out with each inhalation.

He cursed himself, but looked his fill.

Her mouth worked. "I . . . I . . . can't ru . . . run."

"What the devil were you . . . oh, never mind."

"He was after me."

"Hallorhan is my man. I sent him to watch over you." He curled one side of his mouth. "I am afraid he is in worse shape than you. You gave him a run of it, didn't you?"

"I thought . . ."

"I know, I know. Hush now. Catch your breath."

Leah closed her eyes and breathed deeply. He shifted against the throbbing insistence of his erection, cursing himself for a weak-willed toad. But, God forgive him, the woman was tousled, half dressed, flushed, and panting. It was so damned erotic he couldn't bear it.

His eyes lowered again to the luscious outline of her full, firm breasts. The tiny peaks were pink and tight, pressing like impudent temptation against the thin lawn of her chemise.

Her hands came up to cover herself and he jerked his gaze up to find her eyes open. They were dark and snapping with excitement, clashing with his until lowering to witness the evidence of his aroused state.

She didn't look shocked or displeased or even bewildered. The corner of her mouth jerked, as if she caught a smile there before it could flower.

So, it pleased her, did it? He swallowed painfully against a dry throat.

"Are you angry?" she asked, her breathing more even now. "You look angry. What is it?"

"I don't know. Sometimes, Leah, I don't know a damned thing in the world but you." He leaned forward, and she went back easily onto the soft, summer grass, snuggled tight under him. Her eyelashes swept down, fringed veils demurring to his impending kiss. Her arms curled around his neck.

She was panting still, but this time it was for a much different reason.

Sometimes, Leah thought on a sigh as she leaned back, eyes closed, wanting his lips to descend on hers, Morgan Gage was really quite a wonderful man. She might balk at his arrogant mien and despair at his stubbornness, but now as he held her so safe in his arms, she could forgive everything.

The soft brush of his lips was delicate at first, almost teasing. He said her name, so soft, and it went through her entire body. The kiss grew more demanding and she responded enthusiastically, folding neatly against him so that she could feel the full length of him against her.

She gave a violent shiver when he took her earlobe between his teeth. "Do you like that?" he asked.

"I . . . ah . . . like everything you do."

That seemed to please him particularly, because he gave a low growl and attacked her neck with more intensity, moving quickly to the heaving swell of her bosom. His hands cupped her breasts and he pressed taunting kisses in the sensitive valley between. "You have the most incredible—" He licked her, eliciting a gasp. "—body I've ever seen."

"Oh, I like that!"

"That? Or this?" In one move, he jerked down the neck of her chemise. She cried out as he bent his head, delicately flicking his tongue over the exposed nipple.

She couldn't answer. His hands were magical, his mouth more so, leaving her quivering, incoherent. She looked upward, seeing the soaring trees, and the dense profusion of leaves. "Sh-should we be doing this?"

"No." He didn't stop, however, and she was grateful.

Her hands tangled in his hair. "Oh, God, this is . . ."

"Mmmm?" His hands were hitching up her skirts.

The brush of his warm fingers on the naked flesh above her garter jolted a bolt of shock through her that held her galvanized. "Oh, Morgan. This is much too wonderful."

"Stop talking." He peered down at her, his eyes brilliant and dark. "I have other uses for your mouth."

His kisses grew wild, and she supposed hers were equally so. His hands slipped under her drawers, cupping her buttocks.

"Morgan? Are we going to make love? Here, outside?"

"We're just playing," he replied, his voice rough. "Just . . . touching. It's just touching."

He found her, lightly cupping her sex. Reaction rolled through her. She was trembling, quaking under him, hungry. *We're just playing,* she thought.

She groaned when he stroked her again.

Biting her lips, she summoned her courage to do what she had not dared last night. Her hand ventured downward. Morgan's entire body bucked when she placed her flattened palm over the ridge of his erection.

He hissed in a breath, closing his grip around her wrist to stay her. Studying his face, she saw his eyes were closed, his face caught in a grimace.

Had it been painful? Oh, God! She hadn't meant to hurt him.

He let out a breath and released her to unfasten his trousers, then guided her questing hand inside.

She let her fingers encroach slowly, overcome by curiosity and wonder. Wiry hair tickled her palm. Then the tips of her fingers brushed against his aroused member. She closed around him. She heard the soft groan that followed and was emboldened.

It was an astonishing thing, as hard as stone, as hot as glowing ash, and as soft as velvet. His maleness amazed her, as well as what it was capable of. With this, he had stroked inside her, finding that thrilling place and bringing shattering fulfillment.

Sliding her legs open, he angled her hips and slipped his fingers inside to stroke her while his tongue played in her mouth. Inspired, she followed his example, sliding her hand down the scalding length of him when his fingers entered her, and up when he withdrew.

"We must stop. This is . . . this . . ." Her voice was dazed, as wispy as the clouds overhead.

"Shhh," he said. "Come here. Like this."

He slid her leg under him, opening her. The air touching her exposed skin felt wildly decadent. No lady would lie like this in the woods . . . would she?

Maybe they did so all the time. Morgan seemed to know naturally how to pull her to him just so, fitting their bodies together so intimately that all he had to do was shift his weight, and she felt the prodding heat of him at her entrance. Then she knew what he meant to do. Grasping him, she closed her legs around his hips. He slid inside her in one slick, gliding thrust.

In a rush of pleasure, she called his name.

"I know," he answered softly. His breath at her ear, the soft rasp of his voice, infused with passion, sapped her strength. "Shh. Just . . . just let me . . . It's all right."

"We're—he's gone, isn't he? The man? You are sure we're alone?"

"We're the only two people in the world."

Oh, God, he had to say something like that. It felt so true. Nothing else seemed to be important but the giddy rush of indecent delight as he drove into her, building her pleasure with thrust after thrust. Her fulfillment rose swift, sharp, detonating liquid fire inside of her. He followed quickly, smothering his rough cries in her hair, thrusting hard until his pleasure was spent.

They lay still, tangled together. Leah stared at the sky over his shoulder, the lace of leaves, the vivid blue of the sky, the flash of white clouds imprinted itself on her mind in the pleasant lassitude.

It seemed incredible that the bliss could be achieved like that. It had been wild, urgent, full of passion, and speaking of something different than the tenderness of her initiation.

It felt depraved. But that was somehow *very* exciting.

Morgan shifted his weight, slipping free of her body. With one flick of his wrist, he tossed her skirt over her long legs. Lying on his side, he placed his chin on his fist and stared down at her. "Your hair is a mess."

She touched a lock self-consciously.

Morgan smiled, taking her hand and kissing it. "You look delicious."

She almost purred. It was a lovely thing to hear afterward. Delicious.

She *felt* delicious, too.

"This was foolish," he said.

"Yes," she agreed.

"You don't sound chastised."

"Neither do you."

"I cannot say I was thinking all that clearly, but I did consider the likelihood of being caught. I would surmise we are fairly safe. There can't be many guests combing through these woods."

That look came into his eyes, that dark intense look. "What?" she prodded. "You are angry about something."

"Yes," he answered mildly. "But I seem always to be angry with you."

"But why?"

"Because . . . because you make me insane. When I'm with you I wind up doing things like throwing you back on the grass and making love to you."

"And you hate that?"

"No." He chuckled. "That's what makes me angry. Come. We have to put you together. We should get back before we're missed."

He helped her to her feet and while she did her best to pull her corset back together, he searched the forest floor for discarded hairpins.

"I found eight," he told her, holding them out as she made the last adjustments to her dress. The pearl buttons were lost. The back panels flapped open. He frowned, yanking the garment and twisting the edges enough to tie an ungainly knot. Below, the material gapcd to show her bared back and the top of her chemise. Her short-cropped spencer hid the damage.

"That will have to do." Holding her arms out, she jerked her chin down to indicate her dress and asked, "How do I look?"

"Like a woman begging to be ravished all over again."

Her face lit up. "I was ravished, wasn't I? Oh, I like being ravished. In Daphne's stories, women are always being ravished. Most times, they don't like it, but it is actually splendid. I find it absolutely marvelous."

"Leah, for the love of God, don't talk like that. I'm only flesh and blood."

She bit her lip and shone with delight at her newfound power. Tucking the knowledge away for the future, she peered down at the hairpins. "You are going to have to do it."

"You are joking."

"I cannot see without a mirror, so I cannot possibly manage anything. Oh, come now, at least help me."

He let out a disgusted breath and shook his head. "Come here, then. Stand still. I am not a ladies' maid, so God knows how this will go."

Leah obeyed. "I almost forgot to tell you. Morgan, I spoke to Glorianna today. She came to me just before dinner."

His fingers stalled, then took up their task. "What did she say?"

"She spoke of you. She said she misses you. Sanderson told her you had delusions about your father's death, even talked as though you once thought she might have had a hand in it."

"What? I never—!"

"It is how he controlled her, don't you see? Making her afraid, pulling her from you so that she would trust only him and making you seem as irrational as an asylum inmate. And there is more. She knows Randall is keeping a close watch on her. My God, she is nearly his prisoner. She doesn't like it, especially his forbidding her from speaking to you. What I cannot imagine is how she doesn't grow suspicious."

His hands stopped, pausing in mid-action. Leah couldn't see his expression. After a moment he picked up another wayward strand of hair, tucking it into place. "Glorianna was like a child in some ways, needing protection and shelter. She's not stupid, but prefers to be helpless."

"Yes. She even said as much. Doesn't she see how vulnerable it makes her to an unscrupulous man like Randall?"

He gave her the pin and guided her hand to where it

needed to be placed. "She may now. She didn't seem afraid of him, did she? There was no indication he'd harmed her?"

"Not at all. There was no fear in her. It could be he truly does care for her. Even bad people care about some things. This wretched boy I knew when I was growing up positively doted on his equally horrible dog. It could be Randall truly loves Glorianna. It would explain why he . . . well, it could be he killed for love."

Morgan nodded. "He loves Glorianna as much as he can love anything. Randall has always viewed people as possessions. He saw her, he wanted her, and he decided to take her. But the motive was more far-reaching than jealousy and passion. Greed, namely. It ate at him that he was not the heir, it always has. It is why he hates me."

"He must have hated your father, too."

"That was a bit more complex, I think. He regarded my father with both admiration and contempt. He wanted to be like him, have what he had, and then, yes, he did hate him at the same time . . . I cannot explain it. No matter how much Father tried to show him kindness, it never soothed that hate because Father would never give him what he wanted, and that was the earldom.

"He thought himself superior, you see. He felt he deserved it. I don't know that it gave him pleasure to kill my father, but he did it, that I know. And then he saw opportunity was ripe to get rid of us both. He is the next in line, you know."

A repellant thought occurred to Leah. "Did he attempt to kill you, too?"

"He didn't need to at first. He thought I would hang for my father's murder. When that plan failed, he might have done something outright but for the evidence I had collected and entrusted to my solicitor. Although I had been discredited, a fortuitous second death that left Randall the earldom would change everything. A fresh flood of scrutiny would make my proof damning. In short, I blackmailed him into letting me live."

"My God, that is . . . Well, it is brilliant." She smiled approvingly. "You are a very resourceful man."

He pulled her to him, leaning close to murmur something in her ear but she held up a warning hand. "My hair!"

He rolled his eyes.

"Well, we just got it put back together."

Raising a brow, he looked at her askance. She patted her hair nervously. "Does it look awful?"

"Considering the entire disheveled effect, we best sneak you in the back door," he pronounced after a thorough inspection. "Let's go before they notice we are missing and send the hounds after us."

As they made their way back to the house, Leah asked, "Morgan, how did Randall arrange to have you arrested? He had to have some sort of evidence."

"Yes. 'Some sort' is exactly the right way to phrase it," he answered sourly. "It was good enough, however, when greased with a liberal amount of bribes. One doesn't falsely arrest a peer of the realm without some clever manipulation.

"In my case, the most incriminating item was a letter found among my father's effects. It was supposedly written by my father instructing Humbolt to have his will changed to increase Randall's benefit. It was an excellent fake and it was judged for a time to be real. It was brought out that my father and I had quarreled before I left. But it was not a great rift. We had no animosity, and he had no cause to disinherit me."

"Well, then it obviously implicates Randall since he was now the beneficiary of the will."

They cleared the woods and were taking the lawn in long strides. Leah, barely winded, kept pace with him, attentive to every word.

"But the letter was not a registered will and testament. It did not hold in the end, and since it did not, it appeared as if Randall had no motive for the deed. But I did. It was surmised that I acted to keep Humbolt from receiving the letter and registering it with the courts so as to ensure my inheritance remained intact."

He suddenly stopped, and Leah did as well, staring at him as he squinted at the house, but he wasn't looking at the mansion. His voice grew husky as he continued.

"We had quarreled, my father and I. I had tried to warn him about Randall, about how he was so attentive to Glorianna, but he had misunderstood. He thought I meant to defame Glorianna or perhaps to insinuate that he could not keep a young wife content. It was a ridiculous argument, but he was adamant.

"He refused to believe Randall would cuckold him or that anything untoward was going on. He was always like that when it came to Randall. He didn't see him for what he was but the idealized vision of his sister's child. In any event, I stormed out, but thought better of it after a few hours at the village pub. Calmer and determined to make him understand, I returned."

He drew in a ragged breath and closed his eyes. Leah braced herself, feeling the tension around him thicken as he went on.

"I went into the library and I saw him. . . . He was slumped over at his desk. I thought he was sleeping. Then I felt a draft, and I saw the glass broken in the French doors. I became alarmed. When I went to him and tried to wake him, he wouldn't wake. You can't imagine the sick feeling that came over me then as I pulled him back into the chair. He was heavy and there was all this blood. It was on my hands, on my clothes. The head footman came in right then. He saw me like that, over my father, covered in his blood. . . ."

"Oh, God, Morgan . . ." Leah grasped both of his hands in hers. They were shaking. She brought them to her lips and pressed anxious kisses to them.

"The letter, the quarrel, and Phelps finding me like that made the case," he said. "In a few weeks, I was in jail. I tell you, Blackie, I thought that was the end of me. I had begun to figure it out. But I was already judged the guilty one and no one would believe a word I said. I might have hung if not for Humbolt."

"But you said he thought you guilty, or at least he wasn't sure."

"Just so, but he is a man dedicated to truth. He determined the letter could not be upheld as a replacement to the standing will, so I inherited. I gained my freedom by using a good deal of money to have the magistrate and local constables paid to release me. They arranged the inquest verdict to be that he had discovered a burglar in the act and was murdered. Does it shock you to know I stooped to the same methods of my enemy? It should. But it was the only way for me to escape the gallows. So you see, I am no better than Randall in the end."

Her voice was sharp with anger. "It is a large difference, Morgan, if you are innocent of murder and he is guilty."

One side of his mouth curled upward. "You can be inordinately fierce sometimes, do you know that?"

"Indeed, when I believe wholeheartedly in something, as I do you."

"Ah. So you believe in the Wicked Earl, do you?"

"I do. I have enormous faith in you."

The soft pleasure in his face suddenly hardened. "You'd best not. I will disappoint you some day if you think me heroic. I promise I will."

"What do you mean?" Disquiet crept into her veins, chasing the beautiful feelings left from their interlude in the woods. She had felt a genuine closeness with him as he'd told her his story, a sense that he had opened up at last. This sudden blast of ice felt like a slap.

"Just heed me, Blackie. Come on, let's get you inside so you can change." He looked grim as he took her arm and led her to the back door. "The kitchens should be busy enough with getting dinner out. Let us hope none of the servants notice that my sneaking you in the back door has become a habit."

T HE FIRST THING Morgan noticed about Sanderson that night when he joined the others after dinner for the final rounds of the billiards contest was that he appeared nervous. This was unlike him, and it raised Morgan's suspicions.

Watching closely, Morgan noticed how he repeatedly jerked his gaze up to the mantel clock. About ten o'clock, a dark-haired woman walked by the open door of the billiard room. Morgan did not miss the sideways glance she cast into the room, nor the way Sanderson appeared studiously casual as he muttered something about the privy and exited the room.

He paused, looking after his nemesis speculatively. Did Randall have a mistress already? Morgan mulled this over, thinking perhaps he might be able to use this fact. He wanted to win Glorianna's confidence. This could be a way. How fortuitous for him that Randall was being so indiscreet.

More immediately, Randall's secret rendezvous meant Glorianna was not being watched right now. This was Morgan's chance.

The other guests were spread out around the house. Most were due to leave on the morrow, so the mood of merriment was high. Spirits were flowing freely and the laughter was louder, more raucous. This gave Morgan a good idea of where to find Glorianna.

The older, more sedate guests often gathered in the cozy salon appointed with rich tapestries and heavily carved antiques. It was a room well suited for those like Glorianna, whose romantic notions of times gone by when things were more "civilized" rejected the disorder going on elsewhere in the house.

Glorianna looked up as he approached her. Her face registered surprise, then pleasure. He detected a sheen of tears in her eyes. His own stung, as well, to his mortification. He suppressed the urge to embrace her.

She had no such compunction about showing her emotion. Leaping up, she took him in her surprisingly strong arms. "You are here. I can't believe I am actually seeing you at last." She spoke barely above a whisper. "I've been waiting."

"Glorianna," he murmured, giving in briefly to the urge to return her affection. It was good to see her again, flooding him with a feeling of warmth, and of home.

He felt closer to his father in that moment when he held her, and it was then he realized just why he had needed so badly to find a way to her. For her sake, yes, but for his as well. Being kept from his father's widow was to have the last connection to Evan, to his whole previous life.

Looking down at her friends, Glorianna presented them each in turn. They responded enthusiastically, sweeping deep curtsies before him.

Glorianna turned her shining face back to Morgan. "I haven't seen you in so long."

"I was hoping you would honor me with your company," he said in a voice that was strong. He hadn't been sure of it, afraid it would waver with the emotion riding inside him. "We have much to catch up on. A stroll through the gardens on this pleasant evening would be just the thing." He paused meaningfully, staring hard at her. "I am certain we will be undisturbed."

"Oh. Oh! Yes, of course. That would be lovely." She beamed to those about her. "If you will excuse us."

It was on the way out the door Morgan noticed that Leah sat with her mother at a card table. There was a devastated expression on her face. He knew she had an irrational jealousy of Glorianna, but he would explain it later.

Outside was cool and clear, with a hint of moisture in the air. The sounds of night sealed them in a pleasant symphony of cricket song and faraway calls from animals best left unimagined.

They were quiet in the darkness for a long time. Morgan said at last, "I came as soon as I heard of your marriage."

"Oh, Morgan, I hope you do not mind."

"I mind only if you do. I only wanted your happiness."

"I know. It always meant so much to me, your friendship. How I've missed that. There were times when I was so sad and very confused. . . . I would have loved to have you to talk with. Remember how Evan and you and I would sit for hours? We would discuss absolutely everything."

"I was afraid we bored you, debating the villainy of Richard III and other obscure topics."

"I loved it. I loved every moment with your father."

"Then you miss him, too?"

"Each day. A little less painfully with time, but no less frequently. He was an extraordinary man."

"But you have Randall now."

She bowed her head so he couldn't see her face. "Yes . . . I couldn't be alone. He was so strong for me, tireless when I needed him most. Without you, Morgan, I had no one. Randall took care of everything and I am so grateful for his help."

Morgan could well imagine how quickly Sanderson had made himself indispensable to the bereft widow. A sudden clutch of rage gripped him.

"I want you to be happy," Morgan repeated, repressing his temper. "Come, walk with me. Tell me of your life now. I want to know everything."

"And you," she said, taking his arm as they set off down the path into the small walled garden. Before them lay a neatly trimmed symmetrical topiary with a brick path wide enough for two. "I want to know especially about this Leah Brodie. I was so pleased when I heard of your association. Tell me of her."

How could he explain a woman like Leah? he thought. Where does one start? And who would believe him if he told the truth?

Still, he couldn't suppress a smile as he began, "We met while riding one morning. She had a bit of a run-in with some locals who had mistaken her for someone else, and I helped her find her way home. It was a brief meeting, but memorable. I found once I had sent her on her way that I couldn't put her out of my mind."

All of which was absolutely true.

She asked more questions. He indulged her curiosity

awhile longer, then deftly turned the conversation. "But we must talk of you," he insisted slyly, "I want to know everything about Randall, how you came to be engaged and married so quickly."

Her laughter trilled into the darkness, "Randall, as you know, is a dear, dear man. It started soon after the funeral when I was quite lost. When you had all that terrible trouble, he was such a good friend. . . ."

Morgan listened, his brain working quickly to assimilate the tidbits of insight she furnished. He asked offhand questions to elicit the details he craved. And he didn't feel the slightest twinge of conscience as she spoke of the man she now called husband.

Not even when he thought of killing him.

Chapter 13

THE NEXT MORNING, Morgan's first thought was of Leah. He wanted to speak with her before her family left. Most of the guests were preparing to depart either sometime today or the next day. When he couldn't find her at breakfast, he figured she had gone out with the group who liked to ride in the mornings.

Morgan went to the barn, hoping to head her off when he saw her coming in. He whiled the time trying to coax a skittish barn cat to him. The animal kept watching warily, taking one slow step at a time toward the enticement of a nice rub in the patch of sunlight spilling in through the open barn door where Morgan was hunkered down. The light was suddenly cut off and the sound of the door slamming sent the cat leaping for the shadows. Morgan turned to see Sanderson in front of them. He stood and turned to face him.

"All alone?" he asked.

"What I have to say is for your ears alone."

"I can hardly wait."

"It's simple. You broke our agreement. I was told of your little stroll with my wife."

"I didn't enter into any agreement with you. I don't deal with craven slime."

Sanderson flashed a look of rage before assuming his usual demeanor of calm. "You leave me no choice but to show you that I mean to keep you away from Glorianna. Not that I expect you two to ignore each other, of course. That would be unseemly. I would have arranged a civil meeting with Glorianna, in public, with me present. On my terms. But you went about it the wrong way. I heard you spent time alone with her. That was foolish. It made me very upset."

"Good," Morgan said, sauntering closer. He was pleased to see Sanderson take a step back, although the glare in his eyes didn't dim at all.

Morgan gave his enemy a look of pure disgust. "Because this is just the beginning. You think you're 'upset' now, I think you'll collapse from the vapors when you see what is coming."

Sanderson's face twitched. "You must have little care for the lovely Miss Brodie."

At the sound of Leah's name coming from Sanderson's lips, Morgan felt a surge of stark rage turn his world red. With an effort, he kept control. "In fact, you bastard, I am quite certain nothing will happen to Miss Brodie. Because if it does, I can assure you I will find new ways to make you feel pain that haven't been dreamt of since the Spanish Inquisition. If Miss Brodie is in any way compromised or harmed or even looked at wrongly—well, let us say you wouldn't want that, you see, because then I would be really dangerous. There would be no reason not to do what I so desperately want to do. No reason at all. You don't want me with nothing to lose, Randall."

In a lightning-quick motion, he reached out and grabbed Randall by the throat. The man yelped, the whites of his eyes glowing in the dimness. Morgan's fingers dug into the other man's windpipe, squeezing just enough to immobilize him.

Exhilaration poured through him. "This scar isn't the only

thing I received while in prison," he spat. "Those guards have interesting ways of subduing uncooperative prisoners. And I, as you may know, learn quickly."

Sanderson swallowed. Morgan felt the lump of his Adam's apple move against his hand. "There exists a method for crushing the windpipe so that lazy prison doctors assume the man died of natural causes. Did you know the windpipe was that delicate? I was amazed myself. Fascinating what one learns in the most unlikely of places. Apparently just one squeeze"—he drew out the word as he applied more pressure, until he felt Sanderson's knees buckling—"and it collapses. I found that utterly fascinating. And the beauty of it is that the death is never known to be a murder, at least a prison surgeon never bothered to figure it out. Would I really get away with it? Perhaps. But it might be worth finding out, if I had nothing to live for."

Morgan felt cold, colder than he'd ever been in his life. It felt so good and clean, like he had been before his life got confused and muddled. Before Leah.

Suddenly, he released Sanderson and stepped back.

He fought to steady his breath. The last thing he wanted Sanderson to see was any speck of weakness, but he had to get control of himself.

He had wanted to kill him. He had held Sanderson's throat, felt the life pulse beneath his hand. He had only to make one small movement, and it would all be over.

He had frightened himself because *he had liked it.*

"You're insane," Sanderson croaked, rubbing his throat as he studied Morgan.

"I've become what circumstances dictate, much of which is due to you."

"Oh, not me. I'm flattered, but I think it is you more than I commanding your demons. I think it is your own conscience that has turned you mean. How it must haunt you that the last words spoken between you and your father were in anger."

Morgan battled the sensation of his own windpipe collapsing. Sensing the weakening in his prey, Sanderson pressed his advantage. "It *is* terrible that your father died believing you thought him unable to please his wife. Oh, I heard. I made it my business to know as much as possible of what went on in that house. Do you think he believed you were jealous of me? You know, I always thought your pretense of brotherly concern for your father's wife a bit farfetched. Rumors had been spreading about you and Glorianna. Oh, the gossip that reached his ears! I should know, I was the one who told him."

Morgan froze. He knew he mustn't listen to the manipulative words, but his heart contracted into a knot. Outside, he remained calm, fixing his gaze into Sanderson's gleaming eyes so that he would know he wasn't winning.

But inside, he felt as if his footing was coming out from under him as one caught in a landslide.

"In good conscience, devoted nephew that I am, I had to let him know about what people were saying. Even if they weren't." He laughed again, an abrupt, jarring sound. "Oh, you should have seen the look on his face. He lapped up every word."

Morgan forced himself to speak. "If indeed you told my father this refuse, it would only prove to him what I had been telling him for years about you. He was no fool. He would have never believed I would betray him. I rather think your ploy served to make him realize how right I always was. You overplayed your hand with him. You are making the same mistake with me."

"Are you so very sure?" Sanderson taunted. "You know your father never would think ill of me. It was his one blind spot. He died thinking you a cad and a bounder, Morgan, and you cannot stand that and you cannot make it right. Why, I don't believe you even have the stomach for this." His eyes snapped wide in realization. "You don't, do you? You hate it. Yes. Let's see. I remember how you were before this. Not a speck of bloodlust in you."

"If it gives you comfort to have your delusions, then by all means, indulge. It will make no difference to me."

Sanderson was wary. He remained silent. That was good,

Morgan thought, because if the man hadn't stopped talking, he was going to have to put an end to the disturbing flow of words, one way or another. His hand itched to feel that scrawny throat back in his grasp.

Morgan continued. "The time will come when you recognize just how badly you have miscalculated. When you look into my face and know without a doubt that death is inevitable, you will know everything I suffered at your hands. You took everything away from me. I will take everything away from you and leave you alive just long enough to know it."

Sanderson licked his dry lips. "Then you would be the murderer you claim you are not."

"It is not murder to kill justly."

"You will never prove anything. The world will condemn you. You will lose everything."

"I have already lost everything," Morgan said.

Sanderson snapped his mouth closed and appeared disconcerted, unsure of himself for the briefest of moments.

"Now get out of here because Miss Brodie is due back from riding any moment now. And if I ever see you so much as look at her, I'll rip out your throat and feed it to you."

Sanderson's lips curled, but he kept his counsel and left.

Morgan stood in the shadows, still as a statue, clenching his fists against the trembling rage rippling through him. So still, in fact, the timid cat came to sniff at his heels, staring up at him with her diamond-shaped eyes surrounded by unearthly gold. Her hackles rose as she picked up his tension, and she darted away. Leaving Morgan quite alone.

And aching.

L EAH WAS RETURNING from posting two letters, one to Julia, the other to Laura in Ceylon, when she met Morgan in the downstairs hall.

Her guard came up as she remembered the tender scene she had witnessed the previous day between him and Glorianna. She knew Morgan's interest in the woman was not of a romantic nature, and she accepted that. But as she had watched him lead his stepmother outside for a private stroll, she had felt every bit the outsider she was. It was a sad, sober realization.

She had decided she was not going to get sensitive about this. It might not be in her nature to be retiring and patient, but neither was she the type to sulk over anything for long. She was restless and brash and many other faults that were less than ideal, but she was an optimist to her core, and forgiving to a fault. And Morgan's eyes, warm and soft when he looked at her, had only to meet hers and she felt a thrill.

"I've been looking for you," he said.

"I've been here," she said, wincing at the inanity. She wanted to say, "I've been here waiting for you to remember me—where have *you* been?" but that would start an argument and she didn't want to argue with him. She wanted to kiss him.

"I suppose your family is getting set to leave soon. Will you be riding out today or tomorrow?"

"First thing in the morning. We are going to Weymouth next. The regatta. But we will not stay out the entire week. Mother wants to return to London for a brief respite from the society whirl. Julia is accompanying Raphael there when he travels for business and it will be a reunion of sorts. We all cannot wait to see Cosette."

He nodded, then lifted his gaze and ran it from left to right, surveying their surroundings as if he expected someone was watching. Taking her hand, he said, "Come here," and led her down the hall into a small parlor that was empty.

Pulling her into his arms with one arm, he grabbed her chin and jerked her head back for a long, thorough kiss. Leah melted, yielding to the tender demands of his mouth, sighing in contentment.

"Listen to me," he said roughly, leveling a serious gaze at her. "I am not coming to Weymouth. I wish I could. I hate abandoning you now, but I have to go to London. I have to take care of some . . . some business."

She swallowed and nodded, incapable of speech. Her eyes were fastened on his mouth and although she heard and understood him, all she really could think about was how much she wanted him to kiss her again.

He touched her face, lightly tracing the contour of a prominent cheekbone with his fingertip. "I don't want you to be afraid. I've got my men watching over you. They will take shifts so there will be someone with you at all times, even at night. When I get to London, I will arrange for better detectives, trained men who can ensure you are safe at all times. Until then I want you to cooperate with Spencer and Hallorhan. And have mercy on them. The poor fellows don't know what they are up against."

She nodded, feeling light and dreamy in his arms. His scent was making her dizzy. "I will."

"You aren't afraid, are you?"

"Not about my safety," she assured him. "I know poor old Hallorhan can do his duty as long as I don't take him for a trot in the woods."

He grinned. "That's my girl." His smile vanished and his brows jerked down. "I don't want to leave you."

A flutter of panic rose in a giddy wave, taking her by surprise. She was suddenly gripped by an irrational fear that she would never see him again.

The warmth drained out of her and she closed her fingers around his hands, clasping them desperately. "Then don't. Please. Don't."

He frowned. "What's this?"

"I don't want you to go."

He chuckled softly. "I know. I'll come to you soon. I'll give you my direction so you can send me a message when you arrive in London."

"No." She looked away, biting her lip. "I am absolutely serious about this, Morgan. I don't want you to go."

He regarded her curiously. "Blackie? What is it?"

"I mean that I am afraid all of a sudden. Oh, not for me—for you. Randall is dangerous. He's killed once. The proof of his guilt you hold over him may not save you if he thought you were becoming more of a threat—he would take the risk, wouldn't he? I understand how you hurt, Morgan. I know what he did to you, but what will you gain out of it all? Nothing will bring your father back. Would it be so difficult just to let things be as they are?"

He released her, his expression incredulous. "You cannot be serious. You know what he did. *You know what he took from me.*"

She closed her eyes. "And he's still taking. No. You're giving it—the whole of your life to that man. It won't end until it destroys you."

He made a sound of disgust. "This will *never* be settled until Sanderson gets his due."

"And does it not matter what you wind up with in the bargain? Not even if it leaves you dead! Is it so selfish of me not to want to grieve for you? And what if I do the same as you are doing now and decide to avenge you—would that be a good idea? Shall we all sacrifice our lives for something that's lost and gone? Why not keep it going until Randall wipes out all of us, for bloody hell!"

His expression grew fierce. "I don't have the luxury of doing anything else. This is not my choice." Dropping his arms, he scowled darkly and turned away.

She felt immediate remorse at her outburst. "I didn't want to quarrel. Morgan, please just think about what I've said, consider the future, a different future. Surely things have changed since we started. The way we feel—"

"Nothing's changed for me," he snapped, his tone so cold it brought Leah up with a start. "Perhaps for you, but I am just as determined as I always was. I will not let that man get away to live the rest of his life in peace."

"So you will give up your own peace and that of everyone who cares for you for revenge."

"Justice," he corrected sharply.

She jutted her chin out. "*Revenge.* You may fool yourself, but I know what you want. It is nothing so gracious. It is common and cheap. Revenge—plain and simple."

Spinning on her heel, she went to the door.

"Leah," Morgan barked, coming to lay his hand over hers as she reached for the doorknob. "Keep Spencer or Hallorhan with you at all times. Cooperate with them."

She did not turn around. "You are the one who needs to be safe. Please, Morgan, *please* be safe." She wanted to say more, but the tears were in her voice and she knew Morgan hated when she cried.

He released her hand. "I'll see you in London."

She hoped he was right.

THE REGATTA AT Weymouth was tedious. Lady Dahlia was there, with Phyllida by her side, and they were both bristling with malicious curiosity.

"Waring is not with you?" Dahlia smirked.

"He has family business to attend to."

Exchanging a smug look with Phyllida, Dahlia replied, "I'm sure." As they sauntered off, the sound of their giggles drifted back to Leah. She looked away to catch her mother's concerned look. She was sorry to have her mother disconcerted.

It was not beyond Leah's abilities to put Dahlia in her place, but she wasn't feeling up to it. The confrontation with Morgan had left her deflated, and feeling like a fool, begging him to stay with her as she had.

She supposed he was in London, counting himself well rid of a clinging vine. It was different for a man, she knew, for dalliances were a part of masculine life. For women, it was a matter of the heart, not just the body. She'd deluded herself that the intimacy they had shared would make a bit of difference.

He'd said as much.

And she had made a terrible mistake.

She went upstairs, seeking a quiet spot, and found herself in the nursery where her sisters were busy playing with the other guest's children. Immediately, she knew it had been a good idea to come.

"Leah!" Marie sang with a happy smile and ran to embrace her. The small arms around her felt so good.

"Come play with us," her littlest sister requested.

Leah allowed herself to be led by the hand into the group of children. "All right," she said and organized them in a game of blindman's bluff. This was delightfully diverting until Freddie Mickland, a thirteen-year-old viscount who was supposedly rendered sightless by the blindfold affixed across his eyes, raised his hands precisely on level of Leah's breasts and rushed unerringly toward her. She rapped him soundly on the head before he could make contact and took the girls off to play doll party *without* the boys.

When it was time for tea, she sent a maid to say she had a headache and headed for her room. She dreaded facing the twisted smiles on Dahlia's and Phyllida's faces and all the other speculation that would, by now, be buzzing about her as to precisely where the earl of Waring had gone now that he wasn't playing the suitor.

She hadn't taken to her bed but ten minutes when Desdemona knocked and came in. Standing with her hands on her hips, she regarded Leah with a stern eye.

"Brodie women do not hide," she announced, coming to the bed and throwing off the counterpane Leah had been clutching like a child's security blanket.

"If you and the earl have had a falling out, you are not to show one trace of it being of any consequence to you, do you understand? I did not raise any of my girls to shrink away from a challenge. You hold your head up and comport yourself like the well-bred miss that you are. Now get dressed and come down into the salon before there is talk."

"But I have the migrims—"

"You are lovesick, that is all. Now, unless you want the entire polite world to know it, you will do as I advise."

Under her mother's supervision, she dressed in her best dress, looking long and slender and lovely in the lavender-sprigged muslin. Her eyes wore shadows under them. Relenting from her usual strictness over cosmetics, Desdemona allowed Leah to smear some color onto her cheeks and soften her drawn appearance with a light dusting of powder, then examined her closely for flaws.

Her gaze was keen as it coolly appraised her daughter. Leah held herself stiff and straight because suddenly she wanted to fling herself into those capable, safe arms and wail like a babe.

Wiping away some of the rice powder, Desdemona nodded her approval. "We mustn't look as if we're trying. There. You look lovely."

"Thank you, Mother. I'm sorry for this."

"There's my brave girl. Any man who would not see your worth is obviously a fool, and the Brodie women never suffer a fool for a husband. Now. Make me proud."

"Oh, Mother," Leah choked. "I never seem to be able to do that, and I want to so much."

Desdemona stiffened, a look of astonishment on her face. "Why, what makes you say such a preposterous thing? You have *always* made me proud."

Leah was stupefied. "But . . . but I . . . I'm so impulsive and sometimes . . . Carl Enders . . . the soufflé."

Waving her hand, Desdemona dismissed Leah's concern. "You are like a cat, Leah. You always land on your feet. I will not say that was the most glorious moment of my years as a mother when I learned you were responsible for Mr. Enders wearing French cuisine, but I'm made of sterner stuff than that." She reached up and tucked a stray strand of hair into its pin. "And besides, I was to blame somewhat for rushing you into marriage. It was the end of the season, and I thought you would never choose and after what happened to Julia, I just wanted you safe." She sighed, her face softening. "Your father keeps telling me I push too hard. If I do, it is only because I want the best for you."

"Mother," Leah said brokenly, her emotions rising to a dangerous pitch.

Her mother drew herself up at the break in Leah's voice and her sternness returned. It was effective to douse the hot sting of blood in Leah's cheeks and the prick of tears scalding her eyes.

"We have an appearance to make." She gave her daughter a bracing smile. "Are you ready?"

"Yes. I am ready, Mother." Leah's voice was calm, full of self-assurance.

Her mother grabbed her hand and gave it a squeeze and the two women headed out the door.

THEY WERE IN London three days when Julia arrived. She and Raphael, holding Cosette, came out onto the terrace to join the afternoon tea taken alfresco.

Leah leaped up and ran for her niece. Recognizing her, Cosette leaned out from her father's arms, hands outstretched. The baby smelled fresh and clean and wonderful as Leah hugged her close. Cosette gazed into Leah's eyes, waved her hands in the air, and said, "Gah!"

"Here, let her see her grandmother," Desdemona said, shouldering up to take the baby from her.

Julia embraced Leah. "I am so glad we've come although the journey was a trial. I haven't traveled at all since the baby because she hates being confined. She cried terribly at being cooped up in the carriage."

They went to the settee to sit together. "Raphael had some business of sorts in London," Julia explained. "I thought it might be a good time for me to break out of my cocoon. Oh, who am I kidding—nothing could have kept me away when I read your last letter." Her expression sharpened. "How are you faring?"

Unable to speak, Leah averted her eyes.

"Oh, Leah, you poor girl." Julia put her arm around her shoulders and said, "I am here, now. We will sort all of this out when we can talk later."

"I am so happy you've come," Leah said, then glanced at the others in the room. Cosette smiled up into Leah's face, showing off a single tooth.

It was good to be with family. Although it couldn't take away her loneliness, it did give her a sense of peace. She'd never known the people she'd grown up with, fought with, stuck her tongue out at, and cried over were this wonderful.

Then she thought of Morgan, who had no one. She steeled herself against the welling of sadness, telling herself it was his own choice.

He didn't want anyone, and that, it seemed, was final.

⟵——————⟶

R APHAEL LEFT HIS wife and daughter at the Cravensmore mansion and made his way the short distance to his own palatial town house where his solicitors were already convened in the library and waiting for his arrival.

He was immediately informed on the whereabouts of the earl of Waring. The address of the fashionable rooms on St. James Waring used for his London residence was handed to Raphael, and he immediately dispatched a footman with his calling card.

Then he went on an urgent appointment, from which he returned whistling. Waring's reply was waiting for him. Raphael was to call the following afternoon.

He freshened his appearance and went to collect his family. He slept well that night, noncommittal when Julia repeatedly asked him what had him looking like the cat that swallowed the canary.

The next day, Raphael rapped upon the solid mahogany door of Waring's rooms at the appointed hour and was admitted by a stern-looking butler. He was shown into the library where Waring sat behind an immense carved desk.

His appearance of polite pleasure did not completely mask his tension, at least not to Raphael's discerning eye, as he came to his feet. "Monsieur le Viscount, what an unexpected pleasure to have heard from you yesterday. To what do I owe this honor?"

Raphael surveyed the man as the two exchanged greetings. Waring had a closed look to his face. Lines roughened his skin. He had a certain presence Raphael had noted before, an air of steely resolve that was underscored by the direct look in his eye, eyes not warmed by the welcoming smile fitted with precision over his mouth.

"Indeed, I intend to make that quite clear," Raphael retorted, giving the man his own cool look. He sat in the chair Morgan indicated. "My wife is upset, Waring. I told you I would not tolerate that."

Taking the seat opposite, they both faced a huge hearth, banked now and unneeded in the warmth of midsummer. Waring continued to appear relaxed despite Raphael's words. "I am sorry to hear of it. May I be of help?"

"Most assuredly. The source of the situation is her concern for her sister whose affiliation with you has brought nothing but unhappiness. A recent letter had the viscountess so alarmed she insisted on accompanying me to London despite her resolve not to subject our daughter to lengthy travel."

Morgan didn't move a muscle. His gaze stayed firmly on Raphael. "I regret any distress I have caused."

"Yes, well, that does nothing to aid me. The problem is you are a stubborn mule, I gather from my wife's conversations with Leah. Your situation is hopeless and still you persist."

"Pardon me?"

"This quest you are on. It has Leah quite overset. She fears you will find nothing but a tragic end."

"Not so. I expect success very soon."

"So you got Humbolt to speak to you, did you?" Raphael noted the widening of Waring's eyes. "Don't be alarmed. Yes, I read the letter Leah wrote to my wife, at my wife's request, but none of the information went any further, I can assure you. I can be the most discreet of men when I wish. I am assuming you are in London on this plan of yours to expose Randall Sanderson."

Waring considered him, obviously making up his mind whether or not to trust Raphael. He seemed to reach a decision swiftly.

"It is true, I have been gathering evidence against Randall since the day I was released from prison. I have spoken to or corresponded with witnesses who can put together a fairly convincing case to incriminate him."

"Can you convict him?"

"I don't believe I will be successful in doing so. The local officials would have to admit they'd been bribed, first by Sanderson, then by me. I've resigned myself to the fact that there will be no satisfaction gained through the courts."

"Then what is your redress?"

"The court of public opinion, sir. It is imperative to my plan that the most damning evidence that is as sensational and tawdry as possible be disseminated at the right time."

"Ho, my lord Waring, I see your game. It is a duel you are after. Not legal, exactly, but no one would censure you, would they, under the circumstances? It is quite clever. Yes." He narrowed his eyes at the man, reassessing him. "Indeed, I might have come up with something like it in your shoes. Now, my sister-in-law seems to think a Mr. Humbolt is central to this plan. She acquainted me with your dilemma in this matter, and I gather you have yet to impress upon your late father's untrusting man of affairs the wisdom in aiding you. Toward that end, I have devised a plan of my own, and executed it as I am impatient in the extreme."

"That is rather presumptuous," Waring said. Raphael sensed the anger held in check.

"Are you not at least curious?" Raphael inquired.

"Naturally."

"You see, it occurred to me that the key to this whole thing lies in that letter that was found to disinherit you. It was the most incriminating piece of evidence against you. It occurred to me if there was a false letter—and of course it was false, wasn't it?—then there would be real letters, as is common to use with one's man of affairs, giving instructions, directing how the estate is to be invested and so forth that would be equally as persuasive, hopefully to the opposite end as the forged one."

Waring shot forward in his chair. "By God!"

"Don't trouble yourself to admire my brilliance. What with all you have on your mind, I took it upon myself to contact this Mr. Humbolt through my own solicitors and found him not adverse to listening to my reasoning."

"Humbolt spoke to you?"

"Well, I am not you, am I? He has no grudge against me. It seems the fact that, as your family's solicitor, he was aware of how you utilized your inheritance to bribe your way out of prison, and this left a sour taste in his mouth. But I assured him anyone would do the same to save themselves, guilty or not. In addition, once we had gotten a look at the correspondence he's kept, he was full of apology. I am afraid you are due to be subjected to some rather intensive pleas for forgiveness."

Morgan snorted, disbelief mixed with wonder. "Do you mean to tell me he has suddenly decided I am innocent?"

"He realized that these letters would contain clues to decide that very thing." Raphael smiled at the way Waring tensed with interest. "His office was incredibly well organized, and he was able to lay his hands on several letters immediately. I have copies of them with me today." He produced a packet of papers from the inside pocket of his coat. "Which goes to show there is no substitute for a good man of affairs."

There was a long silence. Raphael raised his brows. "Well? Are you not pleased?"

Morgan looked at his guest sharply. "The question that begs answer, however, is why you would go through so much trouble on my behalf."

"Waring, allow me to explain something to you. I am a perverse fellow. I find I have the means and the time to follow whatever diversions interest me. You interest me. From that first conversation, I became curious."

Darkly, Morgan said, "I'm flattered."

"I would rather think you are not. You are not the kind of man to welcome another's interest, as am I. Aside from my wife's curiosity about you, or rather her concern as to whether you are pleasing her sister, I find myself intrigued."

"What exactly do you want from me, Fontvilliers?"

"Right now I want you to look at these letters. Your father

speaks quite highly of you in that first one there. Observe the date."

Raphael felt a sense of intrusion, as if he were spying on something very private as Morgan handled the documents with an air of reverence. To fill the silence, Raphael said, "That first one is dated three days before he died, you'll see. In the letter, he speaks of Mr. Humbolt's duty to include you more in the running of the estates, expressing his conviction that you will have good business sense. Hardly the sort of thing a man about to disinherit a son would be apt to write, is it?"

Raphael paused, stroking his chin. For no good reason, he decided to add, "I found myself rather impressed with his sentiments. You see, my own father cannot abide me. In any event, the effusive confidence is evident. It was this letter, when Mr. Humbolt reacquainted himself with its contents, that swayed him into cooperation."

Morgan's gaze narrowed. "He didn't remember it?"

"I mentioned the man is obsessively organized. It is my experience that this is usually the antidote for forgetfulness. Mr. Humbolt appears the type whose precision in his duties is a cover for chronic absentmindedness."

Nodding, Morgan mused, "I recall my father mentioning the man was occasionally tedious with regard to that particular problem."

Raphael gestured to the other letter in the file. "That one is dated the month before your father's death. You'll see the section I've indicated." Raphael pointed.

Morgan's right hand went to the scar on his cheek, tracing its lines as he frowned over the carefully lettered missive. "He merely makes mention of a new servant about whom he wanted Humbolt to check references."

"References your father wanted Humbolt to *double*-check. The initial checks were done before his hiring, but apparently your father had some question about the man."

Waring's head snapped up, his face ablaze. "*That's* how Sanderson did it—he hired someone to pose as a servant."

"It would seem. Your Mr. Humbolt never did check the

references again. Your father's death erased all need for the precaution."

Waring came to his feet, suddenly restless. "I never could see Sanderson doing it himself. One cannot imagine him having the stomach, or even the strength. My father was not a small man, and still robust. He wouldn't have been easy to overpower, even with a weapon. Randall knew he had to have someone else to do it."

Raphael diverted his gaze. "Well, my good deed is done. The rest is up to you, Waring, although I urge you to resolve this in a prompt manner so that you may again address the matter of your intentions toward my wife's sister. And then my wife can stop worrying."

Morgan gave a gruff laugh. "You've apparently spent so much time delving into the past, you are not au courant. I am afraid I am no longer in Miss Brodie's favor. Which is a damnable nuisance as the chit is proving hard to put out of mind."

"Really? How odd that Julia would persist in believing otherwise." Raphael shrugged. "In the end, it doesn't matter. The detecting game amused me. Do let me know how it turns out. Oh, I instructed Mr. Humbolt that you would more than likely be interested in those references mentioned in the letter. I advised him that he should be prepared for a visit from you very soon. No doubt, you will take charge capably from here."

He rose, reaching for the gloves he had laid on the table next to him. The gesture seemed to snap Morgan to attention. He stepped away from the hearth and gestured to the sideboard where port and whiskey were decanted in cut-glass crystal. "I apologize for my rudeness, monsieur le viscount. I neglected even to offer you a drink."

"It is rather early," Raphael said. "Once, it wouldn't have mattered, but my talent for imbibing spirits has waned over the years. Thank you anyway."

"Then join me for dinner tonight at my club."

"Very well," Raphael replied. "I'll see you this evening. I would be most interested in hearing the tale of your estrangement from my lovely sister-in-law. I am certain my wife will be quite put out to hear of it. She had her mind made up that yours was to be the *grande affaire*."

Waring pursed his lips, looking troubled. "I fear she is destined to disappointment."

Chapter 14

LEAH HAD GROWN quite used to her bodyguards. Morgan had secretly arranged with the head footmen to have his men pose as servants, so they were fairly unobtrusive in their guardianship. No one seemed to take especial notice of Spencer keeping a watchful eye over her, or Hallorhan's long frame shadowing her whenever she went out.

She wanted Morgan to receive good reports on her behavior. She had promised, after all, and at least he wouldn't have that worry, she told herself when she trotted tamely in the park while dreaming of open moorland and the scent of heather. It wasn't as if there was anything fun to do in London anyway. The city was all but deserted, the ton having fled the fog-filled heat for the cooler climes of their country estates. She was glad to be here, however. Her father came home every night and Julia's family was frequently present.

She thought of Laura often. This London reunion didn't seem complete without her lively spirit. Leah dashed off letters full of chatty nonsense and bundled them with pictures drawn by Hope and Marie for the post. Laura was writing to Leah often these days, telling her of the wonders of Ceylon and begging for more news from home. Leah was always careful to put only happy things in her letters, wanting to offer a cheerful diversion in case Laura was feeling homesick. Not that Laura ever indicated she was. She seemed to be enjoying the exotic beauties of that far-off land and the devotion of her successful husband.

She seemed to be surrounded by lovers. Laura spoke glowingly of Nicholas in each letter. Raphael had a way of looking at Julia that made the air crackle and Mother was enjoying the close companionship of Father, smiling frequently these days, displaying a softness that always made Leah happy to see. It made Leah feel more alone.

She thought of Morgan often, and then always forced herself not to. This was a struggle repeated with maddening frequency throughout each day.

Morgan finally called at the end of the week, and by that time, Leah was prepared. She had promised herself she would be cool, aloof, filled with a regal dignity to make her mother weep with pride.

All of that went out of her head, however, when she swept into the parlor where Morgan awaited her. The sight of him took her breath away. He had the habit of doing that—taking her breath away. Not that he looked any different or especially grand. Just his same self, but that was enough to turn her knees watery and raise a lump of longing in her chest.

He came to her and took her hands, hesitating as if he would like to do more. "I have missed you," he said.

Leah stared stupidly, battling the swell of blistering joy. Then she remembered she was supposed to be cool, aloof, and regal. "It is good to see you again, my lord," she replied primly.

It wasn't as cool, aloof, and regal as she had planned, for Morgan looked to be fighting a smile.

She disengaged her hands and stuck out her chin.

"You are still angry with me. I thought you might be. In fact, I thought you might not receive me."

"I am not adverse to speaking with you," she told him. "We may remain friends."

"Friends?" He struck an insolent pose and let the smile go.

Spreading his hands out before him, he said, "So, let me have it, then."

"I do not know what you mean."

"You are spitting mad and trying to hide it—doing a miserable job of it, by the way. Freezing me out isn't your style, Blackie. You're too much a passionate person for it. So go ahead. Rant, scream, rail, and berate me. I'll admit I deserve it."

She smirked prettily at him. "I fear you do not know me as well as you think." She strolled behind a settee, trailing her hand over the carved back. "As for my ability to restrain my emotions, I will have no choice but to be insulted if you persist in calling me undisciplined."

His amusement was still evident in the way his eyes sparkled. "You haven't been at the champagne again, have you?"

Her back went ramrod straight and she blazed a glare at him. "I am not in the habit of taking spirits, my lord. How ill-bred of you to remind me of one tiny lapse."

He offered a shallow bow. "My apologies. I am a knave to bring it up."

"Indeed, that is exactly why I have reconsidered our association and I have come to the inevitable conclusion that there is no choice but to end it. You see, we have little in common—"

She was about to launch into a speech about how he was not the man she had thought he was and she was worthy of much more and all other manner of haughty things she'd rehearsed in front of her looking glass this week—but at that moment he grabbed her by the upper arms and pulled her to him. Leah caught only a glimpse of the determination in his face before he kissed her hard on the mouth.

She didn't resist, nor did she surrender. Remaining stock-still, she felt the gentle warmth soak into her bones in reaction to the skillful pressure of his lips. His scent lightened her head. The hard bite of his fingers was like a vise, but it felt good. The feel of his solid body along hers felt very, very good.

He broke away and stared into her eyes. "We have plenty in common. Do you want me to show you again just how much?"

Frantically, she searched for what she had planned so carefully to say to him. "You never really wanted anything . . . er . . . you got what you wanted. You are part of . . . um . . . society again. . . ." His lips were moist from their kiss and too diverting. What had she been saying? Oh. "You have what you wanted and . . . and . . ."

"Blackie."

"Yes?"

"Shut up."

He kissed her again and she felt that melting sensation begin to take over. It really was a nuisance when she had made her mind up to resist his effect on her and stand firm.

Twisting away, she struggled for breath. She broke out of his grasp and went to the window, seeking distance from him. "That is enough of that. Why did you come here, Morgan?"

He cleared his throat. "I would like to tell you all of what has been happening lately. That is *partly* why I have come." He quickly explained about Raphael's intervention with Humbolt and his subsequent success in gaining his confidence. "I suppose I have you to thank for that as well. Although I don't care for my business being discussed among your family members, I cannot be resentful of the results."

She said in her most haughty, sarcastic voice, "I am so glad I can be of service."

"Is that what you think? That I use you because you are of service?"

"I believe it is exactly the bargain we struck a few months ago. Is that not the case?"

"I need you," he said hoarsely. His hands fisted at his sides as he stared at her, rooted on the spot, his eyes blazing darkly. He meant it, she realized.

Leah was relieved that he did not reach for her. She very much doubted she could resist him right now. "I know," she said. "You needed me to get Glorianna. Now you have her."

"That's not all. Things *have* changed."

She couldn't suppress the hot flare of desperation that charged her voice. "What has changed, Morgan? Have you changed? Do you want anything different than you did?"

He blinked, and something shifted in his face. Looking away, she saw the throb at his temples from his clenching his jaw tightly.

"You see," she said. "It is just as it has always been. I don't blame you, you know. You never lied to me. You never promised me anything different. It is I who am at fault. I deluded myself because I wanted you to be someone you are not. I wanted you to feel something you cannot feel. At least I can be honest with myself. And I'm glad for what happened, truly I am. Sad, but happy. And not angry. Or at least, I'm trying hard not to be."

He said nothing.

She took in a deep, bracing breath. "Please leave now. And do not come here again. I think it's best if we see less of each other in the future."

"I am going to the Cravensmore ball," he said. "And don't ask me not to go. I will be there to keep a close eye on you."

Leah shrugged, pretending a nonchalance she didn't feel. "I will not cut you. We can remain friends. As long as you never touch me again."

He gave her a crooked smile and bowed low. "You ask too much." He grabbed his hat and gloves.

⌒

MORGAN ARRIVED EARLY at the Cravensmore estates the first day of the party. Leah had taken especial care with her toilette that morning, donning a pale persimmon frock that was one of her favorites for the way the soft material floated around her ankles when she walked and the flattering shade on her complexion. She took a moment to have Debra weave the matching ribbon into her hair and decided she looked quite well.

"My dear, you are shaking. Have you caught a chill?" the

duchess of Cravensmore inquired as Leah watched Morgan enter the room.

Leah smiled at the duchess seated next to her. Seeming ancient, the dear old woman had a wrinkled face, lively eyes, and a ready smile. She and her husband were their hosts, but the Brodie association with the Cravensmores ran much deeper than that.

"I am fine, your grace. I . . . I am a bit hungry. I suppose I should have eaten more at luncheon." She knew her tendency to jabber when she was nervous was starting, but she was helpless to stop it. She could feel Morgan's eyes on her. "The partridge was delicious, but I prefer it roasted, not baked. I cannot abide carrots, and although they were pleasantly glazed, I couldn't bring myself to eat them."

Out of the corner of her eyes, she could see Morgan was conversing with another group. He glanced at her from time to time, and she would have to jerk her eyes back to the duchess to keep from being caught staring at him.

The duchess nodded, patting Leah's hand. She was very hard of hearing—a malady she refused to acknowledge—and often misheard in conversation. "Yes, I agree Madam Bartram's affectations are quite faked. I can hardly abide her company myself." She frowned, seeming a bit confused. "But I don't believe she owns any parrots."

Used to the woman's peculiar responses, Leah smiled sweetly. "I agree, your grace."

The fine hairs on the back of her neck rose like a riled cat's, and she knew Morgan was staring. She refused to look at him. She absolutely would not, she promised herself, but her gaze crept sideways without her permission, made contact with his, and snapped back.

He was coming over!

His every advancing step kicked up her tension. She tried her best to divert herself, chattering frenetically to the duchess beside her, who nodded and smiled, unable to comprehend a word.

Then he was there in front of her, bowing and murmuring in that velvet voice of his, "Your servant, Miss Brodie."

She found it impossible to staunch the deep flush as he took her hand. "My lord."

His gaze melted her bones. His eyes had darkened into that nether shade that was neither green nor brown.

She gnawed on her bottom lip, angling a look up at him from under her lashes, feeling a sudden rush of uncertainty. She was doomed if it was always going to be like this. It was the two of them, even in this crowded room, somehow isolated and absorbed in each other. She noticed how his scar seemed to blend into the swarthiness of his skin. Other times, it could seem as if it were painted white, but when he was at ease, like now, it was barely noticeable.

She loved his scar.

"I do hope you have a good time at the party, Miss Brodie. I look forward to a dance tonight, if you will grant it. Good day."

The duchess leaned forward, tapping Leah on the shoulder. "My dear, who was that man?"

"Oh, your grace, I'm sorry I didn't present him to you." Leah shook the pleasant fog still clinging to her brain. "That is the earl of Waring."

The old woman nodded sagely and after a moment pronounced, "I didn't think him overbearing. I thought him quite charming."

The woman on the other side of the duchess leaned forward. She was a marchioness, Leah recalled. She was also opinionated and unkind.

"I hear he is quite the scoundrel," she said.

Leah shot her a scathing look. "The earl of Waring? Indeed, have you not met him? He was quite the rage at the Farthinghams'."

A thin, hollow-chested Mrs. Hanover hurried over, obviously keenly attuned to when good gossip was brewing. "I cannot think what you were thinking inviting him here, your grace! He's positively *not* received. *I* heard he was a recluse and didn't go out in society."

The marchioness waved her hand in the air, gesturing at Morgan's back. "There is no lack of speculation about just why he felt it necessary to hide for all those months on the continent. Did he think we'd forget that he'd been jailed? I can assure you that this brain"—She tapped her fork to her temple—"forgets nothing."

"Like an elephant," Leah murmured to herself.

"I say," a pretty blond woman a few years older than Leah said as she pulled up a seat, "my very good friend made his acquaintance recently and said she was quite taken with him. He is all the rage now and everyone wants him at their parties." Her sly eyes swiveled to Morgan. "I can see why."

Leah picked at the kid gloves on her lap. "I heard he was excessively boring."

The blond woman looked askance. "Well, I am looking forward to meeting him."

"I cannot see why. He has that awful scar on his face. He isn't very handsome."

The marchioness turned her small, glittering eyes on Leah. "That is right, I had heard he was keeping company with you. You must know him quite well. And then . . . well, I know these things happen when young people realize that they do not suit, but I do hope you are not bitter, Leah dear."

"I did speak to him several times and was considering deepening our friendship, but he was so deadly dull that I had to turn my attentions elsewhere." Leah cast a gauging glance to the blond woman. "You wouldn't like him, either."

Drawing down her eyelids to half-mast, the woman responded coolly, "I imagine a man like that would be out of the realm of a girl. You are so young. Perhaps his interests are a bit more . . . mature."

Leah fumed, not having any suitable retort at hand.

"What is this world coming to," the marchioness said, sitting up straighter, her corset groaning in protest, "when murderers are considered interesting and received in polite company?"

"Oh, dear," the duchess murmured. "I hope I didn't hear that correctly."

Leah's nostrils flared, like a little bull spying the scarlet threat. Abruptly, she stood. "There are two errors in your statement, madam. One is that the earl of Waring is a murderer. He is not. He was cleared of suspicion. You are hopelessly out of touch with the latest in the beau monde if you are unaware that the earl is now being received by all the best families." This statement left the marchioness gaping like a bass. The rest of the women fared no better as they sat in stunned silence.

Leah continued with prim patience, as if instructing a child. "The second is that your society would qualify as polite."

She sat back down, picked up her teacup, and took a delicate sip. Beside her the duchess blinked with bewildered confusion. "Why would we wish to fly a kite?"

M ORGAN FOUND HE'D gotten used to thinking of Leah as his.

In any event, she was free to flirt, which she did with relish, he noted sourly as he watched her that night from the edge of the dance floor. She had a way of smiling at men that set his teeth on edge. And of course there was that scandalous dress she was wearing. He glared at Desdemona, smiling on as her daughter dazzled, and wondered what a sensible woman like her was thinking to allow her daughter to display her lush body in that way.

It was indecent, he groused, not giving any credence to the fact that most of the other women had far more revealing gowns. It didn't compare, in any event since none of them had Leah's incredible curves. The swell of her bosom over the top of her décolletage was giving him an immense headache.

Glorianna entered the room on her husband's arm. Spying Morgan, she broke away and rushed to him to place a welcoming kiss on his cheek. "How fortunate to see you again so soon," she gushed, smiling up at him.

He offered her a dance, which she accepted. Ignoring the

steely glare behind Randall's false mask of banality, Morgan took Glorianna onto the dance floor.

"Is that Miss Brodie over there?" Glorianna asked.

Morgan executed the steps of the dance. "Indeed, I believe it is."

"She is so lovely. You had better stake your claim quickly, Morgan," she said lightly in a scolding voice. "By the looks of the admirers she's attracting, she shall not wait long for a proposal."

Morgan's face twitched in agitation.

As the dance ended, Glorianna went to greet some friends with a promise to meet Morgan later for an aperitif in the salon. Morgan, to his great frustration, found himself looking for Leah. He couldn't seem to help himself.

He wanted her right now. He needed her, he had even admitted as much. He hadn't been sure what he had meant at the time, but it became clear in the disappointment that had lingered after their last meeting. He needed her, like any human needs another. She provided a singular sort of companionship he had come to crave.

That disturbed him . . . and at the same time it filled him with a deep, solid kind of joy.

His searching gaze lit onto Randall's retreating back and he was jolted out of his thoughts. What was the cur doing? Morgan mused as he watched his enemy lead a dark-haired woman through the doors to the terrace. Recognition dawned and Morgan went into action without thinking.

This was the woman from before, his mistress—Randall was entertaining her right under Glorianna's nose! This was too fortunate. It was exactly what Morgan needed to drive a neat little wedge between Mr. and Mrs. Sanderson.

Slipping outside, he was confident he'd remained unseen. He kept to the shadows as he moved along the outside wall. There were other people milling about occasionally, taking in the night air or seeking some solitude for a private discussion or stolen kiss. It was easy to slip among them with the thick, moonless night as cover. Closer he moved on silent feet to the couple poised at the top of the flagstone steps until he was near enough to hear their conversation.

"Oscar must not see us," the woman said. Her voice was tinged with an accent Morgan placed as eastern European, probably Prussian.

"He is playing cards, madam." Randall's voice was as smooth and cajoling as Morgan had ever heard it. It turned his stomach, but the woman seemed to respond well to the wheedling tones.

"But I think, Rand-all, this is very exciting." She sighed. "And I am so glad to help. How awful that this bad man has done so much wrong and no one can stop him. It is right, this brave thing you are doing. In my country, to go against a noble is to take your life in your hands."

Sanderson took the woman's hands in his. "Elisabeta . . . may I call you Elisabeta?"

The woman twittered. "You must not do so in front of my husband, of course, but, yes, you may, Rand-all."

"I assure you the ambassador will never know of our little trick. The part you play will not only benefit the women this savage man has brutalized in the past, but put an end to his preying on innocents for good. He must not be allowed to continue, and thanks to you, he will be stopped. And . . . I believe each good deed deserves a reward and you shall have yours, eh? This will help you to get what you so dearly want."

"Indeed. When Oscar hears of this horrible attack, he will know how wrong it was to take me from my family and the country I love. I have been begging him to let me go home, but he does not listen."

Astonished, Morgan strained his ears, trying to decipher what Sanderson had just said. It seemed incredible, but the woman seemed to fear some sort of attack, and yet somehow seemed delighted at the idea.

"He will listen," Sanderson reassured her. "He will have to. How can he not after the terrible ordeal you are about to suffer?" They chuckled. "Now, Elisabeta, are you confident you can produce sufficient emotion to be convincing?"

"Oh, you are too English. I do not have the reserve you prize so much here in this cold, damp land. A woman of my country knows passion, and how to use the wiles God gave her with which to control a man. Have no worries, Rand-all. After your man attacks him, then I will be prepared to begin my part. And do not doubt I will be worthy of your brilliant plan."

His man attacks *him.* Morgan struggled to get closer without being detected, wondering if he'd heard correctly.

Randall executed a bow. "If the plan is brilliant, it is so for the woman who inspired it. You deserve everything you want to make you happy, though I shall miss you most grievously when you are back with your mother and sisters."

Elisabeta twittered again.

Sanderson looked over his shoulder, scanning those milling around on the flagstones. Morgan recoiled, fairly certain he wasn't spotted nestled in the shadows.

Randall seemed to sense him, or something. He took the woman's hand and moved down the steps into the garden. Morgan could only make out the faint murmur of their voices, but no more words were audible.

He gnashed his teeth in frustration. He had no doubt the "bad man" Elisabeta referred to was himself. Was he also the one to be attacked? And that would somehow signal her attack . . . wait. Or *feigned* attack—that was what Randall meant about being convincing. The woman was going to pretend to have been attacked. Was this to cover Morgan's attack, make it look like some madman on a rampage?

Still calculating the convoluted possibilities, Morgan went back into the ballroom distracted and concerned. Leah was still dancing, he noted with a sharp twinge of annoyance, but there was more on his mind at this moment. Chief among them was Leah's safety. Whatever Randall had planned, Morgan would make certain nothing would harm a gleaming hair on her head.

He looked and found Spencer, dressed in Cravensmore livery, standing with his hands clasped behind his back and his gaze trained on Leah. Reassured, Morgan wandered into the library where a group of men were smoking cigars and shouting their political views. He poured himself a whiskey and found a quiet seat by the hearth, lapsing into intense concentration within moments.

His patience was wearing as thin as gossamer. Restlessness grew within him, and disgust at this dark burden he shouldered. He found himself wanting to go back to the party, find Leah. Her pleading upon their parting at Farthinghams' echoed in his mind. *Leave it all behind.* He wanted to, he realized. He was sick with the stench of death and hate. Even Randall had sensed it.

Once, he had thrived on it. It had been life's blood to him, sustaining him through unimaginable darkness, and now . . . but what use did it do to think on what was not possible. No matter how much one wanted it.

When this is over, he promised himself, he would live again. He was set to go to Brighton, there to finish it, once and for all. With the prince regent in residence and the resort community packed with the beau monde, it was the perfect setting to unleash his barrage of facts. The rumors would fly. Brighton, for all of its fashionableness, was not London, for there Prinny reigned supreme with no disapproving queen or castigating king to dampen his tawdry tastes. He presided over his own court at the audacious Pavillion, his ornate and bizarre Brighton palace, creating an environment that was equally as undisciplined, indulgent, and raucous as was he.

And if a person, an earl for example, were to be in Brighton at the height of the summer season and a matter of honor arose . . . some rumors, perhaps, that had the ring of truth to them, a matter of death—murder even. It was the perfect setting for a challenge. A duel would no doubt be pardoned in the eyes of the hedonistic atmosphere that prevailed during the summer regalia in Brighton. All was set for Brighton, just a few weeks away.

If all went well, he might be free by the time the weather turned.

He ran his finger anxiously along his scar.

A man's voice roused him out of his thoughts. "I say, Waring, it *is* you. I'd heard you were here."

Morgan looked up to a face he hadn't seen in a long time. Lord Castleton, a great friend of his father's, took the seat opposite his.

"My lord," he said, rising.

"Sit, sit. You do remember me, don't you, son?"

"Of course." Indeed, he had fond memories of Castleton and his frequent visits.

"I wasn't sure. It had been a long time, well before your father's passing. You did receive my letter?"

"Assuredly. It was much appreciated." In point of fact, he'd been flooded with condolences and had not read a one of them. His grief would not be comforted by mere words inked onto paper. He was suddenly sorry to have ignored the kind gesture, at least Castleton's, for it had no doubt been sincerely meant.

"Good, good. I was hoping you would take me up on my offer to come to my Scotland estate."

Morgan's throat tightened. "I had to see to the European properties."

Castleton waved his hand dismissively. "No need to explain, my boy. But look at me, calling you a boy. Well, I suppose I can be excused. You're still a boy to me, old goat that I am. We've got some years behind us, haven't we? Why, do you recall that time when we went quail shooting?"

He began to chuckle, his whole body bobbing in good natured glee, and suddenly the recollection burst into Morgan's mind of himself, his father, and Lord Castleton together with the latter's two sons camping in the woods. The Castleton boys quibbled and Lord Castleton grumbled and his father tried not to laugh at the lot of them. Morgan had bagged the most that day, and they'd cooked the boon themselves that night on the open fire and feasted, "like kings," his father had pronounced as he'd beamed proudly at his son's accomplishment.

"What a day that was! Those brats of mine had me wishing I'd brought a flask with me." Castleton chuckled. "Now they're both at university and traveling with friends on their holidays. I'd give anything to have that day back, even with their wretched squabbling." The older man sighed. "To have all of us together again."

Morgan looked away, uncomfortable. "Thank you, sir."

Castleton settled back, his expression changing. "I wasn't certain about you for a time. There were rumors you'd done him in, you know. Despite the verdict from the inquest, there was still talk."

Morgan stiffened. Castleton noticed and wagged his finger, as if remonstrating a little boy. "Don't go getting your hackles ruffed on me."

"Sir," Morgan countered tightly, "you of all people knew quite well the relationship between myself and my father. How could anyone who understood that believe for a moment that I could be capable of harming him?"

"What an idealist you are. Do you know once I sat by a girl while she cried for hours over her mother's death, only to find out later the chit had poisoned her because the woman made her do too many chores, or so she claimed when she made her confession. If I had doubts about you, it had nothing to do with your character, my boy—ah, there I go again. There's no cure for it, is there? In any event, it wasn't *you* who inspired misgiving, but life's experience."

He leaned forward. Morgan sat perfectly still save for the deep rise and fall of his chest.

"There are many times in life when things are not what they seem. People disappoint, people delight. The human animal is unpredictable. So don't frown at me for having my reservations about your innocence. The important thing is that I am and have been ultimately convinced that the rumors were not true, but I did not make that assessment based on sentiment, but fact. And so, that's why I'm glad to see you've gotten back to the task of living. Pining away all on your own like that for so long—your father would have been horrified. He wanted you to *live,* find happiness, Morgan. I know it's what I'd want for my sons."

Morgan was unable to speak for a moment. Castleton

seemed to understand. "Don't mean to lecture. Have a tendency to do that, you know. My boys hate it. So, have you seen many of your old friends?"

They spoke of this, of old acquaintances and what they were doing these days. Castleton's brusque humor made Morgan laugh. He relaxed in his seat, letting the companionship warm him.

At last, Castleton slapped his knees and rose. "Well, it was good to see you, my boy."

"And you, my lord."

"It is, now? From the first look of you, I wasn't so sure."

Morgan admitted, "Sometimes, it's been hard. I don't think I've always been thinking very clearly these last years."

Castleton smiled broadly, as if this were so obvious a statement as to be a joke. "Of course it's hard. Hard to let go of the dead when they're beloved. But if you stop living, too, then the legacy is truly dead. You can't do that, boy. That's no sort of tribute to a man who was one of the greatest I've known."

Morgan cast his eyes down.

Suddenly, he was filled with a welling of emotions. Castleton had spoken true. And not for the first time, he wondered whether he was right or wrong in seeking revenge.

But it wasn't revenge any longer. It was survival. It was Sanderson or himself. He was locked in this battle and until it was resolved, there would be nothing else beyond it.

Castleton sighed, hauling himself to his feet. "Time to join the ladies. I've heard some talk about you of late. Of a certain charming young woman that has you the envy of half of the men of the ton. Tell me, boy," he said with a grin and a slap on Morgan's back, "any of it true?"

Morgan rose and walked beside him out of the library, his muscles aching from Castleton's affectionate pounding. "There is no one particular."

"Ah. Perhaps you'll meet the right woman in time. She'll settle you down. It will help put all of this ugly business behind you once and for all."

Morgan was only half listening. They were walking by Sanderson, who stood with a group of people just outside the library door talking. His gaze was locked on Morgan, who stared back unflinchingly.

There was a mutual promise exchanged. And that promise was death.

Chapter 15

THE HALLWAYS WERE dark when Morgan ascended to his bedchamber that evening. It was early, not quite midnight. Most of the other guests were still dancing and drinking at the other end of the house. But fatigue weighed heavy in his bones tonight, and he had sought his bed.

His head was reeling from the events of the day, the past weeks, in fact. With Humbolt cooperating and public sentiment already growing for him, he was ready to make his move. He would be ready by the time the ton headed to Brighton.

He should feel happy, or excited . . . or *something*. It wasn't that he looked forward to August with any kind of dread or anxiety, it was just that it no longer seemed to be the end of anything. Instead, he had begun to look beyond it, an end only to a chapter in his life, and the beginning of another.

It frightened him to dare hope for anything beyond that. Would it weaken his resolve? He couldn't afford to be afraid.

He hadn't bothered to bring a candle with him, not expecting to find the wall sconces had not been lit. This was highly unusual. Most hosts spared no expense to see to their guests' comforts and convenience during weeklong house parties. It was a way for them to flaunt their wealth, and they typically missed no opportunity for extravagance, though it might mean the family might have to eat garlic soup the rest of the year.

However, the Cravensmores were elderly, and might have a tendency to be frugal. In any event, the oversight annoyed him as he felt his way up the corridor, bumping into a table along the wall. Something dropped, a dull and solid thud on the carpet. He'd get it in the morning, he thought.

At the second door on the left—his was the third—his eyes began to adjust to the dimness. Along the right-hand side, almost exactly opposite from his room, was a large window, and a bit of moonlight came in from it. He walked with more assurance into the slightly illuminated patch and reached out for his door.

A figure materialized in front of him. He reacted swiftly, sensing danger even before he knew who or what it was. He struck out, making contact with a solid body with his right fist. A glint caught his eye and he dodged a blow coming from his other side. The man had a knife.

A sudden impact of terrible coldness registered as the steel sliced into his flesh, low on his back. He gasped with the pain and surged upward and around, connecting another punch with some part of his foe's face. Ignoring the rapid advance of heat and weakness, he followed it up with a full-body charge that sent his attacker against the far wall.

The shadowy figure came back at him. The momentum took them into the wall. He hit it with a crushing force, and felt himself blink out of consciousness. He fought to remain on his feet. A fist crashed into his skull and he fell onto his knees.

Rolling deeper into the corners, he lay on his back, hoping to remain unseen, unheard. The looming shape of his attacker advanced, stood over him and there was a long moment of suspended time as Morgan lay still, gathering his strength, ready for the man's next move.

He felt the spidery embrace of unconsciousness begin to weave a web of darkness on the edges of his vision. Desperately, he grasped along the floor, the wall, searching for some object to use to defend himself. Where was that vase he had knocked over moments before he was attacked?

His fingers scrabbled, he waited, his eyes tearing, wanting to close, and he was fading.

The attacker prodded him with his toe, none too gently, and grunted. Morgan remained still, banking on the element of surprise. Let the bastard think him unconscious, or dead. The trouble was, he might well be one or the other soon. His limbs felt frozen, and the longer he remained like this, the more he doubted his ability to move when he needed to.

The man hunkered down, and instead of the blow Morgan was storing his waning energies to deflect, the man placed his hand on Morgan's waist. He slid it around to his side, touching the wound. Another grunt issued from the man and he straightened.

"That should do." The voice was deep, satisfied. In a flash, the shadowy form had dissolved into the darkness. It took a moment for Morgan to realize his attacker had gone. He was alone.

Blood-soaked material clung to his back. When he touched it he felt the stickiness of it seep onto his fingers. He was feeling more clearheaded now. The blood was not gushing, as he had feared. That was good.

Staggering to his knees, he crawled to his room and fumbled with the knob. When he was inside, he shot the bolt and found the flint box, using it to light the candelabra on his bedside table, which he carried to the mirror to examine the damage.

He peeled away his crimson-soaked shirt, wincing at the pain emanating from the knife wound. Damnation. The cut was shallow enough to have missed doing any damage to his insides, but it would still need stitching. It was the position of the cut that was the problem, way around his side, almost his back. Letting out a long breath, he sank onto a wooden chair and tried to block out the throbbing pain.

There was no question Randall had sent the man who had attacked him. He had to have been the one to put out the lights. He'd lain in wait for Morgan. Scrubbing his hand across his chin, Morgan wondered how he had allowed himself to be caught unawares.

Because his brain was atrophied, he silently groused. He'd lost his edge. He'd been feeling sorry for himself tonight, missing Leah and thinking about the things Castleton had said. He'd let down his guard. Maybe he'd grown soft and sloppy in these weeks among normal life or maybe he was finding he no longer thrived on fantasies of revenge.

He couldn't afford to give it up, not now. Not until it was finished. God, he could have been killed—would have if his attacker had decided to inflict more damage. In Morgan's state he could have done little to stop him. But he'd only seemed to want to assure himself that Morgan was injured.

He was alive only because Randall wanted him to be. That meant he was still afraid of Morgan, too afraid to take a risk that the evidence Morgan held would come out. But why had he been stabbed? To frighten him? Randall would know a tactic like that would not work, it would only incense Morgan, make him more determined.

Wait . . . What was it the man had said as he'd stood over him, "That will do," or something like that?

Morgan's memory flashed to the woman with whom Randall had met. They had spoken of an attack. He concentrated, struggling to remember exactly what they'd said. He had found out the woman's name was Elisabeta Galeanov and she was the spoiled wife of the Prussian ambassador. It was no secret she wanted desperately to go home but her older, overbearing husband insisted she stay by his side in England.

He'd surmised Randall had enlisted her help as a sort of trading of favors. Randall had promised her that he would arrange for her to appear so sympathetic that her husband would be forced to heed her wishes. This was to be accomplished through some kind of attack. She, in turn, believed she was helping Randall get rid of a "bad man" Morgan had no doubts was himself.

Then it dawned on him. He'd gotten it wrong when he'd thought this attack they spoke of so lightly would be a sham to serve as cover. He'd imagined Randall would make Morgan's death seem a kind of random event, even supply another "victim." But Morgan was left alive, although. conspicuously wounded.

It was a trap. Morgan saw it clearly now. When he went for medical attention for the wound with his story of some mysterious attacker, it would seem eerily similar to how his father was believed to have died. It would sound ridiculous. Even his most staunch defender would have trouble with that outrageous a coincidence.

And then Elisabeta would come forward with her dangerous fiction of being attacked. She'd claim she had wounded the man to defend herself. And Morgan, sporting a fresh stab wound, would be damned. His reputation would be destroyed, this time for good. He'd never recover, not from something like this.

Oh, yes, this was exactly the way Randall liked to operate, this insidious, roundabout approach. He would set up the pieces so that no direct accusations were leveled. It was easy to make people suspicious if one appeared too eager to condemn a particular person. Randall's way was to plant evidence that would do that for him. Then he seemed as surprised as anyone at how it all turned out, and managed to appear unconnected to anything that had occurred. It was how he had always done it before.

Grimly, Morgan realized no one could know about what had happened tonight. That meant he could not seek medical attention. He had to pull himself together, tend to the injury himself.

While he knotted one of his expensive lawn shirts around his waist, disjointed thoughts teamed in his head. His head began to feel fuzzy and incredible tiredness came over him. Perhaps he'd lost more blood than he thought.

He needed help, but it was a game of shadows that he played, and if he were clever enough, he could cheat Randall out of his boon, and that conniving Prussian bitch as well. He grabbed the lamp and went back out into the corridor.

WHEN LEAH CLOSED the door to her chamber, a familiar voice cut through the darkness. "Where the devil have you been?"

This would have startled a cry out of her if Leah's mouth hadn't been clamped at the very moment by a hand closing over it. It took only a second for the identity of the intruder to register.

She whirled to face him. "Damn bloody hell, Morgan, you know I hate being startled. What do you think you are doing—" She stopped short, her expression changing to guarded alarm. "You look terrible."

"Light the bloody lamps, will you. I need you to do something for me."

"Don't you order me around like that. I demand to know—"

"Just bloody do it!" The insistent whisper was more effective than a shout.

Leah took a taper and opened the glass casing on the wall lamp.

"Go get some whiskey," he commanded her.

She turned and stared at him. He was in the process of easing himself into a comfortable chair that was one of a pair drawn up to the fireplace.

He winced, then said hoarsely, "There's some in the library. No one should be in there now. They're all playing cards or passed out in their beds, I'd imagine."

His dark hair was tousled and his head was angled to one side. He seemed strange. "What is wrong with you?" she asked with unease.

"Do you have a sewing kit?"

She blinked, confused. "Of course I do, but I—"

"Silk thread?"

"My God!" Falling onto her knees in front of him, she peered into his face. The scar was vibrant white against his unnaturally pale cheek. His eyes looked lazy, their hazel dimmed to an indeterminate flat brown. "What has *happened?*"

A movement down by his side drew her attention. She looked and saw him draw his hand away. It was drenched in blood.

She shot to her feet. "Oh, God! Oh, God!"

"Don't—" His hand shot out and closed like steel over her wrist.

"I've got to call the surgeon!"

"No!"

"Yes!" Straining against his grip, she heard his command, calling her in a voice that cut through the fog in her brain, "Leah!" and stopped struggling.

"Come here," he demanded roughly.

She shook her head, whipping her hair around her face. He repeated his order, softer, and pulled her back to him.

"Let me fetch help," she whimpered. Sinking back to the floor in front of him, she felt the terror paralyzing her. "Please, Morgan. Are you . . . are . . . are you dying?"

"No, for God's sake. It's a stab wound, but not fatal. I'd stitch it myself, but I can't reach the damn thing. Just get the things I told you to. And ring for tea."

She looked incredulous. "You want a cup of tea?"

"I want the boiled water. You will need to clean the wound. Tell the servant you will steep it yourself, that you like it weak or some such nonsense."

The strength was out of her limbs. Her body felt like wood, stiff and not alive. "You can't mean . . . Morgan, you know I—"

"Yes, I know you're a flighty-headed fool." He cupped her chin, holding her captive. "But you're strong when you want to be. I need you to be strong for me."

A surge of giddy panic made her voice high and shrill. "I can't believe you are doing this to me! You blighter, you . . ." Her arsenal of epithets failed her. She couldn't think of anything vile enough to call him.

"Calm down." His voice was clear now, full of authority. She resented it, casting about in her frightened mind for a way to defy it. "No one else can know about this. It has to remain secret. Don't ask why, just do what I say. Promise. *Promise,* Blackie."

He was starting to shiver. She could hear the clatter of his chattering teeth as he struggled to force out his words.

"This is Randall's doing, isn't it?" Her words came in a panicked rush. "You said he couldn't kill you, you said you were safe."

"He wants to discredit me, not kill me. Then I can do nothing to discredit him."

"Well, damn it, you shouldn't have been so *damned odd!* You had to go to the Continent for a whole year, didn't you? You had to skulk around crashing polite society parties and glowering about the place. It made you seem odd, Morgan. No one wants to believe in you when you're odd."

He smiled indulgently. "Yes, I see how this is all my fault."

"Don't be ridiculous, it is not your fault. It is Randall's." She straightened, sniffed. "I don't want that bloody cur to win."

He nodded wearily. "Good girl."

"But, Morgan, you can't expect me to do this!" she wailed, suddenly weakening. "I'll faint and you'll have to call in help then. And what will you say to explain it? Think of it, not only will you be bleeding all over the place, but you'll be in the bedroom of a society debutante, and her in a swoon!"

"You won't faint. You can do this, Leah. I need you to."

She swallowed painfully, fighting the part of her that rebelled against his outrageous proposition. He needed her, he said. Damn those words.

"I'll fetch the brandy," she muttered.

"Whiskey," he corrected. "And have the tea sent up. Wait. There's blood in the hall. Before anyone comes up, you should take care of that. I'd have done it myself, but—"

"Never mind. I'll see to it. Just relax. Please, you look awful."

"All right, Blackie. You calm down, too. Now go do what

I said. And see to that blood. If anyone sees it, it will give us away."

"I'll take care of it. Please, just rest until I get back."

She rose on wobbly legs and crept into the hall and down to the first floor, ducking into the kitchens to tell the sleepy staff that she wanted a teapot sent up to her room, then hurried to the library. She opened the door to the music room, the family withdrawing room, the morning room, and began to despair, but at last she found the library and hurried to the sideboard where there was a discouraging jumble of decanters. She picked up one and flew back upstairs.

She went to Morgan's bedchamber, lighting the wall sconces as he'd warned her she'd have to do. There she found smears of blood along the wall and on the tiled floor. Fortunately, the patterned carpet that ran lengthwise along the hall hid the blood that had spilled on it, so she concentrated on swabbing up the other stains using the wash basin water and a towel from Morgan's chamber. Then she bundled everything together and ran to her room before she was discovered.

She was no sooner inside when a maid arrived with the teapot. Thinking quickly, she ordered another pot sent up, this one of strong coffee. The puzzled maid bobbed a curtsy as Leah shut the door.

"You seem too tired," she explained to Morgan. "I don't want you to fall asleep. There is no possible way I could do this alone."

"I might not wake up, is that it?"

Her body started violently. In a low voice, she said quite soberly, "Don't talk like that. Don't even joke. Or I'll call the surgeon, I swear it."

"All right, it was a stupid thing to say. Now bring me your scissors from your sewing kit. You'll need it to cut away the—"

"I know what to do!" she snapped. "My goodness, you'd think I didn't know to cut back the material. I may not be a surgeon, but I certainly know that much."

"Calm down, Leah."

"I'm calm!" she shrieked. Fetching the sewing box, she retrieved the knife and held it out in front of her. Her hand shook violently.

"Take off your dress," he said. "It will get bloody. Strip down as far as you dare."

She froze, stared at him. "Are you daft?"

His gaze was impassive. "I've seen all of it, remember?"

She toyed with several responses, none of them sufficiently scathing. In the end, she saw the sense in what he suggested. Taking off her dress, she flung it in a heap on the floor. She removed her corset and kicked off her slippers.

She was dressed in only her chemise, her drawers, and stockings.

"Don't move," she said gravely, kneeling between his legs. She took no notice of the way her body wedged intimately between his thighs. Leaning over him, she concentrated on snipping away the sopping cloth.

"I can't see," she said. "I'll need you to hold the lamp."

He obliged and she began to peel back the material. He winced and she jumped. "Oh, my God!" Springing back, she retracted her hands quickly. "That hurt, didn't it? Oh, Morgan, I cannot do this!"

"You'll do it. I'd have thought you would have liked a chance to get even with me a little."

"I'm not a ghoul." Leah concentrated, her eyes stinging from the sweat trickling off her brow. Cutting into the expensive fabric caked with drying blood, she carefully exposed the damaged skin. "I'll hate you forever for making me do this," she muttered as she drew away the last of his makeshift bandages and ruined shirt.

A rumbling chuckle emanated from deep in his chest. His exposed skin was warm to her touch. In the flickering lamplight, she let her eyes wander, taking in the beauty of his nakedness. His masculine body never failed to send a thrill into the marrow of her bones. Shaped differently than her female softness, he was hard and vital and pulsing with power. It fascinated her the way his chest was overlaid with thick musculature, deep grooves delineating the plains of his chest, the bulge of his shoulder and upper arms, the sensuous flat of his abdomen. His skin was smooth and warm, sprayed with the tantalizing softness of masculine hair.

She swallowed and forced herself to focus on her task. "Twist to the side, please. I cannot see the wound." She gave a soft, helpless cry when it was exposed to the light. "It's deep, Morgan. It's too deep."

His face was still, as bloodless as a ghost's. "Get the needle and thread. And give me some of that coffee. Put whiskey in it. Then put whiskey on the needle and on the wound."

"Oh, God. I think I grabbed the brandy!"

"Hell, it doesn't matter."

"Stop yelling at me." He wasn't, but he didn't correct her. She picked up the needle and thread, put it down, poured the coffee, handed it to him, tried to thread the needle, put it down, went for the whiskey, handed it to him, and tried to thread the needle.

"Want me to do that?" he drawled, squinting at her efforts.

"Oh, shut up!" She was almost hysterical. "This is horrid, absolutely horrid. And you are a horrid, horrid man! How can you make me do this—sew up your skin like a sock with a hole in it? And I don't darn socks anyway! You might as well ask me to extract your spleen for all I know about doctoring. Of all indecent things to ask a woman to do."

"I'm surprised you wouldn't enjoy that. Taking out my spleen, I mean."

"I agree you've got far too much of it. Oh! I got it!" she cried, holding up the threaded needle.

"Leah, keep your voice down."

"I got it," she whispered, smiling happily. She dropped the needle, and the thread slipped out of the eye. "Bloody criminy!"

"Good God. Take a swig of the whiskey. It will steady your hand."

She grabbed the bottle, surprising him by obeying. The draught she took widened his eyes. Her satisfaction at shocking him was short-lived. She was immediately seized by an agonizing fire in her throat and a sudden inability to breathe.

"It's not champagne, Blackie," he cautioned.

She cast him a murderous look, gasping precariously.

The liquor did steady her hand. She got the needle threaded again.

"All right," he said, taking another long drink of the spiked coffee. "Sew."

"Morgan Gage, you are the lowest, most vile, worm-ridden piece of scum to make a gently reared lady perform such a disgusting task. You are without conscience, below contempt, completely devoid of any decency—" She took a deep breath. "Now don't move."

"I have no place to go."

"I mean keep still. I . . . I'm not sure I can stand this."

"Just do it. Did you clean the wound?"

"No, I didn't clean the wound. You never told me to clean the wound." She thrust her hands on her hips, glaring at him evilly. "How the devil am I supposed to know to clean the wound?"

Morgan sighed. "Why don't you clean the wound?" he said dully.

He tried his best not to notice the outline of her breasts was particularly prominent when she struck this position. Or the gentle way they swayed at every movement. Rolling his eyes to the ceiling, he turned his focus away from their exquisite shape, the memory of them heavy and warm in his palms.

Pain cut through his consciousness when she poured the whiskey on him. He was grateful for it, for each bite of agony leaping in long tongues of fire into his side. It kept his mind from the fact that her scantily clad body was pressed over his.

"All right," she muttered softly. "All right. I'm going to sew now. Don't—"

"I won't move."

She nodded. Bending over him, he smelled her hair, and was shocked to find his body was responding to her state of undress, her nearness, her breasts smashed against his lap. A new pain, much less bearable, asserted itself in his groin.

Why couldn't she have small breasts—better yet, tiny,

nonexistent breasts? And no curves. Straight as a board, with a large belly. And wiry, rough-textured hair, not this skein of silk.

Yes, if only she were grotesque, this would be much easier.

Filling his head with the most repulsive images of freakish female forms, he settled back and refused to look at her. He felt the first prick of the needle. Then she hesitated.

"Go ahead." His voice sounded rusty. "It doesn't hurt."

He felt the needle slip in. Pain flared as the thread whispered through his flesh.

"Oh, God," she moaned.

"Go on. That's a brave girl."

"Oh, God."

"I can't feel it," he lied. "It's numbed from the whiskey."

"Oh, God."

She got through it with several hundred such prayers. God must have been listening, for he gave her the strength. By the time she was through, however, Morgan's head was spinning wildly.

"More coffee," he grunted.

On her way to get it for him, a knock sounded at the door. She stopped dead in her tracks.

"It's Debra, Miss Leah," a voice called.

"I . . ." She looked appealingly at Morgan.

"Tell her you've already undressed, that you were too tired to wait."

She repeated the message. Debra hesitated, then replied with an uncertain, "All right, miss. I'll see you in the morning, then."

"Yes. Thank you. Good night."

There was silence. She brought the coffee, splashing a liberal amount of whiskey in it before shoving it at him.

Morgan took a sip and grimaced. "You are a hell of a cook," he said, and glancing at his side, added, "And a damn fine nurse, too."

She sat down on the bed with a flop, blowing a tendril of

hair out of her face. It flew up and landed in exactly the same spot. Morgan smiled, leaning back, taking in the sight of her.

His groin still ached, but he ignored it. Something soft had come into the room, diffusing in the air, settling the mood. Perhaps it was the exhaustion of his body, or the gradually subsiding ache after the pain of the stitches. More likely, it was the alcohol.

It was pleasant, whichever the reason, and he gave into its lure, suddenly tired of resisting and maybe a little grateful for it. It felt good. When he was with Leah, he could feel normal again. That was, when she wasn't driving him insane with desire. But no, even then, there was something about her . . . a sense of coming home.

"How are you doing?" he asked, reaching out to touch her shoulder. "Are you sure you are feeling all right?"

She smiled and drew her legs up. Her long limbs, encased in sweet pink-colored stockings, showed from under her knee-length drawers. Slim ankles, delicately arched feet, slender, feminine, and tantalizing, drew his gaze.

He jerked his eyes from their tempting feast, focusing instead on the contents of his cup.

"I'm fine," she said, with a touch of wonder in her voice. "I think I'm actually fine. I have just amazed myself. And I think I amazed you, too, didn't I? You kept telling me I could do it, but you didn't really believe it."

"I didn't have a choice. I needed to believe in you."

Shyly, she gave him an underlook that twisted the knot of fire in his belly. "I was rather brave, too, wasn't I? I mean, really brave, not just clever or brazen or . . . well, all the things we *incorrigible* children are naturally good at being. I was so frightened, Morgan, *really* frightened, but I didn't let it stop me. I was just like the women in Daphne's stories."

"When you weren't squealing." He held up a hand when her brows forked over eyes glittering with insult. "I'm just teasing you. You *were* quite brave. I knew I was right to put my faith in you."

She rewarded his contrite offering with an approving smile. "Are you comfortable? Do you need a blanket?"

"No. Don't fuss. It annoys me."

"You are a wretch sometimes."

"And you . . ." He stopped, his playfulness fading. "You are incredible. I've never known anyone like you, Leah."

"I don't know if you mean that as a good thing," she replied with a nervous laugh.

"It is indeed the very best thing. You are a hellion—"

"Oh, dear. If you mean that as a compliment you are going to have to do better."

"You have enormous will," he went on. "Like iron. When you set your mind to something, you can move mountains."

"I didn't realize you noticed."

"I notice everything about you." His voice grew husky. Gooseflesh rose along her arms. "I notice the dress you're wearing on a particular day and I notice the way you wear your hair, especially if I happen to like it. I like it down as a rule, as much down as is decent. Well, at least in public. I notice who you're talking to and who is looking at you when you're not paying attention. I notice who you flirt with."

Her sideways look was wary. "And do you get jealous?"

"That was why you did it, wasn't it?"

Pursing her lips, her eyes wandered with studied innocence. "Not everything I do is concerned with you, Morgan. You have an inflated view of your importance."

He laughed. "I like your spirit. God, I miss it when I'm not with you. Damn." He looked away, suddenly uncomfortable. "I'm babbling. Must be the brandy." He gave a soft laugh. "Or you. You get to me with those wretched soul-stealing eyes of yours. Did you know you appear sometimes to look straight through a man? It is the most disconcerting thing."

"I wish I could see through you, into your heart. Then I would have all my answers."

"Come here, Leah." He lifted a beckoning hand. "I will give you all the answers I have."

As Leah unfolded her long limbs, rising from the bed, Morgan felt his body constrict with the fierce surge of want. Not just her body, although that was where it had begun and where most of his desire was still centered, but for *her.* To have a woman like her, call her his own, and have her belong to him was the paramount desire of his heart.

She sank to his side, hunkered down like a child before a storyteller, eyes limpid and glassy in the lamplight. He took her hand in his, studying the slender paleness of it. His blunt-tipped fingers looked impossibly large intertwined with her long, tapered ones.

"You are so young," he said softly. He cupped her face with his free hand. "So beautiful. Beautiful beyond any man's dream of beauty. What the devil are you doing here with me?"

Her eyelids drifted downward and she turned her cheek into his hand.

"I am getting maudlin. I suppose I had better go," he said. But he didn't move.

"No!" She looked at him like an angel, a luscious, mussed angel, her head thrown back, her slender neck like a swan's, the sultry smile she didn't even know was seductive as a siren's curling on her lips. "You don't want to," she said.

He waited a heartbeat, then admitted, "No."

"Morgan?"

"Yes, Blackie?"

"Do you want to make love to me?"

He sucked in a long breath. "Always. I think about making love to you until my insides are crawling and I can't think straight and I'm pacing a rut into the carpet."

He released her and rose. Standing, he took her into his arms. "And, no, I don't want to leave."

He pushed her backward and lay down with her on the bed.

She said, "Your wound—"

"I don't think severed limbs would impede me tonight," he grunted, then smiled and she relaxed into the cradle of his arm.

She touched him, gliding her hands lightly, her gaze following the path of her questing fingers. "I suppose I am horribly wicked," she said, "because the moment you took off your shirt, I was thinking about how much I wanted to feel your skin."

"Ah. Then we make the perfect pair, because no amount of pain seemed to be able to drown out my wanting to do this," he replied, cupping both her breasts in his hands.

Their first kiss was pure fire.

His hands worked quickly to rid her of her clothing. She returned the favor, insisting he let her do it when he kept trying to help her.

"Stop," she chastised, and he tipped her onto her back, covering her with kisses until she lay gasping for breath.

He kissed a path down to her shoulder, then over the rapid rise and fall of her chest, quickening the pace of her breathing by teasing her unmercifully until she dug her fingers into his hair and whimpered with pleasure. Lower still, he laved the hollow of her navel. She trembled, caught in waves of sensation and shock at the bold liberties he took with her body.

And reveling in each and every feeling he evoked.

His hands parted her thighs and she felt her first tremor of unease. As he slipped his fingers inside her, she froze. The stroke elicited a deep groan of satisfaction. He found a spot so sensitive that his slightest touch rolled pleasure throughout her entire body and she lay still, letting him touch her.

When he parted the sheltering folds to expose her center of pleasure, she felt the flush of uncertainty. Then he closed his hot mouth over her and she arched off the bed, crying out in a mingling of protest and delight. Pushing her back down, he didn't stop, his tongue flicking in maddening light strokes that brought such intense pleasure, any further protests were impossible. Her body strained against this unimaginably wicked kiss, pushing furiously to the completion she sought. Suddenly it exploded, lifting her on a wave of incredible rapture.

It held her aloft, endless and bottomless, then eased into eddies of shivery delight. Morgan moved, hovering above her with his hands braced on either side of her head. "I told you, Blackie. You were made for passion."

Pulling his head down to her, she kissed him ravenously. Her hands slid down his back to his buttocks and she pulled his hips down to hers. He needed no more encouragement, grinding the hot ridge of his arousal against her sweat-soaked skin.

Leah welcomed him, opening herself eagerly. Shifting, he buried himself deep inside her in one smooth movement. His mouth pressed kisses in between groans of enjoyment as he moved in and out, driving deep with each thrust.

He gazed down into her eyes as he rocked hard into her. She watched with growing excitement as the pleasure built within him. His body strained, muscles bunched, cord-like tendons showing against his skin. A protracted series of spasms shook his body. He pushed deep within her, buried completely until the storm subsided.

When his body was still, he rolled with her. They were quiet, wrapped around one another and content for a long while. Then he leaned up on his elbow and kissed her as if they hadn't just made love, as if he were still hungry for her. Leah slipped her arms around his broad, thickly muscled shoulders. They cuddled and kissed and talked in whispers, muffling their laughter as the hour grew late. They touched each other with lazy caresses until the passion rose up again, swiftly, urgently, and they made love once more.

Chapter 16

M ORGAN DRESSED, SLOWLY in deference to his injury and with a few winces that raised Leah's anxiety. When she wanted to check that the stitches were holding steady, he scowled and told her not to fuss. Then with a lingering kiss, he slipped out of her room before the sun arose.

After he left, she sat in the window and looked out at the burgeoning dawn, wondering what she was feeling. She had resigned herself to having to get over Morgan, steeled herself against the anguishing longing she felt, and now she had completely abandoned all of that resolve and made love with him again. The afterglow was still with her. Yet there was an undercurrent of disquiet lurking on the fringes of her thoughts.

It seemed, when he held her in his arms, when he looked at her that way he did when his thoughts and his heart were with her, she could believe she was the most important thing in his world. Her woman's instincts told her he cared for her, yet he had never given her a word of love. Perhaps her woman's instincts were wrong—twisted by hope and the aching pieces of her broken heart. She wouldn't be the first who had mistaken a man's lust for deeper feeling.

Still, she loved the fact that she could command his desire. It was an incredibly powerful feeling to know he wanted her fiercely, even obsessively. But it wasn't the same as love, and it wasn't enough.

She had been embarrassingly susceptible to him tonight. That bothered her. What had come over her? All the man had to do was appear in her bedroom in the middle of the night possibly mortally wounded and demanding she do barbaric things to save his life, and she was clay in his hands.

She bit off the laugh that almost erupted. This was serious. She had to remember not to let down her guard again. Nothing like this could happen again, no matter how precious she regarded each moment spent with him.

She let out a lengthy sigh and began to bundle up the bloody clothing for disposal. After a moment's deliberation, she lit a fire and dropped each piece in to be consumed. By the time Debra arrived to see to her morning ablutions and toilette, there was nothing left in sight to give evidence of what had occurred in the room the previous night.

M ORGAN INTRODUCED THE viscount de Fontvilliers to the other men in the room.

"Humbolt, you already know," Morgan said indicating the man sitting in one chair, twitching his foot agitatedly, then swept his hand to another, "and this is Mr. Bruce Roberts, a former Bow Street Runner, who heads an elite group of specialist detectives and bodyguards out of London. I have acquired his services for the trip to Brighton."

The men were seated. Morgan set his elbows on the armrests and folded his hands in front of his chin. "My reason for calling you together is to have an open and frank discussion of what we are about to undertake in a month's time. When we are at Brighton, I want everyone perfectly clear on their part and what they can expect from the others. Humbolt, let us begin with you, as the entire enterprise will, in effect, originate with your actions."

Humbolt adjusted his spectacles. "I am the logical choice to circulate the rumors about Randall Sanderson that Lord Waring wishes to be out. As it would seem obvious if I, as Lord Waring's man of affairs, put out these accusations, we have adopted a pretense of having parted ways. It is to seem as though upon perusing my files to forward to his new solicitors, I found the relevant letters, which in actuality the viscount and I discovered, indicating there was no intention of Lord Waring's father to disinherit him. These and other letters produce enough speculation to be of interest. I am to go to the authorities and seek help from prominent members of the peerage in London under the guise of seeking some venue of justice so as to redeem myself to my former employer."

Morgan added, "In actuality, none of these men will have any authority to do anything, but they are all gossips, married to gossips, and socialize with the most rapacious wags of the beau monde."

"That's good," Roberts said, smiling. "Once it gets out, they will remember that false letter. As it benefited Mr. Sanderson, it should be obvious where it originated."

"Dashedly easy." Raphael chuckled. "Sanderson's head will be on the block."

"Mr. Humbolt must appear to be operating only under the prodding of his conscience."

"Which he is," Raphael drawled.

Humbolt cleared his throat and blinked, clearly uncomfortable.

Raphael raised his brows. "What? I merely pointed out he had grossly misjudged you, Waring, which was the truth and very convenient for our present purposes. In any event, the plan is sufficiently subtle. I doubt any will detect the conspiracy. I am chillingly impressed."

"I learned from a master, Fontvilliers—Randall Sanderson himself. As I do not naturally have a diabolical mind, I have had to resort to imitation. These are the same tactics Randall has used all of his life. Turnabout is fair play."

"And in the end prevail, we hope. What else do you have, Waring?"

"I have enlisted the aid of Lord Castleton, an old friend of my father."

"Hmm." Raphael raised his brows in speculation. "He is socially prominent, constantly at his club or making calls. Considered trustworthy, a good fellow. An excellent choice to spread news. What is it he will contribute?"

Morgan rose and paced to the window, deep in thought. "My father's valet went to work for a mutual friend of our family and Castleton's. He and I both know this man to be honorable, loyal. He had strong opinions about what happened the night my father was stabbed, but his testimony was suppressed. I have corresponded with him and he has confided some incriminating details on Randall's behavior and actions that he observed immediately after the murder. These were corroborated by other servants. As this was left out of the official reports, it is virtually unknown, but Castleton will disperse this information now."

Roberts leaned forward. "I've arranged with a reporter to release the story on the local Yorkshire officials suspected of accepting bribes. I've got some solid witnesses and some damning stories to tell. I guarantee it will raise the suspicions you need."

Morgan said, "Each foray of information is timed, a series of blows following one quickly upon the other, exciting public interest and turning the tide of opinion against Sanderson. I need not prove his guilt in a court of law, only set the stage for my being able to call him out without eliciting any prejudice."

The meeting lasted another hour as the men hammered down the finer points of the schedule. Raphael appointed himself devil's advocate, a role, he ruefully observed, well suited to him. However, he raised some relevant challenges. Morgan made adjustments and the men adjourned.

Raphael stayed behind at Morgan's request. The other two men had refused Morgan's offer of cigars or libation, but

Raphael helped himself to both now, reclining in a comfortable chair and staring at the ceiling thoughtfully.

"Excellent," Raphael said, admiring the flute of tobacco. "More whiskey?"

"I prefer answers. Although I am flattered, I assure you, I admit to being a bit bemused as to why you have included me in this meeting."

Morgan flashed a smile. "Because I wish something from you. Two things, actually."

Raphael nodded. "How uncharacteristic. You have proved tenaciously independent up to now, even foolishly so. There is hope for you yet, Waring. I will be pleased to comply with whatever you wish if it is within my power."

"I asked you to attend today because I wanted someone beside myself to have the entire scope of this plan. Humbolt and Roberts have excellent reputations, but they do not have titles. You do. And you've been willing to help before. The authorities will listen to you."

"What am I to tell them?" Raphael asked, his tone careful as if he already knew what Morgan was after.

"If something goes wrong, or if I fail, you must see if there is some way to salvage this. I want you to contact my solicitors and release the documented information they hold. I want you to release it to anyone who will entertain it. It is similar to what we discussed here tonight."

"Ah. A sort of 'second' in this intriguing little scheme of yours. I accept the honor. Now, you mentioned *two* things."

Morgan hesitated. "I wish you to keep Leah safe."

Raphael's eyes snapped. "What the devil do you mean? Blast it, man, is she in danger?"

Morgan gave him a brief explanation of Sanderson's threats and the measures he'd taken so far to keep her protected. "I've replaced the men from my own staff with Roberts's men, who are better trained for this sort of thing, but still I'm not satisfied. I want you to take her back to Cumbria with you. There's much to amuse her there and she will be in surroundings easily controlled."

Raphael snorted. "My wife's sister is not a person 'easily

controlled' anywhere. It is a term contrary to the entire family."

Morgan shrugged. "If you find the task too daunting . . ."

"Don't try to bait me, man, the task is impossible. In the first place, what do you intend to tell her parents to get her to Glenwood Park? They have already accepted at least a dozen invitations to take them through the end of summer and into fall. Unless you tell them of these threats—and I assume that is out of the question as you would have done so already— then she will be where they will be, and that is everywhere in England. After all, this is Leah's season. There is still the matter of a husband to find for her."

"Indeed, a husband for Leah is a priority. It is a matter that I plan to take care of immediately," Morgan said, taking a long pause to puff on his cigar, then blowing out the smoke while he studied the glowing tip. "I can solve all the logistical problems by becoming that husband."

Raphael reacted with strong surprise.

Morgan shrugged. "It is an obvious course of action. Her parents will accept it, since I am, if you will excuse the lack of modesty, a fairly desirable catch. As her husband, I will send her to you. *Then* and only then, when I am assured there is no possible way Randall can use her to get to me, will I proceed. I have to know she is safe, first and foremost."

A guffaw erupted from Raphael. "Oh, our Leah will simply adore that—being ordered about. She will view it as being kept prisoner, even if it is for her own sake."

Morgan was grim. "She will have to accept it is how it must be. For now."

Raphael's laughter rang louder. "God help you if you try to cage that one."

"Will she not vow to obey?" Morgan shot, eyes blazing.

"Oh, she'll say it, for it is required. But will she do it?" He raised his brows in question, one they both knew the answer.

"She must. I go to Brighton after our wedding. Everything is set to proceed in just a few short weeks. I will speak to her, make her understand this is the best thing for the time being."

Raphael was still chuckling when he threw up his hands.

"You have more confidence than you should. Of course you can send Leah to us. I will make certain she is safe. She will have Julia for counsel and my daughter is ample distraction. She dotes on the child, which is completely understandable." He grinned. "Cosette is superior in every way."

He exchanged a look with Morgan, one that said he knew he sounded like a gleefully doting father and didn't mind at all.

Hesitating for a moment, Morgan said gruffly, "I thank you for your help. And your friendship."

Raphael escaped the awkward moment with a wave of his hand. "I give you credit for your willingness to take on the virago as wife. But something tells me it is not exactly a dreaded task. You two will suit, I suspect. But what of her—does she concur? I wonder if she will consent to the marriage."

Morgan focused on the smoke curling into the air, choosing his words carefully. "I am rather confident she will. It is not an onerous choice for either one of us. It is my hope that she will even be pleased. I have reason to believe she will."

"It's like that, is it?" Raphael replied. "Hmph. I am not sure if my duties as brother-in-law role require me to call you out or not."

"As I am already content to do the honorable thing, it appears redundant."

Raphael agreed. "Quite so. What a relief. I would hate to have to kill you after all of this trouble I have gone to in order to save your life."

"Indeed," Morgan countered, fighting a smile, "a duel would prove distressing for me as well. Either way."

"Are you suggesting that you could take me?" he cried indignantly.

"I suppose we shall not find out."

"We shall have to box, then. After you return from this curious honeymoon you plan with your enemy instead of your wife, I will meet you in Gentleman Jackson's rooms and we shall put the matter to rest."

Morgan chuckled, agreeing to the friendly challenge.

Raphael grew serious. "Waring, have you considered that Sanderson could prove dangerous? He might not sit idly while you draw the noose tightly around his neck, socially speaking. It is possible that he would make some move, perhaps even rash, as the gossip begins to simmer."

"That is precisely why Leah must be safely under your care. And I have Roberts's men set to shadow all of his movements in Brighton. There is no victory without risk. I accept that. But if I move carefully enough and quickly enough to ensnare him, I will win."

Raphael gave him a look. "You show more patience than I would be capable of. I would have shot him dead long ago."

"Make no mistake. I will kill him. But I'm not giving him a damned minute more of my life. He's taken enough. I can't lose everything again."

"Yes, of course. You thirst for justice."

Morgan was startled. He'd been thinking about Leah, not justice. "Yes, of course."

"One thing, Waring." The viscount's expression was stoic, hard. He said, "Make certain you do not come to harm yourself. I don't want to have the duty of consoling a newly wedded widow. It would be too grim."

Morgan worked the tension from his shoulders. "Very well, Fontvilliers. I'll make the utmost effort to save you the trouble."

LEAH'S FATHER'S SUMMONS to the library made her a little uneasy. Since Francis Brodie worked so much, he was usually found in the parlor during his precious hours with his family, playing chess with his wife or making a fuss over Marie's new doll or Hope's latest watercolor. He didn't do business at home, therefore he never had cause to be in the library. Unless he was going to deliver a lecture.

But she wasn't a child any longer, full of daring and uncontrolled spirit that had brought her before stern-faced parents more times than she cared to count. She was a woman.

And her mother had told her she was proud of her. She had known, then, that her fear that she had been born a disappointment to her parents was wrong.

It changed everything. Or maybe Morgan had changed her.

She rapped upon the library door and entered at her father's summons. She stopped short. Morgan was seated inside.

Her newfound sense of herself didn't prevent her from dropping her jaw in astonishment to find him here, apparently having a private conversation with her father. Immediately questions flew to her tongue, but she bit them back and waited.

Her father came to her, smiling, and gave her a soft kiss. "Waring wishes to speak with you, darling," he said, and to her bewilderment, he left the room.

Morgan stood. He cleared his throat and smoothed his hair. He appeared distinctly and uncharacteristically awkward.

"Your father and I have been talking . . ." He stopped suddenly, startled.

Leah was alarmed. "What? What is it?"

"You are standing. You should be sitting."

He pulled her into a chair. She sat cautiously.

"Your father and I were talking about your future," he began again. He *was* nervous. This was so startling, Leah stared in amazement as he continued. "I wanted him to know—and you to know—that I mean only the greatest respect in saying that your future is paramount to my concerns, my personal concerns, and as such I have come to the realization that the logical steps that face us seem inevitable—"

"Morgan," she cut in with impatience, "what the devil are you saying?"

Morgan blanched, passing his hand over his eyes. "God, I'm botching this hugely. Leah, your father has given his permission, providing you agree, for our engagement. Now, I didn't discuss the true reasons with him, of course, but I know I can speak plainly to you. The situation we find ourselves in forces my hand. I am determined to protect you completely. I know you will agree with me that this is the best way."

He couldn't possibly be meaning what she suspected. "What way?"

"Marriage, Leah. I want you to marry me."

There was a short silence while Leah gaped. Her mouth working for a moment, she finally managed, "M-marry me?"

She stood, her face beaming up at him, her eyes glowing with shimmering tears. "You are asking me to marry you?" She covered her mouth, bubbling with delight.

Morgan closed his eyes against the beauty of her at that moment, refusing to acknowledge the flood of emotion that threatened to overwhelm him. He was trembling. Why the devil was he trembling?

Yes, it was true he had some primitive urge to make her his, to appease the possessive impulse he could not explain. But foremost, he was taking care of his own. It was a completely rational choice.

He could not get carried away here.

Suddenly she stopped, her expression changing instantly. "Wait. Did you just say the situation has forced your hand? You want to marry me to protect me?"

He winced. "I said . . . well, I did say that. Perhaps it is not the point we should be concentrating on right at this moment, but surely you understand it is a major consideration. I just want you to understand, is all, that it is a dire set of circumstances we find ourselves in."

It was obvious from her expression he was making it worse. He tried again. "Marriage is the best solution to our problem. Once you are my wife, I can take care of you without constraints."

"The best solution to our problem?"

Leah reared away from him, looking every bit the virago her brother-in-law had named her. "How dare you! You see me as an *obligation*. That is what you are telling me."

"I didn't say that. I just pointed out that logically . . . Leah . . . be reasonable."

"I am!"

"All right, all right. I've done this badly, I admit, but you have got to see it is not so bad an idea. Think about it, Leah. We are, after all, largely compatible. We've managed to find resolutions to our disagreements. We respect each other. We like each other." He offered a grin. "Sometimes we even find each other's company rather diverting."

She bit her lips and looked away. "How romantic. You will win me with logic."

"Marriage *should* be a practical matter. We've a better start than most have," he said. He moved closer, encouraged when she didn't shrink away. He touched her face, the silken smoothness of her skin too inviting to ignore. Her lashes drifted closed, fanning so prettily against the soft blush of her cheek.

He leaned in close, his lips brushing against her ear. "You know I find you exciting. And, dare I say, you harbor a similar desire. Frankly, we cannot seem to keep our hands off each other. Look at the risks we've taken so far to be alone." His hand slid up her arm. "This will solve that problem, at least. We will be man and wife. There will be no limits, then. I thought that would please you."

Flushing hotly, Leah recoiled from the last words. Is that how he viewed her, like some . . . God, like some bitch in heat?

She wanted so badly to refuse him. This wasn't what she wanted at all. He'd hurt her pride as well as her heart with his mangled proposal that was no proposal at all. She whirled and walked away, wishing with all her heart to fling open the outside door and run away from him.

Coming up behind her, he said. "Leah, I am sorry I don't have romance and flowers and protestations of my devoted heart," he said. "I am not a man of such flourish and fluff. You know that. I am just not capable of such things. But I know women want that."

She could feel the heat of his body along her back, he was standing so close. "All right. I'll try my best. Listen to me, Leah. I care for you. I want to take care of you and keep you safe. I respect you and I promise I will always act honorably. I will never hurt you purposefully and I will care about your feelings above my own. You will be my wife. You will be my family. You know what that means to me. I will never disgrace or betray that. And I am not just doing this because I have to, or because of duty. I want to. I truly want to marry you. I want you to be my family, for all the reasons I just said and more that I cannot."

She closed her eyes, steeling herself against the persuasion of his words, but she could feel herself weakening.

If she married him, she thought, then she would never have to hear the dreaded news in the future that he had taken another wife. She wouldn't have to take another man as her husband, or bear a stranger's intimate touch. Or give birth to children not Morgan's and spend her life wondering where he was and if he ever thought of her.

And fondness grew in time, didn't it? It had with Mother and Father, and look how devoted they were to one another. Theirs had been an arranged match but they had grown a deep and abiding love.

"Ask me," she said hoarsely, not daring to look at him.

"What?"

"I deserve that much, even if it's merely a formality. I want you to ask me."

She thought he would balk. He wasn't pleased, that much was certain. There was a long silence.

But then he grabbed her shoulders and turned her around. Taking her chin in his hand, he tilted her head up and made her look at him. He said in a rough-edged voice, "Marry me, Blackie. Please marry me. Do me the great honor of being my wife."

She searched his face, hoping for more than just the words. His face held regret, but begrudged her anything more.

How hopeless she felt and trapped between pride on one hand and desperate, secret love refusing to relent on the other.

"Yes," she said, not sounding at all happy. "Yes, Morgan, I will marry you."

M ORGAN OBTAINED A special license for his marriage and headed up to Yorkshire, where Leah insisted the ceremony take place. He would have preferred the convenience of some place closer to Brighton, where he would head immediately after Leah was bundled off safely to her sister's, but he would just have to cope with the inconvenience.

After agreeing to marry him, Leah hadn't asked for a single other thing. That made him reluctant to deny her this, especially when he knew how much she loved her cousin Daphne. Even her mother's wish to have the celebration at the Cravensmores' country home would not dissuade her. She said simply she needed to be "home."

Therefore, he didn't mind so much. In fact, he thought it a pleasant idea to be once again in the place where he grew up, the place where they had met. As he made his way up to the blessedly coolness of the moors, he felt himself relax, despite all that lay immediately before him, and that word . . . *home* echoed comfortingly in his head.

Daphne's house, to which he had been given direction, surprised him as he rode into the narrow courtyard in front. It was nothing more than a cottage, although admittedly larger than the typical countryside dwelling. The half-timbered facade boasted mullioned windows, and a thatched roof made the place look like an oversized mushroom. It sprawled over a maze of well-tended gardens, all in profuse bloom.

It actually seemed rather idyllic in a strange, wild, and earthy sort of way. As enchanting and ethereal as the woman who had emerged from it and taken to the moors like a wild-hearted sprite that day in early spring.

He was let in by a robust housekeeper and shown into an empty drawing room. He was left with the reassurance that the housekeeper would find the family and tell them he was here.

That proved to be quite a task, apparently, for it was a good while later and he was still sitting alone in the strangely appointed room, taking stock of his surroundings. All manner of oddities littered the place. The statuary favored figurines of the primitive type, not the classical busts and nudes so popular these days. Some were frightening, others comical, with naked, rounded bellies and grinning faces. There were objects that were unidentifiable, apparently artifacts or souvenirs of some kind. Daphne, or someone else who lived in the house, must have undertaken some extraordinary travels. They filled him with curiosity and a rumbling of his own wanderlust, frustrated by his sense of duty that had cut short his travels and kept him tied to home.

He stood, wandering about to view the huge paintings on the walls, examining the depictions of jungle animals and mounted tribal artifacts. Exotic prints trimmed with scarlet fringe were draped at the windows. He fingered them, wondering about their origin.

Sighing, he consulted his watch and sat. Even the furniture was unique, very large and carved in fine detail that was boldly out of fashion. He found, as he sank into a deeply-cushioned settee, it was also sinfully comfortable.

Morgan was gaining a growing appreciation for Leah's fondness for her very interesting, if eccentric, cousin—she who filled girls' heads with stories of abduction, love, the bliss, and birth control methods. He made a mental note not to allow his future daughters to spend too much time here without close supervision.

There was a scuffle out in the hallway, a burst of giggles and two little girls appeared in the doorway. Not noticing him at first, they entered, one slightly taller with long spiral blond curls and one shorter, darker, adorable with Leah's eyes and hair a deep, rich sable.

He'd met these two before, Leah's sisters. Marie was the dark one, the baby of the family. Her sister, whose startling aquamarine eyes and full mouth promised the blessing of astonishing beauty when she grew into her womanhood, was named Hope.

They stopped and gaped at him. They must have recognized him, for they did not appear alarmed, only surprised. The older one, the blond with the mesmerizing eyes, dropped a curtsy. "My lord," she murmured, then elbowed her sister to do the same.

The little one bobbed quickly, eyes huge, mouth hanging open just a little. Morgan rose and swept a low bow. "My ladies."

Hope looked horrified. "Oh, we aren't ladies. I mean, we are *ladies,* but we don't have a title. You mustn't address us so."

"You so impressed me, I find that surprising. You are, of course, Miss Hope and Miss Marie."

Marie smiled, pleased that he should know her. "And you are the earl of Waring. I remember you. You are Leah's Morgan. You're to be our brother!"

"Marie, you mustn't. This is the earl—"

Morgan cut off the flustered child. "Yes. I am Leah's Morgan. I much prefer you call me by my name. A title is so impersonal."

Marie beamed. "Raphael says that, too. He is our brother by marriage. Raphael is a viscount and Mother says we should call him Font-vee-ay but he hates that, so we don't. He says we shouldn't."

Easing back into his seat, Morgan chuckled covertly, not wanting her to think he was laughing at her. Her mannerisms were so like Leah's it punched an ache straight through his chest.

Was this what their daughters would be like? he thought suddenly. He seemed to have his future offspring on his mind a great deal of late. He had never before thought about children. Suddenly, the idea held amazing appeal.

Hope nudged her sister and sent her a chiding glance. "I am sorry, my lord. Please do not fault my sister. She is young."

He almost did laugh, then—right out loud, at the serious,

solemn girl. She was more like Julia, this one, already showing surprising poise and a dignity well beyond her years.

"I assure you, I am not so easy to offend. After all, we are to be family, and family are allowed a certain degree of familiarity, don't you agree?"

Family. His own voice forming the word jarred him.

Hope smiled. "Yes, of course." She looked to Marie. "We should be getting upstairs. We were to come to tea, but I think we are too early. We will go and wait so we do not disturb you."

"Please don't go. I don't care to be left alone. We should get to know each other, don't you think?" He motioned to the settee, which Marie promptly bounced onto.

"Are you waiting for Leah?" Marie asked. "She takes a long time to dress. When I am older, I shall have pretty dresses, too, and someone to make up my hair."

"You will melt hearts," he assured her. Looking to Hope, he asked, "Will you join us?"

She sat next to her sister after a moment's indecision.

Marie regarded him pertly. "Do you have brothers and sisters?"

"I have a stepmother only."

"Oh. I am sorry."

"Indeed, why would you be? She is a great friend."

"Oh. I thought she would be awful. Cinderella's stepmother was *very* awful."

"Actually, she is a lovely lady. You may meet her some time. She is unable to come to the wedding, however." He hadn't invited her. With Glorianna came her husband, the last person he wished to see on his wedding day.

"Where's your real mother?" Marie asked.

"She's in heaven, with my sister. They died many years ago." Hope looked horrified. Morgan said, "Don't be alarmed, I don't mind that you've asked," he reassured her.

"I'm so sorry," Marie said. "But you still have your father, right?"

"He died a few years ago, a long while after the fever took the others. We were very close, and I miss him a great deal."

She looked stricken, her bottom lip sticking out and trembling. "That's sad." Her face crumpled. "That's very sad."

"Marie!" Hope hissed.

Morgan found himself on his knees in front of the child, her small chubby hands clasped in his. Her huge eyes swimming in tears stared at him. He could see the fine curve of her brow, her pert nose. Just like Leah. So much like Leah, but simpler. Ah, yes, well, it was much simpler without the complication of desire.

That was how he knew the urge to hold her was completely from the heart. He didn't, of course, but he couldn't resist smoothing the little girl's hair. "You mustn't be sad for me. It was a long time ago, and I've learned to live with it. It doesn't hurt any longer, not like it used to."

"You are very brave," Marie said, twisting to look up into his face, hers full of amazement.

He recoiled, feeling a fraud in the face of such honest admiration. "Oh, no, that is not true. It is just that you cannot feel badly forever. The people you loved wouldn't want that." He paused thoughtfully. "I was told that recently, and have found it very true."

"I would weep all day long," Marie insisted, then brightened as a thought occurred to her. "But you have Leah now. You can have all of us as your new family."

Liking this idea a great deal, she bounced in her seat. "Just like Raphael. Oh, I told you about him. He's funny. He tells us stories and plays with us. Sometimes Julia scolds him because he lets us do stuff we're not supposed to. He lets us run outside and one time, when it was raining, we went splashing in the mud!"

She stopped, her face screwing up in concentration. "Sometimes, though, I don't like him so much, because he kisses Julia and it is just awful, all smushed up. Ugh."

He chuckled, sitting beside her. "Don't you think you will ever kiss a beau?"

"Never!" Marie declared.

Glancing at Hope, he asked, "What of you?" Her indecision was easy to read on her face. He cajoled her by saying, "Or do you already have a beau?"

"No," she answered seriously. "No, I do not. I . . . I do not think I wish to marry."

A startling confession from this prim little creature. Morgan was intrigued. "And why not?"

"I think . . . I imagine that I would like to live on my own, without having to listen to anyone tell me what to do. I fear I am rather . . . independent." She confessed this as if it were a great liability. "I simply like being with my family, or by myself."

Morgan nodded. "I can understand that. All people, women and men, yearn for freedom to pursue the things they love."

"Mother says she's too pensive." Marie struggled with the last word, but got it right.

Morgan saw that Hope felt this a disadvantage. He said, "I myself admire those whose thoughts run deep. Pensive people tend to be wise, that is if they steer clear of brooding. You don't brood, Miss Hope, do you?"

Her face was alight with pleasure. "Oh, no. I am simply quiet."

"There. You are to be envied."

The gorgeous child blushed, pleased, and Morgan felt a sense of satisfaction at having allayed her fears.

Marie asked, "Do you think we'll have apple tarts today? I love tea with apple tarts. Sometimes Leah gives us extra because Mother says we shouldn't have too much, but I don't think it's too much, except sometimes my tummy does hurt. Oh! I said tummy. I'm not supposed to talk about parts of my body. I'm sorry."

"You can say tummy," Morgan said.

She relaxed. "I forgot it is all right to say that to you. You are going to be our brother. I'm glad. I like you."

"And I like you, too."

Hope smiled shyly and ducked her head while Marie beamed.

Leah spoke from the doorway. "I hear you giving away

our secret. Didn't I tell you that the sneaking of sweets was never to be told?"

The admonition was not meant to chide, but Marie sprung to the defensive. "But I only told Morgan. He won't tell anyone else, Leah."

"Indeed, I will not," Morgan assured them as he rose. His gaze swept appreciatively over her. She wore a new dress today, a smartly tailored muslin in pale peach sprigged with beige florets and tiny green leaves. Her hair was neatly arranged. She looked uncharacteristically prim, but no less appealing than when she had been windswept and breathless that first day he'd set eyes on her. "As it happens," he stated, not taking his eyes off her, "I am excellent at keeping secrets."

The warmth in Leah's face dissolved. A mask fell over her smooth features, one he was getting used to seeing these last few weeks since they'd become engaged.

She sailed past him, avoiding his eyes. To her sisters, she said, "While we wait for the others, why don't we four play a game? Not only is the earl good at secrets," she said, arching her chin and swinging back to pin Morgan with an over-the-shoulder look, "he is also *outstanding* at games."

Chapter 17

On Saturday, Leah and Morgan spoke their marriage vows in the small village chapel. When the vicar said the words, "I pronounce you man and wife," Leah turned toward Morgan, her eyes lowered, and he kissed her chastely on her forehead before turning the two of them to greet the flood of well-wishers surging from the pew.

Back at the cottage, the wedding breakfast was laid out and waiting. Flowers drenched the air with fragrance, vying with the sumptuous aromas of fine food. Champagne flowed freely and there were people everywhere, talking, laughing. A pianoforte was tinkled in the background by some person unseen, tucked away discreetly.

The celebration gave every appearance of commemorating a very happy day. Leah did nothing that would either enhance or dispel this. A group of older women clucked when she appeared a bit dazed during a conversation and murmured about the wedding night making her nervous, smiling with forgiveness as Leah blushed profusely and excused herself.

Morgan found her and insisted she eat. As he filled her plate, he made conversation she knew was forced.

The sour feeling in her stomach increased by the minute. This was wrong. How could she have made such a dreadful mistake—how had she not realized how impossible it would be to love this man with all of her heart and never have that feeling returned? It would have been best to have left him, she now realized. Maybe it would have been horrible at first, but in time she would have come to see it was better than to have the elusive promise of what she so desperately wanted before her always.

Looking at him now, so tall and straight and dressed impeccably, she never felt farther from him. Marriage had made things worse, not better.

As evening approached, the local guests began to take their leave. Leah and Morgan planned to spend their wedding night at the nearby inn in the village. They drove the short distance. Acting as her attendants, Julia and their mother took their own carriage and met up with them in the common room. The two women escorted Leah up to a spacious suite while Morgan waited downstairs, sipping a brandy.

Debra had come earlier to make the place ready. Leah's brushes were laid on a table and a flowing confection that seemed to resemble a nightgown, only much more shocking, lay across the bed. Leah glanced at this, then did a double take.

Desdemona came to take Leah's hands in hers. When she saw the direction in which Leah was staring she rolled her eyes. "A gift from your sister," she said flatly. "I daresay her husband had a hand in its selection."

"It was to be mine, but the color is wrong for me," Julia explained. "I've never worn it before, and as the plans for the wedding were made so quickly, I didn't have time to have one made especially for you. I hope you don't mind."

Leah pulled her eyes away from the shockingly sheer garment. "No. Not at all." She looked at her mother, who seemed to be blinking as if she had a piece of dust in her eye. Then Leah realized she was batting away tears and felt a lump rise in her own throat.

Desdemona said. "I am so very confident that you and Morgan will have every happiness."

The pressure in Leah's throat grew painful.

"You have made an excellent choice in your husband. I cannot say I was always sure of this, but Daphne reminded me today of how he looks at you, and I realize it was that all along that calmed my doubts. I never cared for the talk that surrounded him, but I gave him a chance, and now it's come to this. You are a countess! More importantly, however, you are with a caring man who will take good care of you."

Leah couldn't take her eyes off her mother while her thoughts raced. *If only you knew, Mother. I think I've made a terrible mistake.*

"Now, I have asked Julia to speak with you, as she is more of an age." Releasing Leah's hand, she exited the room, pausing at the door to say, "I will wait in the carriage for you, Julia."

Julia laughed softly when she was gone. "For all of her forcefulness, Mother is endearingly awkward with these matters. She asked me to talk to you about a wife's duties because she just couldn't face doing it herself." She walked to the bed and picked up the negligee. "I cannot say I am looking forward to it either. Of course, I am aware that there is a possibility that such a talk may not be necessary." She cast a sideways glance at Leah. "I wouldn't be shocked."

"You wouldn't?"

"No. But I am glad we have some time to talk together. I've been watching you, and, frankly, I don't understand your mood. I thought you would be so happy today."

"I am," Leah said quickly, not wanting to admit to her sister the torrid thoughts that had plagued her all day. Besides, what good would it do? She had already taken her marriage vows. Any regrets were too late. "I am just a bit overwhelmed."

Julia looked doubtful, but seemed to decide not to pursue it further. "Dear Leah," she said, giving her a warm hug, "I'm so glad we've become friends as well as sisters."

"I am, too," Leah said with sincerity.

"I hope you will confide in me when you are ready. Until then, the only advice I can give you is this: Believe in love, Leah."

She gave her a quick kiss and left Leah to Debra, who had come in just then. As Debra combed out her hair, Leah stared at her reflection. She was a wife now. Morgan's wife. Stepping into the beautiful negligee, she surveyed herself in the mirror.

A shivery feeling rippled through her. Could she believe in love?

Staring at her image, she felt impossibly vulnerable. She turned away as the door opened and Morgan came in just as Debra left.

He was dressed in a loosely belted wrapper over his trousers. His hair was tousled, as if he'd run his hands through it too many times. He stopped cold when he saw her, his eyes taking in the negligee. He definitely approved.

That made her feel entirely more confident. The shivery heat that always accompanied the first stirrings of arousal unfolded over her.

"You are gorgeous," he said, and his voice sounded strange, as if he didn't quite have enough breath. He closed the distance between them. Very gently he took her hands in both of his and pulled her close. "You looked unhappy today."

"I think I've made a mistake," she blurted, although that disturbing sensation she had felt before was fading now, almost gone.

His eyebrows jerked upward. "Do you? Why?"

"Because you can't love me."

A slow smile crept over his mouth, curving it in the most exquisitely sensual way. "Oh, Blackie, that just isn't true."

She would have asked him what he meant, was about to, in fact, when he took her face in his hands. She tended to be very stupid when he looked at her like this, all capacity to think flying out of her head in an instant. Perhaps, she considered dreamily, she should shut her eyes to block out the soft look of him, stop this wonderful melting feeling and demand answers, but she didn't.

She searched his face with eager eyes, wanting some sign, some knowledge of what was meant by those words.

Did she dare believe in love?

He kissed her, slowly, gently, speaking to her with that gesture. Her body moved to respond without her volition, leaning into him and clutching his shoulders. She craved words, but the kiss filled her after a moment.

Pulling away far too soon, he locked his gaze with hers and slowly peeled the sheer peignoir from her shoulders. It fell like a whisper into a puddle at her feet. His eyes swept over her and she felt a violent surge of exhilaration at the smoldering expression as he looked at her.

He removed his dressing gown and led her to the bed. His breath caught when she reached up and twined her arms around his neck, her fingertips digging hungrily into the hardness of muscle, gliding greedily over his warm skin. He crushed her under him, kissing her until she couldn't breathe.

She *did* believe in love, Leah thought. Quite unexpectedly, she did.

His hands were reverent, touching her as if she were something very precious to him. His mouth was eloquent as he kissed her, tasted her, nibbled her into weak-limbed ecstasy. She began to think these sweet moments of pleasure were surely strong enough to last the rest of their lives. To take them into the future together, to eradicate all of the distance that threatened her peace of mind and fulfill the desires that burned more deeply than the fires of the flesh.

In his arms, Leah very much believed in the power of love. She believed because she needed to believe. She let herself go, surrendered, soared with him until they curled, exhausted, into the warm shelter of each other to sleep.

But the morning found that conviction of no more substance than a dream.

Leah awoke to find Morgan had adjourned to give her privacy for her ablutions. He returned within a short while to share a private breakfast at a table he had arranged to be set up in her room.

Something seemed to be on his mind. She noticed immediately a reserve in him that was incongruent with the magic they'd shared hours before.

At last he said, "Leah, I want to talk to you about our plans. I think it would be best for you to go to Glenwood Park. Raphael has invited you for a prolonged visit and I think it is a good idea."

She was astonished at this news. "Really? That would be wonderful. When do we leave?"

"Today. But it shall not be 'we,' Leah. You are to go alone." He flashed a look at her, as if he were feeling guilty. "I need to go to Brighton."

She frowned. "Brighton? Why the devil are you . . ." She stopped, giving him a daunting look. "Oh. Oh, Morgan, what are you about?"

He took a labored breath. "Please don't ask me, Leah. It would only worry you—"

"Oh, really! Well, that completely reassures me!"

His tone was full of patience, but with noticeable effort. "You have to trust me. I need to finish what I started. And I need to know that you are safe. Now, I want you to go to Julia's and stay with her until I can send for you."

She felt her emotions converge like thunderheads before a gathering storm. "You bastard," she whispered. "You are sending me away. I should have known—you never meant for us to have a real marriage."

"What? This is not about you and I. It is a matter that must be settled between Randall and myself."

"Which is the only relationship you care about!"

"I cannot have this conversation with you now. I have to prepare for my trip. I wish you would just accede to my wishes. For once, would it kill you?"

"Oh, yes, you *will* have this conversation, and now. As far as killing me, that is not the issue. Killing you is—which I may do myself if Randall Sanderson doesn't do so first."

"He is not going to kill me."

"Morgan, you lied to me."

He was taken aback. "I did not."

"I thought you were giving me a future when you asked me to marry you. Just yesterday, you pledged until death do us part. Well, that wasn't such a big commitment, after all. One day!"

"For the last time, I am not going to die. I . . ."

She stared at him, her large eyes wide, a knife and fork held in each hand like weapons. "I know what you are planning to do, at least I have a good idea of it. And Randall Sanderson will destroy you before he allows you to."

"I will be all right. It is all carefully planned. Now, no more discussion." Morgan rose, threw his napkin on his plate, which he'd barely touched.

She shot to her feet. "You really think you can simply discard me, is that it? You will just dismiss me and I'll scurry off like a good little wife."

Morgan turned and walked out of the room.

Breathless, seething, Leah yanked open the door he'd just closed. It crashed against the outside wall, the sound deafening.

Stepping into the hall, she shouted at his retreating back, "Now that you've had your tumble, you shall send me away, like a tidy little pet—is that the idea? I suppose I am to trot off and await the next time you deign to make time for me in your oh-so-important life." She followed him to the top of the stairs and down into the common room, deserted at this hour. "I'm a damned bloody nuisance, aren't I? Come back here!"

The innkeeper, who was folding napkins in one of the small dining rooms off the main room, looked up, shocked.

Morgan stopped, turned around, and said in as calm a tone as she ever heard, "I would appreciate it if you would manage some decorum and go back into the room and pack. I will explain everything when I return."

"Oh, certainly, I shall hie myself off immediately and disappear—so sorry to have inconvenienced you, *you blighter!*"

The innkeeper fled.

"You will watch your language," he growled, his brows drawing down to shadow his eyes.

"Oh, bugger off. The day I allow you to dictate my behavior is the day I stop drawing breath." Crossing her arms over her chest, she stuck out her chin. "I am not a child, nor a . . . piece of chattel to be shipped off subject to your determination of my usefulness. I refuse, do you hear? I shall not go. If I am an unwanted intrusion in your life, I shall take *myself* off, to wherever and whomever I please."

He let out a soft explosion of frustration. "I am trying to protect you, you daft little chit. It has nothing to do with what I *want*. I need you out of the way."

To her utter disgrace, fat, hot tears ran in rivulets down her cheeks. "I know you didn't want this marriage. But I thought you would honor it. I thought we would *try*. . . . I never imagined you meant to put me aside like this as if I were nothing more than a damned mare you purchased to brood for you."

"Leah." He was fast losing patience. "It is not like I am casting you aside. I am your husband, and I must have the obedience—which you promised just yesterday at about this very hour. You will go. I swear it, you will, even if I have to wrap you in a burlap sack and have you toted in the back of a wool wagon."

She felt cold, colder than she'd ever been in her life. She suddenly didn't believe in love. Love for Morgan was hot passion in the dark hours between dusk and dawn, but it was like all things that flourished in the night, unable to withstand the harsh reality of day.

"Of course," she said, bowing her head. "I wouldn't dream of inflicting myself on you. I don't even want to any longer. You can be damned, Morgan."

Turning on her heel, she went into their room and shut the door.

A terrified servant knocked hours later, disturbing Leah's brooding.

"Will you take luncheon, my lady?" the trembling girl inquired.

"No, thank you, but send up some tea, please. Thank you."

The servant brought the tray very quickly, placed it on the table they had used for breakfast, and scurried away. Pouring herself a steaming cup and dropping in a cube of sugar, Leah took it with her to one of the chairs by the window. She placed it on her lap and forgot it as she chewed upon her thumbnail.

For the thousandth time, her thoughts returned to the argument she had had with Morgan that morning. She now knew why he was so eager to marry her. He had to rush the wedding to be able to ship her off to Julia's so that he was free to go to Brighton. What was going to happen in Brighton?

But she knew. Her stomach clenched. Even if she hated the man at this moment, she still loved him. Fear engulfed her as she imagined the dangers he most certainly would face.

For the thousandth time, she wondered why hadn't she fallen in love with another man—why this stubborn, complicated, unfeeling beast with absolutely no regard for what he was putting her through? What of someone like fun-loving Kingsley or any of the other beaus who'd vied for her hand and who would have done anything she wished, she had only to ask?

And for the first time, she stopped in the midst of her raging with a sudden thought. Morgan had never lied to her, never made any pretense of being anything other than what he was. He hadn't promised her anything he was now taking away. Therefore, how could she fault him? He was the man he was and perhaps it was precisely the things that had her railing were what made her love him most.

Most of all, he was not to blame because she loved him. It wasn't her right, furthermore, to have love in return. After all, she hadn't chosen to fall in love with him. If he didn't return the same desires she held in her heart, then she couldn't fault him as if it were something he'd done wrong.

Love must be freely given, or not given at all.

She smiled ruefully at her musings. *What do you know? I seem to have finally found some sense.*

Picking up her cup absently, she sipped, grimaced at the tepid temperature. She must have lost track of time while lost in thought. She returned it to its saucer and stood.

She rang for the servant, who entered the room moments later with eyes wide with trepidation.

As sweetly as she could manage to make up for her earlier show of spleen, she said, "Please fetch my maid, Debra. I must have my things packed. I will be departing first thing in the morning. Make certain the grooms are alerted to have the carriage ready."

She departed, looking very, very relieved to hear Leah was leaving.

THE NEXT MORNING, Morgan watched from the window as his carriage pulled out of the inn's forecourt, bearing away his wife.

He frowned, placing his hand on the glass.

Oh, but there was much more than the thick, uneven pane keeping Leah and he apart. Little fool.

Little brave, beautiful, lovely fool.

He heaved a sigh, grateful that she'd gone willingly. He'd meant what he'd said; he'd have dragged her to Cumbria if he'd had to. When this was all over, he'd make her understand, he'd tell her she'd been wrong. She'd see. He'd be different when this matter with Sanderson was over. And God help him, he'd never let her go, never again.

The carriage disappeared down the lane, swallowed by the trees. He summoned his valet.

"We leave for Brighton tomorrow."

THE DAYS OF Brighton's being the epitome of summer social entertainments was beginning to fade. The streets, once the exclusive retreat of the aristocracy, were attracting the demimonde and middle classes. Gawkers lined the Steyne as the well dressed partook of their promenade, and there was a pervasive air of seediness that one couldn't quite escape.

Morgan rented rooms at the Old Ship Inn. The social life of the seaside resort didn't interest him, nor did the therapeutic waters purported to restore health and vitality. During the day, he walked the streets idly, more to while away time than out of enjoyment. Sometimes he'd go into a shop, pick up an item, and think of Leah. He'd wonder if she would like this particular bauble or that bit of lace. He'd reach for his purse before realizing what he was doing. Sometimes he would put the item back. Other times, he'd purchase it anyway, take it to his rooms and tuck it away for when he saw her again.

He kept thinking about that, when he would see her again. It was a maddening diversion as he waited for all the players to arrive and play their appointed role.

The Old Ship had assembly rooms, used for balls and card parties and massive teas, each activity delegated to take place on a different night of the week. These he attended regularly. It was in the second week that he first got hint the wags were working the news. The gossips began to buzz. At first it was just a comment, a stare, a raised brow in interest. He heard there was talk again of the murder.

He had been prepared for some backlash—once the subject was brought up, he would get some of his own old scandal resurrected. That did occur in addition to several looks askance at such a newly married husband at Brighton, hardly a haven of propriety, without his new wife.

Those were bleak days. The Wicked Earl restored to his legend, he reflected morosely, and wondered if he'd grossly miscalculated. But the interest in him died down quickly when the story broke in the newspapers of corrupt Yorkshire officials. The drone of talk grew louder, like hornets stirring angrily as Castleton arrived in town and began to stir the nest.

When Sanderson arrived, Morgan was informed immediately that he and Glorianna were staying at The Castle. Roberts and his men, all former runners, were making themselves inconspicuous in the crowds of the resort. They kept a constant watch over the couple, with strict orders to send word to the Old Ship the moment either one of them made a move.

More waiting. It occurred to Morgan that he'd never done so much damn waiting in his life. He just needed one tiny sliver of opportunity, one sign that the mood had shifted against Randall and the time had come, and he'd move. It was coming; it was coming fast. He could feel it. He waited.

When he received a summons to meet Glorianna in one of the private dining rooms in his hotel, his thought was of a possible trap. Dashing off an acceptance, he positioned Roberts at the door and checked the matched set of pistols he had stuck in his waistband. They'd been primed, but their hammers were down to prevent any accidental firing. He pulled one back, and adjusted his morning coat to cover it. His hand rode the cocked pistol as he entered the room, his mind calm, set. Ready.

Glorianna was seated in the far corner, turned away to watch the people outside the window. As his footsteps scraped, a sound that seemed impossibly loud in the empty room, she turned, greeting him with a troubled smile.

Morgan paused, tensed to strike if Sanderson should appear.

"Are we alone?" Morgan asked.

Glorianna's eyes darted to her left. Every muscle bunched, tightening for action as his gaze followed hers. His hand splayed, ready to grip the pistol and bring it to bear on his enemy.

From behind a fluted column, a soft, distinct, infuriatingly familiar voice muttered, "Bloody hell."

Leah stepped out into the open. Anticipating his reaction, she had her hand held up before her, a gesture not at all contrite or penitent. It was commanding, as was her tone. "Listen to Glorianna. You and I shall sort out our differences later."

He was still grappling with this stunning development of seeing his wife here when Glorianna stood, drawing his attention. "Leah and I have had a long talk, Morgan." She looked weary, sad, and strangely needy. "She's told me everything."

He started, feeling as if he'd been punched. "What?"

"I know you mean to kill Randall," Glorianna said. "And I'm here to ask you not to."

He was surprised—shocked into silence for a moment. He'd never told Leah his ultimate plan to kill Sanderson during a legal duel.

But she had guessed. She knew him better than he had ever surmised. And she'd betrayed him.

He drew in a breath, gathering his wits. "I don't expect you to understand, not when you feel as you do about him, but he *did* murder my father. I have proof and everyone will shortly know of it. Every single fact is true and can be proven. He did it, Glorianna. He did. I have to kill him. You must understand that."

Glorianna bowed her head, burying her face in her handkerchief. "How can I believe that? I know you wouldn't lie, but I can't imagine it, Morgan, I can't!"

Glancing at Leah over the aggrieved woman's head, he gave his wife a forbidding look.

With an air of rebellion, she said, "It occurred to me that I didn't want to end up a widow. So, halfway to Cumbria I ordered the carriage to turn around. I sent a message on that you'd had a change of plans, but I suppose Julia and Raphael will become concerned after a while. You might want to send word that I am here."

"Your capacity for deception is amazing."

"Yes." She narrowed her eyes and gave him a smirk. "I'm

coming along nicely, aren't I? I suppose it is in the quality of my instructor."

"When did you arrive?"

"A few days ago. I sought out Glorianna immediately. I thought it was time we pushed all of this out into the open." She paused, her stony exterior slipping. "I didn't do this for spite, Morgan. I just don't want you to die. And I couldn't bear it."

"And what, pray tell, does Randall make of your sudden appearance with his wife?"

"Well, I am not a fool, Morgan. I was careful. I made sure Glorianna understood the risk. I met her at the pump room, and Sanderson thinks Glorianna is taking in the waters whenever we met to talk. He knows nothing about me and suspects nothing about this meeting."

"You think yourself clever."

"I am clever. She is here, is she not?"

"That doesn't mean there is no danger. The risk you took, my God! How could you be certain Glorianna wouldn't go directly to her husband with what you told her? She trusts him and thinks I'm a lunatic for my accusations."

She gave him that regal look of disdain that never failed to annoy him. "I did what I thought was necessary. I knew I could speak with her, woman to woman, as long as she didn't have that dreadful Randall hovering over her—really, Glorianna, I hate to speak of you as if you aren't here, but it seems unavoidable." She looked pityingly at the other woman, who was dabbing her eyes and looking miserable. More gently, she said, "How did you fail to see through him, he is so obvious?"

But Morgan was still very angry with his wife. "You didn't trust me, Leah."

"That is unfair," Glorianna interjected. "Morgan, please. If you wanted a fainting miss who did your bidding blindly then you have only yourself to blame. Leah was right, after all. I have listened to her and kept her secrets. I know she believes in you, and I've come to speak to you, hear what you have to say." Her voice faltered. She swallowed hard and began again. "Is it true you have proof? I want to see it. I need it. I believe you, I do, but it is so hard to accept that Randall would be capable of such an unspeakable crime." Her face collapsed and she covered it again and sobbed.

He went to her, put a hand on her shoulder. Immediately Leah was on her other side, comforting her.

"Go ahead, Morgan." Leah's voice was soft, gentle, and strong at the same time. "Tell her."

Slowly, softly, Morgan told Glorianna everything. "I knew when the fake letter was 'discovered' among Father's effects that Randall had to have done this. I had known he wanted you. It was what Father and I quarreled over that night. Then, in the days after, when the local officials refused to properly investigate the crime and I was arrested, it was all too incredible. I knew my cousin. It all came down to one inevitable truth.

"There will be others to corroborate this with further proof." He outlined the phalanx of rumors recently released among the peerage, adding, "Each man who has agreed to help me is a man of good character, a man of honor who has offered to do this because he knows the truth. This sum total is irrefutable, Glorianna. There are documents, testimony, all I need to prove every word I am saying is the absolute truth."

"Oh, Morgan," she cried, "can he truly be that vile?" She looked at him appealingly. "And I that foolish? I am married to a murderer."

"No. Do not blame yourself. You could not have known. It does no good in any event. He's fooled many people over the years, my father included, and he was a hard man to deceive. Randall is very good."

Glorianna wiped her cheeks. "He killed Evan. He killed my love. Morgan, listen to me, I promise I will help you any way I can. Please, just don't leave me, Morgan. I'm so afraid."

Morgan grabbed her. "Of course I won't. I should never have left before."

"I was alone. I can't stand to be alone. I . . ."

"It's all right. I'm going to get you away from him, I

promise. The first thing, though, is that you understand that you mustn't tell him any of this. You cannot even hint that anything is amiss. With the pressure mounting around him as the scandal grows, he may become unpredictable."

"I won't, of course I won't. Just tell me what you want me to do."

Leah came up beside Glorianna and put her arms gently around her, drawing her away from Morgan. "You are over-set right now. You need to think about all of this, let your brain get used to it. It is rather a big thing to digest. Go back to your room and rest. You can talk to Morgan again." She looked at Morgan. "Does that sound acceptable?"

"Yes," Morgan agreed. "Glorianna, if you need to reach me, just have one of the hotel staff send word to me. I will not be far, I promise. You will not be alone again."

The delicate woman pressed a hand to her temple, squeezing her eyes shut. "Yes. I need to think. I just need a little time, Morgan. Thank you."

"I'll call a hansom for you."

After Glorianna left, Morgan took a deep, bracing breath and turned toward his wife. "I am not sure if I want to strangle you or kiss you."

"That is nothing unusual."

He advanced on her. "You deliberately defied me."

"Again, not unusual." She didn't seem at all sorry. In fact, she stared back at him, mildly defiant, but not as she'd been before. Not reckless or impetuous, but with a cool self-possession that gave him pause. She was too remote, disturbingly so.

He said, "I wanted you safe, in Cumbria."

"I was on my way, actually. But I kept being haunted by the thought that I would never see you again. It was cruel what you did to me, Morgan. Not in sending me away, that part I understand, although it hurt to be shut out again. But by the same need that made you have to see to my safety, I had to assure myself of yours. It was unbearable not to know what you were doing, yet knowing you were going to challenge a man who had murdered once, and who hated you. I knew I could do one last thing to help you."

"What do you mean, last thing?" he asked sharply.

"I love you, Morgan," she said, ignoring his question. "And love is love. It isn't ownership or possession. It's giving. So I wanted to give you this. I thought it would help you if Glorianna were told of the truth, and you knew she was on your side. You always needed her so badly. It also would make it easier to leave if I knew you had Glorianna. You would have your family restored, then."

Watching as she moved a few paces, he noticed how stiff she was, how straight her back. Leah had always moved like a breeze, a wide stride, long, loose movements that suited her lithe form. She was always full of confidence and ease. She'd changed.

"Leah, what is this about 'leaving'?"

She wasn't looking at him, but off into the distance, lost in her own thoughts. Her voice was soft, breathy, wistful. "I used to try to imagine ways to get you to tell me your secrets. All your hardness, all your self-contained darkness was like a brilliant scarlet sash waving madly in front of a bull. I wanted to know everything about you, not just facts or explanations, but what you felt and what you thought, about anything, everything. And then . . . as I was steaming over your sending me away, thinking about all of this, it came to me. Just like that, I understood, you see, and then I wasn't so angry any longer."

Morgan watched her with gathering disquiet.

"Your heart is locked away," she said. "And I have no key to unlock it. I have only one means to affect you. Lust. Perhaps duty, too, that need to *take care of your own* that was ingrained in you so well that you would marry and protect me."

She spoke with no vehemence, no passion. Somehow, that was the worst of it.

"Lust and duty . . . I know it's not your fault that you can't return my feelings, but that doesn't change that it simply isn't good enough for me, not anymore. I believe you were right all along. I do deserve something better."

She turned to him, and he saw she wasn't completely untouched. Her eyes glistened, as brilliant as stars. "I hereby surrender. I've given you all I had, Morgan. I loved you. And you never wanted any of it. Well, all right, then. It is time I accept that. At least now at last I've managed to give one thing that matters to you. Glorianna. And you will get Randall Sanderson, one way or the other. You are too driven, too clever, too cold . . . too unable to accept anything less to fail. I hope for your success, I do. That is what I will pray for, and that is what I will believe because I can't bear to think otherwise." She drew herself up straight, her face rigid, her marvelous eyes losing their luster in a few transforming blinks.

Now they regarded him with a return of their former coolness, flat and dull.

"I shall go to Cumbria, just as you *requested*—" There was a flash of familiar impishness in the word and the emphasis she put on it. "—and leave you to your . . . business." She paused, rolling her lips together to bite them. Her brow twitched into a crease, then smoothed. "I will have Father and the duke speak to the archbishop about an annulment. As for your guards, I will cooperate as long as you see the need. But I need to be away from you. For good. It's hard, Morgan. It's the hardest thing I've ever done, but it's one big hurt. I don't think I could survive a lifetime of small, deadly hurts each and every day living with someone who can never love me."

"Leah!" His voice was like a command. Only he knew it was panic that made it sharp.

She shook her head.

"Don't be foolish," he said. She stopped, frozen, still not looking at him. "You . . . you don't understand."

He saw her shoulders square. "But I do, Morgan. I am afraid I do."

He swayed. God! His throat was closed, making breathing difficult. Words were impossible. He felt cold, hot, empty, weak and at the same time a rage burst inside of him, but it was trapped, railing impotently at the confining strictures of his pride. Was it pride? Or simply habit?

"Leah, what do you want from me? To give up now, to sit like a tame dog at your heels?"

She sighed wearily. "It's not about Randall, Morgan. It is about love."

He grew angrier. "It is so easy for you—you have everything you need, mother and father, sisters and even protective brother-in-law. Of course, it is merely a matter of getting on with things, to just forget the past. Well, it isn't like that for me. Do you think I don't want it to be different?"

"Then make it different," she cried.

"I can't, damn it all! There isn't room for love, not until I purge this hate. I never wanted it—I didn't ask for it. But it's mine and I am stuck with it. I have to *finish* this, I have no choice."

She shook her head disbelievingly. "You have every choice."

He looked away, frustrated. She waited for him to respond. When he didn't, she went without another word, eyes down, back straight. Beautiful. Leaving him. Leaving him.

Alone, he stared blindly into the middle distance, his thoughts rising into a roiling pitch.

She was wrong—she was simply wrong. Injured pride was all it was. She was as high-strung as a thoroughbred. Her own emotions had been bruised—he'd make that up to her, yes, he would!

He was not cold, for God's sake, not like she said. He had reasons for everything he did. He was *trapped,* damn it—how could she not see that? It was life or death, and she thought he loved it? How could she not see? He *hated* it. He'd never wanted any of it, and now he was trapped and he hated every moment.

Swallowing against the choking feeling in his throat, he whirled, trying to get his eyes to focus on something. Of course she hadn't meant what she'd said about an annulment. It was her hurt, her feelings of rejection talking. . . .

What if she truly didn't love him anymore? Shock sapped the strength from him and he realized how much he'd depended on her love. On her, Leah, always waiting. Giving. Loving.

She was his, damn it. His future. His family!

He squeezed shut his eyes and commanded his thoughts to settle.

It was a bad idea to give into the impulse to chase her. So much of him wanted to. But he had to stay. The plan was in place, everything was set. Mere days and Randall Sanderson would be gone and out of his life forever.

And he'd go to Leah, then, after it was over. He'd make all of this right. He'd spend his life making it up to her and telling her that she was wrong about him. He wasn't cold. He could love, he *did* love her.

He . . .

He loved her.

Swiping roughly at his chin, he fought for steadying breaths, but there was no room inside him for air. God, he loved her with a fierceness he had never known before. She was his life, his heart, his world. He needed her to *breathe*.

His feet moved, taking him quickly down the flight of steps and out onto the street, but she was already gone.

Chapter 18

"THE COUNTESS DEPARTED for her sister's yesterday, my lord," Roberts said to Morgan. Seated at the small escritoire desk, he consulted his notepad, ticking off items with a flick of his quill. "I have Jacobs on her, keeping his distance this time. He will not be so difficult to shake off, I guarantee. He'll send a messenger when they've arrived in Cumbria."

Morgan nodded, running his fingers absently along his jaw as he paced behind Roberts. "My brother-in-law will take care of that. I've written to the viscount, explaining the delay in my wife's arrival and requesting he send word when she is safely in his care."

The detective continued reading his report. Roberts was nothing what one would expect from his reputation as a keen mind for tracking the criminal and a crackerjack team of agents. His slightly pudgy body came to Morgan's breastbone so that when he looked down at the man, he received a generous view of the balding top of his head, which perpetually glistened with sweat. He mopped it with an apologetic joke, claiming his brain heated his cranium when it was working.

That might in fact be the case, for what Roberts lacked in physical impressiveness, he more than made up for with his quick mind.

"Nothing unusual from the mark, my lord." Roberts always referred to Sanderson as "the mark," never using his name. At first, Morgan had found precautions like these a bit overdone. But after considering the damage loose talk could cause, he had to agree it was for the best.

Roberts continued, "His normal routines are not interrupted. He rises early, keeps to the Castle Inn, and stays by his wife's side as much as possible. Except for the pump room, he is usually watchful. As for the dispersed information, it has saturated the populace with surprising speed. I daresay the mark has caught wind of it."

"But he doesn't know enough yet to guess the plan. Not yet, but soon."

"He will no doubt begin to feel the pressure."

"We will be well under way by then." Morgan stretched away the stiffness of his limbs. Since his confrontation with Leah and Glorianna two days ago, his nerves had been riding a thin wire of anticipation.

"Excellent. Meanwhile, I have been thinking about the man Sanderson hired to attack me at the Cravensmore party. How likely do you think it is he's the same man he had murder my father?"

"Very. The criminal mind tends to repeat the same pattern, to stick to what's familiar and deemed safe. If the mark has a man who has been dependable and discreet before, he'll use him again. But so far, there's no indication that Sanderson is communicating with anyone that fits the type."

"Tell your men to take note of *all* of the company Sanderson keeps. He could be using an intermediary to communicate and I want that man." Morgan worked his neck and shoulders.

"Very good idea, my lord. I shall take care of it."

Morgan bade him farewell. Standing for a long time, his gaze drifted down to the street, studying the bustle below.

He watched the people. They all seemed so ordinary, so

normal. Two children ran directly in front of the Old Ship, squealing and laughing. Their harried nursemaid hurried behind, desperate to keep up. A couple almost collided with them, scowling, obviously disapproving of the mischievous antics of the children.

Morgan's eye caught the round form of a matron and her wisp of a daughter following behind, looking sullen. A gentleman passed and the girl straightened and flashed a smile. He looked back, and she turned, fluttering her eyelashes at him over her shoulder. All was unseen by Mama. When the prospective beau was out of sight, the girl collapsed into ill posture again, like a flower wilting all at once and she and her mother disappeared around the corner.

It was all so incredibly, wonderfully normal. He felt a longing to be bored, to have nothing better to do than stroll along the Steyne, sit and take in the sea air along the promenade, or step into the cool respite of one of the restaurants for a bit of lunch.

With Leah, of course. He closed his eyes for a moment against the sudden welling fear that he would never know that pleasure. Down there, below in the streets, those people's ordinary lives made his stomach twist in envy.

He went to the desk to consult his files and notes. He concentrated on the details, knowing he could afford no mistakes, no miscalculations. He was planning the final confrontation.

It had to be perfect.

He was still at the desk when a rapid knock jolted through the silence. Consulting his watch fob, he saw it was merely three in the afternoon, far too soon for Roberts to return with another report. Unless there was a development.

Rising quickly, he opened the portal to find Glorianna standing in the hallway. He had only a moment to take in her tearstained face, the way her hands wrung at the handkerchief clutched to her breast, before she launched herself into his arms.

"There now, what has happened?" He was glad he

sounded calm, as if there weren't a thousand panicked questions exploding in his brain.

"I did something dreadful, Morgan. I couldn't help myself. I was so upset. I didn't mean to ruin everything, but I think I did."

He brought her to the comfortable chair and pulled up another directly across from her, leaning his elbows on his knees. "What has happened?"

She swallowed, fear in her eyes as she raised them to his. "I confronted Randall with what you told me. I had to. He saw how nervous I was all the time, how I couldn't sit still or . . . let him touch me. He kept asking me why, what was wrong, and I tried to lie but . . . I had to tell him. He was furious, Morgan. He went wild."

Morgan's face must have shown the flood of searing emotion, for Glorianna rushed on. "I never meant to betray you, you mustn't think that! I only . . . Oh, Morgan, I *had* to find what he would say to defend himself."

This was no time for recriminations. He took a steadying breath. "And what *did* he say?"

"Well, he denied it. He said it was your madness and that he could prove it. But I told him about the letters you procured from Mr. Humbolt. I know I shouldn't have, but it simply came out of my mouth. Was that wrong, Morgan?"

"I don't know." He was trying not to react, because if he did he would grow angry. Glorianna would curl into a ball if she felt attacked and it was important to keep her talking to find out all the information he could. "What else happened?"

"Nothing. He was so strange, Morgan. Angry at first, but not as much as one would expect. Then he grew thoughtful." Her face collapsed. "And that was when I knew it was all true. I could almost see it happening behind his eyes—the slyness I never saw before. He wasn't indignant or consoling, or any of the things I would expect from an innocent man. I grew afraid—what if he was so calm because he planned to murder me? I fled without taking a thing with me. I came right to you, just as you told me to. Oh, Morgan! I've ruined everything, I know I have."

"No, it's not ruined, not at all." He said it reflexively to assuage her guilt, but after a moment's reflection, Morgan decided this was fairly true. He had allowed for the possibility of something going wrong in his plans as one never knew if they'd foreseen every eventuality. That was why he had hired the best. Roberts and his men would deal with whatever surprises occurred. Randall could not make a move without being observed.

Perhaps it might even work to his advantage, if Randall acted rashly. Self-protection was a better excuse for killing a man than a debt of honor.

Taking Glorianna's hand, he drew her to her feet. "The first thing we shall do is secure a room for you here. I will arrange it. Then you must not venture out, so that I know you are safe."

She sniffed, nodded, regarding him as sadly as a penitent child. "What will you do?"

"I shall have to give that some thought. Stay here, please, and lock the door. Do not answer for anyone but myself."

Morgan found the runner assigned to shadow Glorianna waiting outside, and gave him instructions to alert Roberts. He was speaking to the innkeeper about making arrangements to transfer Glorianna's belongings and personal staff when Roberts rushed into the room.

"Sanderson has left Brighton. I have two men with him."

Morgan dismissed the innkeeper curtly and pulled Roberts into a private corner where the detective gave his report, detailing Sanderson's movements since leaving his rooms, presumably after his confrontation with Glorianna. "It was just after noon, my lord. He went directly to a public inn and ordered a meal. He spoke to no one, but we believe there was a prearranged signal that triggered a series of events to facilitate his swift departure. When he left there was a carriage waiting. The odd thing was, my lord, that there was a woman inside who was obviously the ambassador's wife. Her attire is rather distinctive."

"Elisabeta?" Morgan murmured, wondering why this disturbed him. "Why would she be involved? It was not an amorous association between the two of them, it was strictly business. Their trick failed, however. So, what use does he have for the disgruntled ambassador's wife?"

Roberts looked disturbed. "I cannot even venture a guess. But there was a third member of their party, and I believe you will be very interested in this. He was a rough-looking man, very large, powerful in a brutish way. He had an arrogant air, a swagger of the kind of man that likes to inspire fear. He could be Sanderson's man, the one who attacked you and carried out the actual assault on your father. It would make sense. They took the road east across the downs."

"Damn, that's Eastborne, Hastings, or Rye—all port towns, where he can easily slip onto a ship for the continent. We've got to follow immediately."

"I don't recommend it," Roberts said, holding up a staying hand. "Let my men track them. They will relay messages back, and we can plan."

"No." Morgan searched for the source of screaming certainty that something was dreadfully wrong. "This isn't right. Sanderson is deliberate, calculating. It is completely out of character that he would flee. He will not give up without fighting for his social position. That is everything to him. All that stands in the way of his having everything he's wanted is me, and he wouldn't allow me this victory so easily."

"He panicked." Roberts shrugged.

"No, this was planned. You may have the advantage, my friend"—He acknowledged Roberts with a nod—"in knowing the criminal mind at large. But I know *this* man. He is very intelligent. He doesn't make mistakes, and he doesn't rush off half-cocked."

"But, my lord, how could he plan this? He had no knowledge of what you were doing,"

Morgan caught Roberts's eye. "Maybe he did. He could have had more than enough time to prepare. If he knew his wife came to me nearly a week ago."

"But she didn't speak with him until today. Do you not believe her?"

"Oh, I believe her. But Glorianna is not possessed of a cunning mind. I think it very possible her coming to me with Leah that first time did not go unobserved by Sanderson. He must have had her followed."

"But my men saw no one!"

"We cannot assume you are the only experts in this game. He knows Glorianna spoke to me, I *feel* it. This was planned. He knows Glorianna. He worked on her until he could get her to 'confess' and blurt out the whole story. It was the confirmation he needed, but he had this in the works. Trust me."

There was silence until Roberts said, "Then you suspect a trap."

"He wants me to fly after him. That is why he took his henchman. It is possible he thinks to ambush me on the downs road. Men are robbed and killed by murderous footpads on the highways all the time. It is rather a good plan."

Morgan pursed his lips. "There is one other thing troubling me. The ambassador's wife . . . why would he take her with him? Believe me, Roberts, there is a reason. Randall has a reason for everything he does. . . ."

Roberts scratched his chin. "I didn't know she was in Brighton. I had briefed my men, and none reported seeing Sanderson speaking to a woman of her description. I don't understand this oversight. My lord, my agents are rarely mistaken."

A heavy silence fell. The men looked at one another as they both came to the same conclusion.

"Bloody hell!" Morgan exploded. "It's not the ambassador's wife with Sanderson. The bastard has Leah!"

They sprang into action, both of them knowing the decision to follow the eastbound carriage was no longer in debate. As they were headed to the carriage house to get their horses, they were intercepted by one of Roberts's men.

"Buttelman is back, sir," he reported, "and he says they took the Eastbourne road."

"To the cliffs," Morgan growled. "The Seven Sisters and

the marshes." He met Roberts's stare and saw his own concern mirrored in the man's troubled face.

The Seven Sisters were sheer walls of chalk rising clear out of the channel. And more men were rumored to have been lost on the marshes just slightly inland from the shoreline than in the Battle of Hastings.

It was a place where a person could disappear without a trace. Even a person who was supposed to be leagues away, headed toward Cumbria.

They primed their weapons while they waited for the rest of the men to assemble in the stables.

"No doubt Elisabeta took the countess's place," Roberts said grimly. "We sat by and watched her ride off toward Cumbria."

"He had to have taken her almost immediately after she left me. And all this while, she has been with that maniac." Morgan dug his hands into his hair. "Christ, I'll go mad if I think about that."

"He wouldn't harm her, my lord," Roberts reassured him. "We know she was well this morning since it was she we saw with him. And forgive my presumption, but by all accounts of the countess she is purported to possess a rather lively spirit."

Yes, Leah was resourceful and brave and clever. Leah. God, he wanted to howl her name. His one and only love. How strange that the knowledge of loving her had settled so tamely in his mind. It had become completely a part of his world. Loving Leah now seemed the only important thing.

Iverson, one of Robert's men, rode behind, scanning the sides of the road with a flintlock rifle laid in front of him in the saddle. Roberts and two others were similarly armed, all carefully assessing each cluster of trees for possible danger as they advanced down the road to Eastbourne with what seemed to Morgan to be agonizing care.

Morgan wanted to shout at them to hurry up, to never mind the ambush. He had stopped paying attention to the potential danger points an hour ago. Instead, he thought of time and distance and Leah, and wanting her so badly his body vibrated with fear.

They neared Beachy Head, paused to confer, and decided to keep to the cliffs. They were filing back onto the road when a cracking sound split the air as a shot was fired. The men reacted, rearing their horses in every direction to disperse quickly.

Morgan bolted, feeling a crawling sensation along his skin as he wondered if he were right now in the sights for a second shot. Then a twinge of pain pinched his shoulder, and he looked down and saw blood.

He looked close, tense until he noticed it was just a graze. Looking up, he scanned the rise anxiously.

Another shot rang out, and then two more followed in rapid succession. These sounded closer, sharper, and louder. These were his men firing. Roberts was calling for Morgan to take cover, but he didn't want to be out of the way. Eagerly, he kicked his horse forward, charging toward the enemy.

Iverson sped past him toward a bend in the road bordered narrowly by a small clump of brush and full-leaf trees. Having discharged his rifle, he tossed it aside and produced a pistol from his coat, thumbing down the hammer without slowing down.

Morgan followed, swerving to the right when Iverson's horse reared as a man leaped out into the road in front of him, a pistol in each hand trained straight up at Iverson. The sound of the shot was like an explosion. Morgan's horse skittered, whinnying in protest. He struggled to control the headstrong beast, pulling hard on the reins with both hands.

Iverson fell forward, grasping his mount's mane to stay astride. Startled by the shot and the lax bit, the horse took off. The pair raced out onto the downs, as the man in the road raised the other pistol and took aim at his back.

Morgan yanked on the reins and kicked his horse hard in the flanks, his face drawn into a determined grimace. He raced straight at the man in the road. He reached for the primed pistols he had tucked into the waist of his trousers.

He shouted, and the man swung around. His eyes widened. He brought his weapon to bear. It was a blur of movement. Morgan saw the barrel aimed straight at him. He fired.

L EAH REGARDED RANDALL Sanderson seated across from her in his carriage with an eloquent flash of her glittering brown eyes. Bound, gagged, and exhausted, it was the only way to communicate her loathing of the man.

He had drawn the windows, so she had no idea of their whereabouts. The violent swaying of the coach and the speed with which they traveled told her nothing of their direction or destination, only of their urgency. She could still smell the sea, so she supposed they were traveling along the coast, although she didn't know if they were headed up Dover way or down to Land's End.

Within the sweat-scented confines of the coach, Sanderson glowered, mopping his glistening forehead and peeling back the curtain to catch a breeze and perhaps check their location. All Leah could see from her position of lying across the squab was an occasional glimpse of green and the blue of the flawless sky.

Randall flickered a glance at her, looking murderous as his handkerchief touched the oozing welt she had given him on his forehead. Blood glistened at the corner of his mouth. He touched his tongue to it gingerly, his eyes narrowing.

She'd kicked him soundly before he'd tied her feet together. The wooden heel of her boot had split open the flesh just over his left eye in a neat line. It was bleeding like the devil. The sight of the blood smeared with his sweat was gratifying.

She hoped the wound would scar him. It would be just recompense for the weal Morgan had received because of him.

Her wild attack had taken Sanderson off guard. Since her capture several days ago, she had been meek as a mouse, waiting patiently for her moment. If there was one thing this summer had taught her impulsive spirit, it was the wisdom in timing.

She'd been snatched the very afternoon she'd walked out of the Old Ship Inn after that last meeting with Morgan, grabbed off the street by Keenan, Sanderson's hired man, and stuffed into a carriage with no one the wiser. She had then been spirited to a seedy tavern outside of town where Sanderson had awaited her arrival with an air of agitated excitement.

He'd fired question after question at her. She'd replied, in a tone befitting her state of loathing for him, exactly what his chances of getting any information out of her were. She'd shown off her rather unconventional vocabulary. The look on his face had been one of astonishment and deep offense. What had the man expected, for her to swoon?

To Leah's surprise, Sanderson had pinned his hireling with a scathing look and told him in no uncertain terms that he was not to "trouble her" with his filthy, common person, and then he had left her in the care of the brute. Leah had thanked God for Sanderson's quirky snobbery and completely irrational ethics. Keenan brought her her meals. He didn't speak to her, he didn't look at her. She was left in peace for three torturous days to contemplate what Randall might plan to do with her.

She knew he would use her to hurt Morgan. She fought panic and despair, knowing she had to be calm, be sensible, be strong.

When Keenan had fetched her today and put her in the carriage, she hadn't fought. It would have been no use if she had. Keenan was a huge man who could crush her in one hamlike fist. It was more likely he'd think her blows would tickle than that they'd do any damage. But more important, she had to wait for her moment.

She'd sat as docile as a tame bird. The men had muttered to one another as they'd raced out of Brighton. Keenan disembarked along the downs road, and Leah gathered he was to lie in wait for Morgan should he be following. Only a single pistol was left behind with Sanderson, tucked safely out of the way for the moment.

Once alone with Sanderson, she'd sprung into action. Her initial foray had been to scratch furrows of blood into his face with her nails. He'd wrestled with her, showing a surprising amount of strength for a man of his slight build. He'd cried like a nicked lamb at shearing when she'd punched him. However, he had overpowered her eventually, binding her feet together with the sleeve of his coat, which had been torn off in their struggles. Smug, he had sat back and smiled tauntingly at her, so sure there was nothing she could do.

She'd not hesitated to prove him wrong, launching herself at him as soon as she'd garnered her strength. She wasn't afraid of the pistol. If he'd wanted her dead, he'd have saved himself a great deal of trouble and done it right away. That knowledge made her fearless. She'd only had to hoist herself up onto her shackled feet and fall down into him to be able to reach him with her small, balled-up fists. A few knocks to the head were all she could manage before he'd wrestled her back to her seat. His trousers had torn in the scuffle, so he ripped the rest of the strip off and used it to bind her hands.

He'd been shocked when she treated him to a colorful diatribe on her opinion of him. He was positively squeamish in the face of her foul language. That was when he gagged her, using a swath of lawn from his expensive shirt tied over a length of his cravat he'd shoved into her throat. She'd managed to bite him before he could get this accomplished, and when he'd sat down, nursing the bleeding finger, she'd gotten in two excellent jabs with her bound feet by leaning back and kicking like a mule. That was when she thought—she hoped—she loosened some of his teeth.

Bloody, bedraggled, his clothing in tatters, he now sat in uncertain victory. She could tell he was still afraid of her.

"Keenan, sir!" the driver called, his voice shrill enough to carry over the clatter of the wheels. "Coming up fast from Beachy Head."

Sanderson grinned. "Stop the carriage. Let us wait for

him." He lowered his gaze to Leah and smirked. "He must be finished with his duties. Allow me to be the first to extend my condolences on the loss of your husband."

Leah closed her eyes and jerked her head away, not wanting him to see her tears.

Chapter 19

A SOUND, A sad, terrible sound, came from the back of Leah's throat.

"At last," Sanderson hissed, laying his head back and grinning up at the ceiling. "I have wanted that man dead since the moment I walked into Blackheath Hall. Evan was just an old man, and Glorianna so easy to seduce, but Morgan . . . he had shrewd eyes. I hated the way he looked at me. He saw things. . . . But now," he said, his voice growing giddy, "those eyes are closed. Forever."

Leah stomped, twisted, tried to bury her face in the upholstered seat. Her sobs were muffled, indistinct, and yet they seemed to fill the small space.

"Do not worry, my dear," he purred. "You will join him shortly."

She heard the sound of the rider approaching. Keenan would kill her when he arrived. Sanderson would never do it himself. He was deluded by his own cultured veneer, and like all snobs, had his hirelings do his dirty work for him.

The carriage jolted and Leah fell forward onto the floor between the seats. She looked up, dazed and shocked. The driver called something that she couldn't hear. But she saw Sanderson's reaction.

He went white. Parchment white, and his hands rose up in front of his blind eyes, twisting, fingers curling, making impotent gestures of frustration. Of wrath.

She lay still, feeling her heart jerking rhythmically in her chest and fighting with herself: pragmatism against hope. She didn't want the white-hot flare of hope. She was afraid of it, but it was relentless and she had to admit that it was possible that Randall's disappointment could only mean one thing.

Morgan was alive. And he was coming.

She began to sob again, this time quietly.

Sanderson turned around, peering out the window. "To the cliffs," he shouted over the clatter of the carriage, and an answering "Aye" drifted ghostlike down from the driver's box.

They rode hard. As she was jounced against the hard floor of the carriage, her head hit hard. She felt a wave of dizziness sweep over her. She fought for consciousness, determined not to surrender, not now.

The carriage stopped abruptly. She watched as Sanderson checked the priming on the flintlock and pulled back the hammer. He held it, the muzzle pointed upward, and then he looked at Leah.

She tensed, filled with terror. She had been wrong; he *was* going to kill her himself. Instead, he grasped her with his free hand and pulled her up, shoving her through the door, which had been opened by the driver. She stumbled, unable to manage the steps with her feet bound, and fell to the ground. Pain lanced through her. She lay motionless and helpless.

Cursing, Randall untied her feet. He was nervous, repeatedly glancing over his shoulder to gauge the rider close on their heels. She had fallen facing the opposite direction. With her ear close to the ground, Leah could hear the hoofbeats of Morgan's horse. Steady, growing louder, closer.

Unfortunately, Sanderson was not so distracted that he didn't remember to jump clear once her feet had been freed, and she missed another opportunity to maim him.

The soft explosion of a flintlock pistol popped into the air and something crashed onto the ground beside Leah. She twisted her head and saw the driver, his face turned toward her. His eyes were open, staring. He was dead. A rush of blood, brilliant red and glistening, began to run down the side of his head and pool in the dirt inches from her face.

Leah screamed into the gag.

Sanderson pulled her to her feet and dragged her with him. She whirled, seeing that he was taking her toward the edge of the cliffs, where the gentle green of the downs bleached into chalk before falling abruptly away into the sea. Crumbled limestone crunched noisily under their every step.

She went limp, trying to catch him off balance, slow him down. He struggled with her dead weight, but managed to haul her toward the precipice. All she won for her efforts were scrapes from the sharp rocks.

He threw her down and she landed on her knees and her hands, which were still bound together in front of her. The pain of a thousand tiny knifes slicing roughly into her skin assailed her. Her palms were skinned badly, and bleeding. She winced as she was forced to use them to prop herself into a sitting position.

Sanderson pulled down her gag. Using her tongue, she worked the cloth out of her mouth and strained to peer around Sanderson as he swung to face Morgan.

He *was* here. She could see him, and the sight filled her with painful emotion.

"Go ahead," Randall purred, "call to him."

She bit back the cry rising in her throat. If Randall thought she would help him he was wrong.

Morgan reigned in his horse and dismounted in a single fluid movement. He began to walk toward them.

Leah made a sound that was both a sob and a gasp. Sanderson braced himself.

Morgan's stride was full of confidence. The wind ruffled his hair. His face was set, immobile, his scar livid on his cheek. He stared at Sanderson, his eyes never wavering. He seemed mythical, those impossible shoulders as strong and wide as the mighty Atlas, and his long, loose frame making him appear larger than life.

He was walking to his own death, and he was not afraid. She knew he was thinking of her. He had come for her.

No. She mustn't fool herself, not now of all times. He had come for Sanderson.

She could hear the sound of her own breathing, her heartbeat, and the sea, churning thunderously below them. It was only three steps away to the edge of the cliff.

A pressure at her temple made her glance up. Sanderson had the flintlock pressed against her skin.

"Don't come closer," Sanderson shouted.

Although Morgan stopped, his manner was one of being completely in control. His gaze was insolent and full of contempt, his posture relaxed.

He gave Sanderson a long once-over, and a corner of his mouth lifted at the man's bedraggled appearance. "Rough trip?" Morgan asked.

"Your wife is quite the termagant. You should thank me for saving you from a lifetime of hell with her. So, have your laugh, even if it is at my expense. It will be your last."

"Don't you want to know what happened to your friend?"

"I assume you dispatched him. I didn't think that likely. You are, apparently, an excellent shot." He jerked his head at the dead driver. "I didn't know that, but I should have. After all, you've been doing the impossible the whole time. You got out of jail, you saved your reputation. And now I find you've actually retained some friends. They have been circulating some rather unpleasant things about me. I didn't think you had anyone left who would believe you. What an inconvenient time to find I was mistaken."

Morgan's gaze flickered for just a moment to Leah. "You've always underestimated me. Or thought completely too highly of yourself. Well, enough reminiscing. Let us negotiate for my wife's release. It's me you want. Let her go. She can take my horse back to Roberts. I've ordered him to stay a short distance down the road. I wanted you and I to finish this."

"How chivalrous. But utterly impossible, of course." Sanderson grabbed Leah's shoulder and pulled her painfully to her feet in front of him.

Leah stared at Morgan, willing him to look at her. He did not. He kept his burning gaze trained on Sanderson.

What did he want her to do? He was unarmed—why the devil did he come here unarmed?

Sanderson jerked her up against him and in one move, pushed her right up to the cliff's edge. At the same time, he brought the nose of the pistol from her temple to Morgan.

Who had somehow produced a flintlock of his own, and it was pointed back at his enemy.

"I suspected you might find a weapon on you somewhere if I gave you a chance. But I don't think you will shoot me," Sanderson taunted. "Even if you manage to avoid shooting this irritating baggage and hit me, I would fall off the cliff. I doubt if you'd want me to take her over the edge with me."

"You have one pistol, loaded and primed. You can only use it once. So you have only one choice. You will shoot me and push her over the side." Morgan's manner was stoic. There was a calm reason in his voice. Leah waited, heart pounding with furious rhythm, trying to guess what Morgan would do.

She could feel Randall's tension, his uncertainty. The gun aimed at Morgan wavered.

Morgan's eyes took in the unsteady hand and said, "It's much different, doing the killing yourself, isn't it? Since you only get one shot, you had better make sure it is fatal, which, I might add, is not as easy as one might think. Unlike me, you are not an excellent shot. If you don't kill me, then you will be defenseless. You know I will kill you. And I might not be very civilized about it. As it happens, I am quite fond of that 'irritating baggage,' as you call her. I might be a bit irrational if any harm came to her." An edge came into his voice, hardening it. "There are ways to toy with pain, prolong death that I feel certain would amuse me if I were in such a state of mind. I don't think, however, you would find it at all enjoyable. Therefore, you might wish to give serious consideration to removing my wife from that edge."

He raised his flintlock and closed one eye, as if taking aim. Sanderson snatched Leah back to him and held her in front to act as shield. Relief at being away from the dizzying precipice flooded her.

"That makes my shot more difficult, but not impossible," Morgan observed. "You've seen the evidence of my marksmanship. We appear to be at an impasse."

She felt Randall's tension behind her like heat, burning into her back.

"There is only one solution," Morgan continued. "Untie Leah's hands and let her take my horse. When she is out of harm's way, I will lay down my weapon."

That was his plan? "Morgan, no!" Leah cried.

"Do as I say, Leah," Morgan responded. "I'll give you what you want, do you hear me, Randall? Me. *If* you let her go."

"I'd be a fool," Sanderson says. "I could never trust you."

"But you can. That is the thing of it, you *can* trust me, and you know it. I give you my word, my solemnly sworn oath of honor. The word of a Gage is binding, that you well know. And Leah is bound by that honor as well. She knows that the sacrifice I make is for her, and as her husband, she will obey me. Will you not, Leah?"

She wanted to scream that he was insane. But he finally looked at her, and his sharp eyes compelled her, commanded her silently and she couldn't deny what they asked. "Yes. I will speak of this to no one. I swear."

"This is absurd. You don't expect me to believe you. Morgan, you're a fool. I'd expect you to die for your precious code, but this vengeful minx—"

"My wife will do as I say. She is a woman of integrity. Need I remind you that she would be honoring the last wish of a dead man? Once you kill me, you ensure her obedience. She will not betray me, and therefore she will not betray you."

Sanderson's voice lowered, mocking and caustic. "In a

pig's eye she will. And what of you? Do you actually expect me to believe you would give me my freedom after all this? Did you think I didn't know how you've dedicated yourself to avenging your father on me? And now you would give me absolute freedom, and your own life in the bargain, all for what? Love of this insane creature you claim as wife? If you know me at all, Morgan, you know I am no fool."

"I no longer care about vengeance. And I don't give a damn about you, either. I wouldn't die for you, or even for my father. He wouldn't wish it. All I want is Leah to be safe. That is the only thing I would die for." Morgan spoke as if to Sanderson, but Leah realized that he was talking to her. "I want her to live and be happy and love again. If I can be assured of that, I will give you all you've ever wanted. Think of it. You have coveted the earldom, the fortune, the fine homes, and the status you've craved all of your life. It would be yours. Just send Leah to the horse."

Randall's tone was scathing, but there was an edge of excitement to it. "She is nothing but a silly bit of a girl who is more trouble than a roomful of angry cats. You can't think I'd believe you'd sacrifice yourself for such a woman as this."

"I advise you to make your decision quickly. I've never possessed a great deal of patience."

There was a long pause. Should she do something? Leah wondered. Make a dash now—what? What did Morgan want from her?

Taking her cue from the preternatural stillness Morgan maintained, she waited. She refused to believe he truly meant to give himself up for her. He had to have some plan, she knew he did.

Morgan said, "I give you thirty seconds. That is all I can spare as my wife is in mortal danger. After that, I will have to take my chances, poor as they are. Although, I can assure you, if you will forgive my braggadocio, that I think I just might be able to hit you without harming a hair on her head. In any event, we shall see. I am quite admittedly desperate."

How could he be so calm? Leah thought wildly.

"It is a ridiculous proposition!" Sanderson exclaimed.

"Just so. But there is an attraction you may not have considered. Think of this, Sanderson—*you will have me utterly at your mercy.* On my knees if you wish, completely defenseless. I cannot help but think that might be more than agreeable to you. I could beg if it would help. As a matter of fact, I beg you now. Take the deal, Randall. I beg you, let her go. I lay all my pride out on this ground in front of you and plead without reservation. All you have to do is free her. So. Make up your mind."

Sanderson hugged Leah tighter. She could hear the rasp of his panicked breathing at her ear.

Morgan looked nonplussed. "Twenty-five seconds."

There was a pause. Morgan said, "Fifteen."

"All right." Sanderson wiped the sweat from his lip with the back of his hand. "Get down on your knees, then. I will have you licking my boots."

Morgan didn't hesitate. He bent one knee onto the small, razor-edged rocks without flinching, keeping his weapon trained on its target.

"Put the pistol down!" Sanderson shouted.

"Not until she's on that horse. You have my word. I will not fire unless you do anything to harm her. Once she's safely away, you will have what you want."

There was a long moment before Sanderson shoved Leah away from him.

"Go, Leah," Morgan said, his voice sharp and cutting. "Go on."

She took a few steps away and stopped. "Morgan?"

"To the horse," he shouted impatiently. "*Go,* now!"

Leah walked toward the horse, closing her eyes and making herself do it. She had to trust him. She had to let him do this his way and believe he had a plan. He wouldn't dare leave her to live without him. He'd have to know she would rather die in his place.

The sound of Morgan's voice stopped her. "One thing before you go."

She looked over at him. His gaze remained fixed on his

enemy, but his voice was soft, for her ears alone. "I love you, Blackie."

"Now the pistol," Randall said sharply.

"Go to my horse," Morgan commanded, his voice flat again.

No!

On numb legs, she did as he told her.

As soon as she was out of range, Morgan placed the flint-lock on the gravel in front of him. Sanderson barked an order for him to push it out of reach. Morgan sent it skittering across the gravel, the sound of it like bones clattering. Sanderson's face lit with triumph and he broke into a smile.

Leah froze, fighting the impulse to go back, to do something, anything!

"I'm going to enjoy this," Sanderson purred, striding cockily up to Morgan.

Leah saw Morgan's glance, read his anxiety. He was very still, looking at Sanderson but she knew all of his concentration was on her. She could sense it.

He wanted her to go to the horse. How could she? How could she leave him to die for her?

Forcing her limbs to move, she headed for the horse, not looking back.

T HE MOMENT LEAH was safely out of pistol range, Morgan's body blazed with relief. The breath he'd been holding flew out of him, slow and steady. Now. Now he could concentrate.

Sanderson was standing in front of him, squinting as the sun blazed in his pale hair. The wind whipped it around his head like it was live fire. Morgan had taken care to position himself so that he had the sun at his back.

He was waiting, waiting. Unmoving, his muscles bunched, taunt. Waiting.

Sanderson moved slowly, deliberately, his predatory smile transforming his face to something ghoulish. "I am going to splatter your brains over these cliffs and toss your body to the sea. You will never be found and the legend of the Wicked Earl of Waring will end in mystery. I might sow a rumor or two to make it interesting, seem as if you really were guilty after all and had come to a just end to your evil ways. You know how excellent I am at these things."

"You do have an eye for opportunity," Morgan said. "However, you are not very original."

"But effective. Well, if something works, one should stay with it, eh? I like the idea of ruining your reputation. I could never stand how self-righteous and superior you always were. God, I could hardly believe my luck when I heard you fighting that night with Uncle Evan. I'd already hired Keenan, you see. I'd wished Uncle Evan dead a thousand times, but when I saw Glorianna, I knew I had to have her. But I never imagined you would provide me with so excellent an opportunity to blame you."

"Yes. I suppose it was a perfect scenario."

"And then, to make it all the more delicioius, you came in right afterward and discovered him dead. My God, you were even found covered in his blood! The letter was an inspired idea that came afterward, when I saw the possibilities. It was rather a good fake, wasn't it? To this day, people think you killed to keep yourself in the will."

His chuckle rode the wind, wrapping around Morgan, filling his brain with a hot tide of fury. He fought it back, steeling his thoughts on his next move.

"And it almost worked," Randall cried, enjoying the moment thoroughly. "Oh, this is lovely, Morgan. I really am enjoying it immensely. You never did appreciate my genius. Maybe now you will."

"I think you are swine."

"But I am a rich, titled swine, thanks to your death. And when that annoying chit is dead, there will be no one who will ever know."

"You never intended to let her live, did you?"

Bringing the barrel of the weapon to bear, Sanderson

smirked. "You should not have trusted me. I would have thought you knew better."

"Of course I didn't," Morgan muttered, and threw himself on the ground. As he rolled, saw the confusion on Randall's face as he drew his other pistol from under his coat, where he had it tucked in the waistband of his trousers. It was cocked and primed, the pistol he had surrendered being the one he had spent shooting the driver.

The move took Randall completely by surprise. He leaped back, his hand with the pistol in it shaking badly. Morgan pointed his weapon in one clean, easy arc and discharged it at point-blank range.

The force of the ball hitting his shoulder sent Randall careening toward the edge of the cliff. His arms were outflung, his fingers tangled in the trigger mechanism of the pistol so that it hung from his nerveless hand.

Time slowed down. Morgan rose to his feet, feeling as if his legs had been glued to the ground while Sanderson back-wheeled out of reach. He lunged forward.

Sanderson teetered on the precipice of the cliff, arms grasping the air frantically for balance. Morgan reached him. He grasped the man's empty hand just as he went over. Leah screamed again.

The impact as he hit the ground knocked all the air from his lungs, but he held on to Sanderson. The weight of the man's unsupported body strained his muscles, pressing his arm—the one grazed by the sniper's shot—into the sharp angle of the cliff.

Shutting his eyes, he concentrated all of his strength into pulling Randall up. The man swung free, legs kicking wildly. This action raked Morgan's good arm across the crumbled chalk, scraping the skin off and he roared for Sanderson to be still.

"Hug the cliff," Morgan shouted.

Sanderson scrabbled to the side, finding footholds, leaning in, steadying himself after a few terrifying moments.

Morgan heard the crunch of footsteps behind him. "Leah, stay back!"

"What are you doing?" she cried, but he didn't answer her. "Let him go, Morgan, for God's sake. He'll take you over with him. Oh, God, please!"

He braced his knees into a secure position. "Sanderson, listen to me," he called. "Climb up. I will pull. Try to help as much as you can."

Sanderson tipped his head back and looked up at him. His lips peeled away from his teeth and he began to laugh. "You are trying to save my life, Morgan? I thought you came here to kill me."

"I came for justice," he said. "I don't want your death on my head. I will be free of you, completely, do you hear me?"

"There will be no justice for you. Or for me. Do you think I could bear it? I would rather die."

Sanderson threw his head back and brought up his other arm.

In it he still held the pistol. It flashed, the metal catching the sunlight like mystic fire. "But I shall die with the satisfaction of knowing I take you with me."

Leah screamed.

Morgan released his grip an instant before the shot fired. Rolling free and unhurt on the gravel, he landed on his back, staring at the sky, the echoes of the explosion dying out slowly in fading echoes in his head.

Then there was silence. Then weeping. Leah was weeping.

Leah. He got to his feet and stumbled to his wife.

"Don't cry," he said, and gathered her into his arms. "Don't cry. I hate it when you cry."

He smelled her scent, filled his whirling head with it. He pulled her closer, shutting his eyes, letting the terror bleed out from his veins. She was safe, here in his arms, thank God.

Leah sobbed, her face pressed into his shirt. Her body quivered like a leaf in a gale. "Shush," he told her, wrapping her tight. "Shush now."

"D-don't you dare t-tell me not to cry." Her voice was muffled, but not inaudible. "I am *not* going to stop crying,

Morgan, and don't you dare get angry at me. I c-can't help my . . . m-myself. . . ."

He smiled. He wanted to cry, too. And he wanted to laugh.

"Leah," he said, closing his eyes, savoring her feel, loving saying her name. Rocking her, he kissed her hair and whispered into her ear. "All right, then. You go ahead, you go right ahead and cry all you want. I've got you. And I'm not letting go."

H E WAS TRUE to his word, keeping her tightly ensnared in front of him on his horse as they traveled north to Alfriston, a small village outside of Eastbourne. Leah laid her head on his shoulder, closing her eyes. She was huddled in to the strong bulk of his body. He felt solid and real behind her, around her, keeping her warm and secure. For the time being, they didn't speak, and she was content to have it so.

They took a room at The Star. Neither one had a desire to return to Brighton, so Morgan sent a messenger to collect their belongings. With a solicitous arm around her shoulders, he took her up to the large suite.

The old timbers of the ancient inn gave the chamber a warm, mellow atmosphere. Morgan led her to the bed. Slipping off her shoes, he pushed her back onto the counterpane. Then he stretched out next to her and wrapped her up tight again.

"I am not cold."

"You are shivering," he explained.

"I think I am still afraid."

"No, love. No more."

They fell asleep like that, neither one of them moving so much as an eyelash. They woke early the following morning, still locked in each other's arms.

When Leah awoke, she felt better. Blinking away sleep and knuckling the strands of hair from her face, she twisted around and glanced up at Morgan. Her movements had roused him. He smiled down at her and she sighed, settling down once again.

He nuzzled her hair, kissed her temple. Leah could feel the abrasion of stubble against her brow.

"What time is it, do you think?" she asked, stretching her toes.

Checking his fob watch, he said, "Just before six. Are you hungry?"

"Mmm," she said with a nod. "But I don't think I want to move."

"Let me. I'll be right back."

He went to the door and called for a chambermaid, giving instructions for two pots, one of coffee and one of tea, and breakfast.

Leah sat up, curling her legs under her, watching him as he hunched over the washbasin and splashed cold water on his face. He peered into the mirror and rubbed his hand over his grizzled cheeks. "I hope our things are not too long in arriving. Maybe we should have gone back."

"No. I don't want to go there again."

He looked at her over his shoulder, his brows drawn down. Coming to sit before her, he touched her face gently. "I'm so sorry, Leah. I will never forgive myself for what happened."

"But it wasn't your fault," she protested. "You didn't want me there and I should have listened to you. I should have been in Cumbria. But I'm safe now. That's all that matters. I'm safe and I'm here with you, so let's not fret about it anymore."

"When I realized Sanderson had you, I went mad, I think. It must have been a nightmare for you."

"No. Please do not worry about that. I told you, he was quite civilized." She gave him a twist of a smile. "And I think I rather enjoyed attacking him. I don't suppose that speaks well of me. The only truly awful thing was that dreadful outfit he made me wear so that I would look like that ambassador's wife."

She leaned into him, wrapping her arms around his neck and peering into his face.

"Shame on you for joking about such a thing," he admonished, but a smile played in the corners of his mouth. His hazel eyes sparkled, beautiful and smoky.

He was so handsome. Hers.

Touching the pad of his thumb to the soft cushion of her bottom lip, he said, "I was so stupid. I love you, Leah, and I should have told you that a long time ago. I am not asking for forgiveness—what I did is unforgivable. I hurt you. I let you think you didn't matter to me."

She leaned back and closed her eyes, a sublime smile on her face. "You love me," she murmured, as if savoring the knowledge.

"With my whole heart and soul, Blackie. I would have given Sanderson his freedom, waved him off on a bon voyage, paid him, given my life—*anything* to keep him from hurting you."

"But what of your . . . justice?"

He drew in a deep breath, held it, and released it slowly. "Do not mistake me, I never stopped wanting that. But I stopped *living* for it. I just . . . I just couldn't find a way out. I had lived for a year thinking of only one thing. I thought it was all I was. I didn't even want to live, and I sure as hell didn't want to love, not anyone. But, damn, you are too much for me, with your delirious spirit, your beauty, the way you fill every moment with this incredible, irrepressible appetite for life. I couldn't fight you any longer."

She smiled. "I love you so very much." She kissed him, tenderly and deeply.

"Are you still chilled?" he asked, rubbing his lips along her skin.

"No. Not at . . . ah . . . oh." She broke off on a sigh of pleasure. He'd lifted her hair and found the spot behind her ear that never failed to send her into a fit of delicious tremors. "Ah, in fact, I am growing rather warm."

"Perhaps if we remove your clothing, it might help."

"I think that will not cool me. In fact, this is the sort of heat that would increase if we begin to discard clothing."

"Ah. That kind. I fear"—He licked a path down to the sensitive curve at the back of her neck—"I may also be afflicted. I do know a cure, however."

"Yes. I believe you do."

"It is all in the touch. Like this." His hand closed over her breast, teasing just enough to elicit a soft, breathy sigh. "That will ease you, do you think?"

Her breathing was ragged, but she managed to say, "I am afraid my affliction is rather more severe than that. I will need much more of these ministrations."

She heard the laughter in his voice. "It will be my pleasure to serve you."

Epilogue

Yorkshire, England
July 1825

MORGAN PACED ABOUT the salon in the newly refurbished Blackheath Hall. The room was filled with memorabilia from his extensive travels with Leah, but at the moment devoid of any other living person aside from himself. Which is what annoyed him.

He glanced at the mantel clock impatiently. "Come now, Leah," he called out, hearing his wife's steps out in the hall. "It's half past the hour already."

Leah swept into the room. "I am here, I am here."

Smartly dressed in a fawn-colored dress and matching spencer, her bonnet in her hands, she walked into the room at a smart clip. Passing him on her way to the Bombay mirror, she pressed a quick kiss on her husband's lips and turned to her reflection to fit the smart little hat onto her head. "Although I don't know why you are in such a hurry. The fair is in the village for three entire days."

He liked the way she turned her head this way and that,

eyeing her reflection critically. "No," she pronounced. "Oh, bother, this will never do."

He lowered his voice to convey his warning. "You best wear it, or go bareheaded. I'll not have another delay. Where are the children?"

"Of course, if you do not mind that I shall look dreadful," she replied with a pout.

"You look ravishing," he assured her, coming to put his arm about her and kissing her temple. He would have liked to do more, but they were, after all, quite late already.

She gave him a sly look. "It is about time you said so."

"It was monstrous wicked of me to neglect telling you."

Her eyes widened as his hips brushed up against hers. He'd been aroused since the moment she breezed into the room. "My, my," she murmured. "You are feeling wicked today."

"Just living up to my legend." He bent to kiss her.

She pulled back. "What of the fair? The children are waiting."

"I will simply have to tell them that their mother is to blame. You have no business looking like this when we have to go out a full day in public."

"Ah, I remember how you dislike that. How thoughtless of me. I recall that time in Hawkshead, when I showed my bosom . . . I am afraid I forgot all about your aversion to that sort of thing, Morgan. I am so sorry. Will it cause you distress," she purred, swaying her hips forward against his hardened manhood, "do you think?"

She grinned and he grinned back.

"If not for wanting to avoid disappointing your children," he said tightly, "I would toss you over my shoulder and carry you upstairs this instant, just to teach you the just desserts of your little flirtation."

"You are still a very dangerous man," she told him solemnly. They laughed.

Leah turned back to the mirror to fuss with her bonnet.

"Glorianna's letter said she and Roger would be arriving next week. I cannot wait to see your new sister."

Morgan called for the nurse to bring the children down. "For God's sake, Leah, that child is not my sister."

"Well, if Glorianna is your stepmother, then her daughter is your stepsister."

He shook his head and rolled his eyes. "It does not work like that."

"But you will be pleased to see her, I dare say, and you'll spoil her child worse than you spoil ours."

He looked horrified. "I do not spoil them. You are far too indulgent."

Leah shrugged happily. "How can I help myself? I can never be harsh with them. Whenever I look into their little faces, I see you in every feature and I just melt."

As if cued by their mother's confession, four small children burst into the room.

Emma, who was nearly two, ran straight to her father. Morgan hoisted her into his arms, brushing wild wisps of dark brown hair out of her eyes. "Are you excited about the fair, princess?"

Emma nodded, her thumb stuck firmly in her mouth and her little mouth curled into a big smile around it.

"We are all ready, I think," Leah said, pausing to adjust the bow on Bethany's hat, then stroking the soft skin of the seven-year-old's cheek. Their oldest, she was tall like her father. In fact, she was exactly like Morgan in every feature and every nuance of personality.

In between the two girls were five-year-old twin boys, Evan and Francis Joseph, whom they called Joseph. They were presently engaged in chasing one another around a table. Leah commanded them to stop, rushing forward to keep the vase resting upon the jostled furniture from toppling. They froze in their tracks and tried to their best to behave as their mother had commanded until Evan inadvertently brushed up against Joseph and Joseph pushed him back and it started all over again.

Morgan's sharp reprimand brought them to a halt. They suffered their mother tucking in their shirttails and straightening their collars, shifting from foot to foot until she pronounced them ready to leave. The boys whooped and raced for the door, all of Leah's fussing undone by the time they were down the front steps.

Morgan laughed, exchanging an exasperated look with his wife. Emma wanted down, which she indicated by going limp as an overcooked noddle. Bethany took her sister's hand and followed the skipping boys.

When Leah would have followed, Morgan pulled her back.

Looking up into his face, she smiled. Not caring about the fact that the children might see—for they'd witnessed their parent's affection frequently—he pulled her to him.

He was feeling reflective for some reason. On these wild and vast northern Yorkshire heaths, he had met her nearly ten years ago. She was the same in so many ways, and yet maturity had ripened the wild, brilliant heart into a woman of poise and self-possession.

He loved her so much. Each day, more and more.

He kissed her. Not a peck, but a real kiss, lingering and full of promise. She swayed into him. She was still slim, still beautiful. At least once every day, he'd look at his wife and think, *she's never looked more lovely than right now.*

He told her this, whispering it in a husky voice in her ear. Her hands slipped inside his coat. "Oh, Morgan. I . . . but the fair . . . the children . . ."

"They can wait a moment longer." He bent his head to kiss her again but she avoided him.

"Oh, Morgan," she admonished. "It's too cruel to make them."

"And what of me?" he teased, refusing to release her. He only intended to start the fires simmering. He wanted her and he wished her to know it. All throughout the happy hours at the fair, he intended to stoke the coals, reminding her of what awaited when they finally arrived home again tonight. "Shall I be kept waiting all day for a simple kiss from my wife?"

She leaned into him, pressing her body close, brushing her hips into his in a movement he was certain was deliberate. "I am afraid that you *will* have to wait. But I promise I will make it worthwhile."

He caught his breath and laughed, realizing she'd turned his own game about on him. She was delighted with herself, whirling away with a coquettish glance over her shoulder and he took her arm, descending the steps to where his children were bouncing excitedly in the open carriage.

It was spring, the air alive with sounds and fresh, fragrant scents. Morgan was filled with a sense of exhilaration. He gazed at his family, his hand lingering on the small of his wife's back as he handed her up into the carriage.

"Father, sit by me!" Bethany cried. He took the seat between his wife and his eldest daughter. Across from him, the boys were trying their best to sit as still as their excitement would let them. Emma reached for him from Leah's arms, and he tucked her tightly into his lap. He angled his head to look at her. She was all Leah, her dark eyes wide and greedy, watching the world with the same wonder and delight as he had often seen on her mother's face.

His family.

Once it had seemed impossible this life or anything remotely like it would be his. And now it was familiar, ordinary, taken for granted most times. But on a day like today, a man noticed.

Settling back, he smiled. Leah raised her eyebrows in silent question as to what was so amusing.

He only shrugged and said, "Surely, no man has ever had more."

She blinked, appearing affected by his words, and then she smiled, too. Reaching out her hand to his, they wrapped their fingers together and settled in for the ride.